WHO WILL LOVE <u>GRANDMA</u>?

- fans of Mark Twain, Garrison Keillor or Forrest Gump
- people who want "funny," but not "R-rated"
- 'boomers paroled from public or Catholic school
- lovers of Americana
- '50s and '60s country people

- AND ANYONE ELSE WHO WANTS TO LAUGH AND RELAX!

Growing up in '50s Ohio, Paul is a born eccentric. He stands ideas on their heads relentlessly, and is completely opposed to modern times. To him, Indians, the woods life and Robin Hood are reality, and he develops ingenious methods to protect himself from the world's invasion.

> *"My most elaborate plan for dealing with punks never had to be used, but I came close one January with Lenny Totterhouse. We were to run six miles up the railroad (after swimming the icy creek), following up with my usual workout of rope-climbing, pushups, sit-ups, and hanging by the neck... We would make a glorious end with the fight, if he made it through the hanging."*
> – Chapter XIV, "Modus Operandi"

<u>Grandma</u> is a *tour de force* – an intensely-written memoir, beginning when Paul is six with the title story, and ending with his first year of college. Thoughtful, feisty, and fresh as a March wind, it's surprisingly literary but comfortable to read. The book has an odd kick to its gallop – at times momentum rushes on powerfully, catching the unwary reader off-balance. Yet it's ingenuous as Forrest Gump, and the slow-paced rhythms of a small town and country living recall Garrison Keillor.

It was a time when kids could still roam their world freely. Some of us were there, but for those who missed out or want another look, Paul Pfarr brings it uniquely alive in these true stories.

<u>Grandma Does His Duty</u> is a classic of American storytelling, with that timeless feeling of Tom Sawyer and Lake Wobegon. While you're busy with Paul's utterly sincere gyrations, the atmosphere is quietly working its way into your heart.

Tho' much is taken, much abides; and tho'
We are not now that strength which in old days
Moved earth and heaven, that which we are, we are;
One equal temper of heroic hearts,
Made weak by time and fate, but strong in will
To strive, to seek, to find, and not to yield.

- from "Ulysses" by Alfred, Lord Tennison

GRANDMA DOES HIS DUTY

The hilarious memoir
of a '50s American misfit

paul j. pfarr

Choosing-Natural-Health.com
2012

GRANDMA DOES HIS DUTY

© 2012 by Choosing-Natural-Health.com
3000 Priceville Road
Bonnieville, Kentucky 42713

Publisher's Cataloging-in-Publication Data

Pfarr, Paul J.
  Grandma does his duty : the hilarious memoir of a '50s misfit /
Paul J. Pfarr.
    p. cm.
  ISBN-13: 978-0-615-47340-6
  ISBN-10: 0-615-47340-7
  1. Baby boom generation—Fiction. 2. Wit and humor—Fiction.
3. Ohio—Social life and customs—Fiction.   I. Title.
PS3616.F36 G73 2012
813—dc22

                                         2011910703

Printed in the United States of America
First Edition

Copies of this book can be purchased through:

www.choosing-natural-health.com/grandma.html
Amazon.com
Barnes & Noble.com
CreateSpace.com

or

Fine Bookstores Everywhere

GRANDMA DOES HIS DUTY

Table of Contents

GRANDMA DOES HIS DUTY

Table of Contents, continued

GRANDMA DOES HIS DUTY

Table of Contents, continued

ACKNOWLEDGEMENT

I am deeply indebted to Justice Valentine, my editor,
for her tireless work in arranging and polishing.

Although I can write a good tale,
her exquisite sense of language and artistic eye
have made this all I hoped for.

P. J. P.

GRANDMA DOES HIS DUTY

Original Illustrations
reproduced in black and white

With gratitude to the artists

Other Original Illustrations
in the public domain

*   *   *

The cover and all remaining illustrations
are also in the public domain.

DISCLAIMER

Nearly all of the events in this book are true,
to the best of my recollection, and most of the names
are real. Like a painter, I have occasionally rearranged
the details for more realistic effect.

These happenings took place some 50 years ago.
At that time, there were many attitudes, perceptions
and stereotypes that we no longer accept today.
While I have included them where they relate to the stories,
I do not endorse them in any way.

Likewise, I have changed my own behavior and perceptions
over the course of a lifetime, like my old acquaintances
whose youthful exploits are told here.

P. J. P.

GRANDMA DOES HIS DUTY

Chapter I.
Grandma Does His Duty

I was smothering.

A slow, rhythmic panting began in the blackness.

No! – please, not again!

I stood on a dark plain of grass, with the light from our front door beaconing distantly.

"RUN! RUN FOR THE DOOR!"

I tried to scream, but there was no sound. My legs were stone.

Focusing all my will, I broke free, moving in agonized slow motion toward the house. The Wolf displayed no such handicap – he was running easily behind, gaining fast. The panting accelerated, crescendoing like an approaching steam engine, and then he was right behind me, snapping. I had a-l-m-o-s-t reached the front door – I lunged for the handle, and struggled to open it –

Relief! It gave way, and my parents grabbed my arm – but the Wolf seized my shoe! Racked between them, I prayed wildly to my guardian angel... and the shoe slipped off! My parents kicked the door shut in the Wolf's face.

I woke up sweating, my heart thudding, and heard a locomotive receding up the valley.

The dream recurred throughout my childhood, a familiar, terrifying bout with the Wolf. If I had been especially disobedient, I would end up in his stomach, a black pit of nothingness. There was a message, and I knew it.

* * *

There were seven children in our family, the Pfarrs, all a year and a half apart. The oldest was Angela, who had suffered oxygen-deficiency at birth, and would never mature beyond the age of 12. Next came Timmy, solitary and taciturn. Bea was third, a tomboy till the age of 13, and Gregory fourth, serious and temperamental. After him came Paul (me), Nicholas and finally, Peter.

It was a chilly but shining morning in March of my first year in school, when fitful winds alternated with heavenly calms, and tiny blue flowers bloomed in the grass. After the tyranny of the school week, *Saturday* had come, and real life could resume.

Around 11:00, I was playing with Greg and Nick near the back door when our eyes lit on the old chicken-coop. Greg lifted the latch and we went inside. The chickens had gone years before, but the musty smell of dried manure and hay lingered. Sun streamed through the south window and tiny feathers floated to the floor, stirred by our entrance. It seemed a warm, ideal place to live, and we felt the unaccustomed urge to set up house. Since it was near lunchtime, I said, "I know what, let's fix a meal of hot dogs and beans!"

Greg and Nicky eagerly agreed.

As Nicky's elders, Gregory and I took responsibility for laying down rules. "I'll be the father," Greg decided. "Paul, you play the mother."

I didn't feel very comfortable with that role. Girls didn't have as much fun as boys, and then, when they grew up, they had to be housewives and do dishes, which I despised. As for wearing dresses – Yuck! I reluctantly agreed, in order to get on with things, but at least I could pass on the discomfort. "Okay, Nicky – you're Grandma!"

Nicky just studied his feet, awaiting instructions.

"Fine!" Greg nodded.

Now that we had defined the social order, we were ready to begin family life.

"Listen, Grandma!" I said. "I want you to go to the store and get us some paper plates and matches."

"Okay," Nicky replied dutifully, "but what are the matches for? Mama said never to play with matches..."

"To light our stove and cook dinner, dummy! And of course she told *you* not to play with matches – babies don't know what they're doing!"

Nicky still looked worried, so Mother reassured him: "Look, nothing is going to happen! Now, mind you hurry, Grandma – lunch has to be on time!" I was starting to warm to my role.

Nicky departed on his errand, and Mr. Greg and Mrs. Paul made preparations for lunch. Mr. Greg, as basic provider of raw goods, found an old cotton blanket in the corner and spread it over the chicken wire platform under the roosts. "Our table and stove!" he announced exuberantly, flinging his hand out, magician-like.

Mrs. Paul sang a little tune to establish domestic harmony while waiting for Grandma. She didn't notice, but Father looked annoyed. After only a few minutes, Grandma Nick returned with the required items.

"Where's Mama?" I asked.

"*You're* Mama," Nicky answered trustfully.

"No, I mean *our* mother!"

"In the basement, doing the washing," he replied.

"Okay!" I was pleased. It was always good to know the location of people who might interfere. "Let's set the plates!"

Father and Mother bustled about amicably (for the moment), setting clean paper plates on the faded pumpkin-and-white blanket.

"Now it's time to cook the pork and beans!" Father exclaimed forcefully.

So Mother took the matches from Grandma, and struck one to light.

How wonderful the flame looked! Oh, the power and satisfaction of being grown-up! I held the match to the blanket (I mean, the stove), and it began to eat into it slowly. Dinner would *definitely* be done soon!

Then I noticed that Nicky looked troubled, and started shuffling his feet when he saw the blanket catch fire. Soon he began to edge nervously toward the door.

"What's the matter?" I snapped.

"I don't think you should..." Nicky hesitated.

"Aw, don't be a baby!" Father told him crushingly.

When the flames quickly reached a foot high, Greg and I tore our eyes away from the mesmerizing sight of dinner cooking, and stole another glance at Nicky. He was gone! The shed door closed softly.

I hissed at Gregory, "He's going to tell Mama, the little tattletale!" and lunged after the traitor. Sticking my head out the door, I yelled at his retreating form, trotting toward the house.

"You come back here right now, Grandma! We'll get you for this!"

Irritatingly, Grandma had developed a mind of his own. He didn't even reply, but just laid his ears back, and kept right on going. As he slipped in the back door I barked one last order, "*Grandma Pfarr – you - get - back - here - now!*"

Mr. and Mrs. Greg-Paul were furious, and started to enumerate the things they were going to do to Grandma, but I will leave out the details, since it sets a poor example of how to treat elder parents. Our diatribe was cut short by the flames, which were now three feet tall and began to claim our full attention. This was getting to be a *little* scary, but Gregory and I possessed the raw materials of strong character, and were still confident that our powers would be equal to the task. So we held our ground, but dropped our family roles and got down to business.

"*Quick, Greg!* Let's wet on it – that'll put it out!"

Both ex-parents followed that sage advice, using their own built-in watering equipment. The water supply ran out all too quickly, however... and the smell! (As a firefighting technique, I would give it a D-minus.) We were dismayed when this creative idea failed, and the fire was still growing. Grief over the ruined dinner, which the firefighters had dealt its deathblow, was forgotten. Now we were *frightened*, feeling not older than our years, but somewhat younger and possibly not grown-up at all! It was time to run and get the real Mama.

As we fled, yelling, "Help! Mama!" we ran into her, coming in the door. Boy, were we glad! She was calm and relaxed – not even running, as though this happened every day! With great *sangfroid,* she grabbed the blazing blanket by an unburned edge, and dragged it outside, to roll and smother it. We felt extremely foolish – a simple solution had lain before us, while we wasted precious time on nonsense! It was a humbling experience, and so undeserved.

Mother took a good look at us, after the fire was out. We were smoke-grimed, with tears streaking down our faces, augmented by the certainty of impending retribution. Our fingers were slightly burned, and we had almost singed the watering devices. Greg and I were looking our most penitent, hoping to mitigate the force of the switch.

Mama didn't have the heart to discipline us just then, but stated after lunch that our father would do it when he got home. We relaxed surreptitiously. He hated disciplining us, and would comply with the letter of the law, but that was all. Our mother whipped us with more enthusiasm, probably because she suffered firsthand from our misdeeds, while he had only hearsay for his motivation.

So when the requisite whippings were delivered and supper eaten, it was time to go to sleep like the erstwhile chickens. Nick and I lay in our bed, snuggled up amicably. Greg, who wasn't so lucky, was in Timmy's bed, and therefore not snuggled at all. By now we had forgotten the earlier day when the shed almost burned down, Grandma was sacked, and our pretend-dinner ruined.

But the Wolf was not asleep. This time, he cornered Greg and me in the coop, roaring that he was going to *r-r-roast* us!

As far as I know, Nick slept peacefully. Grandma had done his duty by getting Mama and saving the shed (and perhaps our precious persons, though I wasn't ready to believe *that*). Even today, I am still a little peeved with Grandma for betraying us.

Chapter II.

The Grand Inquisitor

Along the creek embankment, the sun speckled the ground under the two great elms. Mama had just carried laundry out the cellar door to hang on the line, and set it down to see what I was doing by myself. Greg was gone – taken by "school," like Angela, Timmy and Bea. What I heard from them made it sound like prison. They always complained of problems, and even worse, I saw them miserable over homework. (Why did there have to be *homework*, too, after all day lost?) Right now I was worried because Mama was talking about sending *me* to kindergarten. I never wanted to leave my creek, garden, fields and woods. But she gave me good news this morning – no kindergarten, just first grade next fall! I was so happy that I ran all the way around the house twice – free for another year! It seemed like forever.

The day came, though, right on solar schedule. After breakfast, the five of us set out together, but Timmy, who was 11, quickly disappeared down the road ahead, not caring to be burdened with our company. The walk was only three-quarters of a mile, but seemed much farther to me – up to the top of Pfarr Lane, down Jackson Street to the bridge at the bottom of the hill, and crossing over to Sewards' driveway just past Bear Creek. Sewards' narrow property had once run down to the creek, but previous-century stonemasons had built a 10-foot-high stone wall straight up from water-level and filled behind it, giving the owners room to build while the creek stayed its course below.

The problem was that their garage, built hard against a large maple tree overhanging the creek wall, blocked our shortcut. On its other side, there was a chain link fence confining an obviously mad dog, and the only way to get by was to "walk the plank" – the 12-inch top of the wall, crowded closely by the tree. That always needed a little skill, so it appealed to us. The safest way was to hug the tree with your back to the water, edging sideways. In time, we found other techniques, the trickiest of which was to skip right through the pass, walking straight ahead. You did that if you wanted to impress someone you were bringing home after school.

Past the bottleneck, we crossed Perkins' lane, where a little black boy made of cast-iron held a ring for hitching horses, and took a path leading up the wooded hillside. That first morning, surrounded by warm, shining September, I thought, *this isn't so bad! Maybe school will be all right...*

We emerged just opposite St. Columban's. On the school grounds, cars were dropping off students, parents talking to teachers, and hundreds of kids milling around, some of the little ones crying. Girls skipped rope and boys played with marbles, all one confusing *fortissimo*. I was scared, so Bea, who was nine and in fourth grade, took my hand and drew me through the swarming kids, uphill into the building, where I was handed over to an ancient nun, Sister Mary Rumalda. "I'll be back after school," said Bea, and sprinted upstairs to her own class. Sister led me to my seat.

After five more minutes, while kids were delivered by brothers, sisters, or parents, the class was gathered, hands folded neatly on the desks, waiting for we-knew-not-what. The bell rang to signal the start of the day and pull in stragglers, and Sister Rumalda closed the door. But, as she turned to address the class, there was a commotion in the hall, and we jumped as the wooden door sustained a splintering blow. Then we heard a child crying, "No, Mommy! I don't wanna go! **P-P-P-lease!**"

A knock quickly followed. Sister opened it, presenting her best affable manner and political smile. I knew that act – my father used it when he had to deal with people he didn't really like.

A woman stood there, holding by the hand a little red-haired girl with braids, hiding behind her mother as much as she could.

"Hello, I'm Mrs. Doherty, and this is–"

But, "*N-o-oo...* Mommy, don't make me!"

Sister Rumalda recouped quickly. "S-o-oo nice to meet you." Then bending toward the girl, "And who's this?" in a syrupy voice.

The girl didn't buy it. She glowered, stuck her thumb defiantly in her mouth and buried her face in her mother's dress, refusing even to look at the nun.

Conceding momentary defeat, her mother answered for her, "This is Molly Doherty." Then, in a forced whisper, "Now, Molly, you *know* you have to go to school! *And take your thumb out of your mouth... you got over that years ago!* It'll be all right, you'll see - just do as the teacher says!"

She tried to pry her daughter loose, but Molly began to scream again, "*No! I won't go! I won't! I hate you!*" It was unclear whether this was addressed to her mother, Sister Rumalda, or merely the situation in general.

Mrs. Doherty managed to push Molly to the threshold, but the little girl fought like a frenzied badger, so Sister grabbed hold of Molly's classroom side and began to pull her in. The class sat paralyzed by the dreadful spectacle, but shortly the potential student was forced inside the room, and the door kicked shut. *Wham!*

So far, so good, but this maneuver created two problems: *One*, the girl's dress was now caught in the door, which gave the nun the advantage in the fight, but would present a logistical problem when Molly was freed. *Two*, the kicking, biting wildgirl was now inside, but with only one opponent, and it was evident from Molly's continued vigor that no surrender was imminent.

A vicious battle ensued. At one point, Sister caught her breath long enough to quaver, "You naughty, wicked girl, I'll settle *your* hash!"

But Molly riposted, yelling, "I'll break your glasses, **witch**!" An ominous silence descended. Sister Rumalda gasped, but recovered quickly from this leveler, and flung back, "You **devil!** Why... why... I'll call the police!"

The old nun finally realized that things were going to get uglier, and perhaps in front of the class was not the best place to carry on. So she tried to drag Molly to the coatroom, forgetting, in her rage, the girl's dress, still caught in the door. (Well... not for long!) A loud **R-R-R-IP** was heard, and a goodly patch was left behind.

But Sister had more important things to attend to, and barely noticed. She stuck to her task with the conviction that she was fighting the devil herself, who would undermine the pillars of the Church, the bastions of Society, and the World As We Knew It.

Molly was hauled to the coatroom and finished off in a very primitive finishing-school. We couldn't see the proceedings, but heard more than we wanted to. Sister Rumalda mastered the situation, using in tandem the classroom pointer and the continuing threat of sending Molly to jail. It was too much for a little girl, however determined, and she finally capitulated. Silence fell, and Sister Rumalda shortly emerged from the coatroom victorious, stiffly holding Molly's hand. In spite of her red, tear-stained face and the rent in her dress, Molly's head was held high, and around the mouth lingered a mulish expression.

What our class got out of this was that you couldn't get past Sister Rumalda – right or wrong, martial law ruled. If you crossed her, she would call the police, and then you would go to jail. Didn't we hear her say so? None of us doubted she would make good her threat.

Perhaps Molly hadn't made the acquaintance of nuns before, but had only seen them at church, dressed in their floor-length black robes. The reality of being handed over to one of those strange creatures, especially one who was very old, wearing gold-framed spectacles, may have been too much. (Or perhaps she was just behaving very badly. I know – nowadays, it's usually the parents and teachers who are punished. The kid is merely counseled, to prepare him or her for a life of incarceration, I suppose.)

Molly was led to her seat at the front of the class, and Sister Rumalda started over, in a slightly trembling voice. "Welcome, children, to the first grade."

There was no more trouble that day, but thereafter, the class treated Molly with respect. She was nicknamed "Mad Molly," and eventually went on to lead the underground resistance. Never again did she engage in a knockdown/drag-out fight, but chose instead to work behind the scenes, contradicting and undermining what those in authority taught, especially if she thought it was a cover for wrongdoing. Towards the end of grade school, she said things like, "Faith is largely a smokescreen to gloss over bad logic and appease foggy minds." The New Age had infiltrated St. Columban's.

Molly tried to avoid trouble, but couldn't always help herself. Once, when Sister was teaching us to read, Molly raised her hand, and when called on, corrected her, saying, "The way you're making the class pronounce 'a' in 'A ball rolled out into the road,' is wrong. It should be 'Uh ball' not 'Ay ball!' Nobody talks like that." Sister was furious. She gave Molly a paddling, and made her sit in the corner.

The old grade school was a plain, three-story brick building with a flat roof, on a hill overlooking Old Loveland. It had the feeling of a country school, with a little "old neighborhood" thrown in. Approaching from below, the first thing you saw was our church, dominating road and wooded slope beyond. The school grounds were fenced, except for the church entrance, to keep kids and balls from the road. Beside the church sat the large, brick rectory, with the school building behind. There were also a rundown garage and a tiny, yellow house in the parking lot, looking like something out of The Wizard of Oz. It had served various needs throughout its history, including a classroom for the seventh graders. I was always sorry I never had a class there.

When I first came to St. Columban's, the nuns lived on the third floor of the school. It was instant death to be caught anywhere near the top floor, or even the first step of the stairs leading to it. Due to burgeoning enrollment, they later moved into the rectory, which had been renovated to accommodate separate quarters for them.

What added spice and drama to our existence was the proximity of the public grade school. The two properties abutted, separated by a chain-link fence. This fortuitous circumstance gave us the opportunity to scrutinize the heathens in their pen and thank God that we weren't born in captivity on that side of the fence. It never occurred to us that *los otros* might have felt the same way.

This, of course, was some years prior to Vatican II – toleration of other religions wasn't *in*. From our earliest days at school, the Baltimore Catechism, a long series of questions and answers about what we believed, was a major part of Religion class, and right along with it, we were spoon-fed information about "the Public." Anyone belonging to other religions, and especially *those others* across the fence were "the Public," and were never to be associated with, or even talked to. It was a dirty word, synonymous with heathen, barbarian, pagan, and, of course, atheist.

"The Public" was an enemy, huge, silent, and with few civilized principles, waiting to undermine our morality. They weren't quite as bad as the Communists, but, yes, there was a member of the Public under every bed. We must always be alert and strictly adhere to our teaching. It was our duty to defend the Faith, at all times and in all places, especially including correcting and attempting the conversion of those pitiful folk who were not Catholic. (By contrast, the "Gentiles" we heard about in the Gospels on

Sundays conjured up a peaceful image. My brothers and I kept a lookout for those Gentiles, planning to treat them properly, as Scripture required, but never met anybody from that group, that we knew of.)

The real Communists were even worse. It was not so much "one under every bed," but they were *admittedly* working to destroy the Church and the Western World. The nuns' stories made it clear that *This Meant You!* Small kids were not excluded – we were told vivid tales of the treatment of clergy and children just like us, behind the Iron Curtain. We could be nabbed at any time, even from our beds, so we had to be ready to be Christian martyrs! It was terrifying, but we were determined to be brave.

On the local level, the nuns fed us regular reports concerning the reprehensible behavior of ***those kids next door***, detailing what this or that confirmed-felon kid had done, and reiterating their fates. *Why, they didn't even have the benefit of baptism* (other churches didn't count), and were therefore unwashed by true divine water, unshriven, and unforgiven (at least by us).

I don't know exactly what the old guard meant for us to do with this information about "the Public." (Were they planning a *Jihad?*) For instance, if the Public was to be reviled, why did Sister Geraldine, our principal, act so friendly whenever we saw her talking to Mr. Mann, the principal next door? It was several years before we would be able to understand all the subtleties and complexities of that "P" word.

Inevitably, a kid broke the rules now and then, when taunted beyond what mortal flesh could bear by the heathen through the fence. Then, due to his rigorous training, and fueled by an excess of religious fervor, he felt morally obligated to loosen his tongue and tell the infidels just what he thought of them, and what would happen to them in the afterlife. This naturally made the recipient of that Good News mad enough to want to thrash the messenger, and to taunt him, "If you dare to come over here, I'll show you what *I'm* going to do." I guess the kid who was told he would be damned in the hereafter decided to pound one of the Chosen *now*, while he still had the chance.

"I doubt if you could do anything, with God on my side," the Elect might reply righteously (but snottily). "Even if you do beat me up, it will only increase your torment in hell."

Someone would invariably throw down the gauntlet: "I'll meet you after school – or *right now*, if you have the guts to climb the fence."

The other kid hardly ever turned down this opportunity to defend his pride, his *alma mater*, and religion, all in one stroke. It seemed like a divine mandate. They would meet in battle, heedless of the fence and Sister Geraldine's wrath, and one-on-one soon became many-on-many, as kids from each side swarmed to their hero (or antihero, depending on point of view).

The nun who was playground-monitor would run and fetch Sister Geraldine, shouting, "The Huns have invaded from the north!" The principals from both sides, with all the teachers that could be mustered, would converge on the battleground, blowing whistles and cuffing hardened miscreants who were still engaged in throttling the enemy and biting his ears.

Such a *mêlée* provided Sister Geraldine with a particularly good reason to call one of her punitive school assemblies on Friday, and she always seemed satisfied when a week could end up like this. Though we seemed to receive a mixed message from her: She made it clear we had done wrong, but looked as though she wouldn't have minded a go at them herself. Following her scholarly bent, Molly looked up "Geraldine" in a book of names, and found that it meant "Spear-ruler." It certainly seemed to fit.

The pastor was noticeably absent from the disciplinary assemblies. With regard to the school, he kept himself separate from those engaged in mucking out the stalls. (Interesting, how the class system is never really shaken off, no matter how many revolutions have occurred.) He mostly just inspected the stables after they were clean, and gave pep talks to our classes now and then. It helped him to preserve his dignity as a spiritual leader, while running the parish smoothly, saying Mass and administering the sacraments. From class, we would see him go by on some parish errand in his dignified black cassock, biretta atop his head, looking to us truly like God's representative on earth.

All the kids, especially the boys, loved Father Imbus. He was cut in the mold of a country squire, keeping Beagles at the rectory, and hunting them in season. There were always a couple of hunting stories circulating about the parish... "I called him to administer the last rites to my father, and I was never more surprised – he came straight from hunting, with his Beagles and his gun!"

Father had some endearing traits. Although he left St. Columban's when I was in the 3rd grade, I never forgot him. Once, at the school festival in 2nd grade, he won a big spinning-top, the kind you pumped, at one of the games. Our family could never afford toys like that. He turned around, saw how hungrily I was eyeing the top, and said, "Here, son. You take this home." Nothing like that had ever happened to me. I started playing with it right there on the blacktop. Father Imbus was like that.

He played with the kids at recess, too. It wasn't unusual to find him squatted down on the playground in the center of a noisy group, shooting marbles, yelling and shouting with them over a good shot: "Wow! That was a great one! You got my boulder! Hey, shoot again, Mike!" putting an arm around his protégé's shoulder.

The passionate energy emanating from marble competition made the Sisters uneasy: It bore a remarkable similarity to a crap game. Not for *nothing* had they been thoroughly trained to detect all the stratagems of the devil! Fortunes in purees, boulders, cat's eyes, old-fashioned clay marbles and ball bearings were won and lost daily, and the nuns observed the unrest generated when squabbles occurred due to cheating or larceny. Their consciences urged them to action – gambling was wrong! But it presented a dilemma, like the problem of Father's smoking. How could they effectively interdict what their very own pastor (Christ's representative on earth!) obviously sanctioned?

I suspect the frustration of having their hands tied in some areas produced an over-zealous attitude in others. The nuns had a closet where articles impounded "for cause" were kept. Its contents were legendary, seen only in snatched glimpses and described apocryphally to succeeding classes. Past generations of boys had contributed divers goods, some by playing with them in class, others illegal anywhere on school grounds. There were slingshots, dice, packs of cards, whoopee cushions, peashooters, yo-yos, airplane gliders, marbles, squirt guns, pocketknives, and comic books – especially Zorro. He was considered to have Nazi leanings, because they felt that the "Z" he made was part of a swastika, and were afraid the kids would draw the rest. (We thought that was funny, but some of the nuns had recently come from Europe, and World War Two had ended only nine years before.) There was even an arrow, so prized by the constabulary that it was hung inside the closet door, a symbolic victory over the "Robin Hood nonsense," which embodied the heresy that you could virtuously steal from the rich to give to the poor.

The girls' contributions to the closet were more insidious, but nonetheless dangerous, especially articles manifesting the incursions of incipient vanity: in that category were lipsticks, perfume, combs, compact mirrors, improper articles of clothing, and teenage magazines, as well as a couple of gaudy rosaries. There were also a few jack-paddles, a hula-hoop that had wandered too far from home, some contraband jump ropes, and a beret with a crude effigy of Elvis on it. (As far as the Sisters were concerned, he was prominent among the fallen angels.)

Once impounded, items could only be released to their bereft owners by the pastor's intervention. Otherwise, what disappeared into that closet was gone. The nuns knew that most parents in those days would never bother to make an issue of it, and they were right.

The treasures that accumulated year after year were probably reassuring to the Sisters, testimonials to their effectiveness in the ongoing battle with the Archenemy. All the boys hungered to get in that closet, but never, to my knowledge, succeeded.

In 1954-55, Walt Disney brought out the "Davy Crockett" TV series. We didn't have a TV, but I saw episodes at my grandmother's house. Soon, every kid in the land wanted a coonskin cap, and we were no exception. I *pined* for that cap, but my parents couldn't afford one, let alone five of them.

Father Imbus would come out of the rectory at recess with the Beagles following joyfully, and call out, "C'mon, boys, gather round!" We eagerly obliged, and he would lead the group in song, many of the boys in their coonskin caps, singing at the top of their lungs:

"Born on a mountain in Tennessee

Greenest state in the land of the free

Raised in the woods so he knew every tree

He killed him a b'ar when he was only three!

 "♫ Davy, Davy Crockett,

 King of the Wild Frontier! ♫"

Father knew all six verses, too; we were much impressed. The Beagles howled gleefully along, and a merry time was had by all.

I could tell that some of the nuns would have liked to relax and enjoy it, too, but they were concerned about nuts and bolts. Their reasoning went something like this: Davy Crockett and the *wild* frontier were secular. Davy couldn't possibly have attended Mass out there. And the very word "wild" troubled them. They figured the kids were wild enough, and might go *completely* wild on them with a tad of encouragement. Moreover, hero-worship reminded them too much of false gods. Some of the older nuns would have liked to stamp out the coonskin caps (and maybe some of the kids wearing them), but again, could hardly do so with the pastor visibly supporting them. (It <u>was</u> a warm hat, after all, however silly by adult standards.)

* * *

Sister Mary Geraldine, the principal who ruled our grade-school days with an iron fist, was large, red-faced, and angry most of the time. Sensitive and shy kids trembled when she rustled by them in her black robes, an emblem more of God's vengeance than His love. (She might even have been pleased to know that.) She seemed to epitomize all the repressive nuns we knew, and we wondered sometimes why so many nuns seemed to be mean. Could it be *that* bad to live a religious life and teach kids?

Sister Geraldine saw the world as an unending procession of rules and crimes against them. Every child under her authority was a lawbreaker – it was just a matter of degree and discovering the particulars. Her policy was to hunt down and interrogate them, and <u>make</u> them repent. Molly called her "the Grand Inquisitor."

Sister employed various methods for accomplishing her goals. A favorite was the use of upperclassmen as her eyes and ears, and as a posse, when needed. Regrettably, her judgment in selecting spies was deplorable – she invariably chose either those who were actually behind the "crimes" or were bullies, delighted to have a legitimate pretext for abuse.

There was one time when someone had "wrung" an outside faucet during recess. Sister Geraldine and her henchmen visited all the classes, searching for the miscreant(s), and she angrily addressed Greg's third-grade class: "Some wicked boy has wantonly wrung the faucet outside, and we're going to find out **who he is!**" (She omitted the girls from this speech, since by its nature it had to be a male crime. It was assumed that only boys would be interested in things of a mechanical nature. Not all of the discrimination in those days was *against* the girls.)

The kids weren't old enough to know what a wanton was, and in fact didn't know what a wrung faucet was, but it sounded pretty bad.

Sister continued, "My good boy Ronnie is now going to take the boys' pulses." Ronnie was a cadaverously thin, stoop-shouldered eighth-grader, standing six feet two inches tall, with round, black glasses perched above a sharp nose. With jet-black hair, white shirt and black pants, he looked remarkably like a large, brooding heron about to dive on a fish.

Ronnie had convinced his principal that he had a talent for discovering the guilty by taking their pulses, with results comparable to a lie-detector test. This God-given ability was too tempting for her to pass up, so he enthusiastically put it to work in the service of truth and right (and only incidentally power among the proletariat).

The tall, sinister boy-man advanced slowly down the aisles, stooping to peer at each boy, and doing something mysterious to all their wrists. All the third-grade boys were terrified, and Greg watched the proceedings with a sense of fatality. At eight, he didn't really comprehend what was going on, but knew it had to be important, since adults were taking it so seriously. He was shivering, and his heart and pulse rushed faster every minute. He felt instinctively that they *intended* to hear a confession. *Maybe confessing wouldn't be so bad*, he thought. *At least it would all be over.*

At that moment, his attention was drawn outside to Father Imbus, playing with his hounds. Golden leaves were fluttering to the ground, and the dogs were jumping, barking and licking his hands. Father was smiling, calling their names and petting them. Greg ached to be in that heaven, away from this awful dream, but he felt the noose drawing tighter, and *knew* he would be in it. Could he bolt for home? *No* – one of Sister's liegemen was guarding the door.

Then Ronnie stood before him, took his wrist, feeling the erratic pulse, and exulted to Sister Geraldine, "He's the one, Sister! He done it! Never fails!" Even though this was poor English, and St. Columban's prided itself on high standards in that area, the principal chose to overlook the infraction.

"I didn't do anything!" Greg protested. "What's wringing a faucet?"

But now it was the Grand Inquisitor's turn. Chastising the sinner was the Lord's work. "You wicked boy! You have willfully destroyed school property! Do you know how much it costs to run a school?" she demanded. "You're wasting your parents' money that they tithe to keep you here! Confess, boy!"

"I didn't do it!" Greg persisted tearfully.

"*What!* How dare you lie to me!" She slapped Greg's face. "Look, boys and girls, see how the devil already has this boy in his clutches!" Then, turning to the class, she smoothly shifted gears and spoke in a sugary voice. "Remember, children, God will always forgive you if you confess your sins, even though you must still atone in Purgatory."

This didn't seem like a very good deal for the confessed – first Sister Geraldine's punishment, then the fires of Purgatory and eventually forgiveness. It sounded like usury.

"I'll tell you what's going to happen to this boy *now*," she said slowly, emphasizing each word with satisfaction. "*He's* going to be expelled from school!"

There were moans from the class. The only thing worse than being expelled was excommunication from the Roman Catholic Church. Not that Greg would mind staying home from school – it was the shame of it. That only happened to *really* bad boys.

That night, Greg had to carry home a note stating that he was expelled, and why. However, it didn't turn out the way Sister intended. Our mother knew hogwash when she heard it, and successfully fought the ruling. Gregory stayed in school, and shortly afterward, the janitor confessed to having committed the crime. The evidence, a faucet handle, was found in his lair. A former St. Columban's student, he had apparently become nostalgic for the rigors of grade-school life, and, with time on his hands, had wrung the faucet in order to sit back and watch the manhunt and trial. It reminded him of his own school days, and he felt so much better that he didn't mind confessing. For his punishment, he had to wash all the windows in the Convent and make a special novena to the Blessed Virgin Mary, supervised by Sister Geraldine personally, to make sure it was done right.

No apology was ever given to my brother. Things just weren't done that way back then, and they figured that unmerited chastisement wouldn't do him any harm. After all, kids were always guilty of something, weren't they?

Chapter III.
The Pied Piper

Jimmy Ackerman was the neighborhood marvel. He stood about five feet tall when he was twelve, with dancing hazel eyes, short sandy-blond hair and skin that reddened and freckled in summer. I can see him standing – hands in his front pockets, legs apart, and a slingshot stuck in his belt. With his head tilted a little to one side and a quick smile, he had an elfin air that reminded me of Peter Pan. At almost-thirteen, he was *magic* – more alive than everyone else. The whole vastly exceeded the sum of his parts.

He loved make-believe, word quips, and intricate movements with his hands and feet, often alternately snapping the fingers of his hands while hitting one palm to the other fist, to make a sound of trotting horses.

Where Jimmy was, excitement gathered. He told the most captivating stories, some about his own exploits, and others from TV or the movies. When we were off alone, he could create an atmosphere of gripping drama, and we were entranced.

At the core of Jimmy's adventures was Rudolf, an omnipresent, omniscient threat, and bad clean-through – the Moriarty of our world. Jimmy fought a continuing battle against him, in defense of all free kids in the neighborhood, and Rudolf was constantly trying to destroy him. None of us had ever yet seen Rudolf, but that only meant he was more dangerous than ordinary criminals.

Sometimes Jimmy would suddenly exclaim: "Did you see him over there under the trees?"

"Who?" we'd ask, startled.

"Rudolf!" Jimmy would whisper fiercely. The day's mood would suddenly shift into stealth-mode... we'd have to look sharp if we weren't to be taken!

Jimmy was Bea's age, halfway between Timmy and Greg, and three years ahead of me. But, despite this spread, he managed to be friends with most of us at the same time by maintaining separate cliques, each with unwritten rules and a strictly observed hierarchy. He and Timmy played with bows and arrows and built camps together, or Timmy might invite Jimmy to go somewhere with him, but Timmy was in charge, and Jimmy was expected not to invite Greg or me. Jimmy couldn't just go get Timmy whenever he wanted, either.

Timmy was never there when *our* club was in session – he didn't often include Greg and me in his activities, except as slave labor. But Jimmy was more of a democrat, and would admit anyone who passed his ongoing ordeals. When I was eight, the Ackermans had a nutty dog named Pan. Black and fierce, with white whiskers of age on his nose, he stood about knee-high, and would certainly bite if you didn't freeze until someone called him off. Pan was Jimmy's divining rod, to factor out the chicken-hearted, and you had to keep undergoing it every time you went there – his way of keeping everyone honest. The very first time, I *knew* I mustn't show any fear, and just waited quietly for Jimmy. I was instantly inducted – he wasn't going to let a resource like that get away.

Our club consisted of Jimmy, Greg, Billy Martin, me, and sometimes Jimmy's younger sister Eve. As a girl, she was discriminated against to some extent, but since she was also a tomboy, the first to take a dare, and could throw a baseball like a boy, she was hard to overlook.

Billy Martin was the same age as Greg, but always seemed younger because of the way he acted. Of average height for his age, dark-skinned Caucasian, with black, short-cropped hair and even features, he would have been a nice-looking kid if he hadn't lacked confidence and suffered from emotional problems at home. I don't think he ever possessed much natural courage, and, as the youngest in his family, he had to take a lot of guff. With his brothers riding him hard, he couldn't win, so he learned treachery, to compensate. Billy had also failed a grade in school, and it made him feel inferior. He was like a ruined dog – a supplicant, but not one to trust if you weren't watching him. If you depended on Billy, he would let you down, then laugh, low in his throat, like bullets thrown from a machine gun. "Unh–hunh–hunh–hunh–hunh–hunh–hunh!" It was painful to hear.

Billy didn't exactly pass the ordeals – he was afraid of Pan, and everybody knew it. But it amused Jimmy, and Billy seemed to contrast well with the rest of us, showcasing our virtues and balancing the forces of good and evil in our games. Jimmy would tell little anecdotes about how Billy gobbled and ran for it on this occasion or that, but he was sorry for him, too.

The men in Billy's family cussed nonstop, but Billy admired us because we didn't swear or lose control. He did, often. *He make heap bad Indian*, we thought, but that was all right. When you play war games, someone has to die, and he was made for the role of the doomed bad guy. (He tried to cheat at that, too.)

The Ackermans lived in a big house off Jackson Street. We called it a mansion, because its attractions included three stories; 20 rooms; 13-foot ceilings; a ballroom; a large dungeon-like basement; an attic large enough to live in; and, at the very top of the house, a small tower with glass windows. It was a regular warren, and seemed to us like something out of "The Arabian Nights." In their kitchen, the floor, walls and even the ceiling were covered with beautiful tiles in many colors, some of them etched before the clay was fired to show biblical scenes. Their living room had a huge fireplace, stained-glass windows, and a chandelier. We thought the Ackermans were rich.

One summer day when Greg was eleven and I was nine, we went up there. Jimmy was polishing his dad's 1950 DeSoto station wagon – you know, the one with the walrus grill in front. It was forest-green, with lots of real oak paneling all around, even on the tailgate. Our station wagon was actually newer, but we wanted *that* one. While he was finishing up, Jimmy said in a hushed voice, "There's something I've got to tell you!"

"What?" Greg asked.

"Shhh! Not *here!*" Jimmy whispered. "I think Rudolf is listening!"

"Where? How?" We hunched close to Jimmy, beginning to shiver with excitement.

"I saw him just now, disappearing into the trees over by the fence line."

"Oh! Okay!"

"We'd better go down cellar," he continued. "It's safer there."

Goosebumps attacked the hair on my arms. It was only early summer, and boy, was it starting *right*! We hurried after him into the old sandstone-block garage, through the massive cellar door, and down the long stairway to the bottom.

The cellar was huge, extending under the whole house, with ceilings at the edge of vision, and dark except for a couple of bare light bulbs, burning dimly, far apart. There was a dank smell, discarded junk lying around, and lots of cobwebs. Every now and then, we would see the glow of greenish daylight from small windows set high on the walls in the cavernous rooms.

Jimmy led the way, using his penlight where electric light was lacking, to a remote back-cellar room, far under the house.

"Have you ever seen any ghosts here?" I asked nervously.

"Sure have!" Jimmy said, in a sinister voice. "I could tell you some hair-raising things about what happened to Evie and me down here last Halloween, but not now – later! After I show you something."

We wanted to ask if it was safe even now, but it wouldn't have been manly. Jimmy answered our thoughts, though: "Don't worry, I used some holy water that Gran brought back from Jerusalem to get rid of them. It'll hold for a while, except on Halloween."

We came to a blank wall. Jimmy stopped and faced us, saying in his most serious voice, "What I'm about to show you is secret. No one else knows, not even Mom and Dad. Not Evie, either. She's a good egg, and I wouldn't mind telling her, but she's a girl, and I'm not sure she can be trusted!" He put both hands in his pockets, rocked back on his heels, and grew very still. "Can I *really* trust <u>you</u> boys?"

"Yeah!"

"Will you swear on your mother's name and a stack of Bibles, cross your heart, and hope to die?" The sacred intent was unmistakable.

"We swear!" we answered unwaveringly.

"OK, then, but remember, it may be harder than you think to keep this secret. If Rudolf captures you, he'll torture you... Are you ready for that?"

It was a recurring theme – the nuns were always preparing us for martyrdom with gruesome stories of children who had to die for their beliefs. *"Yes!"* We couldn't say anything else, and keep our self-respect.

"Great!" Jimmy approved, rubbing his hands. He stooped to pick up a small ladder lying on the floor, and leaned it against the wall, then scrambled to the ceiling and raised a trapdoor, disappearing through the hole. We followed with alacrity – this was what we lived for!

The space was large and about four feet tall, built by Victorian carpenters between the basement and first floor. We couldn't quite stand up, but that didn't matter – it was another dimension!

Jimmy had divided a section from the rest of the crawlspace with old blankets and cardboard, to make a clubhouse enclosure. It was outfitted with a mattress to sit on, candles and matches, comic books like "Tom and Jerry" and "Donald Duck," and a battered copy of <u>Tom Sawyer</u>. There was even a cookie tin for comestibles. It was *perfect!* Greg and I were mightily impressed, though we said little, not wanting Jimmy to think we were babies, to be swept away by the arrangements.

We sat down on a scrap of rug, and Jimmy turned to us, with a grave expression that held us silent. This was our leader – so earnest and sincere that we were ready to follow him anywhere!

"Gentlemen, Rudolf has been causing a lot of trouble lately. He hounds me everywhere I go. Recently, he captured me and held me in the old Brock house basement for a *week!* I can tell you that was not a fun time – there was nasty water six inches deep on the floor, with broken canning jars in it, and the place was crawling with rats and poisonous spiders. He tied me up and wouldn't give me anything to eat or drink, and then he whipped me with a cat o' nine tails. I begged him for mercy – just one little sip of water, I cried. But Rudolf is a coldhearted bastard, and I just pray that *you* never get caught by him!"

We silently vowed again *never* to give up our secrets to torture.

"How did you get away?" I asked, appalled.

"Oh, I used a clever trick that I learned in Boy Scouts. Rudolf was going to let me die there, but I outwitted him! He forgot and left a candle burning, and I used it to burn the ropes and free myself. It hurt something fierce, but like my Dad says, you *do* what you *have* to do, when the going gets rough..."

Jimmy paused for effect, and then showed us burns on his wrists.

After a stunned pause, my brother whispered, "Why did he *do* all that?"

"Because he wanted to know where the cave was."

"A *CAVE?*" we choked.

"I can't tell you any more, unless we become blood-brothers. If we don't, our club secrets won't be safe, or any of the kids around here. I know way too much about Rudolf and his crimes. It's too big a risk, without a blood-oath binding us to silence."

We had just nodded solemnly, when Billy Martin's head popped through the hatch.

"I thought *we* were the only ones that knew about this!" I complained.

"Billy's already a blood-brother. Boy, did he squeal when I took a little blood!" Jimmy quipped.

Billy hung his head. "Well, it *hurrrt!*" he protested, in his Kentucky twang.

"How did you get past Pan, anyway?" Greg wondered.

"I expect Gran was feeding him inside, lucky for Billy." Jimmy was getting his bloodletting equipment ready, watching surreptitiously to see if we would bolt. There were a couple of wicked-looking curved upholstery needles, instead of the traditional pocketknife.

"Since you're here now, Billy, you want to do it again to show the Pfarrs how it's done?" Jimmy teased.

"No way, dammit!" Billy whined. "*Shi-i-it*, once was enough!"

"Hey, cut that out!" Greg yelled. "Or we're going to leave!"

"Okay – okay! I won't do it again." Billy tittered painfully.

Beginning to eye the dark spaces edging the partitions, I asked Jimmy, "Are there many spiders down here?"

"Sure, I saw a couple of Black Widows last week." It never failed to amaze us how many things Jimmy had seen – copperheads, water moccasins, Black Widows, and one-legged men.

"*You did?*" Everyone exclaimed, on cue.

"Sure... Look!" he pointed. "There's one on Billy now!"

Billy screamed and rolled over satisfactorily, clawing at his shirt and head.

Jimmy started laughing. "Got you, chicken-liver!"

Billy jumped on him then, and they started tussling on the mat. But this spectacle was interrupted when Evie thrust *her* head through the trap. Everyone groaned.

"You're not supposed to know about this place!" Jimmy accused.

"Oh, give me a break! I've known since the first day you and Tim Pfarr broke in here."

"Criminy, who *else* knows?" He demanded. "Anne? Jean? Mother? Father?"

"Of *course* not! What do you think I *am*? Anne's so busy with her new boyfriend and her car, she doesn't see or hear anything." She pursed her lips, rolled her eyes, and patted her hair in imitation. "'Ooh, la *la!* I do *so-o-o* love you!' It's sickening!"

"You'll be just like her, when you're Anne's age!" Jimmy taunted in a falsetto voice.

"I WILL NOT! *Pig!*" With that inelegant remark, Eve left promptly through the trapdoor, before Jimmy could retaliate.

"Never mind – I'll get her later," Jimmy said. "We have important business. Give me your hands."

We bravely stuck our hands out, and Jimmy pricked my thumb, then Greg's. Billy Martin giggled mirthlessly, but neither of us showed any pain. Then Jimmy pricked his own finger, mixed all the blood, and declared us blood-brothers. "Sure you don't want to be a part of this, Billy?" he taunted. "It's not too late..."

"Hell, no!" Billy bristled.

"You'll only be a blood-brother with me, then, and half a blood-brother with them." (This was OK with us – we didn't want to get any closer to Billy, anyway.)

Billy wasn't speaking.

"What's that red stuff you put on the needles?" I asked Jimmy.

"Iodine. It's an antiseptic, so you don't get blood poisoning and go mad. Then they'd have to chain you to a tree." And he paused to share with us the grisly story of such a man, courtesy of late-night TV (which, of course, he wasn't supposed to be watching). Whenever Jimmy or Billy described what they'd seen on TV, we were enthralled, since we only got to see it at someone else's house.

Billy said, "Hey, man, I've gotta go... Mom wants me home for supper at 4:30, or Dad'll whip me." He threaded himself down the ladder, and left.

Recapturing the spotlight immediately, Jimmy held out a small book to us. "Swear!"

"Tom Sawyer?" I asked, staring at the cover. It seemed appropriate, in a way, but not what we'd expected.

"Oh! Sorry, wrong book." Jimmy grinned, picking up the King James Bible (the one with all the *thee's* and *thou's*). "Do you solemnly swear on this Holy Bible never to reveal our secrets to anyone, especially Rudolf, so help you God?"

Greg and I placed our hands on the Bible, and gravely swore: **"We do!"** This was just like church. Nothing could have made us feel more real, purposeful, and one with the divine plan.

"OK! Now you're real Indian blood-brothers. Let's go to the *cave!*" Jimmy exulted.

"Where is it? How did you find it?" Greg asked excitedly.

"I dug it out of a bank. Wait – you'll see. I needed a place Rudolf couldn't find me, where I could lay up for weeks at a time... C'mon, let's go while there's some afternoon left!" Jimmy disappeared through the trap door.

"Okay!" We shouted, firing ourselves down the ladder.

Emerging from the dark cellar, blinking, we found that a small thunderstorm had passed, and the sun was shining again. Trees and grass were winking with drops and prisms, and the sky was washed like a watercolor painting – blue, with blinding-white clouds.

Jimmy led us down the freshly mown lawn, with its stone benches and summer furniture, under the lengthening tree shadows. We passed the old barn, and crossed the field where long use had scribed a footpath through a young wood. Soon we came upon the board camp he and Timmy had built, fairly large, with a tin roof, window, and board door. We looked longingly, but Jimmy hurried us on. "We don't have time today, but don't worry – I'll show you later."

A little farther on, we came to the Ackermans' boundary, a fence line that cut across our path at the brow of a wooded hill. To the right was the old Brock property, but our way took us left until we reached the corner where Hortons' land adjoined. Pulled down at the corner from the immemorial climbing of local kids, the fences had once contained grazing animals that roamed no more. We crossed automatically.

Three choices of direction lay before us now. Left were a field, Hortons' Pond, and another way back to Jimmy's house. The straight path continued along the fence to the Grailville farm, and to the right, a leaf-strewn cart track slanted down through the woods to Bear Creek. It lay in deep shade, beckoning, and Jimmy turned that way.

The land fell steeply to the right, and lordly beech trees towered above. A dim, greenish glow spread underfoot, and the sun transmuted soft young leaves overhead to a translucent green-gold. We walked in unusual silence, and instinctively remembered that this was the first church of ancient men. Greg and I were half Druid already, and these were clearly trees to be worshipped – they even bore carved wooden placards, with their Latin names in Old English script. *Fagus Grandifolia* was American Beech, *Acer Saccharum* American Sugar Maple, *Carya Ovata* Shagbark Hickory, and there were many others. The lack of English didn't bother us, since we already knew the English names of all local trees. It was neat! We wondered who had put them there, vaguely supposing that Frank Horton's Boy Scout Troop had done it.

Soon we heard the sound of water tumbling over falls. Wood thrushes were beginning to trill quietly to each other, mirroring the water's chuckle. It was always such a remote, ethereal sound, as though they stood in the doorway of a magic world.

Jimmy interrupted. "Hey, we've gotta go on – it's getting late."

We had forgotten the cave. "The cave! Yeah, let's go!" Greg shouted.

We pelted down the path, only slowing to bear right along the stream as it took its way toward the O'Bannon Creek and thence to the two big rivers. It wasn't long before we came to the falls. Here the water slipped over a rock ledge, dropping six or seven feet into a pool. We were surprised – the pool seemed large for such a small creek.

"Boy, that looks like a good place to swim this summer!" I said.

"It *is*!" Jimmy said.

"Can we dive from the top ledge?" Greg asked.

"Sure, if you're up to it. We did all the time, last summer. In a few days it'll be warm enough, and we can all go swimming, if you're not afraid of cold water and heights," he added flippantly. We knew he was trying to take the pulse of any weaklings, and silently vowed he would find none here.

The falls sparkled from the spring's recent cleansing, and we stood watching until Greg suddenly noticed, "Hey, where's Jimmy?"

We looked all around, but couldn't spot him. Then we heard stifled giggling from somewhere above. Roots hung down the bank under a huge red oak tree, and we scrambled up, parting the stringy beard to reveal a hidden enclosure.

"Wow!" I said, looking around.

Jimmy was delighted. "You should have seen the looks on your faces when you noticed I was gone!" he chortled.

We didn't respond, not particularly wanting to celebrate our foolishness. But the cave drove away any embarrassment.

"Boy, this is neat," Greg grinned. "Who dug it all out?"

"Oh, me, and your brother Timmy, and Billy Martin."

"*Billy* knows about this?" (Not *again!*)

Playing to the house, Jimmy said, "I figured it would be best, in case no one else was around, and he had to rescue me someday from Rudolf."

"But how can you ever trust him?" I burst out.

"Rudolf?" Jimmy asked, startled.

"No! *Billy!*" I said.

"Well, I know he's a lily-livered coward, but he can sneak and slink like a weasel, which might be an advantage, if Rudolf finally gets me... Think about it! What's Billy good at? Ratting on somebody! He can sneak off to the police or my parents if I disappear, at the same time he's pretending to Rudolf that he worships him."

Still disgruntled, Greg said, "Well... if you put it that way, it sounds better, but I still don't like it!" Greg had experience with Billy's treachery. You never knew when he might shoot you in the back with his slingshot, or throw a rock at you when you weren't looking.

"Candy bars, anyone?" Jimmy produced a tin from a makeshift shelf.

Greg eagerly took a "Baby Ruth," and I grabbed a "Snickers." Jimmy chose a Hershey bar.

We looked around as we ate. Jimmy had discovered the natural opening under the oak tree and enlarged it considerably. Roots still showed in the ceiling, and the place was rough, but we weren't thinking about dirt or spiders. It was a CAVE, and it was *ours!*

The room was large enough for four kids, sitting down. There was even a small roof exit, in the back corner. Jimmy's impish eye caught mine. "The ceiling fell in on Billy Martin when he was digging back there. You should have seen it! Only his feet were sticking out. Timmy and I had to pull him out. Billy looked like a little pig that had been burrowing in black dirt, with only the whites of his eyes showing. He was madder than a wet hen, but every time he tried to swear, he couldn't, because he had a lot of dirt in his mouth! It was so funny, Timmy and I nearly had a conniption fit, laughing. I told Billy to keep his mouth shut next time, because you never knew what might fall in it! But, anyway, we have our bolt-hole, if we need it."

The next thing we knew, Jimmy was telling a fishing tale involving his father, but I interrupted. "How did you ever *find* this place?"

Jimmy didn't mind. "Now *that's* a story. I was on my way home from school one day, and decided to take a shortcut through the old haunted Brock place."

"*Haunted!*" This was news to us.

"Yeah, but never mind that, right now. Anyway, as I came around the corner of the house – you know the place, by the cellar doors between the house and the pool–" We nodded, and he went on. "–well, there Rudolf was, blocking my way home, and I didn't even have a slingshot or pocketknife! 'Sweet Jesus!' I said a prayer right then, and promised I would be a good Catholic when I grew up, if I lived.

"I was in a bad fix. There was a steep ravine on the left, and I knew I couldn't outrun him – he was too fast. He just stood there, smiling evilly, his head hanging to one side, and those black, curly locks falling over his forehead. In his right hand, he had a bullwhip, and in his other – a broken cross!

"He said: 'You've given me a lot of trouble, boy, but I've got you now, and I'm going to *whip you dead!*'

"Well, I started to say my very last prayers to myself, when I had this idea. I begged Rudolf, 'Please just let me say one little prayer!'

"'Haw! Haw! Haw!' he sneered. 'That's a good one! But I *would* like to see you kneel!' So he took me by the shoulders, and shoved me down.

"I began to pray out loud, in an addlepated way, 'God bless Mother and Father...' and so on. Rudolf was gloating over that display of sniveling weakness. When I finished, I used my right hand to grab some dirt while getting up. With an evil grin, Rudolf cracked his whip, and it hit my arm and tore my shirt. Boy, did that hurt! But I quickly threw the dirt in his eyes, and jumped back. He clawed at his face, but then blindly lunged for me, and almost got my shirt! But I escaped by swinging across the ravine on a grapevine.

"I could hear him stomping back and forth, raving like a madman, and swearing vengeance on my body. But I was beginning to feel smarter than Peter Pan, so I shouted across the ravine, 'You'll have to catch me first... Ha-ha!' and started running. Then I heard Rudolf croak, 'I'll send your body to your parents in pieces, for Christmas!'

"I knew it wasn't over, so I ran to these woods the way we came today, and down to the creek. Rudolf wouldn't give up that easily, and I knew he'd get his bloodhounds to track me. So I tramped upstream through the creek all the way to Rt. 48, to throw off the scent, then took a roundabout way back, through fields and woods.

"I came out of the woods right below the pool here, desperately tired and hungry. I had to have somewhere to lie up safe for a while, since I knew all roads would be watched. Lying here exhausted, I happened to look up and see roots overhanging the bank, so I just crawled up under them, into the hollow behind. I stayed there, dozing, till I knew Rudolf had gone home to dinner and bed, and then I went home in the dark.

"I was wet, muddy and scratched, and my clothes were torn, not to mention losing my schoolbooks. But all my father said was, 'I won't ask what you've been doing, son, but it looks like some kind of initiation, which I know is a matter of personal honor and can't be divulged lightly if you've been sworn.'

"'Yes, sir!' I said. They sent me to bed without supper, but that was a small price to pay, since I probably would have been dead by then if I hadn't been lucky. Gran sneaked some food up to me later."

"What did your father mean by an initiation?" I asked.

"Oh, he was remembering something from his college days," Jimmy replied. "He used to belong to a club called a fraternity. To join, they made him do all kinds of stuff. Once he had to run naked back to his dorm from the clubhouse. And they made him swallow a frog, too. Near the end, there was a huge guy waiting for my father with a club. Dad was sure he was going to hit him, but the guy just tapped him lightly on the shoulder. Dad was so relieved at that moment that he said he could have kissed him. The only problem was that he had purple urine for a week."

"Purple urine!" we exclaimed, shuddering. "How awful!"

Jimmy paused long enough for us to savor the full horror, then continued, "My dad went to the doctor, and he said they'd given him a purple dye in his food, but not to worry - it wouldn't do any harm."

Greg and I felt icky and embarrassed, but wouldn't say so. We thought dying would be better than suffering such indignities, and weren't sure whether Jimmy's father was brave or foolhardy. One thing we *did* know was that we would stay clear of fraternities!

We came back to the present with a jolt - Jimmy parted the roots and we saw that the sun was gone from this low spot in the woods.

"Uh-oh!" Greg said. "It's getting late, and we're going to miss supper."

"Yeah, me, too!" Jimmy agreed.

We scrambled out and slid down the bank, then streaked for home, making a racket running upslope through last year's leaves.

At the turnoff to Jimmy's house, he said, "Bring your dog Rusty next time. I'll bring Cindy, too." Jimmy imagined a romance between the two dogs, and swore that Rusty had once brought a rabbit to lay at her feet.

"Okay - see you later!"

"Bye!"

When we arrived home, winded, Mama asked what we'd been up to, remarking that our clothes sure were dirty.

"We were with Jimmy Ackerman, exploring."

"All right, this time," she said, "but try to be here when supper is on the table, in the future."

"OK," we agreed.

"Your supper's still warm in the oven." We were ravenous, and couldn't eat fast enough. Succotash! Hush puppies! And hot dogs!

Later that night in bed, we whispered to each other. What a way to start the summer! We had become blood-brothers with Jimmy, discovered two hideaways, and found a secret place to swim, all in one day!

Greg, who slept with Timmy, quietly whispered across the room, "It's going to be a good summer!"

"Yeah!" I whispered back.

Timmy's deadpan voice rang out, "***Shuddup!***"

Well, we couldn't say much to that, since Greg was sleeping in an enforceable zone. We were used to this treatment, so the only reply we made was to fall completely and deeply asleep in one minute flat.

Jimmy never did explain why he hadn't just gone to his house in the first place, when he escaped from Rudolf. It was *right there*. But we never asked. I suppose we were too preoccupied with the heroic struggle between good and evil to notice such trivial points.

Chapter IV.
School Days

Our school was integrated, if not with the public-at-large, at least with Catholics of a different feather. There were two "foreign" families in our school: the Romanos, newly arrived from Italy, and the Parkers, a black family hailing from "Colored Town," across the river.

Early on, I don't think our town fathers were any better than their counterparts elsewhere – they didn't intend the black citizens to be a real part of Loveland, though they technically resided within its bounds. I figured that was why they were perched over there, out on the edge. There weren't many places of interest to anyone else in their neighborhood, like restaurants or businesses – they had it all to themselves. It looked ramshackle and grungy, but then a diet of leftovers can do that.

Around 1959, though, people realized that Old Loveland, built on low ground along the river, was a liability, not the boom it had been when boat traffic plied the great Mississippi River system. That commerce had died out almost a century ago, with the proliferation of the railroads, and now, when the ice melted in spring, Old Loveland was a flood trap. Worse, from the point of view of business, it was hemmed in by the railroad, river and hills, and had no more room for expansion. People began eyeing the higher land across the river. It was fairly level, and there was plenty of room. But businessmen were chagrined – "Colored Town" was sitting right on the gateway to "New Loveland." The unwanted land that the blacks originally took up was now valuable. (Oops!) And gone were the days when such land could be seized without difficulty under the pretext of the public good alone. I can just imagine some of the older black occupants chuckling, as they rocked on their rickety front porches, in the middle of their born-again real estate.

Not too many black people around there were Catholics, and we weren't used to seeing them at school. It was amazing, the way Ferris, Marilyn and Ritchie Parker stood out at our school assemblies, especially on Mary's feast days, when the girls wore white. I felt embarrassed for them, but had no real inkling how they must have felt. (Though one later incident gave me some idea.) It was complicated, too. Fate had so arranged it that the two boys were possessed of doubtful character traits, and might not have been admitted, had they been Caucasian. But the mode of the day was acceptance (at least of our own), so we had to live and let live.

The Romanos were brought there under the aegis of the Italian-owned Rozzi's fireworks company, where many poor people were employed (including my father, at times). My introduction to them began one fall morning, arriving at the school grounds on my first day of the fourth grade.

Our new pastor, Father Urbain, was standing near the church sacristy, in earnest conversation with a tall, olive-skinned boy who had black, curly hair. I later learned his name was Luigi, and he was around 16 years old, the same age as my sister Angela. His clothing looked odd to me – the pants of wool, woven in a black-and-white herringbone pattern, coming only to just below the knee, and on top, a white shirt with bow tie and a wool vest matching the pants. Later I realized the pants were actually knickers, and he was probably wearing his Italian school uniform.

Luigi couldn't speak English, and was trying to talk to Father in Italian – I knew how that sounded from listening to Dad's associates at the fireworks factory. As eldest son, he had been chosen spokesperson for his family, and was evidently trying to explain their situation. It was also obvious that Father Urbain could understand him only a little, and was answering in fluent Ecclesiastical Latin, which the boy could hardly follow. After 5 minutes of halting speech and sign language, both of them were scratching their heads. And every time Father repeated a certain phrase, the boy would flare up, stomping his foot and drawing his finger across his throat. He also said something that sounded like *"basta,"* and *"Mamma Mia! Loco! Loco! Per Dio!"* and then added forcefully, *"Santa Maria!"*

I don't think our pastor had any trouble understanding those last few words and gestures, but couldn't imagine any reason for them. Finally Father threw up his hands, and said to an eighth-grader standing nearby, "Go get Father Angelo!"

Father Angelo was a priest of Italian extraction, staying at the rectory. (Sometimes priests were billeted for extended periods, either between assignments or being groomed for Assistant Pastor.) He came promptly out of the rectory, and began to address the boy in his native tongue. After Luigi had calmed down, Father Urbain asked, "Why was he so upset?"

Father Angelo explained with a straight face that the boy thought Father Urbain wanted to date his sister!

Luigi was a fast learner, though. That was the last time he appeared in public in that rig. His younger brother, Antonio, wasn't so fortunate. He was in my grade, and had to wear that suit all through the school year. His family probably couldn't afford new clothes. A friendly chap, though – he tried to talk to me, even though he couldn't speak a word of my language. I never got to know him well, because of that barrier, but I remember him standing off alone sometimes on the playground, in his strange suit, when the others were playing. It was just that way, back then. I didn't think about it.

* * *

Sometimes events made us question what we'd been taught. My brother Greg was playing baseball once with some boys at recess, and accidentally broke a window in the public school. Sister Geraldine was outraged, of course, and sent them to see Mr. Mann, the principal next door. She probably hoped he would lecture and paddle them over there, in addition to whatever she had planned.

But Mr. Mann's behavior didn't conform to the suit that had been tailored for him. The boys were nonplussed when he treated them kindly – how come *he*, the heathen, was nice, when Sister Geraldine wasn't? Being kids, they didn't worry for long about inconsistencies, but were just relieved at unexpected mercy. However, they did know Sister Geraldine, so, before returning to her, they rubbed their eyes with their fists to make them red, and produced tears by staring long enough without blinking. Then they shuffled into her office, sniffing and hanging their heads.

"Well? What happened over there, children?" she inquired archly.

Mike stepped forward, drooping, and said, "Mr. Mann had this huge paddle, and gave each of us an awful walloping." The other boys nodded in agreement at his cue, and rubbed the seat of their pants glumly.

Sister brightened visibly. It was going to be a good afternoon. She was so pleased that she actually forgot to add *her* punishment. It was Greg's first experience with "win-win" business dealing.

* * *

Molly added spice to our lives at school many times. One day Sister Margaret told the cautionary tale of a bad girl and a scapular. The scapular was two holy pictures mounted on cloth, connected by long cords, and worn around the neck so that the pictures hung in back and front. It had been blessed, and the Sisters told us that, if we died wearing one, we couldn't be taken to hell.

The girl in question was wicked (so bad that Sister wouldn't even tell us the details), but always counted on her scapular to keep her safe. But one day she was in a car accident, and the doctor unknowingly took the scapular off. At the very next moment, she died, and the devil took her soul. We never forgot the lesson: *Always wear your scapular!*

Molly didn't raise the issue in class, but later told anyone who would listen that, if there was a hell, God was an idiot if he kept someone out of it just because they wore their scapular faithfully, whatever bad things they might have done. Nobody was that dumb, she said – why, even a businessman couldn't stay afloat if he was no smarter than that.

* * *

Lunchtime was a shining oasis of freedom. All the students were on the playground at once, instead of just a class or two at a time, and we had 45 minutes to play, since no kid (except maybe a *girl*) would take more than 15 minutes to eat lunch, whether brown-bagged or cafeteria fare.

Seventh and eighth graders were allowed to leave the school grounds and eat at Deerwester's, right up the road. Deerwester's was *the* hangout place, with sodas and malts, hamburgers, French fries, candy, fried chicken, pop, ice cream and comics. It was a kid's dream, and those favored upperclassmen sometimes sponsored younger kids to go with them. If you were one of the chosen, and had the money, you could be popular for a day by buying your host a soda. But woe betide you if you were caught there without the official *cachet*, or reported to the constabulary in black. Escaping the nuns themselves might not be too strenuous (though they were pretty sharp) but evading their informers was tough, because they were hard to spot.

A couple of times I managed to sneak up there undetected with my friend Jimmy Schoerer. It didn't do me much good, since I rarely had more than pennies to spend, unless Jimmy was kind enough to share. I usually bought those colored drinks that came in tiny wax soda bottles and cost only two cents each. First you bit off the top and drank the colorful contents, and then you could chew up the wax bottle for a long time.

One hot day in May, when I was in the third grade, three eighth-graders, Tommy Sheen, Ferris and Ronnie Hall, actually left the school grounds and went down past the old Civil War Hospital to the swimming hole in the river. Unfortunately, that was situated hard by the pool hall, a den of sin and iniquity, and forbidden to us on pain of Sister Geraldine.

The three boys were reported by informants and punished, but didn't seem to care much, because they knew they would be graduating in a month. Of course, the Grand Inquisitor's first impulse was probably to fail them, but maybe she realized she'd rather see them gone. Their successful foray inspired the rest of us with thoughts of freedom, but in the flood of 1959, the pool hall was washed away. The Sisters must have felt wonderfully vindicated.

Some lawbreakers paid heavily for their crimes, though, by Sister Geraldine's favorite method, public execution of character and confidence. There were two hapless eighth-grade boys once who dared to go into the boiler room, and that heinous act triggered a special session of the school and faculty after morning recess. On this particular day of wrath, we were going to be treated to a double-feature: first a "trial" and diatribe by Sister Geraldine, and then singing school songs together, a regular weekly part of our curriculum. I had been pulled from Schola practice to attend.

Sister was already on stage at the erstwhile pulpit. A hush fell on the assembly. Two boys sat in the side wings like condemned prisoners waiting for the *auto da fé*. Excited whispers of speculation about their crime rippled through the hall.

Sister Geraldine began the show by shaking the podium and slapping the microphone, which caused loud knocking and whistling noises to bound through the hall. Absolute silence fell, and she opened her address: "As God is my witness, in all my years as school principal, I have *never* seen such an act committed by students! Those wicked boys sitting over there, Willard Hatcher and Ritchie Parker, actually dared to go into the boiler room!"

The podium took a beating, since she punctuated each word with a blow. When she paused, the girls gasped audibly, and all the onlookers began to suspect that the least sentence inflicted might be the death penalty, with the fires of Purgatory to complete the process.

When Sister was done with her furious fulmination concerning punishment in this world and the hereafter, she turned her awful gaze toward the live victims. Now, these boys were large for their age, but right now they looked a lot smaller than anyone remembered. She ordered them forward, barking, "Get over here, right now, and don't dawdle! Hurry up! Quit shuffling your feet like that, and take your punishment like men!"

They came on slowly, not at all like men, but demoralized like condemned criminals going to the gallows, with the executioner following close behind. Their Sister-bailiff gave them a little shove to help them on their way, and the miscreants finally stood before the principal.

"You wicked boys! You went into the boiler room! Didn't you? *Didn't you!*"

This was somewhat redundant, but we were used to that. We heard a feeble mumble from the boys.

"Speak up, you shamefaced sinners! And quit slouching! Stand up straight! And look at me when I talk to you!"

"Yes, Sister," a weak voice replied. We were amazed – this was the school rowdy and tough guy speaking, made to look nohow, ineffective and weak! The audience sighed with satisfaction at this revelation. Things were looking up!

The boys were wondering how they had been caught up in this whirlwind. It had all begun so normally, playing ball with a group of boys at recess. Then the ball had gone up onto the school roof. Willie and Ritchie had volunteered to get Red Klug, the janitor, to retrieve it for them, but unfortunately he couldn't be located. They figured he must be in the boiler room, his official sanctum, but the boiler room was off-limits, since administration didn't want the school blown up accidentally (or on purpose). But what were they to do? No ball for the rest of recess? Unthinkable!

So they went to the boiler room, but were faced with a closed door that said, "**KEEP OUT.**" There weren't many ways this could be interpreted, but the devil said, "*What if he's inside?*" They decided it would be all right to *open* the door just a crack, and peek. They called his name, but he didn't answer.

Willie said to Ritchie, "Maybe he can't hear us because of the machinery running." So they pushed the door all the way back. It was then that they saw the open skylight and ladder leading to the roof. A shaft of sunlight streamed down like divine approbation, and the devil whispered hoarsely, "*Close the door behind you, and get the ball yourself. No one will ever know.*"

So they did. From that moment on, they were doomed, because, unluckily, Sister Geraldine's new snitch, Debbie, saw the boys just as they were sneaking out of the boiler room with the ball. They would never have been spotted if she hadn't stopped for a drink of water at the fountain. Instantly she squealed, "You're not supposed to be in there! I'm telling! I'm telling!"

They cried in one voice, "*Get her!*" But in their haste, they collided, ruining their plans to extract vows of silence. At that point, the boys had an awful premonition. The pits of their stomachs told them they were on a fast-moving train, and couldn't jump off. And that snippet of a girl (a *fifth-grader*, for Pete's sake!) had dared to laugh! They felt this keenly, since they thought they were tough men.

Debbie made it to the principal's office by a mile. Arriving breathless, she caught her breath inside the office door, leaning with her hands splayed out. Sister Geraldine exclaimed, "Goodness, child, why are you running? It's against the rules to run inside! Come to think, it's against the rules to run *outside*, too..." she muttered to herself. Her hand started to inch joyfully toward the demerit chart, but Debbie managed to speak by then, and the hand paused. Debbie quickly reported the crime she had witnessed, and the rest became inevitable.

Sister Geraldine kept a progress chart on all the notable kids behind a pull-down wall map in her office. She raised it now. The chart was divided into three columns: Good, Bad, and Undecided, and there were lines for names, points and demerits. Some kids had scored points for good behavior, and a special star was awarded whenever they turned someone in.

After making a few notes on the chart, she pulled the roll map down again. "You're a good girl, Deborah. I'm going to find some special treat for you, just wait and see," she said, in the coy, icky voice reserved for infants and imbeciles. Then she bustled off to apprehend the criminals, her black robes flapping behind her.

At the assembly, the condemned boys sat wrapped in a shroud of their emotions, awaiting doom. They only faintly heard their names called, and shuffled out as in a dream to where Sister was holding forth. Later, they vaguely remembered being paraded across the school stage, while she shamed them and slapped their faces.

Finally, Sister pronounced sentence: "These awful boys shall be suspended from school for two weeks, and *may* not be allowed to come back at all! If they *are* allowed back, they will report to me for rehabilitation. *Then*, we shall see!"

She took a deep breath. "Now, boys and girls, we will lift our voices in school song!" And we did, with an embarrassed Mr. Morrison leading the way:

"♫ *Home, home on the range*

Where the deer and the antelope play,

Where seldom is heard a discouraging word

And the skies are not cloudy all day! ♫"

This seemed singularly appropriate, so much so that my brother Timmy was inspired to sing "Home on the Range" for a solid week. And that was really something for him, because he didn't even talk much.

* * *

A typical recess was filled with games – the boys played marbles, baseball, and war games (frowned-upon), when they weren't trading baseball cards and marbles. The girls skipped rope, threw beanbags or played jacks. Sometimes the boys abandoned their own games to prove that they could skip rope, too, or just to break up the girls' games and chase them, to hear them squeal (also frowned-upon).

Occasionally former students who had attained the remarkable age of sixteen, and were lucky enough to own a car, would drive by slowly, renewing their acquaintance with the school by squealing their tires and revving their engines. This was to let the current inmates see what *gods* they had become, and to aggravate the nuns, whom they still respected, but also resented. When this happened, the nun on duty would narrowly eye the newly licensed juvenile with folded arms and compressed lips, clearly wishing fervently that she could get him back for *just one hour...* Finding that exercise futile, she would turn her eye to potential miscreants at hand, and redouble her efforts to eradicate *their* many defects, faults, and procedural irregularities.

Those same former students, when confronting a sister face-to-face, underwent a dramatic character-reversion – they would be all deference, almost bowing in their obsequiousness to her every utterance. "Yes, Sister." "No, Sister." "I'm sure you're right, Sister." Despite apparent liberation, they belonged to her for life.

I saw a greeting card once that summed up the predicament of all parochial-school boys, back then: A boy stood industriously writing at the blackboard, over and over, *"I am personally responsible for the suffering of Christ."* A nun was standing over his shoulder, grimly smiling, and holding a birch rod, to see it done properly.

The relationship between a student and nun was unique, like sand in an oyster: Both ingredients were necessary to produce a pearl, though not very comfortably for either. Looking back over my life, I have to concede that, despite human imperfections on both sides, they did their work well.

* * *

At noon sharp every day, the bell in our church tower rang out, and playground hubbub would cease. It was time to pray the Angelus. We folded our hands and bowed our heads, and the pastor or nun who was present took the lead:

Leader: *The Angel of the Lord declared unto Mary.*

All: *And she conceived of the Holy Spirit:*

Hail Mary full of grace! The Lord is with thee! Blessed art thou among women, and blessed is the fruit of thy womb, Jesus. Holy Mary, Mother of God, pray for us sinners now and at the hour of our death. Amen. Etc.

This went on for several minutes, and it sobered us briefly, especially since there were enforcer-nuns present to quality-control the prayer session. They made sure you folded your hands and didn't mumble the prayers, whisper to your neighbor, chew gum, or try to finish that apple you were eating when the event started. Even now, whenever I hear a bell, a familiar voice inside says, *"Freeze!"*

The nuns always encouraged us to make visits to church during recess, and there was an occasion when I made an unexpected one. My friend Jimmy Schoerer and I were playing near the church front doors when Sister Mary Stigmata popped out of the door. "What are you doing?" she asked suspiciously.

I stared at her blankly, then turned to my friend, but he was gone! Apparently he'd made his escape around the other side of the church. Turning back to face her, I quickly asked myself, *Was I doing something?* The problem was, there were too many rules: No running - no talking - no walking on the grass - no eating - stand up straight - don't chew your food like that - don't talk when you eat - use your fork on that, and so many more. It was hard to keep track.

So there I stood, furiously trying to think of something, before she could sift the data and tighten the screws. Then it came to me in a flash that Sanctuary lay just on the other side of the door, so I said quickly, "I was just going into church for a visit, Sister, when you came out."

"Hmm... It sounded to me more like two boys yelling."

"I yelled because I banged my knee," I said, swallowing nervously. Then I added, "Sorry, Sister." (*Ouch – one more item to confess*)

"I'll accept that *this* time," she said, wagging her finger, "but you'll regret it if I find you're trying to fool me. I'm glad you're making a visit, though. The Lord will be glad to see you."

Right then, I was anxious to see Him, too, so I pulled open the heavy door and slipped inside. I figured I might as well do a good job of it, just in case the nun had followed (she had), so, at the entrance, dipping my hand in holy water, I genuflected to the Presence in the tabernacle and crossed myself. Then, hands folded, I proceeded up the aisle to the altar, genuflected again, and bore right to the statue of St. Joseph. I put a nickel in the box, lit a votive candle, and knelt at the *prie dieu*. The doleful sound of that coin falling into the metal box represented a genuine sacrifice. It wasn't a bad deal, though. The nun was impressed; my fallen credit restored; the Church gained a nickel; and I received a partial indulgence, which would lighten my sentence in Purgatory down the road. Another example of "win-win" dealing.

* * *

Going home after school was often an adventure, especially in good weather. My mother wasn't very strict, and seldom said, "Come right home!" even though that may have been what she wanted. She knew we would get hungry, anyway. Mother rarely complained, even when we were an hour late, probably because having fewer of us underfoot carried its own blessing.

There were enticements on the way home. If any of us (except Timmy) had any money, we would take the longer way home by road, stopping on the way to gawk at the new "C" movie posters at the theatre, fueled by a morbid curiosity as to *who* would be in hell.

Then we went on to visit Spear's Drug Store, on the corner across from the fire station. That store was a wonder. A bell hung from the door, and rang when you entered. Inside, it was small, cluttered, dirty, and not too well lit, but stuffed full of delightful things like ice cream, malts, sodas, comic books, candy, model airplanes, and other mysterious paraphernalia of unknown use, stacked to the ceiling. A sign on the wall above the cash register read, "*If we ain't got it, you don't need it.*" The place was usually packed after school, since Bud netted all the kids on foot from both elementary schools. Sometimes there weren't enough stools to sit on, but nobody minded, as long as they were lucky enough to be eating ice cream or having a soda.

Bud Spear was a short, dapper little man in a white apron. His head was bald on top, with only grey side hair remaining, and he was usually courteous and cheerful, though he sometimes pretended to be crabby. We knew he really didn't mean it. One cold Sunday morning, when I was in his store alone, waiting for my father to finish dropping off Sunday newspapers to local businesses, Bud gave me some penny candy to help pass the time. He was a kind man.

Some older boys crossed the line once after school, helping themselves behind his back to plain soda water from a tap. He saw them as he turned around, and yelled, "Hey, stop that! It costs money, too, you know!"

I could see by the boys' blank faces that they couldn't figure *how* – it was only air and water. That *had* to be free...

Sitting at the counter was neat. You could spin the stools round and round without stopping... It was worth going in there for that alone, in my book. Under the counter and seats was another marvel – mounds and mounds of gum, stuck there by generations of kids, making a bumpy, weird mosaic. All across America, kids knew to do this – it became a part of destiny.

After leaving the drugstore on the way home, we'd often pause next door to look at the marble display in our Uncle Lou's barbershop window. To attract more business, he ran a contest: If a kid could guess (*after his haircut*) how many marbles were in either of the two gallon-jars, he could take that jar home. One jar was full of ruby-red "puree" boulders, and the other sapphire-blue. They were the most beautiful things we'd ever seen. Greg and I longed for those jewels, but we never could guess the number. (I'm sure Uncle Lou was relieved – we didn't *pay* for our haircuts, anyway.)

If we went home by the woods shortcut, there were other opportunities: the fascinating allure of Bear Creek; Taber's ballfield across the road, which sometimes had a large sandpile to play in; and the tractor trail nearby that led to Grailville's creek bottom. Sometimes we followed that trail, past Billy Martin's house at the bottom of our lane.

One day, coming home alone through the shortcut after school detention, I ran into Ferris Parker at the bottleneck by Bear Creek. His dark face loomed above me, since he was in eighth grade and I was only in third. Timmy had brought him home once or twice, so I wasn't afraid of him, and stayed for a minute, hobnobbing. He seemed friendly enough.

Pretty soon, he said, "I bet you cain't hang from that wall without fallin' in!"

Always eager for a challenge, I answered readily, "I can, too!" I let him lower me down carefully by my outstretched arms, to hang by my fingertips. It was all right.

Then I noticed he was grinning, and felt suddenly nervous. "Ferris, you're not going to leave me here, are you?"

"No, man, I'll pull you back up. Don't worry... boy..."

He didn't pull me up.

When I asked him again, he didn't say *anything,* but just looked down at me with a glint in his eye. At that moment, I think all he saw was *Whitey,* and meant for me to pay a little for the sins of my race. He turned on his heel and walked away, ignoring my cries.

"Ferris, come back! I'll fall in! Ferris! Ferris! *Please!*"

I gave that up, and concentrated on keeping my grip. The water was only six feet below my dangling legs and not deep, but I didn't want to fall, especially backwards, and I didn't want to get wet, either. I would have climbed right up, but the wall was too slippery with wet moss for any toehold, and I wasn't strong enough to pull myself up with my fingers and arms alone.

After about five more minutes, I was ready to drop, when I heard footsteps approaching. I looked up to see Charlie Beale's anxious face. He was in sixth grade.

"Help!" I cried. "I can't hold on!"

He quickly reached down and pulled me up. Then he asked who'd put me there. When I told him, he said, "Boy, that sure was a mean trick! Lucky I came along."

I nodded, still shaky and tearful. From that day on, Charlie was a hero in my book.

Ten minutes later, I arrived home, and went straight to the kitchen where Mother was working. Without looking up, she said there were oatmeal cookies in the jar, and that I could have a glass of milk from the refrigerator. So I sat down at the table with my homemade cookies, and she asked, "Did anything interesting happen at school today?

"No," I said flatly, continuing to eat.

"I don't understand that. When I was a girl I used to love school, and couldn't wait to tell my parents about it."

Well, the nuns weren't riding herd on you, I thought. Mother was a convert.

"*Something* must have happened," she persisted.

"Okay," I said. "I got nabbed outside of the church, at recess, for doing nothing but playing. Molly Doherty got paddled for trying to explain about babies. And Timmy's friend, Ferris Parker, hung me from the wall over the creek and left me, so I almost fell in and drowned."

"Some of that sounds made up, Paul... I meant, what did you *learn* today?"

"Nothin'," I answered, with my mouth full.

Chapter V.

Pirates, Indians and Treehouses

Dawn! Greg and I silently extracted ourselves from our beds and grabbed our shorts, thrown down last night. It wasn't easy to slip out of a bedroom where old box springs creaked incessantly and three other boys slept – especially Timmy, as uncannily alert as he was bad-tempered. Briefly stopping in the kitchen to put on the shorts and grab two cereal bowls, we sneaked out the front door.

Honeysuckle was thick on the air and dew had soaked the grass under a pale-gold sky. Birds chatted softly like an orchestra warming up, and the sun, shimmering abruptly above the eastward hill, slowly took command of its world.

Rusty burst on us, barking joyfully and dripping from his nocturnal travels. He leaped up to lick our faces, trying to knock us down. (He was good at that.) "Good dog!" I squeezed his 'bosky and held his face in both hands, calling him some of our favorite names. "You're my Boo-Woo! My special Boo-Woo!" He rewarded us by shaking himself, sending doggy dew flying.

Greg conferred privately for a few seconds, squeezing the furry nose again, and Rusty, his tanks full of love, bolted around the yard to expend that excess emotion. After this, we had to rinse our bowls at the outside tap, since almost nothing escaped the invading canine tongue. Rusty's general policy was to lick things first, to see what they were.

We headed for the red-raspberry patch at the end of the garden and quickly picked our bowls full, eating as many outright as the bowl saw. Rusty ate right along with us, pulling berries off with his teeth as nimbly as a fox. Sometimes we had to shoo him away to prevent dire loss; he had been caught more than once browsing there by himself. We picked for ten minutes or so, shorts and legs damp from the dew on the bushes. A robin hopped about companionably in the garden, looking for worms, but also patiently waiting for *his* chance at berries for breakfast.

Back at the house, we set our bowls on the picnic table under the English butternut, where our blue '48 Chevy used to sit before we had a driveway. Most summer mornings, we ate at that table, which my father had built last winter during a slow-work period. Greg went inside to get the milk, sugar, cereal, spoons, and two more bowls, while I remained to guard the berries from our pet marauder. Then we got down to the business of eating, without talking – the food was too good to waste time. When we were done with our cereal, and slowly finishing off the remainder of the berries, my brother asked, "What can we do today?"

"Go fishing? Or maybe hike up the railroad?"

"No, I want something new," Greg mused abstractedly.

"I know! Let's build a treehouse!"

"Hey, that's neat! We haven't done that before. But we'll need stuff like wood and nails, and metal for the roof!"

"Maybe Grailville threw some more out."

"I don't know..." Greg said doubtfully. "There wasn't much last week. But we can go look again."

Grailville was an international Catholic women's organization, founded on Peace-Corps-like ideals. With the intention of being self-sufficient, they had bought a 500-acre farm just outside the city limits, and there were sometimes several hundred foreign students in residence. The farm adjoined Grandpa Pfarr's old property line, and ran from O'Bannon Creek all the way to Route 48, a major barrier to commercial development. Along with the railroad and creek, Grailville preserved an extensive area of pasture and woods where my brothers and I ran free. The organization grew steadily, and carpentry was always going on, with the remains deposited in a dump we routinely checked.

"You know what?" I said excitedly. "Let's go see Jimmy! He's pretty smart – maybe he'll know where to get things."

"He might," Greg admitted. "But we need to find the right tree for our house first – let's look out by Dad's blackberry patch!"

We ran off to the back corner of our property, where fence lines met next to a mowed field and the path that led to our own dump. A 20-foot-wide strip of grass ran between the tree-lined fence and Dad's cultivated blackberry hedge, with its thorns an inch long (but never many berries).

When I was about eight, my mother read Howard Pyle's <u>The Merrie Adventures of Robin Hood</u> to us. From then on, wooden swords, homemade bows and arrows, and later, quarterstaves, became articles of the religion, while snatches of high-flown language made a creative alternative to swearing. In the context of Indians, pioneers, and nature-worship, we already felt that living in the woods by hunting was a viable profession, and we were planning to adopt it when we grew up. But Robin Hood elevated that vision to pure magic.

This site had been a favorite of ours, hosting Robin Hood sword-battles, cowboys repelling Indian attacks (from John Hutzel and Billy Martin), and pirates of the Spanish Main. It *seemed* the sort of place where Robin Hood would have a treehouse. We could *see* him here in our minds...

> Up rose Robin Hood one merry morn when all the birds were singing blithely among the leaves, and up rose all his merry men... Said Robin: "For fourteen days have we seen no sport, so now I will go abroad to seek adventures forthwith..." So saying, he strode away through the leafy forest glades until he had come to the verge of Sherwood...
>
> At last he took a road by the forest skirts; a bypath that dipped toward a broad, pebbly stream spanned by a narrow bridge made of a log of wood.

As he drew nigh this bridge he saw a tall stranger coming from the other side. Thereupon Robin quickened his pace, as did the stranger likewise, each thinking to cross first.

"Now stand thou back," quoth Robin, "and let the better man cross first."

"Nay," answered the stranger, "then stand back thine own self, for the better man, I wot, am I."

"That will we presently see," quoth Robin; "and meanwhile stand thou where thou art, or else, by the bright brow of Saint Ælfrida, I will show thee right good Nottingham play with a clothyard shaft betwixt thy ribs."

"Now," quoth the stranger, "I will tan thy hide till it be as many colors as a beggar's cloak, if thou darest so much as touch a string of that same bow that thou holdest in thy hands..."

There were good associations here. It was *our* territory. We carefully inspected the trees, finding most too small. But there were two candidates: one, a hackberry two feet through, with steps already nailed on it and an old platform about 25 feet up that Timmy had built several years before. It was the obvious choice, since it had lots of branches, but none of them had a large slingshot fork for the strong floor joists we had in mind. So we considered the second alternative: a black cherry tree we had never really noticed before. It wasn't that special to look at, but it did have a Y-crotch ten feet off the ground. Above the potential house area, the trunks ran almost straight up, each supporting a thin canopy of leaves at the top, almost 60 feet above the ground. This tree was clearly waiting for our improvements, and we immediately appropriated it.

Twenty minutes later, we walked back to the house, eagerly discussing plans. It was now around 7:00 AM, and a cacophony of sound flowed out the windows, like feeding time at the zoo – obviously everyone was up and clamoring for breakfast. We smiled at each other, feeling superior because we didn't have to compete in that arena. We were ahead of the game, and ready to pursue our private adventure, unless impeded by local authority.

Instantly our mother hailed us, out the kitchen window: "Boys, where are you going so early?" We groaned. How did she *do* that? "Is there something I should know about?" Without waiting for a reply, she continued, "I see you've already eaten breakfast," eyeing the mess on the picnic table. She always went on like that, which made it easy for us not to incriminate ourselves by answering every item.

"Yeah, we did," Greg said, keeping to safe ground, glancing sheepishly at the table.

But I spilled the beans. "We're going to Jimmy Ackerman's to see him about a treehouse!" – thinking that would be of paramount importance to anybody.

But all Mother said was, "Are you sure it isn't too early to go up there?"

I was a little deflated by her indifferent response. Why do grownups always force you to consider nonessentials, just when you've announced something significant? They don't seem to be able to focus on what you're saying, but keep getting sidetracked. *"What's that on your face?" "Stand up straight!"*

We answered together, "Yeah!" It wasn't too early for Jimmy. God only knew what his parents thought, but we never considered them. That way lay madness.

"I guess you can go," she said, "but first I want you to clear away the picnic table, and then get some spring water." We groaned at the delay.

"One thing for sure," Greg muttered to me, "it won't be early for long, if Mama keeps finding things for us to do."

"Did you say something, Gregory?" Parents always ask you to repeat yourself, knowing very well what you said. This is an attempt to get you to tighten the noose around your own neck, but we both knew better than to fall for it.

"No, just talking to Paul, Mama," Greg said.

"One more thing. If you're going up there, at least put on a T-shirt and shoes! You look like savages, with those berries smeared on your chests."

We hadn't noticed, but mumbled, "OK," and went inside to add the required apparel. She hadn't said anything about washing, so we didn't – we had to maintain some shred of integrity.

Bringing our dishes back from the picnic table only took a minute, since Rusty had helped by cleaning up the spilt milk. We fetched the buckets from the kitchen, clattering the dipper as noisily as possible to protest the delay she was causing us.

"Boys, do you have to make so much noise?" *Ah, the sweet sound of an arrow finding its target!* We had made her pay a little for her role of joy-killer-in-the-morning.

Our house was in the country on the edge of town, down a gravel lane named after my grandfather. It felt like a turn-of-the-century country road, with two strips of tarmac where the tires traveled, and meager gravel and moss between – no one could afford more. In summer it was a leafy tunnel, with cool air flowing gently to and from the O'Bannon Creek valley. A small stream of water ran along the bank on one side, vigorous only in spring and fall. Even in late summer, though, you could always find *some* water there if you were willing to overturn rocks and dig a little.

Halfway up the shaded lane was the spring we used for drinking water. It came from under a limestone slab deep in the earth of the field, and was pure, with no taste or odor and always a perfect temperature to drink. The

spring came out of the bank on the far side of the little creek, and a plank made a bridge from the lane. A stone grotto some 3 feet tall and 2 feet deep housed the spring. Dry-laid into the bank with great skill, it never showed any sign of age or collapse after 75 years of use, nor did the bank behind ever budge or bury it.

We used to wonder who had built this marvel in the distant past. All we had to do was clean the spring out once a year to prevent silting up. We were lucky, too, since we traveled *up* the lane with empty buckets, and *down* with the full ones.

When I was very small, I was a little afraid of the spring, especially in late evening, when the large opening looked like a dark mouth – the very place a bogey-man would choose to lurk when looking for tender kids. (And there was no doubt in our minds that he *was* looking!) Of course, the other thing was that I didn't want to fall into the spring, and have the "crawdads" get me.

We never played in it much, except to poke those naughty crawdads with sticks, since we knew better than to foul the water. But all of the creek-bank adjacent had springs, though none quite so strong as that one. They afforded us many hours of amusement, digging pools, rocking them in, and then drinking from them later when they cleared.

Our family didn't drink the water from our drilled well, because it was full of bad-tasting minerals. A water softener helped for washing clothes, but didn't improve the taste any. When we had company and they asked for a drink of water, my brothers and I were delighted to be of service! It offered us two interesting options: A) give them a glass of tap water, with its terrible taste, or B) offer them spring water, with a tiny crawdad in the bottom of their glass - a sort of country garnish, like a cherry or olive. We hoped for an interesting reaction, because most people back then didn't know that crayfish weren't just nasty little bugs but the best water purifiers around. But we didn't really get much satisfaction, since usually the visitors were either country people themselves, or were too polite to say anything. However, they generally didn't seem to be very thirsty anymore. The best marks were Mother's music pupils, or city girls and boys, but we didn't see many of those, unless our third cousins were visiting from California.

After we fetched the water and placed it on the kitchen counter, we heard Angela complaining, "Mama, where's the Cheerios? They're not in the cupboard!"

"Check the picnic table where Paul and Greg were eating."

Uh-oh, we better beat it, we thought to ourselves, giving each other a look. Funny - we remembered leaving the cereal on the picnic table, but hadn't seen it when we cleaned up. *Rusty!* Greg and I ran for it, laughing, before anyone could connect us with the deed. Pelting up the lane toward Jimmy's, we glanced down and saw Rusty running alongside, proudly carrying the missing Cheerios box, clamped in his smiling mouth!

"Bad dog!" we reproved halfheartedly, but he just bounced along, very pleased with himself.

"You know what this means?"

"Hunh?"

"Maw's going to have to eat Wheaties!" I giggled. (*Maw* was one of our endearing names for Angela.)

"Yeah, the breakfast of champions!" Greg laughed even harder.

Just before we got out of range, Mother managed to sing out, "Come home for lunch, you two, and don't play in Jimmy's house on a day like this." She was thinking of Mrs. Ackerman, and the destruction we might wreak to her nerves and property. They had Tiffany lamps, art objects and antique furniture, not like our hodgepodge, that would predictably last only a few years.

It wasn't far to Jimmy's house, and we were only a little out of breath at the top of the lane. Several houses down Jackson Street, we swung left into Jimmy's driveway. From the road, you couldn't see the Ackerman mansion, completely blocked by trees and brush on its rise of land. But we could hear the sound of kids playing, and climbed eagerly up the private road. Halfway up, Jimmy's "Tarzan" call rang out, **"Awh-ih-awh-ih-awh!"** - sounding amazingly like Johnny Weismuller. Jimmy had a real talent for mimicking voices.

"They must be playing on a new grapevine," Greg said.

"I hope so!" I said hungrily.

Their driveway was always a little mysterious. The ravine on the right grew deeper, while the bank on the left rose higher. Near the top, the road bore left into the bank, lowering its grade and pitch. At that point we came under the view of the old Brock place, looming above us on the other side of the ravine, vacant since the death of its elderly owner. Even in the daytime, we were a bit nervous walking under the staring eyes of *whatever* was living there, especially after Jimmy had primed us about dangers living and dead - everything from evil spirits to demented convicts. We tried not to look at the dark cellar windows, and always said a hasty prayer. The $64-thousand-dollar question was, *Could ghosts reach out in broad daylight to get us, or possibly even draw us in, if we stared too long at those blackened windows?* I shivered. We quickened our pace.

In actual fact, what you mostly encountered when you rounded the final curve and arrived in the backyard was... PAN! Ackermans' crazy black dog would be blocking the way, barking and daring you to budge. "Move it and lose it!" was the threat - and you knew he wasn't kidding! Not much of a nature dog, he only seemed to appear, Hook-like, to harass kids, and then return to his lair, where he watched TV with the family or by himself. What he actually *saw*, I can't say, but watching cartoons never improved his temper any. Probably they were too violent.

I never got attached to that strange dog. We tolerated each other, Pan taking his cues from Jimmy's fancy in the moment. But the family seemed fond of him - they even set a place for him at dinner. Once, before going home to supper, I saw him sitting soberly on a chair at their kitchen table, complete with dinner service, and wearing a red bib.

Coming around the bend in the road, we were just in time to see Jimmy give a little crow like Peter Pan and drop lightly to the road from a grapevine. Landing, he pivoted neatly on one foot, making a single motion of it, then bowed to us, and said, "Bless me, if it isn't the Pfarr boys!"

Though we were pleased by Jimmy's attention, we felt sheepish at his exuberance, and said, "Hi, Jimmy," in low voices. He was already effervescing, and we didn't want to encourage him too much.

Billy Martin was sitting on the ravine edge of the drive, his back against a tree, looking down at his new sneakers. Across the drive, Eve lounged on the green bank, a grass stem in her mouth and a ball mitt on her left hand. With brown hair cropped short and a baseball cap worn backward, she looked like a boy.

Our arrival swelled the crew to five, not including the dogs, Rags, Cindy, and Rusty, who were absorbed in boisterously greeting each other dog-fashion. Billy's dog Rags was a black Cocker Spaniel, friendly and humble, the peasant of his race, looking - well, rag-like. Cindy was a dog of a different plume, the same breed but a little larger, with an elegant strawberry-blond coat, and well-groomed - a princess of her kind.

Our Irish setter, Rusty, was a nice dog, but he had a boneheaded streak - even repeated forceful expletives, such as "NO!" (and worse) had no detectable effect. He chased trains, cars, birds, airplanes ("Boxcars" were his favorites), and cats, of course. If it moved, he was after it, but was more a menace to himself than to wildlife.

When the dogs were together, they pretended to be hunters, roving hither and yon, looking for anything that stirred. You could almost hear Rusty saying to Cindy, "You should see what I caught last week, my dear..." The awful truth was, none of them had a clue about hunting. The only thing they had in common, besides being pets, pests, and dogs, was their bird-dog heritage: They all knew how to point, but couldn't figure out what it *meant*. They made up for this with boundless enthusiasm, though. When they surprised some hapless critter, they leapt high in the air, chasing it, trying to *see* over the grass, instead of using their noses. *Boing! Boing! Boing! Boing!*

Only rarely did any of them catch or kill anything.

We humans all started talking at once, catching up on the news and commenting on the dogs. Billy grew a little overexcited with the swelled audience, and, feeling that his moment had arrived, scrambled up, grabbed hold of the grapevine, and shouted, "Watch me!" He kicked off and sailed out over the ravine. When he had reached the apex, he yelled, "Look, one hand!" whereupon he promptly lost his grip, and slid off into the dump. It was like watching slow motion – there was nothing we could do, except watch his frozen smile change to fright as he fell. *Crash!* Then we heard his efforts to extricate himself. Apparently he had fallen into some discarded bedsprings. He was swearing like a drill sergeant, and whimpering like a dog biting his legs to get at the mange. Billy always tried to regain lost face by cussing, but it never worked.

"He must be all right," Jimmy quipped, "or he wouldn't be making so much fuss!"

When Billy finally crawled out of the ravine, Jimmy was leaning against a tree, chuckling. Evie was wild with laughter, clutching her middle. "'Look at me, one hand!'"

Billy's face was red and smudged, and his legs were scratched, but he grinned crookedly and left off the swearing. But when Eve and Jimmy kept cracking up, he glowered, "Knock it off, you two!"

Evie was still chittering. "Your – face – looked – so *funny* when you dropped, just like a cartoon!" she got out.

"I'll rub some dirt in yer face, and see how funny *you* look!" Billy threatened, getting worked up.

Jimmy frowned, since his natural reaction was to defend his sisters, but he quickly grasped the potential in the unfolding drama. "Careful, Billy," he warned. "I wouldn't try anything on her, if I were you – she has a great left hook!"

"*Shi-it*, the day I cain't handle a *girl* with one ha-a-nd tied behind mah back—" Billy's twang always got more pronounced with emotion, and he swaggered up to Evie with a handful of dirt. She didn't even bother getting up, but coolly kicked him on the knee when he came within reach.

"Ow!" Billy yelled, rolling on the ground, clutching his knee. The laws of decency won't let me repeat all the words that came out of his mouth then. All I can say is that I tried one of them on my father, when he was trying to catch me for a whipping. It had an electrifying effect – he was almost propelled through the air in his eagerness to get me.

Jimmy was ready to move on, so, while Billy was still rubbing his knee, he said to his sister, "Okay, Evie, you show 'em how it's done."

"I will, if I can stop laughing," she said.

"You'd better!" Billy glared, making a halfhearted fist.

"Or you'll what? Give another demonstration as Mr. Milktoast?" Jimmy mocked.

Eve swung out over the drop and came back on one hand, landing easily on the road.

"Nothing to it, dipstick," Jimmy said scornfully.

"We-e-ll, my hands were wet with sweat!" Billy whined.

"I'll tell you what – I'll bet Paul, who has never used this grapevine before, can show you how it's done! You want to show him, Paul?"

"Sure," I said, grasping the vine, and took a flying leap out over the ravine, coming back to rest just as Eve had.

Then Greg took his turn successfully. "Boy, this vine is really strong! It should last a long time!" he said.

We all kept swinging and made dares to each other while Jimmy, pleased with himself and events, executed a little dance. He turned in circles and tapped out rhythms with his feet, while snapping his fingers and singing, "Wabbit! Wabbit! What's up, Doc?" It was his way of keeping the stage warm between acts, so he would be ready to slide right into the next scene.

Finally, Greg and I remembered why we'd come in the first place. Greg said, "Jimmy, we want to build a treehouse. We thought you might know where to get wood."

"Gee, I'd like to help you, boys, but my dad is still sore at me for some stuff I took out of the garage to make my board camp."

"Oh!" Greg tried not to sound dejected. "We'll just have to try Grailville's dump, I guess."

Billy, anxious to raise his current standing, said eagerly, "I know wh-u-u-t! You can cob some off Old Man James. I saw some lumber out back of his house, from when he tore down his chicken coop. Hell, he'll never miss it!"

Gregory and I were appalled at this lawlessness. We tolerated Billy, but felt we had to be careful not to be tarred with the brush that got him.

Jimmy replied, "Sure, they could do that, Billy, if they didn't mind ending up in Juvie..."

"'Juvie?' Whut's th-a-a-t?" Billy twanged.

"Oh, it's a place where they send kids who steal or commit other crimes, because they're not old enough to be executed, or go to regular jail. At Juvie, they whip you every day, give you cold baths, and make you eat raw oatmeal. I <u>know</u>. Last year Lenny Lindburger was taken out of the eighth grade. The police came to school and got him right out of my class! They dragged him, kicking and screaming, down the front steps of the school, in handcuffs and wearing a straitjacket." Here Jimmy overdid it, since it's impossible to wear cuffs in a straightjacket. But none of us caught that slip, and he went on, "No one ever saw him again. He probably died of *pew-monia*. That's what happens to most of 'em."

Jimmy always told his stories authoritatively, but with an offhand, smooth delivery. His cheerful manner contrasted oddly with the grisly content, and he had a penchant for being "hip," long before we knew what that was. He went on, "My dad says it's cheaper that way for the County... the quicker they die, the sooner they can get the next batch of bad boys in."

By now, the audience was his, body and soul. Greg and I were stricken dumb, impressed by his superior knowledge of the world, and frozen by the horrors he retailed, thinking how close anyone might come to the gallows, if they put one foot wrong. Even Billy was beginning to sweat, realizing how narrowly he had escaped Lenny's fate, especially the raw oatmeal and the cold baths.

Greg found his voice, and felt it necessary to add, "That's not <u>all</u>! It's a *sin* to steal anything – you'll have to pay in Purgatory when you die!"

Billy, beginning to feel the squeeze between Juvie and eternal fire, relented. "Aw, shoot, I didn't mean it, youse guys... I was just kidding."

We had all drifted toward Jimmy's back yard. On the way, I picked up a bottle labeled "Screwdriver" from the dump in the ravine, and exclaimed, "Hey! That looks like orange juice in the bottom."

Evie said, "It tastes like orange juice, too. I sneaked some once when we had company."

"But, whew! It *does* a lot more," Jimmy sang out in a falsetto voice, moving his eyebrows up and down rapidly, performing a crazy little dance to imitate a drunk person, and singing *"Hava Nagila."* Jimmy always seemed to know about adult stuff, and yet I never saw him play with his father's guns, or take alcohol from the liquor cabinet.

Greg and I looked at each other soberly. It was time for a reality-check, and my brother waded in with a verbal left hook: "Well, I don't know about fun, but it's a *mortal sin* to get drunk!"

I followed up with a quick right: "Yeah, you can go to Hell for that!" – just to make sure no one could recover. Our concerted efforts at least put the kibosh on Jimmy's dancing, if not his spirits.

My brother and I were indoctrinated well by the Old Church. By the ages of eight and ten, we were budding moralists. Our identities were bound up in this, and we felt it was our function in the social group (especially among non-Catholics) to be the spiritual leaven to the loaf. Jimmy never resented this, or took us to task, but was amused and interested by turns. His own father had his roots in Catholicism, though lapsed, and his grandmother went to Mass every Sunday. Once I showed him a shrine to Mary that I had made for the month of May, with wild flowers surrounding a statue on my dresser. He eyed it wistfully, as though he wished he could be a part of what we had and get some of the security that religion gave us.

Meanwhile, Cindy, Rags and Rusty were back from hunting, playing in the lawn. "What's Rusty got, anyway?" Greg asked.

We all looked to see. Rusty proudly displayed a dead mouse, lying on the grass. "Wow! You actually *caught* something!" I teased. Rusty tossed it up in the air in celebration, like a pizza chef, and then all the dogs scrambled for the prize, which vanished in two seconds. One of them had put it in a place of no return.

Suddenly our attention was riveted by the beatific sight of Jimmy's go-cart, sitting on the croquet lawn by the old well. It had slotted scooter-wheels painted Chinese red, and looked like the most beautiful thing in all the world. Until now, we hadn't really understood that 10th commandment: *"Thou shalt not covet thy neighbor's goods."* But now Greg and I looked at each other dumbstruck – we were coveting *real* bad.

We closed in hungrily to inspect all the details. There was a red-leather padded seat, a hand brake on the right side by the rear wheel, and a bicycle horn mounted on the left. Steering was accomplished by placing the feet on the right and left sides of a pivoting front-axle-and-wheel assembly. A single piece of knotted rope, attached close to each front wheel and held in the hands, assisted the feet in turning. An old license plate was tacked to the back of the seat-box, to complete the equipage.

"Man!" I said to Greg. "We've got to build our own!"

"We WILL, as soon as the treehouse is done!"

Our appetite for racing had been whetted by Jimmy's tongue-in-cheek accounts of Billy's recent defeats. Billy remembered, too, and interrupted our thoughts. "I'm gonna get even with you. I fixed some stuff on my cart, and now you're gonna eat my dust!" He had learned this kind of talk from his reckless older brothers, who raced their cars everywhere they went, including their own back field, behind the barn.

"We can't wait," Jimmy said dryly. "Who's driving?"

Furious at the slur, "Me, of course, stupid!" Billy retorted.

"I'm not worried, then," Jimmy told him sweetly. "You won't beat us, chicken-liver."

"I *will so!* You'll see!" He turned and ran off down the drive, pretending he was racing his cart against us, with revving engines and squealing tires.

My brother Timmy materialized almost at Jimmy's elbow, coming up the woods path near Ackermans' garage. He could move awfully unobtrusively when he wanted to. When he was ten, Mother gave him a broken alarm clock to keep him busy, and he took it apart and fixed it. It became his talisman, and for a while, he rang it everywhere he went. We didn't mind – it gave us warning of his approach, like Hook's crocodile. This was especially useful if you wanted to examine his treasures when he was out, though you still had to be careful – I think he already knew how to dust for fingerprints. Even when you had distanced yourself from the goods, he would be scowling and suspicious, sensing that the psychic field had been altered. If we were cheerful, he was sure of it.

Timmy was carrying his Osage-orange bow at the ready, with an arrow-quiver slung over his shoulder. Our Uncle John had made four bows in his workshop, for himself, Timmy, Greg and me. Unfortunately, mine had a flaw near the notch, and broke the first time I pulled it. I was still miserable about that.

"Who was that leaving?" Timmy asked Jimmy, pointedly ignoring us.

"Billy and his go-cart," Jimmy answered innocently.

"Didn't have a cart."

"Yes, well... you know Billy." Jimmy smiled diplomatically. "He's overexcited about his new go-cart, and forgot he wasn't driving it. Says it will beat mine all hollow."

Timmy pursed his lips and brooded for a moment. "Saw it. Won't go anywhere."

"Why not?"

"Too heavy."

"If you say so, Boss," Jimmy said, mimicking Bugs Bunny. "What's up, Doc?"

This was answered tersely. "Let's go."

"Where we going, Boss – woods – town – what?" Jimmy sassed. "My mother told me not to go just *any*where with just *any*who..."

Timmy almost smiled. This took the form of twitching lips, stingily acknowledging a hit. Jimmy was one of his few friends. It took me years to figure out the attraction, but I finally realized they were opposites: Jimmy a fun-loving Gemini-type who got along with everybody, but my oldest brother naturally uncommunicative, angry and phlegmatic. Timmy was like the lead he used to smelt into bullets in our backyard, while Jimmy, with his zany, winning ways, was quicksilver, responding instantly to every atmospheric ripple. He was the only one who could get away with laughing when Timmy was being strange, unreasonable, or just plain mule-headed. My brother didn't feel threatened because Jimmy wasn't *his* younger brother... Also, he had to be more tolerant because the relationship wasn't automatic, like family, and if he wanted to keep it, he couldn't afford knee-jerk resentment.

A few years later, Timmy actually had another friend, Ivan Resner. He was polite and soft-spoken, but for Timmy it was primarily a religious association: Ivan was a good mechanic by the time he was a sophomore in high school, and presided as high priest over the Wizard motorbike *aficionados*. Since Timmy had a broken-down Wizard that he was dying to ride, he attended services regularly.

Timmy stood there bluff, like royalty, quietly waiting for Jimmy's compliance. On his part, Jimmy was always flattered because this older boy actively sought his company. He couldn't turn down that opportunity, so he said, "I'll go get my bow and arrow, Boss. Hey – I've got a new target we can use!"

Nobody said anything while we waited – Greg and I knew better than to initiate conversation. When Jimmy came back, he turned to us and asked about our own new bows. I told him sadly about my bad luck.

Jimmy always looked on the bright side. "Man, you must have a strong arm to break that!"

It hadn't occurred to me. "I don't know... But Uncle John said there was a flaw in the wood, and it might not hold," I told him.

"Gee, that's really a tough break," Jimmy said, putting his arm around my shoulder. "But you can still make your own bow like you did before."

"Yeah, I know," I said, feeling better already.

So the two older boys went off to play bow-and-arrow in the field by the old barn, and all the dogs followed after. Greg and I understood that a different club was in session, and it was our cue to go home. That was okay – we'd had a great morning, and it was almost lunchtime. Besides, we were looking forward to working on our treehouse!

"Race you home!" Greg started to run, and I charged after him. He would probably win, but if he tripped, I'd have a chance.

As soon as lunch was over, we eagerly set out, taking a strong hammer to pull nails and a lard bucket for collecting them. We had baling twine to tie boards together for hauling. It took us ten minutes to get there, over several fields and fences, but there weren't that many places we could get free materials.

We looked hopefully around the dump. There *was* more than when Greg had last checked, but maybe not enough.

"I know what–" I suggested. "Maybe if we dig down, there might be wood from other years."

"Good idea!"

We went to work, pulling items off the top and separating them into piles. There were two-by-fours, bits of plywood, old-fashioned boards, some two-by-sixes, sheet metal of various sizes, and hinges. Some things were so tangled with chicken wire and broken glass frames that we had to take them apart before we could get them out. Others were under tires or old rotten barn doors that had to be flipped. At one point, Greg yelled, "Hey, Paul, look!" He had found an oak-framed glass window, without a scratch on it. "Wow!" I exclaimed. "That's definitely going into our house!"

Finally we were done, and all our materials lay on the grass, tied with baling twine. All nails had been pulled and thrown into the lard bucket, and we were ready to start hauling! We were so absorbed that we didn't hear a tractor approaching, but looked up, startled, when it got near. It was only a Grailville girl. She turned the engine off, and asked, "What are you boys doing?"

"Getting stuff for our treehouse," I said, smiling at her.

"All right, but see that you don't leave anything on the grass. I don't want our cows stepping on any nails!"

"Yes, ma'am," Greg returned. "Don't worry, we'll drag it all home today."

We made several trips that afternoon, taking the most valuable stuff first, in case some neighborhood sneak made off with it behind our back. Some of the salvaged sheet metal served as a sled to drag awkward items. With the weather in the mid-eighties and muggy, it was pretty uncomfortable, but we understood work, and had the calluses to prove it.

The next morning, we started to build. Using Dad's ladder, we nailed the two main supports to the outsides of the crotches. They were a bit wobbly, so we ran Y-braces down to the main trunk. Next, we created a joist-rectangle by boxing in the ends, and put additional joists inside the box, nailed through from the outside. We pieced the floor together from our store of salvaged wood – I would hand Greg some lumber, and he would cut it up on the platform with the carpenter's saw, working each section as best he could.

By early afternoon the floor was done. It was wonderful sitting there in the open air, with leaf patterns and sunlight moving over us every time a breeze blew. And to think it was all *ours*! Lying back on the platform, I broke the silence. "You know, maybe we should leave it this way. Robin Hood lived outside, in the leafy greenwood."

"Yeah, I like that idea," Greg answered, "but we want a clubhouse we can go into when it's raining or cold, and maybe sleep out. Robin and his men must have had caves or something for bad weather."

"That'll be neat," I agreed. Looking up into the treetops gave me another idea. "Hey, see where that little crotch is at the top? We can make a crow's nest, and fly a pirate flag and spy on everyone!"

"Yeah, and launch raids! Wait – we could build it now, before we finish our house. It'll only take us a little while, and then we can start using it!"

We plunged in, making our ladder to the top by nailing one step at a time and standing on them to nail the higher ones. Finally we were ready to build the tiny platform. It took us at least another hour, because we had to haul all the materials up in our hands or pockets.

When Grailville's bell tolled the Angelus we looked up, surprised. Our look-out was finished – perfect, swaying like a ship's mast when the wind blew. You could enjoy events in the neighborhood not evident from below without hearing any sound, like seeing Billy Martin run for the house after his older brother dope-slapped him by the outhouse.

Mama came out to tell us supper was ready, and saw us in the top of the tree. "Goodness, boys, what are you doing all the way up there?" We could tell it made her nervous, but she never said we couldn't go up again.

Our mother partly subscribed to the Charles Lindbergh theory of raising kids (at least when she wasn't imploring guardian angels to save us). He believed kids needed practical experience, even if they sometimes got hurt, and thought overprotection would ultimately prove more harmful. We heartily seconded that. Besides, if you were in shape, there wouldn't be much danger. Greg and I had begun climbing small trees when we were three, and weren't foolhardy. We never once fell from a tree.

That night Mother sewed some eyepatches for us, and Greg made a pirate flag from an old sheet. It was the classic skull-and-crossbones, white on charcoal black, and next morning early, we climbed the mast and hoisted our colors. The flag stood as a warning to all that sailed the neighborhood seas: *"The Pirates of the Spanish Main have taken possession of their territory. Let unfriends beware!"*

We worked steadily on the treehouse for the next two weeks. When the walls were halfway up, we realized there just weren't enough materials to make it full-height. I said to Greg, "Let's just roof it over with what we've got. We won't be able to stand up in it, but it's better than nothing."

"I guess we'll have to, " Greg agreed.

"I'm going aloft to take a look around first," I said. We badly wanted a spy-glass, like the pirates in <u>Treasure Island</u>, but had to make do with an old pair of opera glasses.

"Go ahead, I'll start with the roof supports," Greg replied.

I skittered up the tree, and what did I see from the crow's nest but John Hutzel, Jr. advancing in the direction of our Indian camp, with two of his cousins following. "Hey, Greg!" I yelled. "John's headed up the wash toward our camp again. Let's go ambush him at the top of the hill!"

Greg dived down the tree, and I scrambled after him. We tore out for Grailville's fence line, the longer but concealed way.

We had a score to settle. A couple of weeks ago, John had found the camp, hidden behind the honeysuckle-covered fence, once Grandpa's boundary and now our fort wall. Beyond it stood a towering old pear tree, near some strange mucky pits in the ground that looked suspiciously like old dug graves. More honeysuckle had made a patch of young trees into tepees, one of them especially dense. I kept my treasures there: a tomahawk mounted on a stick, a wonderfully twisted black-cherry cudgel with a burl at the top, and some wooden spears we had fashioned. Just recently, I had left my homemade hickory bow and arrows there, complete with real stone arrowheads, and I didn't mean to see them come to harm.

Barely in time, we nipped behind the hedge and took defensive positions, sticking buzzard feathers in our hair and grabbing a handful of pokeberries for war paint. John's head popped over the hill as he trudged forward, his retinue trailing behind. He was smiling smugly, as though he would enjoy some leisurely vandalism. But as he reached the fence, we jumped up, yelling war cries, and he was caught off-guard. He nearly fell over when he saw our bloodied faces, but bellowed and charged when he recognized us. John tried to climb the vine-covered fence, but Greg pushed him back over when his balance was precarious. When he rushed us again, I drew a bead on him with my bow and arrow, and let fly. The wooden arrow hit him square in the chest and bounced off. *Thunk!*

He'd had about enough, and started to run home, but when his cousins Bernard and Larry arrived, he felt revitalized by the pleasantly favorable odds of three to two. They came on again with confidence, and John made it over the wall this time, heading straight at me. *Uh-oh!* He was older and more heavily built, so I knew I had to trick him. I positioned myself just in front of one of the smelly pits, blocking his view of it. When he lunged at me, I feinted, stepped aside, and gave him a little push. He landed face-down. When he struggled up, his feet made sucking sounds and a fetid odor rose up to choke him.

In the meantime, my brother had taken care of the two cousins. One was put back over the fence by a simple body-throw, and the other one fled when Greg flourished a primitive tomahawk in his face.

A black-faced John sounded the retreat: "C'mon, let's get out of here!" and all three fled down the hill. His parting taunt was, "I'll be back next time with ALL my cousins, and get you then!"

The loser retains always the right to use his tongue as he will. My brother and I didn't pursue – we were happy to have repelled the assault for the moment, so we sat down for a breather. Normally we weren't very violent, but were peeved with John Hutzel just then. In addition to his recent disrespect for our camp, he had hit Greg in the back with a rock last week while Greg was carrying two buckets back from the spring. What kind of person would do that? No, it wasn't over, not by a long shot.

But there was more than that driving us. The Hutzels just rubbed us the wrong way, and today's incident was only the most recent irritation in a situation always ready to flare like bacon grease on the back burner.

To begin with, they seemed hoity-toity, and made us feel apologetic for the way we lived. They had a new car, and new toys. Wilma Hutzel, their mother, kept the house so spotless and antiseptic that we felt like germs when we visited there. Why, the kids had to take *baths* every night, and be exactly on time for supper! It all spoke plainly to us: *We live better than you do.* As a final insult, they erected a gate at the entrance to their driveway, and promptly closed it at dinnertime, winter and summer. The *hoi polloi* were admitted during certain hours only. Greg and I itched to return the compliment through John Junior, in much the same way Tom Sawyer had "messaged" the new boy in his fancy clothes. (It didn't occur to us that the kids might already be paying heavily, under their mother's regime.)

That afternoon we returned from our Indian foray a little tired, but still eager to resume building. Several things interfered, however: Mother wanted us to help with a couple of chores, as well as setting the stage for dinner, and that shot the rest of the day.

The next day was Saturday, and rather purgative, since it consisted of more chores, Confession, and baths. Sundays revolved around Mass, breakfast, a sumptuous Sunday dinner, and a long walk (or nap, if you had overeaten). We weren't allowed to work, out of respect for the Lord's Day. And respect it we did, backed up as it was by the threat of mortal sin and eternal damnation, even though we couldn't really see how *play* was work.

Anyway, we didn't get back to the treehouse till Monday, but the next two days saw its completion, with the roof covering half-high walls. We entered through a trapdoor in the floor and couldn't stand up, and the roof leaked some, due to a shortage of sheet metal. But this was our headquarters now, where many of our games would be played.

Cowboys-and-Indians was a perennial favorite, whenever neighbor boys wandered by and gratuitously shot at us. The rules were simple: If someone got the drop on you, and shot first, you were dead and out of the game. Of course, there was always a lowdown, sneaking cheat (Guess who?) who wouldn't play by the rules and die. When this happened, either the game could get tedious or the cheater would have to be taken in hand-to-hand combat. In cases of extreme annoyance, the defeated would be tied up. More often, though, we didn't bother, but just went on to kill him three or four times. We were willing to stretch the point, since Billy Martin rarely got the jump on us, and it seemed fitting, anyway, that the bad guy should die more than once.

We camped near the treehouse, too. One night in late July, Greg's friend Tommy Wack and the two of us slept in a tent, excited to be out at night on our own, even though it was only in a corner of our property. Tree frogs were making their high-pitched, hypnotic sound, and crickets chirruped close by our tent, while cicadas were beginning their "Katy-did" and "Katy-didn't." Around 9:00, we weren't even beginning to settle down to sleep when Tommy said reverently, "Shhh! Listen to *that!*" My mother was playing the piano, and strains of "Rhapsody in Blue" floated across the night air from the house.

"It's really wonderful, the way your mother can play," Tommy said. "I wish my parents could."

We lay there listening quietly to the crashing chords, piano runs, and impelling jazz rhythms. The still night and the distance gave the music a magical, far-off quality.

The next thing we heard was the morning twittering of birds.

The best time to be in the treehouse was when it rained. Summer storms in Ohio come up very fast, but sometimes, when the wind was rising and we saw it getting black, we would run for the treehouse, climb in, and bang the trapdoor shut. Often, we just made it before the rain came rushing down on the sheet metal roof, right over our heads. Then we lit candles, holding them or using the wax to stick them down to the floor. They fluttered from storm drafts, and lit our faces dull yellow. If the roof started dripping from one or two leaks, we would get out a couple of tin cans, saved for the purpose, and felt cozy and protected, like small animals in a burrow.

The *pièce de résistance* was the single oak-framed glass window, which overlooked the garden. It was really a glass door from someone's oak bookcase, the kind that opens horizontally, but we didn't know that. We mounted it to open inward and fastened it with a hook.

The house was furnished with sundry items, such as Sterno for cooking. For some reason, we really liked the idea, but it smelled horrible and rendered food inedible. There was a tobacco can with a lid, full of fossils and special rocks, and we had comic books, matches, and a pack of playing cards for "War." (We didn't have the patience to learn *real* card games.) In the corners we stored the weaponry of the moment, ranging from slingshots to wooden swords and homemade Indian articles. In a few years, we would graduate to real David-and-Goliath slings. They were introduced by Timmy, the only time he showed any interest in the Bible.

Chapter VI.

The Carnivore at the Carnival

It would have been a good day to consult my personal *horrorscope*, if I had known about such things. If only I hadn't gone to get the mail!

It was late June of '58, and I had just survived fourth grade, my worst yet. I'd passed with an unremarkable "C" average, but the teacher, Isabella, had made my life a misery. (She was a Grailville girl, not a nun, and referred to me as "that Pfarr boy," so I didn't dignify her with a title, either.)

Religion class was the worst. I was very religious, but just couldn't memorize long sections of the Baltimore Catechism. When I got my report card at the end of the first semester, and found that Isabella had failed me for *THAT*, I was crushed. I knew what the catechism *meant* and tried to live it, and she gave me an "F." But other kids who just rattled it off and didn't understand it got "A's." Fortunately, my mother called up and told her how hard I'd worked, and argued my grade to a "C."

Anyway, at the end of the year, I had more than the usual frustrations for the summer to expiate. Whenever Isabella crossed my mind, I realized she was gone forever, and then my heart sang out: *"Free at last! Free at last!"* Like every other kid in the land, I prayed, *"Please, God, let this summer last forever!"* If He had agreed, I would still be living in that summer, always about to be in the 5th grade, and Isabella's vindictive nature would have starved for lack of students to torment in the fall. I didn't care. That was her lookout.

After several weeks of freedom, I felt uplifted and glorious. One fine Friday morning, I went to the top of our lane to pick up the mail, and Davy Monihan hailed me, grinning. "Hey, ma-a-n, what's up?"

I was torn between wanting to be friendly and not being sure how close I wanted to get to anyone in the Monihan family. Besides, when someone comes on strongly, there's a perverse inclination to back away. If the first party seems cool, then you pursue (ever more obnoxiously, if there is no warming trend). So, adhering faithfully to "Basic Psychology for *Dummkopfs*," I studiously avoided matching his enthusiasm. "Oh, not much," I said diffidently.

We spent a few minutes talking about this and that. When I finally started home, Davy called, "Ma-a-n, did you know the carnival's in town?"

I spun on my heel. This changed everything. It was an event of magnitude – it spoke to my parched soul! Later, with native insect logic, I decided everything that happened that day was Davy's fault. The devil, or perhaps one of his henchmen (Screwtape, or was it Tapeworm?) had put him up to it.

"*Really?*" I answered, forgetting to be disinterested.

"Yeah! I talked to Tommy Wimms, this morning, and he said they have all kinds of rides, cotton candy, and a house of horrors with skeletons in it and everythin'! And they have a ride called 'the Rocket!'" he continued breathlessly. "It has two arms that whirl you 'round and 'round, straight up and down... Tommy Wimms said one girl blacked out, and threw up!"

I privately marked that ride down as a *must*. (If you want to be a tough man, like the heroes on TV, you don't talk before you know if you can take it.)

"Hey-y-y!" Davy exclaimed, "I'm goin' tonight! Why don't you come with me, man? It starts at seven o'clock!"

I *really* wanted to go, even with him. I *had* to go! "Okay, it's a deal!"

"Cool!"

"I'll come up to your house at seven o'clock to get you," I promised.

Davy quickly turned and trotted home, pretending he was riding a horse, and I pelted down the lane.

Davy lived in one of five houses on our lane. He was considerably younger, and not my preferred choice of company, but sometimes we would go fishing with him, or hunt pop bottles together. His large family was desperately poor by American standards, with no inside plumbing, and a kerosene heater in the winter. Inside their house, everything was shredded and tangled, stinking of urine and kerosene, and alive with cockroaches. Ironically, they had a TV long before we did — their one lifeline to sanity of the spirit, if not to reality. They didn't get regular meals, or baths, but were easy-going and generous with what they had, if you were brave or magnanimous enough to accept anything. I never ate over there unless it came from a sealed bag straight from the store.

They had a lot of strange habits. One of them was rubbing their cheeks frantically with their fists, a fetish invented by the second-oldest brother, Lonnie, expressing unbearable excitement. It caught fire with the whole family, and sometimes, when I dropped by, they would all be sitting on the couch, watching TV, and wildly rubbing their cheeks.

Being outdoors with Davy, away from his domicile (and the many ragged brothers and sisters) wasn't so bad, as long as you stayed upwind, he didn't get rained on, and you weren't forced to share close quarters.

Not surprisingly, his impoverished life had made him a little odd, though always good-natured and amenable to whatever scheme you might propose. (Who can resist a yes-man?) Sometimes I would test this, to see if he had any wishes of his own. When any particular project was suggested, the questing conversation went something like this:

"Let's go to Loveland on my bike and get some pop."

"Yeah, man, let's go!"

"Aw, maybe I don't really want to go, after all, do you?"

"No, man, not really..."

This caused me to scratch my head, and after many similar attempts, I had to concede defeat. But at least he wasn't going to cause any trouble if I couldn't make up my mind. I don't know whether he had figured out that the best way to get by in his deplorable situation was to be agreeable, or he was just glad to be included in someone's plans, on any terms.

His brothers and sisters were the same way. Sometimes we amused ourselves by getting five-year-old Joey (the one with the speech impediment, of course) to sing popular songs like *"Thinking of Baby,"* which to our delight came out, *"chinking of chaby."* He didn't mind – just glad of the attention.

On my way home, I felt a sense of renewal and purpose. I was actually going to the carnival! I pictured endless rides, cotton candy, popcorn, and winning prizes through my skill...

However, instinct cautioned me to wait till after lunch to broach the subject with Mama. (My father didn't count for this purpose—he was out sign-painting somewhere.) So, after lunch, I followed her outside to where she was hanging up the laundry, and told her I wanted to go to the carnival with Davy. To my dismay, she said curtly, "No, absolutely not! I don't want you out at night in Loveland, especially at a place like that!"

I hadn't dreamed she could refuse. She was normally so reasonable... Then, before I even had time to recover, she had the audacity to ask me to do some chores. I was so outraged by this evil substitution that I sassed her: "I don't care what you think — I'm *going* to the carnival! And I'm *not* doing any stupid chores, either!"

She replied by grabbing me and slapping my face, and that's when I kicked her in the shins. She let go, and I ran for the fence bounding the south side of our property, with Mama in eager pursuit. Just as I was crossing over, she called out, "Paul Pfarr! You get back here right now and get your whipping! It will only be worse later!" I wished she hadn't used my full name — that never turned out well.

Well, I didn't intend to get a whipping, now or later, so this sailed right over my head. I stubbornly put my worst foot forward, and ran. Her final riposte was "You're not going to get any supper!"

"I don't care! I'm running away!" I yelled, sending her an unsubtle message: *I don't* need *you interfering in my life anymore! Leave me alone!* Later on, my stomach came to regret the no-supper part long before my conscience noticed anything else.

I had seen "Pinocchio" recently, but all I'd thought was, *What a stupid story... why, he wasn't even real, just a manikin giving a wooden performance! Nothing could be dumber, with his silly little smile, and bobbing up and down like a complete idiot... What a sap!* I had felt morally superior, since, even though he had a kind master, he had run off to the carnival for no reason, hung out with low company, smoked and even gambled. Normally, I was good at getting the moral of a story, but in this case, Screwtape had directed my attention to the trivial elements of Pinocchio's personality to avoid my noticing other, more germane facts.

Thus it was that the recording angel was forced to write in the *Bad Book* that I was off to town that afternoon, looking very much like Pinocchio. My plans and emotions were askew — it was still early, and I had several hours to kill before the carnival opened. It irked me that I was suddenly an escapee, a fugitive from maternal justice, and in violation of several commandments. *Why* couldn't Mama have behaved more graciously, and not tried to spoil my innocent outing? What was wrong with her? I nursed my injustices, and daydreamed that she would be sorry when I didn't come home for supper or bed. But *nothing* was going to stop me from going to that carnival!

So after wandering around for a half-hour, restless and fuming, I showed up at Davy's house *five hours early*. Of course, there was no reason to tell him about my problems. Wormsnout intimated it was better to put it all aside. I might have to pay later, but, like Tom Sawyer, figured that any whipping was a small price to pay for my blissful night.

Davy saw me approaching, and met me at his driveway. "You're awful early, ma-a-n! What happened?"

"Oh, I just came to see if you wanted to go hunting pop bottles... We can get some more money."

"Hey, cool — let's go!"

We went to his grandpaw's barn to grab a gunny sack for the bottles, then strolled out the lane, scuffling our feet satisfyingly in the gravel as we went. At the curve in the lane, we stopped to pick up some bottles I'd left in an old hollow maple stump, a secret hiding place. Then we hunted all along Jackson Street, first working toward Grailville along the east side, looking in the ditches and putting our finds in the bag, and yelling when we found a large, 5-cent bottle. Then we returned along the west side, finally finishing up at Taber's ballfield, almost downtown.

Bear Creek bounded one edge of the ballfield, and we sat on a rock there in the shade, dangling our feet in the running water. It was so cool and peaceful, with the dappled sunlight on the riffles, and we were in no hurry. We watched the minnows darting and water skaters eternally gliding on the surface. The day was warm, in the mid-80s, and, after resting, we noticed we were powerfully thirsty. I had been told not to drink from streams or ponds, but the water looked so clean that we drank it, anyway. It was wonderful. Next, we waded around, turning over rocks to see what lived under them. Ten minutes after that, we progressed to shying rocks at tin cans that picnickers had lazily discarded. But when some noisy ballplayers arrived in cars and unloaded their gear, we instinctively took cover on the other side of the creek to avoid being hassled, since they were bigger than we were.

That side of the creek was an alfalfa field owned by Grailville and lined with trees on all sides, part of the floodplain that ran along the O'Bannon Creek all the way to Martins', behind our house. A little distance away, I spotted a wild black-raspberry patch. Like a bear, I was almost psychic at finding berries from a distance, by the color of the light falling on the leaves, the way the patch grew as a unit, and *where* - black raspberries love the north side of a wood. And, of course, they attract lots of birds. Wintertime was easiest, though, since the purple canes were unmistakable.

There were a lot of berries today. I made a mental note to come back tomorrow, but, in the meantime, we applied ourselves steadily until we had allocated about 3 quarts between us. It was a little disturbing that I was hungry already, when it wasn't even suppertime. I had forgotten that I sometimes ate six meals a day, including snacks. Half-formed regret misted across my mind - perhaps I had been reckless in my haste to cross the cook...

But after the berries, my insides were more comfortable, so I shouldered the gunnysack and we moved on amicably, unconscious of purple tongues and lips. Taking the old tractor trail back to Jackson Street, we made for Loveland Grocery, where Ella Herbert ruled at the cash register, queen bee of her store. She greeted us with her usual sourness, and when she spied the fifty or so pop bottles in the gunnysack, demanded sharply, "*Where* did you get those!" Then she added, her lips twitching grimly, "Look how dirty they are! And what's that on your lips — you can't be *cold!*"

"No, ma'am, we've been eating black raspberries."

"Never would've guessed," she said dryly. "I swear, you kids think I have nothing better to do than cash these in! Sonny! Sonny!" she yelled to her son. "Come out here and help these kids with their bottles!"

We stood there, nervously shuffling our feet, trying not to look Ella in the eye. She was always cross. When we had bottles, she acted as if she were giving you *her* cash, and wasn't going to be reimbursed by the bottle-man. Or if we bought candy bars, she would say, "Does your mother know you're eating that junk before supper?" We knew from experience that you just had to tough it out with her.

Sonny appeared, smiling, from the back of the store, where his father worked at the meat counter. When Ella turned to the next customer, he winked conspiratorially and led us around to the side door, where the bottles were stored. There were crates stacked up, with names like "Canada Dry Grapefruit," "Barq's," "Nehi," "Orange Crush," "Royal Crown Cola," and, of course, the beer bottles.

"They *are* awful dirty, some of 'em—" I began apologetically, hoping it wouldn't matter.

"Don't pay any attention to my mother," he said cheerfully. "Complaining makes her happy. She feels useful, like a quality-control boss. Her doctor says her attitude has added years to her life. Don't worry — I'll rinse 'em a little. We don't want the bottle man to think we pulled them from the river bottom!" He winked.

"Well, some of them *did* come from the—" Davy began, but I elbowed him so he couldn't finish the sentence. I didn't want to test the limits of Sonny's good will.

"Thanks, Sonny!" I took the bottle receipt from him happily, and went up front to redeem it. She gave us the coins with a sour smile, slapping them down on the counter in a way to make us blink. "*Well...* aren't you going to buy any candy?" she growled. (We knew she didn't want that money to get out of the store.)

"No, we need all the money we can get for the carnival," Davy replied.

"Humph!" Ella snorted.

As we were leaving, Sonny whispered in our ear, "She likes you." Surprised at this improbable revelation (but not caring much, since we had the cash), we left with a sigh of relief. Our meager carnival funds had been increased by another dollar.

As soon as we got outside, we could hear exciting noises coming from a block away. Moving eagerly toward the din, we passed the little stores with their imitation Western facades that comprised the heart of Old Loveland, and stopped for a moment to look at the new Brown's Supermarket, which had replaced the old town square and drinking fountain.

The carnival was being held by the bridge, where they had recently pulled down some buildings across from the old Western Auto. It wasn't a very big lot, but Loveland wasn't a very big town, and they had managed to squeeze everything into the space between Broadway and the river embankment.

There were people everywhere, strolling in all directions, laughing and talking, young boys chasing girls, and people screaming on the rides. All the machinery of the carnival was grinding away at once, each playing its own tune, and the noise was stimulating to our unworn nerves. There were booths selling merchandise, mostly gaudy junk like striped canes and strange teddy bears. Our Chief of Police, John Fritz, was in evidence, walking around with a slight swagger because of the big gun he wore, nodding and greeting the people he knew, an ever-present reminder to everyone to behave themselves.

For rides, there were all the standards: a Ferris wheel, a merry-go-round, and a swing set that simulated flying. There was a dunking booth, and I thought, *"Why couldn't Isabella be up there? That would be something to throw at!"*

There was one ride where you sat in your own car, and were whirled around a noisy hub on an undulating horizontal plane. Out back was a house of horrors whose shape looked suspiciously like a trailer, but I was so scared that all common sense fled. I wondered, *"Could they have gotten real ghosts to put in there?"* When I put this terrifying thought to Davy, he only made a moaning sound like "Unhhhhh...."

Our first objective on entering the grounds was to buy cotton candy from a middle-aged lady with pink hair. "Is *that* cotton candy, too?" Davy asked the lady, pointing to her hair.

"Lord love a duck, *no*, sweetie, ants would be all over me in a second," she giggled. The candy was the ultimate in junk food, retreating mysteriously and shrinking under the questing tongue. And the taste— *ecstasy*! It was very sticky, but only grownups would fuss about that.

"Isn't it *go-o-od!*" Davy yelled over the din, grinning.

"It sure is!" I answered moderately, between massive mouthfuls. Our family didn't go in for an excessive show of emotion over venal things, and certainly not in public.

Davy didn't mind. He just shouted, "Let's ride the Ferris Wheel!"

And we did, a couple of times, but couldn't help furtively imagining what it would be like to fall out. That made our knees hurt, so we decided to try the swings next. I didn't really like them, either, since they made me dizzy and a little sick to my stomach, but I never let on. I was going to be a *man*, and small things like that couldn't be allowed to signify. Every time the carnival came to town, I got on the swings as many times as everyone else. My brother Peter was different, and I believed him a pathetic creature, since his unusual approach was to avoid pain and discomfort. My inner voice said, *"Get used to it, and if you can't, never let anyone know."*

After riding the swings, we were getting low on money, so we went to look at the brand-new ambulance parked out front, which the town was going to buy if the bond issue passed in the fall. It was a Cadillac, with fins that reached for the sky like a rocket. "Wow!" we marveled. It was *huge*, and the engine boasted over 500 horsepower.

I said, "Boy, you sure could take a sick person to the hospital fast!"

"Yeah, that would be neat, man," Davy agreed, fascinated.

We entertained the advantages of this noble profession—speeding to the hospital at 100 miles an hour, sirens blaring, running red lights, warning everyone, *"Get out of the way, you idiots, I have a sick person here!"*– being a hero, race-car driver, and benefactor to the race all at once.

A nearby fireman named Jake asked, "You boys wanna be paramedics?"

"Para-*what?*" I asked.

"Paramedics," he repeated.

"Could we drive the ambulance?"

"Well, now, if you don't mind going to school, and learning how to handle accident victims—"

"*School!*" We both exclaimed, horrified.

"Sure, at least 2 years, after you get out of high school."

That tore it. I wasn't sure I was going to make it through grade school, let alone high school and college. We were out of there!

Jake rolled his eyes, and muttered, "God help the sick!"

We rounded a tent corner, and almost ran into a man playing the accordion. You *know* this man. He lived in everyone's hometown, always entertaining at festivals, weddings, and carnivals. If somehow your town wasn't blessed with him, you could catch him often on the Lawrence Welk Show, or maybe in Norman Rockwell's classic portfolio.

Davy and I stared at him, riveted. The man was slightly overweight, with an aura of the salesman, and must have been around forty, though he looked like an overgrown Mama's boy, still living at home in a hothouse environment that had somehow limited his normal growth. His suit had baggy pants, smelling slightly of mothballs, and he wore heavy-framed black glasses. His hair was black, too, slicked straight back, forties-style, and it was curious to us that his ears stood out slightly from his head, making him appear over-eager. (Well, he *was*, of course...) This ensemble was topped by an oversized polka-dotted bow-tie.

He provided so many uneasy amusements that it took a minute to catch your breath and sort out exactly what you were feeling. Even though we knew he was very clean and a nice guy, we felt instinctively that he presented an excess of everything: goodwill, smiles, happiness, mothballs, and cologne. But none of this was immediately thought of, since he played polkas with great exuberance and energy, smiling continually like Liberace. I almost said the smile was pasted on, but it wasn't—it was syrupy and sentimental, but, oh, how frighteningly sincere! He welcomed everyone to come into his parlor and celebrate. (I didn't go in... I was afraid it was a land of no return, and I wouldn't be able to climb out again.)

There was a small group of people around him, some a little stunned at getting this much of everything all at once, but others, such as maiden aunts and grandmothers, gazed sweetly at him, reminded perhaps of their ethnic roots and their youth. I don't know why, but it scared the bejesus out of me. Davy, on the other hand, no musical judge, took him at face value, but even he bent over double, laughing, and exclaimed, "Gawd!" as we walked away.

It was dark now. The kind of people coming to the carnival had changed. Before, there had been a predominance of kids and their parents, but now the crowd was older and more hardened. Adults and older teenagers came in couples, and the gaiety began to have a forced, desperate sound on the air. Girls' laughter was shrill, and some of the men accompanying them were raucous. A couple of men walked unsteadily, and carried paper sacks with them, from which they took a swig now and then.

"Man, they're *drunk!*" Davy laughed. His background had made him knowledgeable.

But I knew what I'd been taught. "Yeah, but it's a mortal sin!"

"What's that?" Davy asked curiously.

"I'll tell you about it on the way home."

We were out of money, tired, and slightly queasy from the rides and the junk we'd eaten. The cacophony of sound, interesting at first, was beginning to jangle our nerves. We wandered around, a little disconsolate, wishing the fun could be revived, or at least prolonged, by some unforeseen catalyst.

"Hey! Maybe we can find some money dropped by a drunk," Davy proposed.

"Maybe—let's look!"

We didn't find any, but I did spot Jimmy Ackerman and his sister Jean coming out of Madame Cucaracha's fortunetelling tent. They came over, and Jimmy said, "What are you doing here, Paul?"

"Same as you."

"I'm surprised your mother let you come alone," Jean said. She was 15.

Jean was becoming annoyingly mother-like. "I'm not alone," I said, dodging the issue. "I came with Davy."

This was dropped because Jimmy interrupted, beginning to tell us about the startling future predicted for him in the next year. "Madame said that I would have to endure capture and torture, but my worst enemy would be defeated. She said I had to be careful, though, or he would kill some of my friends—maybe even Mom and Dad! Then she said she saw me going to a new place, and I might never see my home again," he added seriously, looking suddenly sad.

Changing the subject, he went on, "Hey, did you hear about the accident that happened to this girl at the carnival in Madisonville? The car she was riding in came loose, and she was thrown to the ground and beheaded!" Having apparently completed his mission now, he said goodbye, and they went on their way.

Davy and I were just about to concede that the day was over when a strange man in the shadows behind a booth called out to us, "C'mere, kid!"

My breath caught in my throat. I looked at Davy. He was scared, too. *God, help me!* I wailed inwardly, and after that, *Mama!* I remembered painfully that I had been forbidden to come, had disobeyed, sassed, and *kicked* (!) my mother. I was a goner – I just *knew* the devil had been told, "He's yours – go pick him up!"

Well, we both started running and just about flew up Jackson Street, probably setting a record for the quarter-mile dash. Davy and I finally stopped to catch our breath after crossing Bear Creek, then went on silently. I forgot to tell him about the fatal effects of mortal sin, and the need for confession. It would have to wait.

We parted company at the Monihans' driveway, and I continued home, down our very-dark lane, still scared. At the house, I hesitated. The lights were out, and everyone was obviously in bed. *They didn't care at all, not even enough to stay up and give me a whipping!* But Tapeworm pointed out that this would aid me in sneaking undetected to my bed. (He was probably looking forward to a good laugh while I was being whipped. It's no risk for the devil—he figures to have a laugh now, and get your soul later.) I vetoed this rapidly, remembering how lightly my mother slept even when her faculties weren't sharpened by anger. (After all, hadn't we guerilla-trained her?)

Then my eyes came to rest on our '54 wood-paneled Chevy wagon. It looked so friendly and inviting in the night that I decided to sleep there. It wasn't locked, so I crawled in and curled up in the back seat. Not the most comfortable bed in the world, but it beat a soft one after the nasty whipping I knew was coming. It was warm, and I could shut out the night and blissfully go to sleep. I was so tired...

But after about ten minutes, my sister Bea, who was thirteen, tapped on the window. I opened the door for her, and she said sweetly, "We missed you... How are you doing?"

I felt so relieved not to be an exile anymore. "I'm fine."

"Here, Paul, I brought you a pillow and blanket to make you more comfortable–" She handed them to me. "–and something to eat. I thought you'd be hungry." She gave me some biscuits, then kissed me goodnight and tucked me in. This bit of sisterly care made me relax and fall asleep instantly.

But five minutes later, my sleep was rudely interrupted by Mother, who came not with sympathy but a switch. I was dragged out of the car by my ear, and she towed me up the front steps into the house, finally coming to rest in the kitchen. This was going to be a public whipping, for the benefit of the community. My mother knew that no doubt could be allowed in the minds of my siblings as to whether justice had been done.

I used all the standard yelling and screaming techniques, giving no consideration to other sleepers, since I had learned this was no time to be stoic. That would only prolong the whipping by affording the disciplinarian no satisfaction in a duty well done.

The end came, and I limped off to bed. Tears not yet dry, I dropped off quickly, without time even to feel sorry for myself. My sleep was deep and untroubled — well, almost. Except for the wolf Boris, sneaking in the wee hours of the morning.

A stage with red hangings appears. A narrator in the wings announces, "A PLAY IS ABOUT TO BEGIN!" and the curtain rises for the opening scene, displaying the title: "The Carnivore at the Carnival."

A wolf is taking tickets from little boys, girls and sheep, who are "baahing." The wolf is wearing a white shirt, bow tie, and armband, and holding an accordion, with a '20s-style straw boater perched on his head. None of the kids (or sheep) seems to notice his scanty disguise. Pinocchio is there, bobbing up and down with that stupid smile on his face, and the kids are jeering at him. This causes the wolf to smile at the audience, showing some large, disturbing teeth. A soft sound like sawing wood begins in the background — whish-whoosh-whish-whoosh-whish-whoosh — gradually getting louder as the drama progresses. The wolf slowly turns toward the audience, searching for me. His eyes lock on mine, and he says sweetly, "Hello, dear!"

"NO!" I scream, and run for home as fast as I can. But it's no use — I can't see in the dark, and can barely move! The wolf is gaining on me by the second, and starting to pant like a locomotive. "Chuff! Chuff! Chuff! Chuff!" which soon turns into "Wuff! Wuff! Wuff! Wuff!"

I desperately make one last effort to master my feeble body, and it <u>works</u>! I leap into the air, and fly the rest of the way home, but it's still too late! The wolf has caught hold of my ankle, and comes along.

I finally reach my house, and my parents are holding open the front door. They grab me, and try to pull me in. But after a brief tug-o'-war, they lose the struggle, and the wolf drags me outside and eats me all up. I disappear into the black pit of the wolf's stomach.

Finita la comedia!

I awoke the next morning refreshed. While my mother was making breakfast, I asked her impertinently if last night were all a dream. Luckily, she was too busy to focus on me, since I was really saying, *"That whipping hardly fazed me at all, and now it's only a memory!"*

Fortunately for Wormface's young client, there was always Confession on Saturday, and by the time church was over on Sunday, I had reclaimed my soul and reason. By Monday, things were *really* shaping up—next week was the Fourth of July!

Chapter VII.

Let the Races Begin

I was down-cellar, cracking black walnuts for Mother's nut bread when Timmy shuffled in.

"Let's go," he said in his deadpan way. He didn't say *where*, and, young as I was, I knew better than to ask. Obedience was assumed. To be included in his activities at all, even on a rainy late-fall afternoon, felt like a privilege, though I knew any treat would have to be paid for.

Take the time when I was eight and Nick six-and-a-half. Timmy took us to Old Loveland Bakery and actually bought us pastries. We couldn't believe our good luck! But our benefactor handed them out as we were heading home, and then started walking so fast that Nicky had to trot as he ate, and got cream-puff all over his face. Just Timmy's idea of a little joke on the "pig."

I had just finished the walnuts, so I ran them upstairs. By the time I got back, Timmy was already halfway out the lane, moving fast. I sped after him, figuring I was being trained like Indian boys. My oldest brother didn't talk as he strode along – slaves didn't need to understand his plans, merely execute them.

At Jackson Street, we went right, then turned up Jimmy's drive. This *was* odd, since it was still raining lightly, and anyway, it was about Jimmy's suppertime. What was Timmy up to?

I found out when we arrived at the top of the drive. There was Jimmy's cart, with its beautiful red wheels, sitting partway in the dump, sodden in the rain. It almost looked as though Jimmy had thrown it out.

Timmy stopped in the hedged lane, 20 feet short of the cart, and we stood there in the drizzle for a few minutes. He seemed to be calculating how to navigate the open space between him and the cart, unseen. Why? Maybe he was following some sort of etiquette—say the owner had given him the cart, but couldn't bear to actually see it taken away... Hmmm. My sensitive conscience was really reaching to explain this suspicious behavior.

The light was fading, and Timmy decided to make his move. (Who would be looking out the bay window at dusk? Not Jimmy, surely!) He dashed toward the cart, and I followed hard behind.

"Get in!" he said. "You steer."

So. It looked like I was the getaway driver in a heist.

Or... *could* Jimmy really have given it to my brother? Maybe Timmy was taking it because he thought it was abandoned. (No kid would ever *ask* in a situation like that – the owner's interest will instantly be rekindled, even if he doesn't really want the item. Far better just to take it, and find out later if it's missed.)

Perhaps Timmy meant to refurbish it, and give it back to Jimmy as a present. Or did he hope to make it unrecognizable, and race it next summer as his own? (Doubtful, since Jimmy's IQ was well over 100.) On the other hand, he could be planning to sell it on the kids' black market after he fixed it up... If he *was* stealing it, was Timmy really willing to sacrifice his friendship with Jimmy for a go-cart? I had to admit it was probably simpler than all that: Timmy wanted it, so Timmy took it. Anyway, it didn't feel right, but I couldn't sort it all out at the time, so I did what Timmy said. He pushed the cart home, and I steered.

We weren't home five minutes before I heard Mother on the phone with Mrs. Ackerman. Jimmy wanted his cart back.

Mother said, "I don't see how Timmy could have done it – it's been raining out, and he's been down in the basement, working on his bicycle." But there was a strain of doubt in her voice. Mrs. Ackerman vowed that he had been seen no more than ten minutes ago!

Timmy and Jimmy went on being friends, probably because Jimmy was amused at such an act of sheer piracy, after he got the cart back.

Jimmy was always generous with his stuff. He used to leave his red 24"
bike down at our place when we were younger, so we could learn to ride.
Before that, it was his red scooter. It meant a lot to us, because we'd always
wanted a scooter, and never had one. Another time, it was Eve's bike that
he left for a month, but Nick wrecked it when he hit one of the low stone
walls bordering our bridge, and fell into the creek. That was one of the few
times I ever saw Jimmy upset, probably because it was his sister's bike.

* * *

At one time or another, all of the boys in our neighborhood built go-
carts to compete with each other. Martins' first model was heavier than ours
and slightly longer. Then there was the Ackerman Special, the one Timmy
tried to steal.

When the Eichelburgers lived at the top of the lane, Mike's father
helped him build one of sheet metal, tapered in front and back like a
racecar. It looked so slick and fast that we were worried, at first, but
mysteriously, it never won any races. Maybe it was too light, and the wind
held it back, or the wheels were under par. It just went to show, looks
weren't everything!

Every year we worked on a cart, either building one or improving last
year's model through trial-and-error and advice from the older boys. The
hardware man sometimes gave us friendly hints, if we had a problem.

Greg and I got our first racing experience in Jimmy's cart, the summer
of '57. We had hoped to get our own cart built that year, but at one point
we didn't have any money, and later, other things came up. But, thanks to
Jimmy, we got to race against Billy, anyway.

When Jimmy wasn't driving, he instantly changed roles, becoming
coach and commentator. It went something like this: Billy and Greg lined
their carts up in the street, waiting for the signal. Jimmy would shout, "Go!
Go!" They would take off down Bond's Hill, with Jimmy hurling advice
after them: "Pass, Billy! Pass NOW! C'mon, *pass!*"

But Billy was always slow to get *on* the horse, and slow to get *off*. He
would delay too long, then finally start to pass when it wasn't safe. Jimmy
would shout, "NO, Billy! Not *now!* Pull back!" And Billy would be forced to
run off the road, screaming and swearing. Jimmy would just laugh, and sing
out, "The Lone Ranger rides again!" Then he would tootle the TV theme,
using his fist as a pretend-trumpet.

Greg and I were more stable, so we won most races against Billy. His cart *was* a trifle clunky, but most of the problem lay with Billy himself. He would always do something stupid, like pulling in front of Greg and slowing down. One time, he got overconfident after a good lead, and then his wheel popped off because he'd forgotten to put the cotter pin back after greasing the axle.

It wasn't till the summer of 1958 that we actually built our own cart. One morning, Greg and I saw Billy coming up the leaf-dappled lane from his house. He was swaggering, imitating the TV cowboys, his slingshot in his back pocket. He started to draw it, but reconsidered when he saw ours in hand. You could never tell with Billy. Some days he would just start shooting at you, with no palaver, and other times, he'd talk and be ready to play games. At any rate, we weren't too worried – he was a terrible shot.

Today he decided to be friendly. "Uh-hunh-hunh-hunh-hunh," he laughed raucously. "I just wanted to see the look on your faces when I reached for my weapon!"

"If you draw on us, you'll get more than a look," Greg said darkly.

With all our slingshots at the ready, the question of skill naturally arose. We began to aim at various objects, animate and inanimate: a tin can lying in the tiny creek, a hapless crawdad in shallow water, and finally some innocent water-spiders skating nearby. There were about three missed shots for every hit. None of us were that good, except maybe Eve Ackerman (but we couldn't admit that). When any of us actually hit a target, we would crow, to subtly celebrate our victory, and the others privately vowed revenge, later, after much secret practice.

Next, we started shooting at birds overhead, fortunately without any success.

"WOW! I almost got that one!" I shouted. (This was reaching hard for glory, but you have to do that when you don't succeed often.)

When this got old, Billy broached a new subject. "Wait till you see our go-cart *this* year! Jimmy's cart's *nothing* – Jerry and Frankie helped me put on double brakes, and a car horn, and a real car steering wheel, and *everything!* I'm gonna whip your butts!" he bragged, an unholy gleam in his eyes. He was still smarting from last year.

Greg and I looked at each other. We weren't really worried about our laurels, but we sure would like to get a look at that steering!

"Do you want to see it?" Billy offered eagerly.

"Yeah!" we shouted, and all ran down the lane to his place.

Sitting in front of the barn was the cart we knew, but with the new steering wheel attached to a shaft and supported by a dashboard. A block of wood screwed-together was mounted in the middle of the shaft, and rope was wrapped around the block in one continuous piece, with the ends attached to the right and left sides of the front-axle assembly. When the driver turned the wheel to the right, the slack rope would wind around the block, preparing itself for a left turn. There were knobs on the steering wheel, and some streamers.

The cart we built that summer was steered at first by the traditional foot-and-rope method. After seeing Billy's, though, we incorporated the wheel and shaft design as soon as we could. But Billy's steering rope had broken once, in the middle of a race, and he cracked up, so we improved ours by using 5/8" nylon rope, kindly donated by Uncle Marshall.

With little money to spend, we mostly scrounged the materials, as usual, salvaging and bartering with other kids. Old wood was found in barns, garages, sheds, or dumps. But nails, wagon axles, wheels, cotter pins, washers, and bolts were harder to obtain, and highly prized.

Barter was the foundation of our local economy. Billy might have an extra axle or wagon wheel that he would trade for something we had. Greg and I never stole anything, but dealt honorably with the kid-in-charge. Parents were not consulted about this or that piece of stray wood, part, or bolt that went missing – this was *kid* business; it equalized the wealth, and contained the rudiments of a cooperative.

That first cart we built in the summer of '58 was more utilitarian than elegant. The frame was a capital "I" lying on its back, constructed of doubled two-by-fours, clinched together with nails. The front crosspiece was attached only by a heavy bolt running loosely through it. Two 2' axles were attached to its underside with U-nails (or bent-over regular nails), and the wheels were slipped onto the axles, sandwiched between washers and held on by cotter pins. The whole front-axle assembly pivoted on the bolt, and you steered it with your feet, assisted by a rope in your hands.

The rear crosspiece was mounted rigidly, with only one axle, and over it we built a low seat. The overall length of the cart was governed by the distance one's legs could reach from the seat to the front axle, for steering.

For brakes, we just used our feet, at first. Later, we copied Billy's braking design, which consisted of a lever loosely bolted through its middle to the side of the seat. When you pushed the top of the lever forward, the bottom was forced back against the rubber wheel and slowed the cart. Billy's cart had one on each side, but we couldn't figure out who was steering if you had both hands on the brakes. Sometimes bad accidents were avoided by using both brake and feet.

In spite of our best salvaging efforts, we knew we were going to be short one wheel and an axle. But we had each gotten some birthday money from relatives, and done odd jobs for neighbors. We also had an allowance of one quarter per week from our father (if he could afford it, and we hadn't made some fatal blunder). With everything together, we had enough money for the parts this year.

Going to town to buy them was exciting. Our dad usually had Saturday-morning business there, and sometimes our errands coincided. We would take care of ours, then meet him at some predetermined place, like the bank.

You never knew what you might see in town on a Saturday. One afternoon Gregory and I headed for Western Auto, by the bridge. The usual hardware man wasn't at his post inside, so I asked the owner where he was. He said Mr. Black was raising funds for the Kiwanis, in the lot across the street. When we came out, we looked over there, and stopped in our tracks, staring.

There was the colorless Mr. Black, whom we knew only as a Western Auto employee (and servant to our projects), standing on a makeshift stage in a parking lot, with a suit, string tie and Western hat, talking enthusiastically into a microphone.

"C'mon, folks, let's raise some money and have some fun!"

He sat down at a piano on the stage, and started playing and singing energetically, *"Look at that gal with a red dress on!"* He wore a ghastly smile, and topped off each phrase with *"All right!"* like the jazz singers.

Greg and I were horrified. It wasn't all right with us! Our innate puritanical attitudes were ruffled by this kind of behavior, especially since he was OLD – at *least* fifty. Why, he was acting like a swinger!

He kept on through all the verses, which I still think caused a girl with a red dress to materialize out of the crowd. She jumped up on the stage and started dancing furiously, with her full skirts flying out straight.

We never knew Mr. Black could *be* like that! Here was a conservative pillar of the community in heavy-framed black glasses, acting in a shockingly loose fashion. Greg and I wondered if we could *do* anything about him (besides pray). Could he be reported to someone – the local League of Decency, or maybe the pastor of our church? It didn't seem practical, so we moved on, trying to recover our calm and sense of purpose, and our surroundings gradually reclaimed us. In time, we forgot all about it, since Mr. Black was always nice to us.

Moving on to the bank, Greg and I stood in line with our father, awaiting his turn at the window. There was nothing to do but look around, so I stared at the black pens chained to their holders on the counters, and read their dread warning nervously:

> **Federal sentencing of**
>
> **10 to 15 years**
>
> **for stealing Government Property!**

If I had needed any proof that those signs meant business, I suddenly saw our police chief, John Fritz, standing in the next line, wearing his gun, pretending to have bank business. But I knew he was really there about the pens. My imagination began to work overtime. What if a pen accidentally came unchained, and ended up in your pocket? You would be torn from your family, and thrown in jail for the rest of your life! The thought was so horrible that I had to quickly find something cheerful to think about, like impending lunch.

Most times, we went to Loveland by ourselves, since the center of town was only ¾ mile from our house. It was a pleasant walk out the lane and down Jackson Street, which was lined with suburban houses and people we knew. At the bottom of the hill, we usually stopped at the bridge to check on Bear Creek, and looked in at Taber's field to see if any C-league teams were practicing. We played on two of those teams – I was center-fielder for the "Phillies," and Gregory pitched for the "Pirates."

Whenever we passed, we always took a minute to stare at Buddy Borger's outrageous pink-and-black '56 DeSoto. It had fins in the back, with three cylindrical lights sticking out on each side. What a car!

Next came the sandstone-block Taber mansion on our side, and the Nazarene church opposite, interspersed with residences. Further down on the left was the Presbyterian Church. Passing those churches, we were always silently thankful we had not been born members, especially when we heard the wild, mournful sound of the Nazarenes singing.

A short block later came the first traffic light, where the town proper really began. Most of Old Loveland was loosely contained by two parallel streets, Jackson and Broadway. Broadway later looped around under the railroad trestle by the river and returned to cross Jackson at the second traffic light, by the bridge. Nearly all the stores were located between the traffic lights. Two separate sets of railroad tracks, the B&O and Pennsylvania lines, crossed in the middle of town, behind Rolke's Feed & Coal yard.

Entering downtown, the intersection at the first light was dominated by the Town Hall on the left – a great, brooding building of German Gothic design with a tower, wrought-iron balconies, and a "gingerbread" slate roof. It housed the police station, town offices, jail, fire station, and an opera house on the second floor, by then condemned.

On our right was our doctor's office. Old Doc Lever seemed about ninety years old, and his bedside manner with kids was rough. It felt more like he was administering discipline than trying to cure you. He poked and pinched (never mind that we were sick), giving a short bark of laughter after he'd done his worst, saying, "Quite the little man, aren't we?" Then he would sock you on your freshly vaccinated shoulder, and hand you a lollipop. Maybe he thought he was doing his small part to prepare us for a tough world.

Spear's Drug Store stood on the opposite left corner, across from the fire bays in the Town Hall. Unlike the doctor's office, Spear's conjured up good memories, with its soda counter, glass cases of candy, and unlimited ice cream.

The far right corner held Red's Mobil station. I always liked the red winged horse on the sign, but more importantly, they helped us repair bike tires. You had to practice a little tact, of course, especially if Red's mechanic, Eugene, was busy. So you would turn your bike upside down on its seat out by the air pump, and start working on it, in full view of the lift where Eugene was fixing a car. Eventually he would get curious, and come out. "That's not the right wrench to do that," he would say. Or, "The air won't hold in that tire – there's probably a leak."

Then you could say, "I've already fixed it once at home with a patch kit." Few mechanics wanted to help you if you hadn't tried to fix it yourself first.

Finally he would tell you to bring it inside. Relief! You followed him happily to the tire-drowning tub, and he would test for leaks. It would shortly be fixed, or at least he could tell you if you needed a new tube or tire.

Today we passed by Red's, crossing the B&O tracks, with the train station on our left. We went by Schoerer's grocery, a converted two-story, white brick house set back from the road, where we almost never bought our treats, even though Jimmy Schoerer was my classmate. They were more expensive, and might tell you they didn't take certain bottles you were peddling. Then you had to go to Loveland Grocery, too, for the rejected ones. That was *our* store, in spite of Ella's brusque manner.

Next came Murray's tavern, always quiet and sleepy in the daytime, and Militzer's Dry Goods. Every time Greg and I passed, it reminded of us of buckle-up galoshes.

Mrs. Nisbet was a widow in her sixties whose family owned a hardware store and lumber mill over on Broadway. Originally from New England, she now lived in a perfect Currier-and-Ives Colonial house on Jackson Street, only a couple of doors from Pfarr Lane. The white house with its black shutters looked like an import from Massachusetts, and to further help her adjust to the Midwest, she had planted an American holly to the left of her front door. It was always beautiful in the snow, with its red berries and prickly greenery. She also planted a birch tree and a cherry that overhung the sidewalk, very conveniently for us. A Colonial lamppost stood by the driveway, nestled in a curve of the hand-laid, serpentine walk. At Christmas, the house showed electric candles in every window, and a wreath with a red bow hung on the door. Everything else about the grounds was perfect, too, including the carriage house out back that housed her 1959 Imperial and her grown son's horse, Rose. It had a cupola on top, with a weathervane.

Greg and I fed and watered Rose (who was fond of nipping), put Mrs. Nisbet's trash out every Thursday, and shoveled her walkway in the winter. She paid us well, and one summer she let us pick the gooseberries that grew out back by the white picket fence. She always bought wild berries from us in the summer.

One snowy morning, when we were shoveling her walk, she noticed that Greg and I had holes in our tennis shoes, letting in the wet snow. That year, our parents couldn't afford new shoes right then, and these were our summer sneakers, which had seen better days. We didn't mind much – lots of socks mostly compensated, and we worked hard enough to keep warm. Still, after a couple of hours, our toes got numb, even though we ran between jobs. Often, we had to plunge our feet (and hands) in cold water when we got home, to warm up slowly and prevent damage.

Mrs. Nisbet said, "Those shoes aren't fit for winter!"

Greg and I looked at our feet, embarrassed, feeling colder and sorrier than we had a minute ago.

When we got home, Mama told us that Mrs. Nisbet had called, and was going to buy us buckle-up galoshes. She had called Greer Militzer, and all we had to do was go down to his store and pick them out.

*   *   *

Next to Militzer's was Loveland Grocery. We always wanted to stop and get some treat there or at the bakery around the corner, but usually waited till after our purchases, to see if there was any money left.

After crossing the second set of tracks, we arrived at Sparks Hardware, in the middle of a row of solid, three-story, Western-fronted stores, including a home-style restaurant and some small offices. On the upper floors were more offices and apartments.

Outside Sparks', there were old men sitting on benches. Until recently, they had sat or played horseshoes in the park across the street, but progress, in the form of a newly built Brown's supermarket complex, had edged them out. Their new location wasn't as aesthetic, but had one strong advantage – they could interview people entering and leaving the store, finding out not only what they bought but what they were up to.

When you first stepped into the hardware store and closed the door behind you, you noticed it was fairly well lit, due to the large display-windows. But as you moved back toward the middle, where the cash register and display cases were, it grew dimmer. There were single fluorescent lamps here and there to minimally light the area. The floor was clean, but made of plain boards that creaked when you walked. Mr. Sparks was friendly, padding about softly and keeping tabs on every potential customer, with a cheerful "What can I do for you boys today?"

The hardware store was one of the main centers of activity. Everyone had to go there, and the storeowner got all types. There was a sign near the counter that said, "If you're so smart, why ain't you rich?" I think it was put there as a slap in the face to all the cranks that argued with the proprietor about politics and religion. But I was puzzled. Wasn't it a virtue to be poor? The saints were poor. Besides, it was being good that mattered, not money or brainpower, wasn't it? Did this mean that the storeowner was a heathen? But he always treated *us* kindly...

When we went in for our go-cart parts, Mr. Sparks took us back to the wheel section, saying, "Take your time, but tell me if you need any help." He went off to help another customer.

Gregory and I looked at the wagon wheel we intended to buy, and picked it up, reveling in the crisp newness of it. Then we opened a lower cabinet, where the wheelbarrow wheels were kept.

"Wow! Look at those fat tires!" my brother exclaimed.

"And with ball-bearings, too!" I added longingly.

"We could win all the races, forever, with those wheels."

"Yeah," I agreed.

Was there any way we could afford them? Then we saw the price, $12.00 each. *Impossible!* Oh, well, we knew we were lucky to get the cheaper one, so we took it to the counter. Then we asked Mr. Sparks if he had any 2-foot axles, and he went to look at his vertical rack. When he came back, he said he was all sold-out, but to try Western Auto. "Do you need anything else, boys?"

That reminded us about the washers, cotter pins, and master bolt for the steering. After five more minutes of selecting these, we made our purchases and headed for Western Auto. Just a door or two further along Jackson, we came up to the town's second traffic light, where Broadway crossed.

Catty-corner was the bank, with Western Auto beyond it, next to the bridge. Across Broadway on our side was the vacant lot above the river where the carnival was held. It, too, had once held stores, destroyed by floods a few years ago.

Opposite the bank on our left was Rexall Drugs, part of the Brown complex. Whenever we passed it, we couldn't help thinking about the time Jimmy and Eve Ackerman almost died from carbon-monoxide poisoning. Their grandmother had parked her '51 Plymouth out front, leaving them inside, with the engine running. That was on a cold, rainy day the previous spring, and we were actually there at the time. It was frightening – the ambulance came, and took the unconscious Jimmy and Eve into Rexall's, where they began to administer oxygen. Jimmy looked so helpless. We had never seen him like that, and wondered if he might die. A small crowd gathered, talking in whispers.

"I hope we aren't too late," the ambulance driver said.

"Wait – he's coming around!"

"Yeah, but will he be brain-damaged?"

"Look, she's coming 'round, too."

Eve and Jimmy were groggy, but awake. The paramedics began to question them thoroughly, to see if they were "all there." Both of them answered all the questions satisfactorily, but there was only one thing the medics couldn't make out – when Jimmy first woke up, he kept muttering, "Rudolf... Rudolf!" They just thought he was babbling, or missing his stuffed reindeer.

* * *

Before going into Western Auto, we always looked down the cellar grate in the sidewalk to see if anybody had dropped money. Today, they had! A dime was shining in the litter below. We stretched out on the sidewalk, trying to figure a way to get that coin.

Greg said, "Let's get some bubble gum and a stick. It'll stick to the gum, and we can draw it up. I'll go to Rexall's – you go find a stick by the river."

We took off on our missions. I went down to the edge of the water to pull a branch off a tree, but instead found an old broom handle that had washed up as jetsam. Perfect! I ran back to meet Gregory, who was just coming around the corner of the bank, chewing bubble gum and looking at the new baseball card. When he got near, he said, "Hey, look – Mickey Mantle!"

I inspected the card eagerly, and we talked about our favorite cards and team – the Cincinnati Reds. (Never mind that they hadn't won the pennant since 1948, the year I was born.)

Soon we were lying on our stomachs again, jabbing at the dime with bubble gum and broomstick. We'd done it before, but today our luck wasn't in. The dime turned over and fell deeper into the trash and litter. Then we felt a shadow pass over us, and glanced up to see Mr. Black, looking curious and smiling. "What are you boys doing with that stick? Did you drop something?"

"Oh – we were trying to pull up a dime that fell down there, but it only went in deeper."

He admired our apparatus for a moment, then said, "I think I can help you out."

A minute later, we saw his arm down below, reaching through a cellar window. Then he came back up, and handed us the dime.

"Wow! Thanks, Mr. Black!" We echoed each other.

"Need anything in the store?" he asked.

"Yeah, we need an axle for our go-cart," Greg said.

"Threaded or unthreaded?"

"Smooth," I said.

"That's the same as unthreaded," he smiled. "How long?"

"Two foot," I said.

"You're in luck – I've got several of those in the back."

He led us inside, and a few minutes later we were headed home with our parts.

We felt like celebrating, so we stopped at Loveland Grocery to get RC Colas, a big Hershey bar, potato chips, and a bunch of bananas. Ella was her usual self, behind the counter, but grimly pleased that we were actually spending money, and not just trading.

"What! No bottles today?"

"No, ma'am, we earned this working for Mrs. Nisbet," I said.

"You won't want any lunch with all that junk - did you know that candy rots your teeth? If you were *my* boys-"

"Yes, ma'am - I mean, *no*, ma'am," Greg said obediently. We would agree to anything at that moment - just let us at the goodies!

We left the store, happily munching and drinking. As we walked back home, Jerry and Frankie Martin came racing through town in their cars, revving their engines and playing tag. Jerry was in front, hunched over his knobbed wheel, and squealing his tires every so often. With curly hair spilling over his forehead *à la punk*, he looked remarkably like pictures we'd seen of Early Man in our history books. His younger brother Frankie followed him, grinning and bumping Jerry's car a couple of times, just for fun. Both cars were vibrating to "♫ *Duke... Duke... Duke... Duke of Earl...♫*." We had no idea what that meant, but it sure was egging the drivers on.

Jerry and Frankie were in high school. I think they actually got their cars early because their father had been killed in a car accident, and they had to help support their family.

* * *

It didn't take long to add the new parts to the mostly assembled cart. Nine o'clock on the following Monday morning saw all three carts gathered in Bond's driveway, at the top of Jackson Street. That drive was an excellent place to reconnoiter off the road before starting. We decided to race only two carts at a time, even though Jackson wasn't very busy - three would be asking for trouble.

Our cart was new, so we raced Billy first. There would be two heats, Greg driving in one and I in the other. Winning one might be just luck - besides, it would give each cart a chance to start in the curb position. The winner would race Jimmy's cart, with an extra heat if no one won both. It might only take four races to decide the champion, or many more, depending on what happened.

We were getting restless. Jimmy called, "C'mon, gentlemen, the road's clear! Time to race!"

Billy and my brother rolled their carts into position, side by side, and rested their feet on the ground, waiting for Jimmy's signal.

"Go!" Jimmy shouted, waving his arm like a flag, and both carts rolled away, gathering speed.

Thirty feet downslope, Jimmy called out, "Hey – Greg's got the lead by a nose! No, wait– Billy's pulling up almost even! But there goes Greg, out front again! Billy's dropping behind... Wow! Look at him go, Paul!"

Greg had reached his maximum speed at the bottom of the hill, and won by two lengths. Both contestants let their carts roll to where our lane joined the street, and came to a natural stop. Greg pulled our cart back up the hill to the starting point, but Billy had to push his, because his new steering apparatus had eliminated the driving rope. He complained, "My brake was rubbing the wheel – that's why I lost."

"Sure, cork-brain," Jimmy mocked.

"We-e-l-ll, it wu-uz!" Billy protested.

"Well, un-stick it, then, peabrain!" Jimmy retorted. "Anyway, you're going to get another chance against Paul, in the good slot."

"I'll win this time," Billy bragged.

"Don't talk, just do it!" Jimmy shot back. "C'mon – line up your carts!"

I was on the outside, and Billy on the curb, by the stone ditch.

"Go!" Jimmy yelled, and we were off, running neck-and-neck and hogging the whole road. It was at that moment that a car appeared around the curve below, heading up the hill.

"Pull back, Paul!" Jimmy warned. I used my one-wheel brake, and slowed enough to whip in behind Billy, hard on his tail. It took the car eight seconds to get by. As soon as it passed, I came out around Billy, gaining an inch at a time.

We could hear Jimmy calling the race – "Man, he's pulling ahead! Now he's got the lead by a nose! I don't believe it! – Paul's *got* it, by half a length!" Then he got carried away, and started imitating Don Knotts in a nasal voice: "Wow! What a cart! What a race! What a driver!" He held his fist to his mouth, as though he were speaking into a microphone.

The next race, against Jimmy, would be harder. He was a shrewd driver, had a good cart, and possessed what people call *luck*. We won and lost to him that afternoon, but had a lot of fun doing it. We weren't smart enough to know all the permutations involving three go-carts, but just played them off as they came. It got a little confusing, since Billy won some, too, and of course got pretty intolerable then – I think he felt that his advanced steering design should have won them all.

So the races went, that summer. Billy did have one day when he won against all our carts, and we were mystified until we noticed our wheels making a dry sound as they turned. Then we got suspicious, and found he had slipped the cotter pins off our wheels, wiped off all the axle grease, and then put them back with extra washers, to slow the wheels when they turned. Older brother Jerry gave him the idea, and Billy couldn't resist counting coup. The silly thing was, he was just as pleased as though he'd won fairly. That was Billy Martin – if he won, he *won*.

* * *

Clouds floated like whipped cream across the great blue bowl overhead as Anne and Eve played croquet on the front lawn, laughing. Jimmy wasn't visible, but Pan was, and rushed at us as though we were turkeys. Jean came out the kitchen door to rescue us. "Pan! Pan! Get back here! What an idiot! He knows you by now..." She dragged the growling and swearing miscreant back to the house.

"Where's Jimmy?" I asked her.

"Oh, you mean 'Superboy,'" she jibed irreverently. "That's what I call him. If you listen, you'll find him – he's been making a racket all morning. It's about to drive Mom crazy, but at least he's out of the house, she says."

She was right – we could hear pounding coming from behind the barn. Yelling our thanks, we ran down the lawn to investigate.

In the deep shade behind the barn, Jimmy and Billy were up a huge oak tree, working on a treehouse. Steps snaked up the tree, and the carpenters were perched in a large forked crotch, 20 feet off the ground, trying to nail a main floor support to one of the "Y" trunks.

"Well, what do you know? It's Greg and Paul!" Jimmy sang out. "Want to come up and see?"

"Sure do!" My brother and I scrambled up the newly nailed steps, leaving Rusty, Rags, and Cindy gaping up at us, and arrived just in time to see the nail they were driving bend like putty.

"Criminy! *Another* bent nail!" Jimmy exclaimed. "It took all morning to get *this* far!" A small pile of twisted 20-penny nails at their feet bore witness to the hardness of green oak.

"This oak's gonna kill us," Billy complained.

"My *dad* will kill me, if he sees all those wasted nails!"

"Ow!" Billy yelled, hitting his thumb as he tried again to put a nail through the 2" x 8" joist.

"Give it up, Fly-Face! We'll have to find another way." Clearly, Superboy was inspired by Dick Tracy at the moment.

Billy objected. "Don't you call *me* that, rat-face – you're not Dick Tracy, you know!"

"Maybe not, but I know a *dipstick* when I see it!" Jimmy scampered down the ladder, chuckling, and Billy swore, throwing some bent nails after him.

"Missed me!" Jimmy taunted. "I'll be right back," he told us. "I'm going to get some concrete nails. Those are the only things we'll be able to drive in that oak."

Billy seized the opportunity to fill us in on Jerry's recent improvements to his '52 Pontiac – new knobs on the steering wheel, and mud-covers for the rear wheels. The front end had been raised even higher. Now Jerry was leading the *cool...*

Jimmy returned shortly with the nails and a hand-drill. "If we bore some holes in the oak first, the 20-pennys won't bend on us. We'll use the smaller concrete nails where the wood isn't too thick to get them through," he said.

"That's a good idea," Greg said, "but you're probably going to need "Y" braces, too, to help steady the two floor-joists."

"You may be right..." Jimmy paused to think. "We'll see how firm they are when the floor is on."

After half an hour, the horizontal floor supports were finally attached. We quickly nailed on the flooring, drawing the materials up in a basket attached to a rope and pulley.

"Whew! I'm tired of this," Jimmy said, throwing down his hammer. "It's been almost three hours, and I'm hungry!"

"I'll say!" Billy echoed.

Gregory and I started down the ladder, but Jimmy nipped past us, swinging down on the hauling-rope, and Billy came down last. "See you later!" he called, and made off home.

"C'mon, you two," Jimmy whispered to us conspiratorially. "I want you to see something." We followed him to the garage, where he picked up a battered car muffler. "Gran just had the muffler replaced on her car. This is the old one. What do you make of that?" he demanded.

We looked closer, and saw two round holes in it.

"Those look like they were made by a drill," Greg said.

"Precisely, Watson!" Jimmy said crisply, starting to pace with his hands behind his back like Sherlock Holmes.

My stomach started to ache at the awful implications.

"That's how Eve and I got sick," he said. "*Rudolf* drilled those holes – and he almost got me that time! He didn't even care that Eve would have died, and maybe Gran, too!" His face was tragic, and there was a catch in his throat. "If you want, I can show you the other holes he made under the back seat, too."

But no further proof was necessary. "What are you going to do?" I whispered, horrified.

"We're going to have to move away. I always knew it might come to this... It's not safe for me or my family to stay here anymore. They'll *have* to believe me now – I told them before, but they thought I was making it up..." His voice trailed off.

"I'm glad Rudolf's not after *us*," Greg said, overwhelmed.

"Well, I've worked hard to keep his attention on me - although he's seen you from a distance. But he doesn't know your names or where you live... yet."

I suddenly thought of something incredible. "We might actually have *seen* Rudolf that day at Rexall's!"

Gregory stared at me for a moment, and then he got it. "That's right!" he exclaimed.

"*What?* You did? Why didn't you tell me before?"

"We didn't know it was him. And then we sort of forgot about it, till you showed us the muffler just now," Greg said.

"Tell me *exactly* what happened!" Jimmy shot back.

"When you were coming to, you mumbled Rudolf's name twice," I said. "And right then, something moved at the window, but when we looked, it was gone. We ran outside, but all we saw was a man in a black raincoat with his back to us and his hands in his pockets, walking real fast toward the river. But he looked back over his shoulder, and I saw black, curly hair over his forehead, like Jerry Martin. And he was *laughing!*"

"It's a good thing you didn't try to go after him," Jimmy sighed. "Rudolf's too dangerous! Anyway, he probably had his escape planned, with a motorboat at the waterside."

We all went home to lunch. Greg and I had a lot to think about.

A week later, Jimmy confirmed that his family would be moving as soon as they could make arrangements. His father, he said, would be staying in the house for a while, to keep up the pretense that they were still there, until their trail was too cold for the archenemy to follow.

"But what if Rudolf decides to kill your dad, to get back at you?" Greg asked worriedly.

"Did you ever see my dad's gun collection?" Jimmy asked.

We had. It was extensive, with everything from antiques to modern weapons. He had a knife collection, too.

"If Rudolf shows up, he'll find a Colt 45 up his nose!" Jimmy said. "That's another reason Dad's staying, I think – he's hoping to catch the bastard red-handed!"

We were terribly impressed at the grandeur of the situation, and honored to be trusted with such an important secret, involving a heartless criminal. But the idea of Jimmy leaving made us feel lost. It was hard to imagine a summer without him.

But there was still the rest of *this* summer. And besides, something unexpected might happen, and then he wouldn't have to go.

And there was more magic, that summer. One time, he surprised us with something we'd never expected.

Inside Ackermans' barn that day, it was dim at first, but sunlight found its way through the many cracks, making slanted patterns on the floor, posts, and walls. Jimmy headed over to one side and lifted something flat from a stack leaning there. As our eyes adjusted, we saw a glittering stained-glass window. The stack was full of them.

"Did they come from a church?" I asked, awed.

"No, my dad says they were left from when our house was built."

We looked through them. Some had biblical scenes, but others were just flowers, or patterns of diamonds or gothic crow's-feet, interspersed with small, round jewels in green, blue, and red leaded-glass panes. A few were broken, but still beautiful.

"Boy, are those neat!" Greg said.

I accidentally kicked up some dust on the floor, and there, sparkling in the dirt, was one of the brilliant ruby jewels.

"Wow!" I exclaimed, and started to sift through the fine dirt, looking for more.

"They're just cut-glass," Jimmy said. "They fell out of the windows. You can have that..."

Greg joined me in the jewel hunt – we didn't believe Jimmy's explanation for a minute. We were rich – *rich!* – stuffing our pockets with the cut rubies, emeralds, topazes, and mediæval-blue sapphires.

Then I got worried, and asked Jimmy, "Can we *really* have these?"

"Sure, Paul, I don't see why not. They've been in here forever."

We had a wonderful feeling about these stones – they *might* turn out to be the real thing! It was a happy half-hour, gathering stones and looking around the barn.

Then we climbed the stairs to the loft. It was rickety there, and you could easily put your foot through a floorboard and fall. To make it more interesting, Jimmy told us about the time Billy *had* fallen through, and had to be rescued (by "Superboy," of course). So we mostly crawled-around on our hands and knees, staying away from the weak places. For years afterward, I had dreams of walking on that floor, and sometimes falling through it.

But there was more. Jimmy took us out through a small side door, and just outside, on the ground along the wall, there were heaps of fired clay tiles, with pictures on them – the kind they had in their kitchen. Jimmy said that they, too, were left over from building the house. Some were plain beiges and whites, but others had geometric patterns on them in an Arabic style. Still others depicted biblical scenes. We rummaged, fascinated – you never knew what treasure might lie just beyond the next turn of tile. Jimmy let us choose some to keep, and I found the best one of all: a green landscape with the yellow sun rising, and Jesus standing in the foreground in a long white robe, holding a lamb in his arms. The artist had somehow captured the softness of spring, with a hint of peach in the morning sky. I thought it was the ultimate Easter morning, and asked Jimmy if I could have it.

"Sure," he said, then added wistfully, "I didn't know *that* was in there... But let's go out to the woods, now. You can leave your tiles here. No one will steal them."

I saw Billy Martin eyeing the Easter tile hungrily. He envied us our religion, and wanted to belong the way we did. He was at an age when a religious item was a talisman to possess - maybe he thought some benefits would rub off on him. I didn't want to leave my stack there, but they were too heavy to take with us, playing, so I set them down reluctantly, and went along.

On our way home, Gregory and I stopped at the barn to pick up our tiles. The special one was gone, as I had half-known it would be. Even though I remembered it vividly, I still couldn't help wondering if it had ever been real.

But when we arrived home for lunch, we found our pockets full of jewels. *That* part wasn't a dream, anyway.

The weather turned hot and the blackberries were ripe. Jimmy came down to our house one sweltering day, and invited us to go swimming in the pool by the falls. Ten minutes later, we were walking out the lane with him, up the woods path that came out by his garage and the stone bench. We took the usual route to the creek, across the field and through the young wood where Jimmy's board camp was hidden. It would have been nice to stop, but we were hot and couldn't wait to get in the water.

At the pool, Jimmy opened the festivities by diving from the six-foot ledge at the head of the falls. A stream of bubbles followed him underwater. When he came up, he called, "C'mon in! It's great!" This established the tone: there would be no fooling around, or adjusting ourselves gradually. We had to follow him off that ledge.

Boy, was that water *cold!* We almost howled. But we stayed for a couple of hours, and were just thinking of leaving when the land grew shadowed, and we heard thunder.

"Get out of the water fast!" Jimmy warned. "If lightening strikes it, we'll be fried like bacon! There was this boy I knew-" A loud clap of thunder preempted this cheering recollection, and large drops began to spatter rapidly. "Uh-oh! Run for it! To my camp!"

We jammed on our shoes, and ran up the woods path. The rain didn't quite penetrate the thick canopy overhead, but we'd barely made it to the camp when it started to *pour*. The wind was wild, and thunder and lightning held full sway.

Inside, Jimmy lit a candle, and we felt safe and secure from the elements. The hut was about six feet square, made of boards, with a window, full-size door, and tin roof. There were wooden shutters that you could pull over the window, in case of Indian attack. Jimmy showed us around, and we sat on various items of furniture – an old metal lawn chair that bounced like a rocking horse, a plain, wooden chair, and a bench in front of a small table.

"Did you ever sleep out here?" Greg wondered.

"Sure, lots of times. Once, Timmy and I went fishing in the creek, cooked our supper outside, and stayed all night. But we were lucky we lived."

"Why – w-what happened?" I spluttered.

"I don't know exactly, but at 1:00 in the morning, something snuffled at the door and growled. Whatever it was had claws, and it was big like a bear. I wasn't too worried, because I was wearing the scapular Gran gave me, that was blessed by the Pope. But in the morning, there were claw marks on the door, and an awful smell. I showed Cindy the marks, and she took one sniff, yelped, and ran all the way home."

Greg and I were relieved that monsters like the "whatever it was" weren't after *us*. Jimmy was so brave, especially since he seemed to attract all those strange, malevolent things like ghosts, one-armed men, and, occasionally, even aliens. While this was terribly exciting, we knew that *we* couldn't cope with it as a steady diet (unless maybe Jimmy was there, too). Rudolf alone would have been too much for us – two more martyrs would have been added to life's tragic book.

It drummed on the metal roof for almost an hour, while we hunched around the table by flickering candlelight, and Jimmy told more harrowing tales. When the rain ended, we all trooped outside. The roof had actually kept us dry! It was late afternoon, and the after-storm light was eerie but beautiful.

When we arrived home, we discovered that a large tree had fallen by the spring. It stayed hung up in the other trees there for many years.

The summer ended with Jimmy leaving, just as he had foretold. He would be starting the eighth grade in some strange city, and hopefully, Rudolf wouldn't find him. We didn't miss him right away. With a large family, there was always something to do and someone to play with, and, just then, we were distracted by the new school year. It wouldn't be until the next summer that his leaving really sank in.

Jimmy's father stayed on in their mansion late into '59, drinking a lot and shooting off his guns into the fireplace. Only my brother Timmy dared to visit him, drawn by the gun and knife collection. We gathered, from what he said, that Jimmy's father was thinking of killing himself. By then, all of us knew the real reason Jimmy's family had moved away – the parents were getting a divorce. We had overheard our mother talking to Mrs. Ackerman on the phone.

Jimmy's father was a kindly man, whatever his faults, and Jimmy thought the sun rose and set in him. He used to look forward so to his father's coming home from his traveling job, telling us what they planned to do together. The divorce must have been devastating to him, and he couldn't bear to tell anyone the truth. Rudolf's predations provided an ideal pretext for the changes Jimmy could not prevent.

In January of 1959, there was an unusually prolonged cold-spell. The creek froze a-foot-and-a-half deep. Then came heavy rain, and all the ice broke up into floating slabs, grinding and crashing against each other, driven by 6-foot-high waves. It was amazing that our placid creek could change into a roaring river overnight. The excess water couldn't soak into the still-frozen ground, and eventually backed up all the way to Grand Banks, which made the summer of '59 a good fishing year, since larger fish swam up the creek to escape the high water in the river. We made a high-water mark on a tree by the cliff path, and when the creek returned to its banks, the mark was 15 feet above normal level. Old Loveland was completely flooded, almost all the way up to the town hall.

When the water finally subsided, huge slabs of ice lay everywhere till mid-April. Martins' bottom looked like a moonscape, with ice stacked at crazy angles, and you could hardly walk.

After the ice finally melted, there was a clean, scoured look to things, with lots of large clamshells everywhere. One damp morning, after the flood water receded, I went down to Theodore's bottom, and was horrified to see a *quarter-acre* of huge, squirming crawdads piled a foot deep: black ones, orange ones, yellowish ones, plain taupe-colored – all sizes and shapes, all angry and snapping. I was revolted, at first, but soon realized it was *food*, and gingerly collected a bunch for dinner.

In the flood's aftermath, Timmy saw another opportunity to acquire illicit goods. Walking along the river, he saw a chained rowboat. He hacksawed the chain and then sought Uncle Marshall's aid to bring home the lost boat he'd salvaged after the flood. Marshall believed him, and brought it home on his trailer, but, in some mysterious manner, the police found out and restored it to its owner. Timmy was lucky to be caught, and even luckier to avoid punishment. He has managed to avoid jail time ever since by staying on the straight-and-narrow.

* * *

Passing by our old treehouse later that summer, we were struck by its shabbiness. "You know, that looks like a doghouse in a tree," I said. "It's not very big, either."

"It does look kind of dumpy," Greg added. "And we can't stand up in it."

"It did *come* from a dump," I said lamely.

"We ought to build a better one, with more windows," Gregory declared. "We could even slant the walls out at the top, along the tree fork, to make more room!"

"And put a real door on the outside!" I added enthusiastically.

Greg started drawing plans, and even consulted our father briefly to sound out the new design. The necessary materials showed up, too, but not in any of the ways we might have imagined.

Ackermans' barn fell down during a heavy thunderstorm in July. We were sorry to see it go, with its good memories of playing there with Jimmy.

It shook us up a little. We hadn't thought it was *that* run-down – maybe it just gave up, when Jimmy left. But the new potential didn't take long to sink in. Real wood! The old barn had been of post-and-beam construction, over a hundred years old, with hemlock board siding, the kind you only find now in very old buildings. This hemlock was the heartwood of the tree, as hard as flint, very different from the sapwood in the lumberyards today. The boards were three feet wide and 20 feet long, so heavy that we had to cut them before we could even drag them. We were a little afraid Mr. Ackerman would shoot at us, and tried not to attract his attention.

Our new treehouse was rather daring - modern and streamlined, with all of the features we'd planned. It also had vertical plastic corner-windows - an afterthought, when we found that there were V-shaped gaps at the corners where the walls tilted out and didn't quite meet.

Leon Jones, one of our parents' musical friends, was visiting with his sons, and cheerfully suggested that we install a "phone," Boy-Scout style, using two open tin cans connected by a wire. It sounded really neat, at first, but then we realized that a link with the house wasn't such a good idea - it would only give Mama a chance to catch us for more chores! ("Get back here and dry the dishes!")

When Billy toured our treehouse, he was consumed with envy, and prevailed on his older brothers to help him build one, when they tore down their own leaning barn. Theirs was built more quickly than ours - about the same size and sturdy, but lacking flair. It had only two small, shuttered windows, but there was an attic - an undeniable advantage. The treehouse was well situated, 10 feet off the ground, in a hackberry crotch, with their garden on one side and a view of the creek bottom on the other.

Billy wanted to show it off, and invited us down to sleep out in it one night. We weren't too surprised to find he had prepared an initiation for us - it might have had something to do with the one we had ready for him last year. Ours was simple - a dripping of hot wax on the hands and fingers till they were coated. But Billy had gone one step further - he had a gallon can of hot wax, melted over Sterno.

We pretended that dipping our hands in hot wax was an everyday occurrence. Billy had been practicing, so he dipped his hands first, making an agonized face in hopes that we would chicken-out and declare ourselves *bona fide* sissies, for once. But we knew the secret of cooling our hands quickly, so they were only red after the wax was peeled off.

Billy's house had a design flaw - the trapdoors lined up exactly, one directly above the other. Climbing up the attic, I slipped and fell to the first floor, then found myself falling through the other trapdoor, which we had left open for air. My arms barely saved me from plunging to the ground.

We celebrated that night with marshmallows roasted over Sterno, washed down with pop and potato chips, then read comics for a while, and finally went to bed. A storm blew up during the night, with wind, thunder and lightning, and rain pelted for hours on the tin roof inches above our heads.

* * *

A year and a half passed before we saw Jimmy again. He took the bus out to Loveland one day and just showed up. Nobody minded – he was always welcome, and bedded down with a blanket and pillow on the braid rug between the bunks in our room. The next morning, we awoke to the heavenly smell of homemade doughnuts, Jimmy's favorite.

Over breakfast, we told him we had built a new treehouse down below, with wood from his old barn, after it fell down.

"Fell down!" he exclaimed. Then quickly added, "It didn't *fall* down – Rudolf sabotaged it! My dad looked at the wreckage, and found that the main support beam had been sawed almost through, so the first wind would bring it down. Dad shot him, though – he found some blood where Rudolf had been working. But I don't think he's dead..."

We didn't challenge his story. Rudolf was part of our lives, by now, the same as Captain Hook and Peter Pan. Better to let sleeping villains lie.

But then, years later, when I was in high school, I was up at the Hortons' house one day, and noticed there was an apartment with "The Rudolfs" in faded lettering on its mailbox. I stopped breathing. Hortons' large, Elizabethan house was right next door to Ackermans'.

I talked to Mrs. Horton in the yard. She told me they'd had tenants of that name about 6 years previous. Feeling a little dizzy, I asked her whether there had been any kids. She said, yes, there was a boy about 18, but he had gone away. "I was glad to see him go," she said. "I never trusted him, though he was good to his mother." A couple of years ago, she'd heard he was in the Navy. Stunned, I remembered that Jimmy had enlisted in the Navy three years ago.

Was this the infamous Rudolf? Could he actually have been *real*? If so, where was he *now*? Following Jimmy's naval career? I shivered.

But walking home, I rethought Jimmy's family situation and his penchant for storytelling, and started to relax. No, I thought. *It couldn't be!*

Chapter VIII.
Watching TV

It all began when Jimmy left. Our feelings whispered that maybe *none* of it would have happened if he'd stayed put. But the goats were in the garden now, and everything started rolling away.

In January of 1959, St. Columban's moved to its new home, out in the country on a piece of property bought from Grailville. Construction had gone on for some time, but students were deterred from sightseeing by hideous threats, so no one saw it until the move. Only the school had yet been built – Sunday services would be held in the auditorium for a while. The classrooms were airy and modern, and I could see cows grazing from the window.

Right after that, the big flood came. The old part of town was never the same, and businessmen started looking for *lebensraum* across the river. Old Loveland would never grow any larger.

That fall, when Gregory and I started the 6th and 7th grades, we were surprised by two new lay teachers, *men*, from Notre Dame. Up to then, we had seen only women in the classroom, most of them nuns. With a new school *and* new teachers, the change in atmosphere was dramatic. Mr. Morrison and Mr. McCallion weren't concerned with endless rules and trivia, just education and enlightenment. They even played baseball with us at lunchtime! The sense of repression was gone, even though the nuns were still there.

At home, we got a new (used) Ford station wagon only two years old – two-toned pink and beige, with fiberglass "wood" paneling! And the following spring, we moved to the old home place at the top of the lane, where my grandparents had lived and my father had grown up. It was just across the field from our old house, but seemed completely new to us, since the Hutzels and others had lived there more recently, and left their improvements. Late in the afternoon on Memorial Day, I brought the last wheelbarrow-load up the hill from our old house, including a cast-iron pot full of hot chili for our supper.

John F. Kennedy was elected president in the fall. There was a social stirring – protesters were gathering, prodded by the Vietnam War and racial integration. There were even glimmerings of change in the Roman Catholic Church, culminating in 1963 with the Second Vatican Council.

Our country was in a race with Russia to conquer space. "Junior Scholastic" magazine said we would be traveling in hovercraft by 1963! Anything seemed possible (if the world wasn't destroyed first by the atom bomb), and there was hope that technology would solve all of people's material problems. We were even told we could look forward to a 4-day work-week when we were grown up.

Television was becoming the universal medium, but at our house, there was still no TV. Publicly and privately, we were against it. It was commercial, venal, and generally contemptible – suitable only for entertaining the masses, who watched soap operas and lived in Loveland Heights, a subdivision hastily built in the late '50s. Its houses were too close together, with no trees, and the soil was bright yellow. Grass couldn't find common cause with it, and "just said No," even when coaxed with lots of chemicals and chlorinated water. Tales had filtered down even to us – tales of termites under the floor, and walls that you could put your foot through. (Though, as reincarnated Druids of the Sacred Groves, we found the rape of nature more shocking than the substandard housing.)

Because of these shortcomings (especially the soap operas), we weren't sure that beings who lived there rated as high on the human scale as we did. At any rate, whenever the TV subject came up, our spring-loaded reply was: "WE DO NOT WATCH TV!"

My brothers and I considered ourselves moral arbiters in these matters. The only problem was that, despite our intentions, we *craved* TV. Desire had rudely pushed principle aside for the duration of many a flawed program. Afterward, we felt a bit used, so we instinctively fortified injured standards by rigorously critiquing what we had seen and endured, using stringent moral and mental yardsticks. When done expertly, this soothed the two conflicting internal giants, carrying us all the way until our next fall from grace.

When we first watched TV at a neighbor's house or with relatives on Sunday, it completely devoured us. We were mesmerized, and afterwards, it was like coming-to after hypnosis. I remember being fascinated by Mickey Mouse and his famous Club, but at the same time embarrassed at the way they behaved – sentimental, goody-goody and... icky! It was the same with Liberace, Howdy Doody, and Lawrence Welk.

The opportunity to have a TV in our house didn't present itself until I was in the seventh grade. Timmy brought home an old RCA that didn't work, gotten from Mr. Rickenbacher, the local TV repairman. We didn't notice it much at first. Timmy was always bringing home orphaned items to fix, sometimes successfully and sometimes not, depending how much time, energy or money they took to repair. That broken TV sitting there was only a dumb device, no threat to any religious vows we'd sworn. Besides, fixing it wasn't the same as watching. (It turned out later that Timmy agreed with that – *his* right to fix did not imply *our* right to watch.)

But one day, when Timmy was fooling around with it, there was a tiny pneumatic sound, exactly like the one a TV makes when it's turned on. Pssst! It *was* the TV! When this happened, a light went out in my head, to be replaced by the light of the TV screen. It was a primal experience, going back all the way to the Creation, when God said, "Let there be Light." At the stupefied expression on our faces, Timmy actually smiled sourly, and said, "*D-o-i-n-g-erl-erl-erl!*"

We had erred. We thought that the device Timmy brought into our world was merely another boring hobby, involving wires, tubes and plastic, and on which he would still be working unproductively when Gabriel blew his trumpet for us all to come home. But not so! After the requisite number of tubes, time, and incantations had been applied, it actually worked!

Now we would have to face TV temptations right in our own bedroom. No longer was it an occasional hazard found at *other* people's homes. Sure, we'd watched it, but felt superior in our minds since *we, the virtuous*, did not have one. Our Code severely reminded us, "Indians do not need TV, any more than they need stimulants!"

The resurrection of this view-box from the dead created some odd behavioral problems in my oldest brother, problems directly affecting our small fraternal bedroom community. The first was quasi-legal, concerning the laws of possession: the TV was *brought home* by Lurch, *fixed* by Lurch; ergo, by beetle logic, it was only to be *watched* by Lurch. The second problem, stepchild of the first, involved the circumstance of four other boys (ages ranging from 9 to 13) having to live in the same room with the sole, selfish proprietor of the aforementioned device, who also happened to be the eldest brother and lord of the castle by divine right. It was a question of Personal Property Rights vs. Community Rights, but in this case, community rights didn't even get a review. The rest of us were going to be the serfs in this little drama. (Ironically, one of the first things watched on the TV was an adaptation of Charles Dickens' <u>A Christmas Carol</u>.)

But Timmy was faced with no small challenge: how could he keep this TV to himself, and not let anyone else watch it? He couldn't throw us out, although he would have liked to, since it was our bedroom, too, and our parents wouldn't stand for it.

The logistical problems were formidable. But he and the devil must have put their heads together to solve the conundrum, and developed some creative solutions that many business entrepreneurs would envy. I always imagined Fork-tongue's silvery advice went something like this:

"*Your lordship, if I might be so bold as to make some small recommendations to you: when watching TV in your bedroom, don't let anyone else in to watch. You may permit them to come in and get something, but not to stay. This way, they will get an evocative glimpse of whatever interesting program you're watching, but must go away hungering madly for more.*

"*Also, I would humbly propose that you put a slide-bolt on the door, to avoid any possible noisy brangling, which we all deplore and might alert any parents who weren't minding their own business.*

"*And, your eminence, when you go out of the house, leave the TV in its place on the dresser. It will be a burning temptation for them to turn it on... They will not see how you can possibly know about violations of your exclusive TV-watching rights, but you will! Remember the last channel you watched, and always feel the TV when you return to see if it's warm, but don't always let them know what you've discovered – keep them guessing.*

If the TV is warm, there are several delicious possibilities:

*"**One***: *The TV is warm, but you're in a good mood, so you give no reprimand. But neither do you indicate that you <u>know</u> your property rights have been violated.*

*"**Two***: *The TV is warm, and you want to make them pay... Show them your extreme displeasure – tell them in plain terms that you know they have been watching <u>your</u> TV. Here, you may justly pass out punishments, either today, or using the payment plan.*

*"**Three***: *Most unfortunately, you can't feasibly throw your brothers out of the room in late evening, since they can claim they need to go to bed. However, if you want to watch a show that is interesting to you, but boring to them (such as "The Dick Powell Show"), leave the volume loud and clear. But if it's a show they really want to see, like "Maverick," turn the volume way down. They won't be able to hear, and will be tantalized by a picture without words. You'll be able to hear, since, as we know, your hearing is exceptional. This will be 'as gall and wormwood' to their parched TV appetites. (How I do love these biblical allusions! 'If they have ears to hear, let them hear!')*

*"**Four:** Might I also suggest, sir, if it's early evening, and they are already present in the room, you may let them watch and hear, since this is only incidental watching, and it's their room, too. (Sigh) But if someone shows up after you turn on the TV, let them stay in the room but do not let them watch, since they are clearly there specifically to watch the TV, which they in no way paid for. Make certain these newcomers put their heads under the sheet for the duration of the program, or require them to stare at the opposite wall. (Of course, they <u>can</u> always go to sleep... Henh-henh-henh!)*

"I have prepared these trifling ideas, your honor, only
to help you conform them to your just bidding..."

All of these methods were put into effect. I remember coming into the room once after he had turned on the TV, and he asked me sullenly, "Whaddaya here for?"

Since I knew it was against his rules for me to watch, I prevaricated, "I'm tired, and I want to go to bed."

While I was climbing into the upper bunk bed, he put his fist to his chin, scowled, and told me, in a deadpan voice, "Put your head under the covers!"

I obeyed, in the light of my pretext. But listening to TV on minimum volume, with no pictures, and trying to piece together what was happening was a real challenge. It usually seemed to go something like this:

Woman speaking:	*"I just don't know what we're going to do!"*
Man replies:	*"Don't worry... (Mutter, mutter)."*
Woman crying.	(Who *was* she?)
Loud noise. Scream.	What happened? Car accident, bomb, or heart attack? No way of knowing...

Half an hour later, my nerves were chafed, but I stuck with it. At least I was in close proximity to the holy relic. And, after all, I wasn't really there for the TV, was I?

When I finally stuck my head out for air, Timmy barked at me, "Get back under there! I didn't say you could come out!" (*Yes, milord! No, milord! I'm sure you're right, milord!*)

There were reprieves and holidays. For instance, when Mother wanted to watch TV, she just came up directly and turned it on, whether his royal nibs was home or not. Her attitude was, "Whyever not?" (She didn't really know what went on in the lower pecking-orders.)

The first time this happened we were taken aback. Such a simple thing

- you want to watch TV, and you just turn it on. *(Hunh?)* We told her Timmy wouldn't like it, but that didn't seem to bother her. Whenever this treat occurred, we enjoyed a relaxed time, and if Timmy happened to come home, it was our turn to revel mutely in his powerless condition. For once, we didn't have to cover our tracks! Oh, how our contented faces must have galled him, and what pygmy revenge would be perpetrated upon us in days to come!

If one of Timmy's friends were there, such as Jimmy Ackerman, the rules also magically evaporated (you wouldn't want your friend to witness such churlishness).

My brothers and I grew adept at posting a lookout at the upstairs window that overlooked the driveway. When Timmy was spotted, we quickly deployed our forces. The TV was turned off and rapidly fanned with a piece of cardboard to cool it. Timmy would arrive after a couple of minutes, leaping up the stairs two at a time. The first thing he did upon entering the room was to scowl, purse his lips, and close the door. Then he would inspect the TV by placing his hand on top in the back, where the perforations were. This was always a silent moment of prayer for him (and for us!), so we didn't interrupt when he was communicating with his Muse. Whatever he learned there never seemed to make him happy.

Sometimes four or five of us would be stuffed into that small bedroom on a sunny afternoon when caught unawares. One pretended to read, another worked on his model airplane, and a third might try to look dumb and innocent, or perhaps idly destroy a magazine by doodling in it. (Unh-hunh - Peter.) What disinterest we affected towards the TV - what nonchalance toward Timmy! Of course, our being there at all was highly suspicious, since he knew we loved to be outdoors at all times. Timmy wasn't fooled, but there might come a moment of sentimentality, uncertainty, or weakness when we could temporarily gain the high ground. *(Not likely.)*

We never complained to our parents, or begged Timmy for clemency. We just pretended to like what he liked, and were always amenable. Neither side gave anything away. But our compliant pose never appeared to soothe him - he seemed to know the difference between the smokescreens and what was really in our hearts. I guess the devil told him.

Eventually, things turned in our favor. Timmy lost his possessive interest in the TV when he acquired his first car, a 1957 Ford (the one with the 'T-Bird' engine). He could escape the family trap, and now it was *"Don't even look at my car!"*

The TV became a community item, of secondary interest. In another year, he joined the Air Force, and that TV was ours to keep! Possession was nine points of the law. (Though if my brother reads this, he may attempt retribution even now.)

But we continued to preach against television. After all, we were highly selective watchers. How could you be an effective critic and moral arbiter without knowing the enemy?

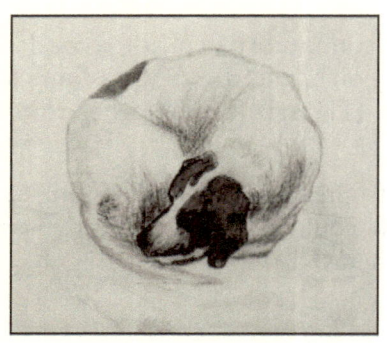

Chapter IX.

Sam's Moral Duty

In the late afternoon we arrived at our favorite campsite, a small clearing near Long Pond cliff. The weather was hot, with a bluish-white sky, and the sun hung in a nest of mare's tails. It would shortly reach the wood west of our camp, and set in an apricot blaze, signaling a warm, dewless night.

My cousin Steve, who was 15, sat on a bench by the old firepit, smoking a cigarette while he undid the fastenings on his gear, strapped to the loaded bicycle. Greg and I sat on our rolled-up sleeping bags, watching. When our eyes met, he said self-consciously, "What? Oh – *this*," waving his cigarette and smiling. "I'd really appreciate it, you guys, if you didn't tell my parents. They don't know, and I want to keep it that way."

We made some reassuring noises, sliding around the issue with the mental reservation that we wouldn't lie, if confronted. Steve knew how we felt about smoking – Indians do not need pacifiers, any more than they need stimulants. Still, the shade of Jesuitry didn't trouble our consciences. We wouldn't rat on him – we didn't see his parents much, anyway, except on special occasions. Besides, we were here to have fun, not be our cousin's keeper.

Gregory smiled duplicitously. "We weren't thinking about your bad habit, Steve – just gawking at that incredible mound of stuff on your bike. I don't think I recognize half of it... what's that thing you just picked up?"

Steve smiled sheepishly, and said, "C'mon, guys, you've seen a Boy Scout knife before!"

"Sure," I said. "But not one with a hundred and fifty blades. Looks more like an archaeological tool... Probably made in Japan. They didn't know what a Boy Scout was, so they put everything they could think of in there, just in case..."

"I *know* what it is!" Steve interrupted. "You *hicks* from the *sticks* haven't seen 'store-boughten' stuff before!"

The bantering continued as he unpacked, Greg and I feeling tolerant and slightly superior in our role of masterful woodsmen.

That morning we had eagerly awaited Aunt Josephine's call. At 9:00, it came, confirming Steve's departure by bike from Dayton, 40 miles away. He would be arriving at our place around 1:00 p.m. It was great news! Greg and I rushed to get our gear ready. We were on!

Steve lived in a model suburb, famous in its day for forward-looking design. His house was a large, two-and-a-half story, square brick bungalow with full basement and cantilevered front porch, in a style popular in the '20s. All the houses were built on a tree-lined circle surrounding an oval park, and in the back, a narrow alley followed the housing row at the edge of the backyards. It was so well appointed, with quaint garages, kids' playhouses and shrubbery that even we loved to visit there.

But last year, at 14, Steve had wanted to assert his independence and have his very own adventure – a vacation from authority, in wide-open country, where he could live in unfettered freedom. He thought our place was perfect, and his parents reluctantly gave their approval.

That first bike-pilgrimage took him four-and-a-half hours on his American Flyer, but turned out so well that he looked forward to the next one all year. He kept his hope alive through the winter months by over-readying his gear, packing and repacking his bicycle, and purchasing new equipment for the venture. It produced some very interesting items for our *country* entertainment, and plenty of grist for ragging.

I'm sure our family looked more than *some peculiar* to him, compared with his own, but he just thought that made us more interesting – par for the course where artistic temperament reigned.

Now it was 1:30, and Steve was a half-hour late. We were just starting to wonder when we spotted him, sl-o-w-ly pedaling up our driveway, tongue hanging out like Bertie Wooster's. Every time he bore down hard on one pedal, the overloaded bike would veer to the right or left, like a sailboat zigzagging a windward course. The rider had also condemned himself to wear a backpack. How he could pedal that load, we didn't know, but weren't going to build him up by telling him.

Our dog Sam took instant exception to the contraption. He approached it warily, growling and sniffing, hackles up, as if he doubted anything human dwelt there. But Steve forestalled a beasty eruption by calling out, "Hallo, Sammy!" and Sam instantly geared-down into wagging mode, as if to say: *Uh... okay, I remember you, of the blood... I guess humps don't really matter...*

The bike-boy was hatless, wearing T-shirt and shorts, with the fair skin of his arms, legs, and face sunburned, but he was grinning, and came to a panting stop at the top of our drive. When he tried to dismount, his backpack almost pulled him over, but Greg steadied him. Our cousin groaned as he eased the pack off and collapsed on the steps, tired but excited to be here. I threw an M-80 into the yard to celebrate, its satisfying boom mildly stimulating – sort of an official signal for the games to begin.

Nick, Mother and Peter came out on the porch. She said, "What's all the noise about? I was taking a nap." Then she saw our guest. "Oh, hello, Steve."

"Hi, Mrs. Pfarr," Steve greeted her cheerfully. He was always very polite and called her *Mrs. Pfarr* (never Aunt Catherine, even though we were cousins and called his mother "Aunt Josephine.")

"Well, I see you got here all right," she said.

"Yeah, I didn't really have any problems," Steve smiled shyly.

"Your mother said you forgot your hat. And she wanted you to call her, first thing."

"Yeah, I know," he said. "I forgot it last year, too... May I use your phone?"

"Sure, come on in."

Steve's phone call afforded us a leisurely opportunity to examine his rig, smiling knowingly over some of his naïve choices. We were growing wiser all the time about the weaknesses of greenhorns and city-slickers, and soaked up all the incriminating details to use as ammunition in the ongoing city-versus-country skirmish.

Steve's bike was heavy-duty, with fat tires and no gears, and he had equipped it with *five* wire baskets - two mounted over the front wheel fenders, two over the rear, and one in front of the handlebars. A sleeping-bag roll and tackle box were lashed on top of the crammed rear baskets, and another small bag was attached to the seat, to hold bike tools. A disassembled fishing rod was strapped to the main bar.

There was only one item that stirred envy - Steve had purchased a generator headlight, powered by the spinning of the front tire. On that subject, we would remain silent, and not be churlish enough to reveal our baser feelings. But at the first opportunity we would acquire one ourselves!

When Steve came back, Greg asked him innocently, "Do you think you've got enough stuff with you?"

"Unh-hunh, just about," Steve replied good-humoredly.

"Well, I don't know... maybe you forgot to bring coat hangers or something... I mean, where will you hang your clothes at night?"

"Ha-ha, very funny, guys! I'm surprised you've even heard about those, this far out in the boonies. I can always tell when I'm close to Hicksville... the hills get so huge, I have to push the bike up them with my tongue hanging out! That's what slowed me down in South Lebanon - that, and a *stoopid* dog who was sure I was one of Hannibal's elephants crossing the Alps!"

"If *you* were a dog, and saw someone on that rig, you'd know why!"

Steve just grinned. Being around him was always pleasant - he was charming, good-natured, and always ready for fun. We never knew him to be mean or critical. His long, oval face was vaguely horsey, but had regular features and intelligent brown eyes, with light brown hair, cut in a longish burr for summer. Sometimes, when he smiled to himself, he had a habit of thrusting his lower jaw out slightly and moving it from side to side, especially when pondering some private joke.

Steve was hungry after his journey, but we didn't think of that — it hadn't been that long since *we'd* eaten. Fortunately, Mother wasn't asleep, and asked if he wanted something to eat before heading out. He accepted readily, even before she had time to list the comestibles - he knew there was always something good to eat at our place. Our mother was a fine cook who not only used many homegrown organic ingredients, such as black walnuts, black raspberries, and maple syrup, but also baked bread from freshly ground wholegrain flours.

Sam, our very own *special* breed of hound (universally known as *mutt*) attended all eating events, if not bodily ejected. He lay under the steel-rimmed table in the kitchen, well protected from pots and pans, but grew agitated, even so, whenever Greg or I came into the kitchen to cook. This was his signal to cut eating-class, and he would rise and prowl about with lowered tail and hunched back, looking for the exit, as though he expected a blow to fall at any moment. If Mom were there, he would stand at the back door and scratch to go out. If not, he would resign himself again to the table's protection, hunched against the far wall, ears flat, licking nervously. Greg and I were a little annoyed. This behavior bordered on the facetious, particularly since Sam was such a calm, even-tempered dog. You could only imagine what kind of deadly force it took to get him into that state.

After the eating ritual was over, it was around 2:30. All of us, including Nick and Peter, headed across the field, Steve wheeling his loaded bike and the rest of us carrying our gear. At the crest of the field, several fan-shaped American elms cut across our view, their leaves yellow in the dry weather, prematurely suggesting fall. The trees lined a small gully that had served as Grandpa Pfarr's dump, before the days of trash collection. You might still see blue medicine bottles, high-buttoned shoes, or a bottomless blue graniteware coffeepot, lying forever beached on old bedsprings.

We meandered past an old strawberry-apple tree, loaded with worm-eaten fruit. Tussocky grass and trumpet vines now covered all the cleared ground. This area was once part of a tiny orchard planted by our Uncle Tony many years before. His dream was abandoned when he left home to become a Jesuit brother, and only a lone Bartlett pear had survived at the edge of the wood. It seemed blessed, and produced some fruit every year, despite almost complete shade.

Though we never harvested many of the wild apples, Nick and I discovered how excellent they were, green, for throwing on the ends of sharpened sticks. They could be catapulted with tremendous velocity, and we spent at least a week exploring the possibilities, until an incident occurred to cool our ardor. Peter and I were playing with apple-sticks out by the asparagus bed, and I hurled one with especially satisfying force. But it misfired and hit Sam smack in the eye. He yiped piercingly, and when I went to look, his eye was all mush. I was sick – I had caused him to lose an eye! How could I live with myself, or face telling the rest of the family? Then I noticed that the mush was green. Were eyeballs green inside? With shaking fingers, I began to pick it out, and, miraculously, underneath it all, his eye was fine! I was so grateful that I didn't do anything reckless for a whole week. Of course, Peter and I didn't tell anyone... it was strictly a case of "need-to-know."

* * *

We arrived in the clearing. Steve brought the bike to rest and eased his pack off, flopping down with a thump. "Whew, it's hot! I don't know about y'all, but all I can think of is getting in the creek." We lived three hundred miles north of the Mason-Dixon Line, but ignored this slur on the native *patois*, and clamored agreement.

"Better not unpack any of your food, Steve, if you want it to stay safe till we get back, " Greg warned. "In fact, you better lift it into the crotch of that crabapple tree."

"Very true, you two," Steve rhymed. "You don't expect bears, do you?"

"No, but one dog could do it," I said darkly.

Twenty minutes later the three of us were in Theodore's Pond. It was so hot that we mostly just trod water over the blessed cold springs, the coolness rippling up between our toes. Heavenly!

Our swimming-hole was located on a bend of the O'Bannon Creek, at the lower end of a rich bottomland running a quarter-mile upstream. A screen of trees buffered us from the field. Spring floods nearly always cleaned out the pond, maintaining its depth, except for one year when it was filled with sand. Whenever the creek jumped its bank, it renewed the field. In the nineteenth century, the Stouder farm's 15-foot topsoil had been proclaimed by the State as the deepest in all Ohio. In our time, it had dwindled to 2 feet, but still grew some amazing cow corn that reached over 13 feet tall.

We stayed for about an hour, until the day began to lose some of its heat. When the shadows grew, we had to go, since Steve hadn't unpacked yet, and we'd begun to feel the claws of hunger.

The woods path ran through the sandy bottom, stair-stepping its way up Long Pond Cliff, and bearing left at the top through a park-like stand of trees to the camp. All around us were remnants of past ventures – a stone-ringed firepit, some rotten steps nailed partway up a maple tree, an old lean-to with withered leaves still clinging to its branches, and a rotting hammock, strung between two trees.

While Steve finished unpacking, he asked, "What was that burned-over place I saw earlier, when we crossed the field?"

Greg and I eyed each other nervously.

Steve caught it. "C'mon, guys, 'fess up!"

"Well... Greg and I sort-of accidentally burned off the field, trying to make a ball diamond..." My voice trailed off.

"You started a *wildfire?!*" Steve exclaimed gleefully.

Greg said, "It was a fluke! It wasn't supposed to spread! We did it the way they said in the books, with a small, controlled fire, but the wind gusted, and it got away... That was last March."

"HEE-HEE-HEE!" Steve exploded. "Did the fire truck have to come down Pfarr Lane, with its sirens and all?"

"Unh-hunh," we admitted glumly.

"Oh, man – you guys are *too much*! Did it come out in the 'Herald?' I can see the headline now – *'Juvenile Hicks set field afire to make ball diamond.'* Did the Fire Chief read you a lecture?"

"Yeah," Greg mumbled.

"Boy, I wish I could have seen you trying to explain it to him!"

We were glad he hadn't. Our faces were blackened with soot from trying to put out the fire ourselves, and we were almost in tears about the fire truck having to come. "It wasn't that bad..." Greg began lamely.

"What did your mom and dad say?"

But we were rescued when an object suddenly towered behind Steve's head, hissing, and Sam started barking.

"Look out!" Gregory yelled.

"*What?*" Steve jumped up, then grinned – it was only his self-inflating air mattress that had somehow released its catch and attacked.

"What's *that* for?" I demanded, pretending I'd never seen one.

"To sleep on, you yokels! I don't like tree roots in my back. Man, don't tell me you never saw one of *these* before!"

"Oh, sure, *we* understand," Greg said patronizingly. We winked at each other. Then he asked innocently, "Did you ever think about the way an air mattress hisses, when you turn over at night?"

"Of course – the air currents keep you cool," Steve replied smugly.

"But the hissing might attract other things, on a hot night like this..." I said.

"Like *what?*" he asked scornfully.

"Oh... like snakes..." Greg smiled sweetly.

"Aw, youse guys! Don't try to con me with that crap!"

Greg bored in relentlessly, "I saw in 'Boys' Life' where this kid attracted a big snake to his bed, just by tossing and turning on his air mattress. He woke up in the morning and–"

"Aw, stow it, youse guys! I don't believe that!"

"Okay, but don't say we didn't warn you!"

"Besides," Steve argued, "there aren't any poisonous snakes around here. You told me that last year!"

Greg paused. "Yeah, that's *probably* true. We haven't seen any, but Jimmy Ackerman said he saw at least one water moccasin, a rattlesnake, and maybe a nest of copperheads."

"Who's Jimmy whatsit?" our cousin asked. "Sounds like a flake."

"Someone up the street. He moved away," I said.

Greg mused, "The poisonous snake population does seem to have shrunk since he left..."

"Maybe he sent them to grass like St. Patrick," Steve mocked.

"He might have... he was a lot like the Pied Piper," Gregory answered pensively.

"He sure could tell stories," I agreed.

Having successfully planted that seed of doubt about reptiles, we moved on. Glancing at Steve's stuff again, Greg remarked with a straight face, "It looks like you forgot to bring plates."

Steve responded unthinkingly, "No, they're right here," pulling them out to show us.

We roared. Stung, he retaliated, "Well, you're such rubes, you've probably never eaten off plates before! It wouldn't surprise me to see you eat beans out of a can with a knife. *You-all* better quit minding my stuff, and look to your own!"

"We already did," said Greg.

"You call *that* getting ready?" Steve pointed at our sleeping area, which contained our unrolled sleeping bags, some fishing gear, a cast-iron skillet, and a container of margarine for frying fish.

"Right!" we replied, pleased at his look of chagrin.

The country boys were starting to look good. Of course, having the home turf helped. Whenever we needed something, we could go back to the house and get it, while Steve had to outfit himself for a whole week, trying to avoid being too dependent on his rural cousins.

I asked him, "How are you going to wash up later, without a sink, Steve?"

"Well, I guess I'll just have to go down to the *crick* and wash up like you and the coons do every morning."

That was a good one. Then Steve started pulling out snack food — cheese doodles, potato chips, marshmallows and pop - all the things that our parents didn't keep around, because they were expensive and not nutritious. We were struck dumb. While our wholesome diet made us feel virtuous, we still craved junk food, and right now we were ravenous! The sight of it almost made us faint.

The immediate problem was how to get as much of it as we could, while maintaining the illusion of rectitude. We eyed those items so wolfishly that Steve was taken aback, though too polite to say anything. He might reasonably have thought, *Look at the hypocrites!* Instead, he was kind enough to offer us some. (♫ *It's a gift to be simple, it's a gift to be free...*♫) I think he *did* mumble something about the appetites of savages, but we couldn't hear very well over the loud crunching of potato chips. After all, he had many inadequacies himself, like being a greenhorn. We weren't being unfair or anything - we only mentioned his shortcomings when necessary, and with subtlety and tact, even then. City people couldn't be expected to meet up to our stringent standards - it would take instruction, practice, some hardship, and maybe prayer.

After a supper of hot dogs and beans foraged from the house and fresh tomatoes from our garden, we were sitting around the campfire, drinking pop and roasting marshmallows. Steve told anecdotes about some of his Jesuit instructors, who apparently passed out demerits like blessings. We didn't have much to contribute, besides the remembered purgatory of grade school with the nuns, because our family couldn't afford the tuition of Catholic high schools.

In the bonfire light, Steve looked around camp and caught sight of the ragged hammock strung between two trees. "D'jou guys put that up, over there?"

"Yeah," Greg said, disinterested. "There were two of 'em. We slept out in them last August."

I started laughing. "You should have seen Greg at 1:00 o'clock in the morning, crawling around on the ground!"

"That wasn't near as funny as *you* wiggling and groaning!" Greg told Steve aside, "He was moving so slow, he looked like a sloth!"

"Why – what happened?" our cousin asked, grinning.

We had found a couple of hammocks in Grailville's dump, and decided to try them out. After stringing them up, we climbed in and lounged around for a while, reading and looking at the treetops. It was great — like floating on air! So we came back at dark and tucked ourselves in contentedly, with an Army blanket each. It didn't take long to fall asleep.

But I kept having dreams about being paralyzed, and a dull ache that wouldn't quit. This misery went on and on, until I finally managed to wake up and found I couldn't move anything but my eyeballs! I hurt like the devil, and my first thought was that I was still dreaming.

Then I heard Gregory moan in the next hammock. *What the–?* "What's wrong?"

After comparing notes, we realized that the only way out (if we ever wanted to walk again) was to somehow flip ourselves out of the hammock, and land face-down on the ground. Not pleasant, but we knew we couldn't stay like *that!*

(Steve was gurgling and wiping his eyes, but I ignored him and went on...)

Well, Greg had turned himself out of the hammock first, and started advising me on technique while still crawling on all fours. I determinedly ignored him, and flipped myself out, landing in the same undignified position. After a while, our backs thawed and we caught our breath. When he finally had energy to talk, Greg gasped, "I'm NEVER going to sleep in a hammock again!"

All I could think was, "Amen, brother!"

"Man, you guys are a two-ring circus!" Steve said.

"Not on purpose," I muttered.

* * *

Steve woke up at grey light. Opening his eyes, he looked straight into the eyes of a snake lying coiled on his chest, and froze. "Guys!" he whispered softly, only his lips moving. Then louder, "Guys! This isn't funny... I need help!"

We slowly sat up in our bags. Greg said, "Don't move, Steve! I was afraid of this, with all that hissing..." He sounded serious, but winked at me, when Steve couldn't see.

"Shut UP!" Steve said, through stiff lips.

"The question is, how do we get that snake off without getting bitten ourselves?" I prevaricated.

"Just get it *off*, I don't care... Oh, God, it moved!"

"You probably got him excited. You move - *he* move," Greg said.

Steve finally decided to take action on his own. I think he figured he might die, waiting on us to rescue him. So before we could get a stick to deal with the serpent, he jumped up, yelling, and flung the top part of his bag away, which sent the snake flying. Sam, who loved drama, immediately pounced on the naughty snake, growling and giving it a good shaking. Meanwhile, a panicked Steve ran around camp in his skivvies, until he stepped on a sharp twig. "Ouch!"

Sam brought the snake forward to appease him, with a speaking look, but Steve backed away. "Keep that damn thing away from me!"

Sam didn't understand English, and apparently thought he said, "Throw it at my feet," so he did.

Steve jumped back. Then, suddenly, "Hey! That's not a real snake!"

"Greg put it there early this morning," I said, laughing. (Score a big one for the hicks!) "You should have seen yourself, running around camp in your underwear!"

Our cousin countered with some heat, "Go ahead and laugh – just keep a sharp eye out, 'cause I'm going to get *you* – and it'll be when you aren't expecting it!"

We didn't care. The joke was too good.

Steve rounded on Sam. "And don't *you* think to turn me up sweet, pretending to be a hero!"

Sam drooped and walked away, as though he understood every word.

Steve's threat had us checking our beds and shoes for a while, but after a day or so, we figured he'd forgiven us.

Three days of Steve's week were gone. Things went on pretty evenly for the rest of his stay – one day he went to the store for supplies, and another time, we took a hike up the railroad. But mostly, we stayed close to camp. All the everyday activities took more time than at home, but that was the whole point. We could run our own show – if breakfast took two hours, we didn't think, *How inefficient.* We were just living in the Zen of a summer morning.

One evening we actually caught some fish, and cooked them for supper. This didn't usually work in hot weather, so it was gratifying, and made us look good. Later, we went swimming in the velvety darkness – there wasn't even a moon that night.

Steve finally got back at us on Friday, when we were snorkeling. He had tampered with the little balls that keep the water out, so Greg and I sucked in a lot of water, leaving us beached and gagging. We took it philosophically, knowing that he needed some release, after the harrowing episode of the snake. Sitting around the campfire later, I don't know what set Steve off, but he reverted to a familiar theme: "Man, you guys are really a bunch of *farmers.*"

"Farmers feed the idiots in the city," Greg returned.

"The kind of farmer I'm talking about is a parasite," said Steve. "The city makes his farming equipment, and then has to bail him out, in the end."

"That's only because the bedlamites in the city won't pay enough for the food they grow!" I said.

"That's a crock! I still say the City supports *them*," Steve persisted.

"Why? That doesn't make any sense!"

"Sure it does!" he insisted, half-joking, "The farmer raises food that even country people can't eat, in its raw form. The city people feel sorry for them, so they buy it real cheap, process it, and then sell it back."

"Then the farmers ought to get it free," Greg said. "You act like they should be *grateful*, when they have to pay more to get it back than they sold it for in the first place!"

"Gratitude would help," our cousin returned smoothly.

"As a spiritual principle, yes, but not instead of bread and potatoes," Greg trumped him.

"Children," I began patronizingly, "I don't think we've been reading the same books."

"Hardly," Steve agreed smugly, thinking of his alma mater's special curriculum and divine mandate. We knew one thing for sure, though – none of his required reading included Louis Bromfield's agricultural works.

Greg characteristically spent a while digesting Steve's peculiar ideas, then recapped, "Let me get this straight. The farmer provides city people with the raw goods to survive, but then, instead of being commended, he is held *liable* for his effort, and ridiculed into the bargain?"

"Sounds like usury, with a twist," I added.

"Yeah, the twist of the *knife*," Greg quipped.

Steve smiled. "Aw, c'mon, you guys – you're taking me too seriously."

"*Dead* serious!" we chimed together.

"*Briars!*"

"*City slicker!*"

That night, a mountain lion screamed in the early hours: "Whow! Whow!"

Steve sat straight up in the dark. "What in God's name is *that?*"

"A wild, hungry puddy-tat – or at least an escaped one," I told him. "Don't worry – he won't hurt you. We can't even catch sight of him."

"You mean all this time, there's been a wildcat running around out there, and you never *told* me?"

"We didn't know you were interested in the fauna, Steve…"

Steve slept poorly the rest of the night. After breakfast, he was sitting on his sleeping bag, smoothing the lumps out, while Sam wandered around peaceably, looking for stray food that wasn't doing anything at the moment. None of us was thinking much of anything until we heard Steve exclaim, "*Christ! That dumb dog!*"

Sam had made a discovery. We looked up and saw him standing there, feet spread apart, greedily scarfing cigarettes as fast as he could chew them up. They dangled ridiculously out of all sides of his mouth, as if he were smoking six at once! He had rifled Steve's shirt, lying on the ground. Our cousin quickly snatched what was left (not much), and stowed his other packs inside the rucksack, away from the miscreant.

But only a few minutes later, we heard Steve importuning the Father again: "*Christ Jesus!* He's got them *again!*"

Yep, there Sam was, chomping more cigarettes, and looking completely innocent, as though he had no clue what all the shouting was about. My brother and I were delighted.

Steve admitted ruefully, "I know swearing is a sin, but, *damn it!* He got almost all of 'em!" (He had brought a whole carton, which Greg and I thought an excessive amount, for a 15-year-old.) We had nothing to say about his swearing. He'd heard God's commandments from the nuns, the same as we had.

For the *third* time, our cousin hid his cigarettes. This time, he nestled his rucksack in the tree crotch, *five feet* off the ground. But unbelievably, ten minutes later, we heard Steve yelling, "Jesus! I don't *believe* it! That damn pooch got 'em *again!*"

We'd forgotten to mention that Sam had a talent for climbing. He had inched his way carefully up the leaning crabapple, just far enough to nose the rucksack out of the crotch, and then proceeded to the ground for the feast. Steve wasn't mean, and hadn't tried to whack the dog yet, but a martial light was beginning to kindle in his eyes. When he tried to save a few last cigarettes from under Sam's nose and the dog growled at him, Greg and I went off into whoops.

Things settled down. Steve sat on a stump, smoking a cigarette from his only remaining pack to calm down. Sam sat there worshipfully at his feet, waiting.

"I know you guys think it's funny," Steve said apologetically, "but this is all I've got for the rest of my stay here." We didn't answer – he couldn't expect any sympathy from us.

Sam provided entertainment for the rest of the morning by shadowing Steve's every move, punctuated at intervals by soulful pleading.

"By the way," Greg said, smiling, "what safe place did you find for your stash?"

Steve was a little sore. "None of your business!"

"He's put 'em in his underwear!" I said, laughing. "No wonder Sam's been sticking to him like glue."

Steve only smiled remotely. It wasn't in his interest to say any more.

Greg and I were content. We had witnessed a morality play, wherein it was shown that smoking and swearing were vices, and Sam had acted as an instrument of the Lord. It was obviously a judgment.

Chapter X.

Sunday, and Born Again

In the dim church, the quiet was palpable. When you closed your eyes, there was almost a sound to the silence, like a horizontal line in the mind, frictionless, but buzzing evenly on the psychic inner ear, a soft *sssssssssssssssssssssssssss* that went on endlessly. The smell of myrrh lingered on the air from past worship.

As your eyes adjusted to the light, the stained-glass windows leapt forward, dazzling, with their jewel blues, reds and greens surrounding saintly pictures. The rest of the interior slowly became visible.

There was a discipline, heaviness, mysticism and bondage to the Old Church that was mysteriously liberating. Perversely, it could soar, like Gregorian chant or the motets of Tomás Luis de Victoria.

I proceeded to a pew, genuflected, and crossed myself before entering. When I knelt down, the pew creaked loudly, and I began to pray: *Help me to be good, and follow the Ten Commandments. Please save me from the devil and the fires of hell. Help my father and mother, and brothers and sisters. Please don't let the Communists take over the world, and, if it's not too much to ask, I'd like to have a sled for Christmas.*

Once, when I visited, there was a nun doing her housekeeping –

making the altar ready, cleaning, and arranging flowers. This was one of the few times that nuns would leave you alone, unless you committed some *faux pas*, like forgetting to remove your hat. That day Sister surprised me, asking me to help her light the red and blue votive candles in front of Mary and St. Joseph.

I said, "But I don't have any money." Of course, there *were* some that cheated and lit candles without paying, but what was the point of that? It didn't make sense.

She said kindly, "That's all right, dear. Every once in a while I have to light them when not enough other people do. We don't want these signs of devotion to go out – what would the Holy Mother and St. Joseph think of us?"

In the old days, the Church had a lot of things sewn-up – you had to fulfill specified obligations or face the graphically depicted penalties. Purgatory and hellfire were always with us. You had to go to Mass on Sundays, Confession on Saturdays, take Communion at least once a year, and meet numerous other stipulations. Another unspeakable threat was excommunication, which cut you off from God in *this* life, and would be followed by hell. It was always a possibility, if you were bad enough.

Being under compulsion sometimes bred an unconscious resentment in members of the Catholic proletariat. As a child, it was no hardship for me to go to church on Sunday, and I felt good about it. But I wasn't tired from working all week, or worried about paying bills, or harassed by having too many things to do in too little time. My father always had headaches on Sunday morning. He often lost his temper, ranting about things that worried him while getting ready and driving us there. I used to offer helpful suggestions on Christian behavior from the back seat, but it didn't seem to calm him any.

At the age of seven, after long preparation and buildup, everyone celebrated their First Communion. Then we were supposed to begin taking serious responsibility for our behavior. In Catechism we learned about what we believed and what God wanted us to do, and we started going to Confession, to face up to our sins of the week, repent, and get a fresh start. Confession was arranged for us during the week in grade school, but as we grew older and our understanding was expected to increase, we had to go under our own steam, on Saturdays.

Despite the strict iron-fist-and-hellfire teaching, I would find myself confessing the same sins over and over. Every week was a seesaw of spiritual ups and downs that kept me in constant flux. It reminds me of a nursery rhyme:

> *Solomon Grundy*
>
> *Born on Monday*
>
> *Christened on Tuesday*
>
> *Married on Wednesday*
>
> *Took ill on Thursday*
>
> *Worse on Friday*
>
> *Died on Saturday*
>
> *Buried on Sunday*
>
> *This is the end of Solomon Grundy.*

The brevity and futility of this poem got to me. And then there was that word "end," that was so final. I *knew* what came next – judgment and retribution, surely, and reward for the chosen few.

By the nuns' reckoning, practically all of "the Public" were going to be in hell. *(Thank God I'm a country boy!)* We weren't members of the Public, no matter what the IRS thought. So I figured that, if I followed the rules, prayed, and worked hard all my life, I wouldn't be among them on the last day, either.

My intentions of constant reform, if a little coerced, were sincere. It was kind of like putting a hot iron to the seat of your pants, and exacting promises of good behavior: Just hearing about the hot iron made you sit up and take notice. Seeing it made you promise a good deal more, but actually having it put to your backside elicited complete metanoia, and a strong declaration that you were going to be a saint.

But, for all that, my religious week still parodied Solomon Grundy's:

- *Fresh slate on Monday* - Praying, feeling saintly, much crisp advice to others who haven't come up to the mark. The scourge of school satisfying all need for punishment, on top of the penance assigned for last week's sins.

- *Holding on Tuesday* - Still saying my prayers. Still giving advice and criticizing others, but not so forcefully.

- *Slipping on Wednesday* – Fog moving in. Absorbed in my own business. Forgetting to pray, not giving any advice unless asked (except to Peter).

- *Fallen on Thursday* - Only *thinking* wistfully about praying, and not giving advice (even to Peter). Feeling mediocre and a little hypocritical.

- *Unconscious on Friday* - Never got up from Thursday's fall. Afraid to pray. Afraid to think. Looking over my shoulder for the devil, who must surely be following hungrily by now. Looking *forward* to the relief of confession, and the reinstatement of Grace.

- *Confessed on Saturday* - A dark weight lifted from the soul. The devil slinks off, dejected. God resumes his guardianship – Benediction and assigned penance prepare for Sunday. Looking forward to redemption.

- *Born again on Sunday* - Lifted to the highest plane on fasting, Sunday morning Mass, Holy Communion, and celebration afterwards. School's out, Sunday morning breakfast and homemade cinnamon rolls!

So many Saturday afternoons during my adolescent years were spent going to Confession. The mood was pensive. Sometimes I went alone, and other times with my brothers, walking or riding our bikes through the same country shortcut we took to go to school.

My father, an artist, had a book about drawing the human figure, with a dull, yellowish cover showing a man who looked like an ancient Greek athlete. It was a very conservative book, I'm sure, and my brothers and I consulted it now and again. (Perhaps we were all thinking of becoming artists someday.) For some reason, we found the male figures boring, and the female studies intellectually stimulating. But after each study session, I felt extremely guilty, and could sense the devil drawing near, gloating over my Achilles' heel. I would vehemently recoil, and long for Saturday-afternoon confession. It felt as though I had been tricked somehow – I *knew* that this interest in the physiognomy of women was immoral and straight from the devil.

Without this serious sin taking me to the edge of the fiery pit, I would only have had dozens of petty ones to confess. It did provide excellent raw material for the confessional.

The following Saturday, I would be waiting there in the church. There were three booths in a row along one wall, the center one for the priest, and one on each side for penitents, with curtains to shut behind you when you went in. I would make myself as small as possible, and slip into an empty cubicle, blessedly screened to hide the penitent's identity from the priest. It was everyone's hope that he wouldn't be able to recognize individual voices.

There were hazards, entering and leaving the confessional. It could be a tricky business. For one thing, people could see you coming and going, or the priest might come out, thinking everyone had gone, just as you were about to enter (probably because you waited for most of the people to leave). Then he would certainly ask, "Are you here for confession?" Whereupon you would hear a small voice, from a great distance, saying, "No, Father, I've already been..."

This only saved face temporarily, because you still had to confess. So your only chance of achieving anonymity was to reconnoiter and wait for more people to come into the church before trying again. And, of course, you would have one more lie to confess, to go with all the other sins. These were venial sins, so the confessor never investigated very thoroughly. But deep down, you knew he *could*, he *might*. You prayed he wouldn't – it didn't bear imagining.

There was also the fear that, when you were in that dark place, alone, confessing your sins, the priest would come out of his cubicle, pull open that curtain and LOOK at you. (!) I had never heard of it happening, but I knew of nowhere that the rules stated he *couldn't*.

"Bless me, Father, for I have sinned. My last confession was two weeks ago... I sassed my mother twice. I called my brother "stinkpot" seven times. I called my other brother "bizpot" four times. I lost my temper and hit my third brother. I disobeyed Mother twice. I stole a candy bar, and–" (in a much smaller voice) "*–I looked at this book with women in it, that didn't have any clothes on.*" My voice dropped away to nothing.

I heard the priest snap to attention. It sounded like he moved too fast and bumped his head. He had probably been half-asleep, enduring another kid-confession, but was fully awake now, and I had his (unwanted) undivided attention.

"*What?* What did you say?"

This was particularly distressing, since now I had to repeat what I hadn't wanted to tell him the first time. I complied, but not without cost. My self-consciousness was raised to a paranormal level. I imagined all the people in the church leaning closer to hear my perfidious words, and when I came out, they would look at me and think, "There goes a hardened sinner, and in the guise of a little boy, too!"

My only remedy was to leave the confessional as quietly and quickly as possible, trying to look humble, pious, and saintly, while hunching down to obtain whatever cover the pews provided. Sometimes the priest actually did come out of the confessional shortly afterward, which was alarming – another reason for leaving church quickly, and saying your penance on the run. It could be really embarrassing if you were the only one there. If he spoke to you, all you could do was make a casual reference to the kid who just left, and disguise your voice. Early on, I thought he really was trying to see *who* that awful sinner was, but later realized he needed to come out sometime, if only for air.

As I got older, it was more difficult to maintain all these dodges, so, like everyone else, I learned to wear a poker face. By the time Catholics learn to play poker (much frowned-upon by the nuns), they've got that part down pat, from years of practice exiting confessionals.

Father always absolved me, but not without a short lecture on the wages of sin and my predilection for being a preadolescent adulterer. My assigned penance was usually five or six "Hail Mary's" and "Our Fathers." It always seemed such a light sentence, considering the seriousness of the sin, the anguish I suffered, and the alternative for the unshriven. From my own small experience with fire, I thought five seconds was pushing it. On the other hand, when I recalled what I had been taught about the boundless mercy of God, it seemed adequate.

There was something highly unstable about these two sides of God – mercy and magic versus hell and damnation – doomed one minute, saved and on the road to sainthood the next. It was a very jerky ride. Once I reached the age of ten or so, I used to worry a little about how this dichotomy would affect the fate of nice people who happened to be members of "the Public," like Mr. Mann, the principal of the public grade school. Once, I asked, but the reply was unvarying: outside the Church, this kind of person was unlikely to evolve, and if it did occur, the most he could hope for was Limbo, a grey place where you exist, but are not "happy" or "unhappy." You just *are*. (Very Buddhist.) I did wonder what would prevent these people from living any way they pleased, if they couldn't go to Heaven, anyway. I suspected that I might, if I knew that being a good person wouldn't help.

* * *

Religious instruction went on all the way through high school. We were taught the fundamentals, beginning with the Ten Commandments, but I have to admit that I didn't always understand these thoroughly, despite the nuns' efforts. For instance, the first and second were always grouped together: "Love the Lord your God with your whole heart, mind and soul, and your neighbor as yourself."

I couldn't figure out quite why these two were linked. The first part was easy. God was good, and I could sincerely say, "I love you, Lord, with all my heart, mind, and soul."

But how did we swallow the second part? There were some terrible people in the world (and I was told that all of them were my neighbors). I definitely didn't like most of them, from what I saw. How could God tolerate them? I was taught that you didn't condone what others did, but you loved them anyway.

Trying to come to terms with these two awfully demanding opposites was going to take more than a little practice. It was going to take lifelong sweat, and, I began to suspect, blood. If only they hadn't been linked together... It's like someone saying to you, "Tell me before you go that you love me, and by the way, would you bring me home a piece of the sun for supper tonight?"

Another one was, "Thou shalt not covet thy neighbor's goods, or his wife, or anything that he hath." *Okay, I guess so*, I thought, but I couldn't see what it would hurt, fantasizing a bit about his motorboat. Coveting his wife was not a problem. Who would want to? I knew the wives in the neighborhood. I couldn't see their husbands coveting them, let alone the neighbors. I guess I didn't really know what it was about, but it seemed an easy commandment to follow, and therefore easy credit. I never even broke it once.

"Thou shalt not steal" was covered in depth. One of the lessons went something like this:

Sister Mary Pain said to one of the fifth-grade girls, "Now, Virginia, suppose you stole a pencil."

"That's wrong, Sister."

"Yes, we all know that by now, or I hope we do." The nun smiled ickily. "But it's only a pencil, and not worth much... Maybe nobody will even miss it. So why do we care so much about it?"

Silence from the class. It didn't sound so bad, phrased that way.

"Because it's not so much *what* you steal as the bad attitude behind it," Sister explained. "As Virginia said, it's wrong to *steal* anything at all. It may start out small, but it doesn't end up that way.

"I heard of a boy no older than you, who started out by stealing a nickel. He wasn't caught, and the boy he stole it from was well off and didn't miss it. But today, that boy is grown-up and living in the State Penitentiary for robbing a bank! And it all started with that nickel. After that, he stole desserts out of his classmates' school lunches, and in a few years, he was stealing toys, then a bike, and finally a car."

"Did he make any money, Sister?" one of the boys, a car salesman's son, asked.

"Don't be impertinent, boy!" the nun barked. (The barking nun, not the singing one, was what we got.) "And let me tell you, it CAN be a *mortal* sin to steal a *penny*, if you take it from someone who's starving!"

There were two important central points: One, the first theft will lead to others, increasingly more serious, and, Two, the moment you steal the pencil, you begin to bond with other thieves, via the unified field. (Putting Einstein to work)

I stole a candy bar from Loveland Grocery once. Even though Ella Herbert has long since passed away, I still feel some trepidation at this public admission. I can imagine her exclaiming, "What!" and immediately starting to harangue, "It'll be charged to your parents' account! I'm not paying for that! And you'd better believe *me*, young man, I'm going to tell them when they come in! Maybe I'll just call them now... I hope you're ashamed of yourself! And a good Catholic boy, too! You'd better go to Confession, or you'll have more than me to reckon with!"

I guess I was lucky it didn't pull me into the hell-bound cycle Sister predicted. She was right, though, that it would cause trouble. When I was 17, I applied for a security job, and had to take a lie-detector test. They asked whether I had ever stolen anything. I answered No, but the lie made me so nervous that I probably drove the machine crazy. But not before it shouted to its operator, "Liar! Liar! Liar!" Another boy from my class was applying for the same job. He seemed to get through just fine, and he'd stolen *bicycles*. Was the machine measuring veracity, or sensitivity?

*   *   *

I always tended either to do something wholeheartedly, or refuse to do it at all. So I believed what I was taught about Christ, the saints, and the right way to live, and tried to adhere to all the Church's precepts. The most basic principle was, *Learn the rules, pray, apply your will, and you will steadily become as close to divine as Man can get.* Ours was not to reason why, beyond the borders of ordinary life situations. Past that point, blind faith was required.

But for some perverse reason my mind flew immediately to those borders, and stood there, looking over the fence, thinking about pole vaulting. This is where you're supposed to trust, fear God, and not go any further. But I always thought, *Why would God give a man a mind if he wasn't allowed to use it?* And my mind wanted to know a lot more.

But some theological things can pull you in so deep that you get thoroughly turned-around. For instance, take the text, "If your enemy hits you on the left cheek, turn and offer him your right." Now, this is really hard to take. We all know instinctively that someone who hurts us is our enemy. But the cheek-slapper has actually provided you with an opportunity for spiritual merit, and that's what we're all supposed to want. So he must *really* be your spiritual friend, right? (I have to admit that I haven't actively sought out this type of friend.) Buddhists might say, "Thank you. You have made the path of my life clear."

From a worldly standpoint, this type of thinking is unproductive, and a long way from "I'm OK, you're OK." But if a person had no enemies or obstacles, he would have no opportunities for spiritual development, right? Therefore your enemies are actually your friends, and your friends are your enemies. The devil knows what your faults are. (Your friends do, too, only they call them virtues.)

The devil also knows your friends. Their help and support make you feel good about yourself, all the while smoothly sliding you down that slippery slope to perdition. Who would want the kind of friend that was looking out for your spiritual welfare, and kept trying to give you the nasty medicine that dying to self requires? (Mixed up yet?)

In a nutshell, that was probably why I was a loner. It wasn't the sort of thing the nuns felt up to discussing, and the priests had more immediate matters to address. Somewhere along the way, I decided it would probably be wiser to change gears and follow Ted Williams' advice: "Remember, if you don't think too *good*, don't think too *much*." I tried that. It worked well for a while, but didn't hold.

I sympathized considerably with the battles Molly Doherty fought in school. One of the most memorable concerned the Old Testament. Protestants have often accused Catholics of not reading the Bible, and it's true that the Church wanted to emphasize the New Testament rather than the Old. Jesus himself had said to do that, and we were constantly admonished to live his teachings (despite any confusing local events that might tend to water them down). I came to learn *why* Catholics were somewhat ambivalent about reading the Old part when Molly laid waste to Religion class in the fifth grade over the story of Sodom and Gomorrah.

What we learned early on about the Old Testament came from abridged and sanitized versions. We had been told that Lot and his family were righteous, and God saved them from destruction, except for Lot's wife, who was turned into a pillar of salt for disregarding instructions not to turn and look back.

They certainly did not teach us the follow-up, wherein Lot's daughters, using beetle logic, get their father drunk, and get pregnant by him, to save the human race from impending extinction. (This, after the Lord has singularly saved them) The daughters seemed to get away with a bit more than Lot's wife. Now, remember, this was the "Family of the Year," religiously speaking, which causes one to wonder what the bad ones were like! (Ask yourself, are we reading this part of the Bible to cheer ourselves up, or to inspire us to become better people? It gives me the willies, just thinking about it.)

We had been assigned to read this chapter from our Bible stories for the next day's lesson. But Molly was a budding genius, IQ tests had confirmed, though the nuns suspected she might be an *evil* one. (Some of them clutched their rosaries and made the Sign of the Cross when she passed them on the grounds.) She considered our Bible Reader a bit slow and childish, and thought to herself, *Why not read the original?* So that night, she went home, took the family Bible to her room after supper, and thoroughly devoured tomorrow's lesson.

The next day, after Sister Clotilde had reviewed the assignment with the class, Molly raised her hand. When the nun called on her, she said, "What about the *rest* of the story?"

Sister Clotilde replied nervously, "What do you mean, dear – what *rest?*"

"Oh, the part about Lot's two daughters. They got their father drunk and slept with him to get pregnant, to prevent the extinction of the human race. What I don't understand is–"

Sister gasped, and before Molly could finish that enlightening sentence, she swooped down on her and shoved her out the classroom door, throwing a forced smile at the class and saying, "Molly has brain fever... I'll take her outside. Be good children, and study your lesson. I'll be right back!" Once outside, she shook Molly viciously. "You evil, wicked girl!"

"But why? I don't understand," Molly wailed. "It was right there in the Bible! I thought you'd be happy, and give me extra credit."

"You *monster!* What you'll get is extra punishment! I'm taking you to see the pastor. He'll fix your wagon!"

Father was enjoying the light lunch prepared by his housekeeper, Fern (who later told her friend Maria all about it), when he spotted Sister Clotilde dragging Molly purposefully down the walk toward his domicile. For a moment, Fern thought he looked as though he wanted to slip out the back door, but he stood his ground, not entirely surprised at the development. He knew Molly, and he knew the Sisters.

So he sighed, pushed aside his lunch, and went to meet Sister Clotilde at the door. "What's going on here?"

Sister turned to Molly fiercely. "You stay right there while I talk to Father!"

Inside the rectory, she began agitatedly, "You won't believe it! Father in heaven! No – I can't tell you–" (breathing hard) "–what *that girl* said in Religion class... the sheer wickedness of it! I have *never* been so mortified and ashamed..."

"Calm yourself, Sister, and tell me... It can't be that bad. We aren't dealing with a monster."

"That's what you think! Oh, dear! I'm sorry, Father," she lamented, rubbing her hands together.

"Now, hold on! Just tell me – *WHAT DID SHE DO?*" Father demanded, exasperated.

"Well – we were studying Sodom and Gomorrah, and how Lot's wife was turned into a pillar of salt. Then, near the end of class, Molly said that wasn't the whole story..."

Father almost choked, trying to suppress a betraying laugh, but managed to say, "Oh, so *that's* it! Molly finished out the story for the class... How far did she get, before you dragged her outside?" he asked.

Sister looked pained.

But Father had a lot of practice in this sort of thing from the confessional. He was almost psychic. "Did she tell what the daughters did with their father, and the reason?"

"The story's *t-t-true?*" Sister blushed and stammered.

"Yes, I'm afraid so."

"Then I can't punish her?" Sister asked sadly.

"No, I wouldn't advise it. It's not a sin to tell the truth, and no one told her she couldn't read the Old Testament."

"Oh, Father, what should I do?" Sister implored.

"You've probably done enough already, I'd say, from the way Molly's looking."

"Well, I did shake her a bit," Sister admitted.

"It's my fault this happened," Father offered. "Her parents came to me and explained that Molly was a genius, and liked to get to the bottom of things. I warned her earlier teachers, but didn't get around to you. I figured, what harm could she do... One thing I can advise: Don't call on her in Religion class, even if she raises her hand! Just smile, and go on. I'll talk to the girl now, and try to smooth things over."

"Thank you, Father. I'd better get back to my class now... It's time for lunch."

Father didn't argue with that, and Sister Clotilde left, sending Molly inside on her way out.

Molly entered the rectory somewhat shyly, but the set of her chin spoke volumes to the experienced. At once, Fern seemed to appear magically with cookies and milk.

"Been reading again, Molly?" Father Urbain smiled at her.

Molly curtly nodded. "*Yes.*"

"Don't worry – I'm not going to yell at you."

She sagged visibly. "Really, Father? What am I supposed to do?"

"All you have to do is less," Father said gently. "You try too hard. There was nothing wrong with reading the Old Testament, though we don't usually recommend it for everyone. But in the future, it would be better not to volunteer anything in Religion class that isn't in the textbook or that the teacher doesn't cover. There really *are* reasons for the way it's done – most children don't have the maturity to make use of your... er... discoveries." (He probably thought to himself, *I'm not sure the teachers do, either.*) "Why don't you come and see me, if you need to talk about something?"

"Thank you, Father. I will try to do differently next time." Molly didn't say "better." She always said exactly what she meant, and meant exactly what she said. Before leaving, she couldn't help asking her unanswered question: "Sister wouldn't let me ask how it was possible to have children by your own father! How could they do that, back then?"

Father could understand why Sister Clotilde was upset, when the children weren't even supposed to know about "the birds and the bees" at that age. But he thought fast, and answered, "It... uh... was... a special dispensation for difficult times."

She asked, "Could it ever happen now?"

"Never!" Father answered firmly, shuddering.

Molly had private doubts, but let it rest. It had been a rough day.

Later that evening, when the pastor and his assistant were having a drink together, Father related the entire incident. Chuckling, he added, "Sister Clotilde nearly died of a heart attack at hearing Molly's unabridged version. I think she would have liked to excommunicate her. Thing was, it was all true. Some people just aren't ready for the Old Book."

My mother belonged to the Rosary Altar Society, which met once a month in various homes. That month, the meeting was at our house, a week later. I was in the kitchen, and paying no attention to their conversation, because it was usually so boring that it made me want to howl. But this time, I heard Molly's name mentioned. Mrs. Maria Halloran, Fern's best friend, was letting the whole story out bit by bit, as several ladies questioned her.

"...and Fern said to me *that she felt so sorry for Molly, with all them brains!* She said, *How Molly was ever going to function normally, she didn't know.*"

Telling this (and everything else) wasn't exactly a betrayal of confidence, though I'm sure Fern didn't intend that it should be spread quite so widely. She always waxed garrulous over a cup of tea, especially when she wanted to impress a friend about the importance of her *inside* position, privy to the Pastor's confidence. This was stretching it a bit, of course, but she tried to enliven things when she had the chance.

The rest of the story I got from Molly herself. Possessing a spark of the same fatal flaw, I commiserated with her occasionally.

* * *

There was another particular Church teaching that I was very comfortable with, growing up, and very unhappy when I was forced to lose it. I probably wouldn't have had many thoughts about dating, marriage, and so on, if the Church hadn't insisted on telling me. But the trap had been baited, and the wide-eyed woolly lamb swallowed it joyfully. (We all know the fate of woolly lambs, both secular and religious.) *What* they told me suited my temperament at the time, so I didn't object. (*B-a-a-a-ah!*) This is what I was taught:

1. <u>Marriage was a holy sacrament</u>. Only the Catholics had it... all others were living in sin. It was God's sanction of the union between men and women, for the Chosen. ("Go in peace... You can now have children.")

2. <u>Conception was a miracle</u>. (How did it happen? Pure magic.)

3. <u>Birth was a miracle</u>. (Even the Public agreed on that.)

4. <u>Both Mary and Jesus were conceived miraculously</u>. (What were intellectuals arguing about? If you accepted ordinary conception as a miracle, it was no stretch at all to accept this, too.)

5. <u>The consummation of a marriage was on an unimaginably high spiritual level</u>. (I thought it must be like dying, and going to some fantastic place of light.)

So far, so good. But what about firsthand information? I didn't have any. What little *secondhand* information I got, I learned from my mother. My father had probably been asked to explain the facts of life to me, but did not really want to be on the same planet with that situation. (*Knowing* my father, I think I'm grateful.)

Apparently, it all had to do with umbilical cords. Babies were connected to their mothers by cords when they were born. From this scrap of knowledge, I inferred that the baby came through the navel when it was ready. Not exactly a magical materialization of man into matter, but my longing for paranormal events was pacified for the moment. How did it get *in* there in the first place? No one knew, except God.

My mother did not have the desire or *chutzpah* to contradict this and explain the facts to my ten-year-old self. (Can't say I blame her.) I did sense that she was a little vague on detail, which I chalked up to the miracle theory. Perhaps she didn't really *know*... Maybe it was like Santa Claus – you saw the presents, but never actually caught him coming down the chimney. Maybe she woke up one morning, and there it was, another miracle, attached to her tummy at the navel. All you had to do was snip the cord and tie it up. Any questions?

So this became the rock foundation of my knowledge of magical obstetrics. You can see I had a sensitive, natural ability to glean information and figure things out, so I was able to add two and two and get ninety-six every time, especially about "the birds and the bees." (By the way, I don't know why people ever used this euphemism... birds are hard to track and observe, bees almost impossible [*Ouch!*]. "Facts of life" is also obscure. Which facts? Too many facts everywhere. Whoever invented these terms was very nervous, and looking for an escape hatch.)

I believed in all the reports of miracles that I heard. (Why would people lie about sacred things?) In addition, people received so many miracles every day, usually in the form of babies, that miracles were obviously not that rare.

Although I felt the foundations tremble now and then during my preadolescent years, it didn't trouble me much, since other interests occupied me. A miracle didn't have to be rooted in this earth, anyway. What would be the point? Furthermore, what my mother told me perfectly dovetailed with what I had learned from the Church through parochial school – the old "Marriage-is-a-Sacrament/Baby-Conception-and-Baby-Born-are-Miracles" teaching (MSBCBBM for short). So I was satisfied. I didn't need any proof. Who would? I couldn't imagine someone demanding more proof from God, when He had already given us a bushel of miracles.

From the end of eighth grade on, I was sometimes puzzled by Father

Bach in the confessional. He would go on about the physical urges of adolescents. I didn't understand much of it, and I wondered if he knew as much as I did about rising above them, the way the Church taught. Maybe I should try to tell him a little about it. In retrospect, I think he was trying to determine, from the scant information I gave, how bad the sin was – whether mortal or venial. He wasn't sure how much I might know, and wasn't going to contribute anything new.

I couldn't see why he was working himself into a sweat. I saw his vague outline in the confessional, and noticed that, the longer he talked, the more often he mopped his brow with a handkerchief. Once I saw him outside, after confession with my eighth-grade class. At first I thought that he was bowing over and over in prayer at the north wall of the church, the way some Jews do when praying at the Wailing Wall in Jerusalem, but then I noticed that his head was actually making contact with the wall. One of the nuns must have seen him, too, and saved his dignity by running out of the convent, kindly taking his arm, and saying, "Father, I have some questions concerning the Rosary Altar Society." He was led off, before the rest of my class saw how he was spending his break.

As time went on, there were questions that I always had trouble resolving. Somehow I didn't feel comfortable asking our priest, and especially not the nuns. For instance, if heathen couples weren't really married in God's sight, how did they merit the miracle of children? What about people who hadn't gone through any form of marriage at all, like young high-school mothers? How could there be illegitimate children, if God had to bless a union and give permission? If God required that parents be (a) Catholic, and (b) sacramentally married, then why could those who didn't meet either criterion have children, just like Catholics?

And why did my mother tell me not to spend too long in proximity to any girl? I don't remember just how this came about, but one day I found myself alone in my bedroom with the neighbor girl, for perfectly innocent reasons. After about 20 minutes, my mother called me down and quietly told me not to be together with the girl for very long. She didn't say it, but I got the implication clearly – "just to be on the safe side." The safe side of what?

It took me a while, but an idea began to dawn on me. I was staggered. Could time and mere proximity to women have something to do with conception? If true, I figured that 20 minutes must be the maximum safe time, since that's when my mother had called me. Imagine! Another ten minutes and it might have been too late! What if Mother had been delayed, talking on the phone to a friend? I was almost a goner, and didn't even know it! There must be a hair trigger!

I tried to figure it out. These seemed to be the rules:

- A distance of 6 feet or more (*more* was definitely better)
- A time limit of 20 minutes, time shortened by any casual contact. (*Avoid it!*)

Maybe all illegitimate children occurred when these rules were infringed, and it activated the miracle mechanism, by mistake. It was obviously a misuse of Divine Law, which somehow couldn't tell the difference between those with Church sanction, and others.

I had never gone in for dating, anyway, but this certainly wouldn't make *anyone* very comfortable with it... you would have to time your dates for 20 minutes or less. From then on, I applied this with the neighbor girl. You never knew when the timer was going to go off, and I certainly didn't want to be hooked up to *her*, compliments of divine accident!

We had a strange conversation once, when we were out for a walk.

"Why are you walking so far away from me? I won't bite," Judy said.

"Oh, no particular reason," I lied. There was no way I was going to explain everything to *her*.

"You'd think I hadn't washed this morning, or had a disease!" she said, fishing.

"Oh, no, it's not that," I prevaricated.

"Well, what is it, then?"

"Oh, never mind. I can come over there by you for about 20 minutes," I said.

"Why, do you have to go to the bathroom, or something?" She was exasperated.

What was wrong with the girl? Was she trying to flirt with disaster? Girls were supposed to take the Virgin Mary for their example, and judging from my sisters and some of the creeps they dated, they seemed to need it. Why were they taking such risks with the hair-trigger miracle mechanism? I wouldn't have done it, in their shoes. You had to be careful, so that at least you'd end up with the *right* family, not some black-sheep, son-of-creep, with no benefit of sacrament! Things were bad enough.

But Judy was awfully cool about it. I concluded that she was either stupid or a hardened sinner already, living deep in the clutches of chaos and the devil.

So, after about 20 minutes, I said, "Gotta go!" and hared off home.

I heard her parting words: "He *did* have to go to the bathroom!"

"No – Confession!" I gasped out.

"Already? I swear, some people!" was her faint reply.

It had to be true. This was how the heathen, without even the benefit of a civil marriage license, could get into the family way. It didn't entirely square with the "MSBCBBM," but... things weren't perfect in this world. I let it slide by.

You can see that inimical forces were at work, beginning to erode the foundations of belief, but I wasn't aware until the floor caved in.

When I learned the real truth from a book my mother gave me over the summer after eighth grade, I was shocked, disappointed, and let down. Some miracle! Human beings were supposed to be so special and so superior, but any animal could do as well! A miracle had evaporated, like a fairy dying.

And they had lied to me! What opinion of them did those who encouraged my religious fantasies think I would have when I grew up? It made me very uneasy. What else were they hiding? Illegitimate urges and interest in the opposite sex became more understandable, but I hated it, because I had to come down from the high plane I had finally achieved.

There was *one* comfort, though – at least I could forget about the hair trigger!

Chapter XI.

Outward Bound

Pale and drained, we stood in the kitchen like strangers. After a day of shallow breathing, shallow associations, and punitive learning, we felt wooden and insignificant. Even the sight of a snack on the kitchen table had no immediate power to jump-start us. It would take deep breaths of freedom and some life-giving idea.

Every schoolday's legacy was the same – the overpowering need to do *something*, fast, before homework could renew the attack on our creative centers. Like any viable organism, we developed daily, weekly, and seasonal defenses against this perpetual menace.

After the advent of TV in our house, we would often watch for an hour – programs like "Cheyenne" and "The Big Valley." Sixty minutes spent that way did much to wipe the mind clean, and a game outside might complete the process. We *never* asked each other, "Did you do your homework?" That nameless activity was relegated to the after-dark, where it belonged – provided it didn't compete with some educational program like "The Man from Uncle," or "Get Smart."

But on bad days, the need to eradicate the scourge was paramount, and we ran straight into the arms of Nature, skipping even the snack. A favorite avenue to freedom was the railroad, far enough distant for the trees and hollows to buffer the noise, but only five minutes away to us. Its rhythms seeped unconsciously into our days and nights, and, like Thoreau, we felt a strong attraction to its quiet song of wanderlust, boundless horizons, and mystery.

The railroad's moods were many – sweltering in summer, we saw heat waves shimmering as we walked the ties and endlessly chased mirages of water lying just at the vanishing point of the tracks, while the satisfying, pungent odor of tar rose at our feet. Wintertime revealed its somber, rudimentary glory in the wind and cold, with patches of snow lying like a tattered coat on the cinders. In late winter, the land lay patchworked in shades of brown, red, gold, charcoal and silver, bright one moment and sober the next, as shadows overtook it. Whatever the weather, the tracks went on, their perspective narrowing to a point at the horizon that beckoned us toward the mysterious blue lands beyond.

I took long walks and runs up the railroad in all weather, sometimes with my brothers, but always in the company of Sam. We would dash across the field toward the creek, thrilling to the chase, and when the wind was bitter, it seemed only a fitting pumice to scour away the day's tedium and loosen the knots inside. Sam considered humans very slow, but took advantage to hunt along the way, and from time to time, we caught his excited yipping. Being a hound, his great love was rabbits. (I think he thought of them as *rarebits*.) But he would show up periodically, panting heavily, to make sure we were still there.

There were always things to see. Tiny creeks were frequently dry, but their tunnels rushed with water in season. The slopes of clay banks and cuts showed soapstone layers, adorned with tangles of honeysuckle, thorny black locust, blackberry, and occasionally bittersweet. Some of the bittersweet made it to the Christmas wreath, but most was left to its wild nature.

Then there was the old watering-place for steam locomotives a short way out of town, looking like a black tower with a witch's hat on top. For a long time, a waterfall flowed out like silver hair from a leak under the hat, a cool shower for us in summer.

Later, when I was in high school, the tower was gone, but the 3-foot concrete piers remained, and we used to jump from pillar to pillar, sometimes assisted by poles cut from saplings. Now, redbud trees, blooming there in the spring, hide its secret from the uninitiated, but water still flows deeply in the dark capped well, its roots delving into the creek nearby, awaiting the day when thirsty giants may have need of it again.

In the early fifties, the locomotives sometimes stopped in town.

Resuming their journey, they huffed and puffed, working hard to pick up speed on the uphill grade, and the whistle screamed as they progressed up the valley. Sometimes a train would pause, with brakes screeching, before the sound reached full-volume, and we knew it was drinking water for its thirsty boilers at the black tower.

On winter nights, sound carried piercingly on the air, and when I was young, I pulled the covers over my head for safety, afraid the train was going to smash our house. If I somehow managed to sleep through the noise, it still colored my dreams, and in the morning, I half expected to see the outhouse destroyed, or at least tracks running through the yard.

Later, when I ran track, I used the railroad for training, alternating running and walking until I was thoroughly warmed up, then going for distance, to build endurance. After several miles, I would cool off by walking again, and might find some grassy, sheltered area to rest. Sam, infallibly sensing a change, would pause in his hunting and nose his way back to check on me. Then he threw himself down alongside, panting from his exertions, and we lounged companionably, sometimes dozing, until we were ready to move on, or were awakened by cold, drizzle, or an approaching train.

In our area, the tracks seemed to avoid civilization wherever possible, and paralleled the creek for many miles. We took advantage to travel far afield – to Cox's Woods, where the wild berries grew secretly in abundance, and our favorite ponds, with interesting names like Grand Banks, High Banks and Cinder Slip, where we camped, fished, swam, or skated.

* * *

By summer, the cumulative effects of education demanded more comprehensive purging. We had to come up with projects of greater scope to banish our bane completely. One late summer when Greg and I were in high school, we set out to find the source of O'Bannon Creek. It was one of those white days in mid-August, hot and dry, as it had been for weeks. By 9:00 in the morning, it was uncomfortable already, and even the maples' luxuriant shade brought no peace. Approving, the locusts overhead gleefully rubbed their papery wings together with satisfaction, as if to say: *"Dry! Dry! Dry!"*

We prowled restlessly about the driveway, finally settling on the front steps beside Sam. The weather chafed, but mostly it was the threat of summer's end. On the radio at breakfast, we had heard some "progressive" educators (lunatics!) discussing the benefits of attending school year-round! Incensed, we hurled fulminations at the universe on this evil subject, then began to fantasize about arranging *their* education. Where did ideas like that come from? Why not kill yourself for entertainment, and have done? Worse yet, we had overheard *Mother* talking to someone on the phone about school supplies - a traitor in our very midst!

But there was no ignoring it. School was only two weeks away, and we were desperate to savor every moment of life remaining to us. Fear seeped noiselessly into the back of our minds, and we screamed inwardly, *No! Let us die young, Lord!* But we didn't talk about it directly - we weren't going to give that spectre any form in reality until we were dragged off in handcuffs.

The immediate problem was to find something we could do *now* to create a lasting emotional shield against the imminent predations. Lurking deep was an unformed hope that, if we did a good enough job of it, we might be caught in a time warp, and never have to return at all...

Greg thought of it. His face lit up and his words fell like a benison. "*I* know what - let's go on a hiking trip to find the source of the creek! We'll spend a week living off the land, and sleep under the stars. We can make it even better by not taking any food!"

The combination appealed strongly. Adventure! Privation! Purpose! We envisioned dramatic rocks, caves, trails, huge trees, and waterfalls, like the landscapes of early American painters. *This* was the <u>real</u> world! The sickly memory of the half-life of school was put to rout!

"That's right!" I returned, in deep relief. "It's been so warm, we won't need our tent, just sleeping bags. We can fish, eat berries, and forage corn from fields on the way." Whether foraging corn qualified as "survival" was a fine point of semantics we didn't care to examine. Our parents and others had done it since time began.

"Let's get our stuff!" Greg exclaimed.

We took a small rucksack, and borrowed Nick's Adirondack pack, which was more like a torture device than an article of service - I think I still have grooves in my back. We would take turns carrying that. I had a Bowie knife long enough to kill a grizzly, and Gregory his Buck hunting-knife, though it was always a little disappointing that there were no bears to challenge us. For hunting smaller game, we took our slings, though we were better at scaring things than hitting moving targets. Fishing line and hooks were tucked into the packs' pockets, since fish would be the mainstay of our diet. Poles could be cut on the spot.

In spite of our primitive intentions, we knew enough to eat lunch first. After all, the official rules didn't apply till we were actually on our way. And we took some food with us for that evening's meal, since we probably wouldn't have time to fish, forage, set up camp, *and* cook, after a long hike.

So we left around 1:00 PM, our heads filled with romantic notions of Daniel Boone, Altsheler's Henry Ware, and other frontier heroes, fugitives like us from the "Church of Perpetual Responsibility."

We had just finished reading Conrad Richter's <u>Light in the Wilderness</u>, with its descriptions of the primeval woods once covering the state of Ohio so thickly that you could walk four days without seeing a ray of sunlight. For us, too, trees figured largely, and we were sick to think of the waste of burning large tracts of virgin timber, back then. There were records of trees as large as 15 feet through – not just priceless timber, but living things, elusive, mysterious dryads, many of them a thousand years old. They were the beings of the Sacred Groves, and an irreplaceable loss to the spiritual world of nature.

Like Thoreau, we were acquainted with every notable tree for miles around. When a line of magnificent 200-year-old white oaks in perfect health were cut down on Grailville's property, near the crossing of power lines but not even in their way (!), we tried to commiserate with Prudence, Grailville's head farmer. But she shocked us by callously replying, "They were going to die, anyway."

This incited us to speculate, *Should people be cut down in <u>their</u> prime, since they're going to die, anyway?* Not a bad idea for *some* people we knew...

*   *   *

Our well-worn trail took us across the field, thick with weeds, small saplings and late summer flowers. Halfway across, we turned to look back at the house. It sat deep in shade beside the garden, which had been mulched with several different materials in patches of red, brown, and yellow. Lima-bean tents and sprawling butternut squash vines accented the design.

Greg reminded, "Come on – we need to get going!"

We started down the back slope of the field, where the yellow-topped cow parsley, with its thick, square stems, was just about finished, and goldenrod and ironweed were beginning to dot the meadow with their own yellow and purple. At the bottom of the field, the path led across a small ravine on a wooden footbridge Timmy had built of locust logs and Osage-orange branches. From there, we followed the wooded edge of Long Pond cliff, then threaded our way down to the water by a steep trail cut in the clay bank.

We were already boiling-hot when we reached Theodore's Pond, and decided to shed our gear and take a 5-minute swim in our clothes. It would keep us cool on the march.

Earlier, we had decided to take the tracks as far as we could in search of our goal. They seemed to follow the O'Bannon forever, and we weren't sure exactly where the branching-off would come. So, climbing out and loading up, we crossed the dry creek near the Indian Stone, embedded in the riffles with its stoic face-carving forever staring upward and reviewing all passers-by.

We were much younger when we first came across that Indian face among the willows, chiseled on the surface of a huge limestone block between Theodore's Pond and Cinder Slip. We were thunderstruck, sure we had found a genuine Indian shrine, though the date carved into it, 1938, confused us a little. We ran home in great excitement to tell our parents. But my father only said, "Oh, your uncle Tony carved that before he went into the Jesuits."

The 2,000-pound block had originally come from West Virginia, part of a shipment imported by the railroad to hold the bank where cinders from the track were rolling into the creek. They had given the pond its name, Cinder Slip. The flood of '38 had loosened several blocks and deposited them downstream, near the head of Theodore's Pond.

We were a little deflated at the commonality of the Indian's origin. Still, the carving was remarkable. It looked like the face on Indian-head nickels, only it faced full-front. We couldn't understand why no one had bothered to tell us. Imagine some kid, thousands of years from now, finding it even further downstream, and wondering, *Did the owner of the face carve it? If not, then who?*

Once across the creek, we scrambled up the embankment to the roadbed of the diesel giants. There were two ways you could travel the railroad: You could walk on the ties, or use the second, older roadbed alongside, whose tracks had been removed in the late '50s. Neither was very comfortable. The ties were irregular, unevenly spaced, and not level with each other, so you had to adjust your rhythm constantly. After a mile or so, it became irksome, and you'd have to switch to the roadbed. The problem there was that it was strewn with cinders, and just as rough in a different way. The best you could do was to alternate, for a change of pace.

Greg and I marched along at pretty fair speed, talking only when necessary and trying to put as many miles behind us as we could.

At Pickleville, an old gravel road ran along the creek for a while, and we left the tracks to follow it. The walking would be easier, and it would give us a change of scene. When we were eight or nine years old, the man who owned that road had mined the creek rocks for a couple of miles, to crush and sell the gravel. (It wasn't illegal then.) It had destroyed most of the natural pools above that point.

Some of his machinery had been left here and there, just standing. We passed one of the dead rock-crushers, rusted and silent.

Greg said, "Remember the noise those used to make?"

I recollected it vividly. "We couldn't even hear each other talk."

Gregory strode on ahead. He was taller than I was, and had thick, black hair, like my father's family. His build was angular, like Mother's, and his legs were long in proportion to his trunk, giving him a rangy gait.

Certain ironies and ridiculous situations in life would catch him unawares, and he would almost snort when he laughed. He didn't like humor that involved him too personally, though. When family members made him the butt of a joke, he was touchy, but more impartial when his friends did the ribbing.

Early on, Greg and I were inseparable, like the Katzenjammer Kids in the Sunday morning comics. We waited eagerly each week to see what new trick they had perpetrated on their frazzled, pessimistic German father. We were same age as the Kids, and frequently at odds with *our* pessimistic German father, who even used some of the same words, like *dummkopf* and *nincompoop*.

Positioned between Gregory and Nicholas, I played with them equally, as happenstance dictated. This meant that, with Nick, *I* was in charge, and with Greg, *he* was - a simple system, containing the rudiments of social order. When walking, it was politic to let Greg be ahead of me, at least slightly, even if we were walking in tandem. To do otherwise would say plainly, *"I have usurped your position, and for the nonce, you will play second fiddle to me!*" When I transgressed those natural bounds, the walk would shift into scrambling mode, marring our peace and shifting the ground from *Nature* to *human* nature. (Definitely not *nurture*)

Of course, when Nick tried to violate *my* natural authority, I put him in his place, too, but I think we were a little jollier about it... more like Little John and Robin Hood at the bridge, probably because Nick was easygoing and didn't get my back up. Greg and I, being both temperamental, fed each other's erroneous zones, since neither had a yielding nature.

I was more of a talker than Greg. That was okay with him, unless I was on a tear and had utterly worn out a subject, repeating myself like a broken record. Of course, when I *did* talk, I didn't require any response from the auditor of my discourse – I just held forth on whatever subject preoccupied me at the time. If the other person couldn't interject his conversation into the small interstices available, I assumed he didn't have anything to say. This, too, worked out well with Greg, who forced his way in whenever he wanted to speak. Sometimes this began with a well-timed sock on the arm.

One of the reasons we mostly got along was that he never shirked responsibility when there was work to be done, like cleaning out the garage, working in the garden, or picking berries. Otherwise, I wouldn't have considered him honorable. Some would argue, *Well, everyone's different. You can't expect people to do chores they detest.* But I wouldn't accept that. I knew the family was a communal effort, and these chores were central to survival... Personal work preferences had to be set aside on principle... except when it came to my doing dishes.

* * *

After passing the rock-crusher, we stopped on the road bluff, looking down on another branch of the creek that split off and returned to itself. Its small waterfall was barely running in this drought. Nearby were the ruins of some old stone houses, abandoned in the 1920s for reasons no one seemed to know. Their cisterns were still there, though, and we used to peek into them sometimes.

Another 15 minutes brought us to the end of the gravel road at a creek ford, the only way to the last house. We scrambled back up the embankment onto the tracks, which crossed the creek here on a bridge built without metal, just timber and concrete piers. You could see between the ties to the water far beneath.

Years before, when Greg was about eight, he and Timmy had been sitting on the concrete abutments down below when a train surprised them, crossing overhead. Startled, Greg had fallen into the water, and come home badly upset. Those old trestle bridges could be frightening places if you were caught there when a train came, even though they did have escape platforms, hanging way out into space. For a small kid, it was alarming just to walk across under the best of conditions, with those gaps in the ties under your feet. But we all learned to walk them at an early age.

Greg and I crossed easily on the unused side of the trestle. I remarked, "Remember when we picked blackberries with Bea in Cox's woods, and afterwards sat down on the tracks to rest?"

A train had come along *absolutely* silently. The engineer blew his horn when he was almost on top of us, and it was so loud, it blew us right off the tracks, spilling our berries.

"Then we picked them up again, after the train was gone, and ate them in the cobbler that night," Greg laughed.

"Well, we weren't going let anything come between us and cobbler!"

We hadn't known that a train makes hardly any noise at 55 mph on a downhill grade. The only sound is the wheels rolling smoothly on steel rails, with a soft whistling. After that, we knew what the whistling sound meant, and kept our ears open.

Wide-open spaces came into view. On our right, we could see across a floodplain to the last house, where a retarded man named Calvin Moore used to lead a backwoods life. Standing on a hill nearby, amidst mounds of soil and rock, was another defunct rock-crusher, looking rusted and forlorn, with devastation all about, as though a war had been waged.

Ahead, the track went on, smooth and almost level to the distant edge of sight, cutting straight through a 100-foot-high hill to blue lands beyond. On our left, the creek traveled in a big semicircle from the bridge behind to another ahead, cradling in its arm another fertile bottom for growing corn.

The wild cry of the killdeer pierced the air regularly. Small bands of them ran back and forth on the tracks ahead like sandpipers on some long-forgotten shore. There were also indigo buntings, who sat on the telegraph wires trilling their sweet song, flashing iridescent purple when they flew.

Soon we came to the next bridge, this one solid, and safer to walk across on the unused roadbed, but without railings of any kind. Sometimes we sat there to rest on the flat concrete girder, legs dangling over the side, looking up and down the creek. You had to be careful, since there were always loose cinders underfoot on the flat place where you wanted to sit. Even approaching it gingerly made your knees hurt – it was a nasty fall into the shallow water, thirty feet below.

Downstream, back toward the bend in the creek, there had once been an excellent swimming place called Bass Hole. Our parents swam there, but now there were no ponds more than waist deep above Pickleville, after the creek had been gutted. Bass Hole had been ten feet deep, with cold springs in the bottom, and you could swing off the bank into the water from a rope in a tree. We knew how wonderful a deep pond like that could be – there was one further down the creek called High Banks, not far from where we lived. It was like swimming in an Olympic-sized pool – wonderfully fresh.

Upstream, there were remains of an old Civil War bridge, with slender towers. The piers were made of stone blocks, put together by masons long-dead, and still bore witness to the skill of their founders. To us, they always seemed like portals to another time, and we often played there, or followed the old cut through a small wood to ruins of still another old bridge.

Just beyond the Civil War bridge were knee-high falls, running most of the year, and a high cliff on the right that marched beside the stream for another eighth-mile.

Greg and I looked for a moment, but we were smothering from the heat, so we shed our gear again by the side of the tracks and scrambled down the stair-stepped concrete abutments to the water below. The pond under the bridge was in the shade, and blessedly cool. We didn't stay more than a few minutes, because it was now around 3:00 PM, and we had to find a campsite soon, so we could be all settled in by nightfall. Tomorrow we would hike on, refreshed.

Climbing back up the giant stair to the top, we switched packs, loaded up, and moved on. After crossing the bridge, we decided to go by the old railroad cut, and find a place to camp along the creek nearby. Midway along the cut, we turned and headed down toward the creek through the gently sloping woods. Last fall, we'd spent a night there in a lean-to of dead wood, bark and leaves. Arriving about dark, I had cut red cedar boughs for our mattresses, while Greg made the lean-to.

"I still remember smelling that cedar all night," Greg said now. "Every time you turned over, you'd get a strong whiff."

"Me, too. But it sure got *cold*, even with the fire in front. We could use some of that chill now... Hey, let's go and see if it's still there!"

We broke course, and traveled a couple of hundred yards to our left, further upstream.

The bones were there, but part of the roof had fallen in. After touching base with it, we resumed our course, and when we came to the end of the next pond downstream, crossed easily without wetting our feet.

Just as evening approached, we found the perfect place to camp on the far bank: a formation of large, flat rocks about eight feet above water level. We eyed the small pond we'd just passed, deciding there should be fish there, and immediately laid out our gear and sleeping bags, built a small fire, and cooked our supper.

Sam whined piteously when he realized it was going to be a survival trip. Where was *his* food? After dinner, he disappeared for about an hour. We assumed he had gotten into the spirit of things and gone hunting, but, when he came back, there was a smell of dog food on his breath! Greg and I looked at each other. Sam *couldn't* have run all the way home, eaten, and then returned, could he?

When the sun went down, it was a pleasant evening with no bugs, though much warmer than we liked. Smoke and flames rose straight up, signaling more hot weather to come. Sitting on our sleeping bags in the dusk, we looked up and saw a brilliant white contrail, with the silver flash of a jet leading it across the sky. The fire sank to embers with the day, and wood pewees called to each other plaintively. One would pipe out mournfully, "*Pee-u-u-WEE,*" and another would answer, "*PEE-doo...*"

This was probably the most remote spot on the creek. The only sounds we heard from outside the woods were the occasional train, a lone dog barking, and the drone of a plane overhead. As darkness fell, a bullfrog boomed out its guttural song, and katydids began their eternal argument. Soon they were so loud that individual voices were indistinguishable – just one overwhelming sound, like a thousand steel brushes scraping on cymbals.

We turned in. Our beds weren't comfortable, but that didn't surprise us. We had no pillows, except for our rolled-up clothing, and there was no such thing as an ensolite pad yet, only air mattresses, which we would have been ashamed to carry. Oh, well, this was supposed to be survival, so we weren't going to complain. We would try instead to enjoy Thoreau's "hard plank of famine."

So we slept badly, restlessly waking every couple of hours. When we woke around 3:00 AM, everything was uncannily quiet. A small moon rayed faintly, and an owl quavered mysteriously. If we'd slept better, we would have missed that moment, with no pressed leaf to mark our book many years later.

The next morning, we realized that this was *it*. The only food we had left was salt and margarine for frying fish. Survival was upon us, so we got busy cutting fishing poles and getting bait.

First snag. There were plenty of grasshoppers, so we tried them for bait. The fish wouldn't touch them. They just looked at us, from their bed of clear water, as if to say, *Is that the best you can do?* I recognized the attitude. They were reacting the same way a gardener does to a plate of boiled zucchini, when there are bushels of it in the patch.

Next, we tried black crickets. That worked a little better. We actually caught a scrawny bluegill, so stunted that we would normally have thrown it back. But *one bluegill* was pathetic. Man, we were going to have to do better than that!

So we went in search of fishing worms. They were awfully scarce, but we were experienced enough to scrounge some successfully. They looked like they were starving, too – very small, and so thin you could almost see through them. It was particularly frustrating because we knew there was a very healthy supply of worms in our leaf pile at home. But never mind – we just used what we had, and got them somehow on the hook.

By 11:00 we had managed to catch, clean, and eat four small bluegills, cooked in the cast iron skillet over the fire. They were bony and fishy, but the margarine and salt (and frying) helped. Well, we thought (glossing over the skipped breakfast), *right on time for lunch!*

By 1:00, our stomachs were seriously cogitating again, and finding the source of the creek had slipped our minds. The need for food had rudely shoved aside adventure.

Well, standing in the hot sun all day, fishing, didn't appeal much, so we left our poles to tend themselves, checking on them every hour. By 3:00, the "catch of the day" added up to two ornery crawdads, one sunfish so pathetic that we *did* throw it back, and a horrendous snag caused by a resident turtle, who humbly took what we had to offer and wedged himself under a huge rock to dine.

Greg saved the day. "I'm going to climb that hill, and try to find a cornfield. You stay here, Paul, and get the fire ready."

Twenty minutes later, he was back with a huge armful of cow corn!

"There was a field right at the top of the hill. The coons did so much damage on this side that the farmer won't miss this."

I concurred heartily.

Cow corn is not very tender, unless it's picked young. It also helps if you have butter and salt. The best corn I've ever eaten was cooked by an Indian method that doesn't need plates or utensils, and that was how we were going to fix ours.

First we put the corn in the creek, husk and all, and let it soak 5 minutes, so the water would fully penetrate. Then we buried the ears in the ashes of the fire. I counted off five minutes in my head, using the time-honored method: ONE-one thousand, TWO-one thousand... Then all we had to do was carefully peel back the husks, add butter and salt, and eat. All the flavor was sealed in, and it was smoked. A real gourmet treat!

We stuffed ourselves. Sitting around the fire talking, that evening, we started to feel on top of things. Our faith was just about restored. Maybe things were going to turn around, and we would be able to finish the quest, after all.

Sam annoyed us, though, by smelling of dog food again. His attitude seemed to be, "Never volunteer for survival... let it find you!"

Peeved, Greg looked him in the eye. "You think you're fooling us, mutt, but I know where you've been!"

Sam only snorted in a self-satisfied way, as if to say, *So what!*

By the time we went to bed, though, there was something wrong with our stomachs again. There was a sort of rolling and groaning. Oh, well, tomorrow was another day. We would get used to the corn, especially when the fishing improved.

After another restive night, we felt a little weary and stretched-thin. On rising, we washed up in the creek, and began eating cold, leftover corn for breakfast. Yummy! Then we set to work again. The fishing continued bad... A crowd of hopeful minnows watched beneath our feet, but no fish of any size cared much to be caught and eaten.

When 11:00 came around, we were restless and hot. It was an exact repeat of yesterday, except that now we had no margarine, thanks to Sam's nocturnal rummaging. And then there was the endless clear weather, and still NO FOOD!

Greg and I sat there staring and sweating, after a pitiful lunch of emaciated bluegills and leftover corn.

I said, "You know, corn must not be that filling... if it was, my stomach wouldn't feel this way."

"I know what you mean," Gregory said seriously.

"Is it my imagination, or is this rock getting hotter each day?"

"It's called a solar collector," he told me absently.

"Then why did we camp on it?" I was starting to get irritable.

"I guess it seemed made-to-order at the time..."

"Yeah, for frying eggs!" I retorted testily. Then...

"EGGS!" we both exclaimed, jerked to attention.

"We're going to starve!" Greg said wildly.

"I'm not! Let's go home!" I entreated.

Greg didn't actually say he agreed, but started packing so fast it didn't matter.

We made that journey home in one forced march – no sightseeing, no swimming and little talk. When I spotted an American bittern, Greg, usually a compulsive naturalist, only said, "I wonder if it tastes like chicken."

I answered tersely that it probably tasted more like fish, since that's what they ate. After the bluegills, fishy bird didn't tempt us.

As we came across that last field, our yellow house with its white porch pillars had never looked better. Maybe coming back wasn't so bad after all. For one thing, there was going to be FOOD! Greg and I dumped our gear in the garage, and ran for the kitchen.

Though we were pulled and ragged around the edges, the inevitable seemed less threatening now. I could tell that Greg was beginning to look forward to his artwork and the French class he would be taking. I wasn't *that* far lost, but food would help a lot.

I'm glad we didn't find the source of the O'Bannon, anyway. It turned out that its headwaters were only half an hour away by car – field drainage ditches in flat, treeless farm country.

Greg still thinks we were way up the creek on that trip. I won't tell him otherwise. (In our minds we were considerably farther out than either of us thought.) At least he still has his dream.

* * *

Our appetites for wild places and wild things were insatiable, but many attempts to immerse ourselves met with doubtful success, though we couldn't admit that. It was too much a part of our identities.

Nick and I tried to escape into a woodlore fantasy one fall weekend in 1963. There was still plenty of wonderful weather left, but we already needed major purification. School always obtruded into that most glorious time of year, and the proverbial question dogged us: Why was darnel always mixed with the harvest? We tried vigorously to winnow it out.

School was for the closet, like raincoats, used only under duress. Our teachers constantly told us it was *an-opportunity-for-self-development-and-a-route-to-higher-education-and-ultimately-the-gateway-to-the-world*. But even if true, this left us holding the bag, because Greg and I never wanted to become a part of their normal world. Our lives should be distinctive and separate, like the saints and Thoreau, and we didn't see how that could be done in conventional society. So, on top of keeping us away from home and out of the woods, school made us uneasy, since we were being forced to work toward dubious goals. Ultimately, we had no choice, and decided to endure it, like a boil, falling back on religious mysticism. Maybe the suffering could at least be used as spiritual credit later, when we passed beyond all mortal care. But the paradox remained: how does one integrate scourge and opportunity, and swallow it without indigestion?

Superficially, it sometimes appeared that Peter agreed, but his motives were always hard to fathom. Nick went along with Greg and me most of the time – I guess he wasn't sure about the feel of Peter's brand.

One Saturday found Nick and me upstairs, restlessly looking through outdoor catalogues and dreaming about sundry articles of the faith – dreaming, since we didn't have any money. Guns, knives, bows and arrows, duck calls (we had no ducks, but they *might* show up) and sleeping bags all called us with their siren-song. But what really got our attention was an aluminum canoe in a catalogue called "Gander Mountain."

This woodsy nautical vessel seemed more wonderful than anything, just then. It awakened a desire for possession so fierce that we might have sold our souls for it, if Daniel Webster's scaly opponent had shown up just then with $350.00. This was out of character, since we were usually pretty restrained when it came to wanting material things. Our religion constantly urged us to follow Christ, and we really tried, though sometimes this produced results that chagrined the people who taught us in the first place. If religion weren't enough, our personal Code reminded us that *Indians need few possessions!* But that argument was weak, since Indians obviously *had* canoes! This struck us as a <u>sign</u>, a mandate that we, too, should have one, even though it conflicted marginally with the ascetic Christian vow of poverty. But the deviation was minimal, since the Indians were stoics, and shared some of the same vital qualities as Christians, being very much into pain, self-sacrifice and self-denial, though rooted in far different metaphysical thrones.

So we sat there on Timmy's old bed, talking about canoeing down the O'Bannon to the Little Miami. We imagined ourselves early explorers (or at least *late* explorers), the prow of our canoe gently parting leaf-strewn water in the crisp fall air...

But the devil didn't proffer any bargains, and we still needed the money.

So I said to Nick, "Do you have anything saved?"

"I dunno," Nick answered noncommittally. "Let's make a list... maybe we'll figure something out..." (Definitely a *No*.)

We went over our standard money sources. There was fireworks-making. Our father contracted with the local fireworks company, and subcontracted frames to us, but it was the wrong season.

Then there was working for our uncles. Both Uncle Pete and Uncle Marshall paid good wages, but how could we beguile them into needing our services long enough to acquire the holy relic? Besides, we had already mowed lawns and dug ditches during the summer, and spent the remuneration. There seemed no way of predicting their mysterious future needs – too bad we couldn't turn them on and off like a tap. And even if they did need labor, what was to prevent them from asking Greg, or one of their own neighbor boys? And Gregory didn't want a canoe just then. It was *our* project.

Our minds spun futilely, sifting the rest of the list.

There was selling berries, but it was the wrong season again. (Besides, I knew from experience just how many berries it took to mount up, at 50 cents a quart. I had slowly saved $28 to buy a bike over a year and a half, during the summers following 6th and 7th grades.)

We thought of collecting pop bottles, but that was grasping at straws, like dogs that worry old bones, and can't understand why there's nothing left in them when they can still smell beef.

Nick and I looked bleakly at each other. How could we get that canoe, short of thievery?

But Nicholas thought of a way out. "Hey, I saw some Indian canoes in a craft book at the library. It showed pretty clearly how the Indians made them."

"Of course! We can make our own canoe *and* paddles, just like they did!"

The solution was so obvious! I had seen those books, too – why didn't we think of it before? It felt right. No money would be involved – we would avoid the taint of commerce, and it would be consonant with our principles. The Indian spirits would smile on us in approbation, *and* it would cause us to work our fingers to the bone for many satisfying, grueling hours. We stretched back and relaxed. Both the process and the goal were going to be worthy. One canoe, coming up! It didn't penetrate that this was a longer-range project – we weren't going to get it *now*...

We were ready to stride forward together, shoulder to shoulder. Nick was always game for adventures like this. (And so was Greg. But not Peter... perhaps he instinctively felt he'd suffered enough.) All that remained was to choose the right materials and methods, using the woodcraft books as a guide.

We eagerly walked many miles that day, searching our favorite haunts for the necessary trees, and discussing tools and methods. There were no birch trees – the only ones we knew about struggled to grow in people's yards. Uncle Pete had one... *No.* We didn't think he would appreciate finding, one morning, that the bark had been stripped off. This evoked a clear picture of him standing there, eyeing the scalped tree, swearing, "Goddammit! For crying out loud!" More than that, we would have to de-bark all the ornamental birch trees in town.

I had an idea. "You know, there's plenty of dead bark on some of those huge elm trees that were killed by Dutch elm disease."

"Hey, that might work!" Nick agreed eagerly.

We found a large dead tree in an isolated pasture, and started to work off the bark with the prescribed pointed sticks. Hmmm... it didn't seem to want to behave. We got some pieces that were roughly 1' x 2', but noticed that there were holes in them, where beetles had made inroads.

"We could patch it with tar," Nick said.

"Pine pitch," I corrected, automatically. (I would never think of buying tar.) But pine trees for sap were almost as rare as birch. And Grailville probably wouldn't have been pleased if we made hack-marks on all the conifers in their tiny white-pine stand.

Nick made a noncommittal sound, which meant that he was beginning to waver about getting *that* elemental, anyway.

Then I accidentally dropped a piece of the bark, and it broke in half.

"It seems awfully brittle," I said. "I don't think it would hold together very long. Maybe the Indians used *green* bark." (*They did.*)

"Maybe so."

Problems were starting to crop up and sting us like sweat-bees. Why was it that, when you started a project, you saw many hopeful ways to accomplish it, but when you actually tried to MAKE the donuts, all you got was holes? All right, maybe we *could* use dead elm bark if we were careful with it, and tarred each piece before using it – but wouldn't it be too fragile if any object in the water hit it?

The next obstacle concerned the reality of felling a large elm tree. They were too big to shinny up (not to mention using tools up there). And whose tree? There weren't any on *our* property. Grailville had some, but we had to avoid being seen. So *when* could we tackle it? At night? Impractical, now that school was in session. (Though it did have its Huck Finn attraction)

How would we do it? Not with an axe – it's noisy, and dead elm is virtually impossible to cut. We didn't have a two-man saw large enough (or sharp enough) for its girth. Uncle Marshall had a chainsaw, but we knew how that would go: "*Uncle Marshall, will you help us cut down a tree on Grailville's property tomorrow night?*" Most of all, we didn't want to be found in the act – "*What are you boys doing, cutting down that tree!?*"

OK, we weren't going to have a bark canoe. But there was still a dugout! This had its own appeal, since it, too, required Indian tools and methods: fire and a tomahawk or stone adz. You selected a large tree and built a carefully controlled fire around its base, using the adz to chip off the resultant charcoal until the tree was gnawed through, and came down. Once it was on the ground, you hollowed it out by the same method.

But this brought us back to the original problems: where to get the tree, and when to burn it down. Dead elm wasn't a good candidate for this, and there were few other dead trees of easy workability and girth. We would never have the heart to sacrifice a living tree that size. In addition, we had to admit that it would take days to burn down a tree, and if it were "bootleg," even our slow County Sheriff would be on to us, after we'd been sending him smoke signals for a week.

We felt a little ill-used. All we wanted was to have fun in a canoe, but were being forced toward the criminal fringe. Our morale was beginning to sink, but I came boring back in. "Don't worry – we'll get that canoe yet! I know – why don't we make some paddles first, then we'll be ready for the canoe!"

It was late Saturday afternoon. Most of the day was shot, and now we had to make new plans. Rats!

By the time school was over on the following Friday, our optimism had renewed itself, and we set off running with axe and saw for Grailville, where a small white-pine grove offered many candidates for our paddles. It didn't trouble us that it wasn't technically ours – weren't we the monarchs of all we surveyed, like Thoreau? But we proceeded stealthily, not wanting to contest with those who thought *they* owned it.

The strictest interpretation of The Code required felling the tree with an axe. No saws were allowed – that would let in the beginnings of corruption! *And* we had to run to and from the site through the woods and fields – the use of roads was prohibited, regardless of weather, equipment we might be carrying, or the log itself... (We didn't acknowledge roads, anyway, unless they were streams, logging roads, or possibly the railroad.)

We managed to get the tree down, utilizing more energy than skill, although it tried to hang up in its brethren. Then branches had to be trimmed, and the correct length sawed from the trunk. (It was permitted to use a saw for cutting-to-length.)

Now we were cooking! The tree was down, and we had used the right methods to propitiate the gods. We were feeling masterful and ready to run with Daniel Boone or the Indians. All we had to do now was pick it up and take it home. We hid our tools in some brush for later retrieval.

I bent down to lift one end of the log, and... it *wouldn't budge!* But we were strong, and pine was one of the lightest woods, right? That's why we'd selected it for paddles. But this log was heavier than any piece of wood we'd ever lifted.

We hadn't read the fine print in the woodcraft manuals. DRY pine is light, but anyone who knows wood will tell you that *green* pine is heavier than oak.

Tough! lashed the Code. *You don't have a choice. You will lift it, and you will carry it!*

So, using all our strength, we managed to raise the log to a vertical, balanced position, and then, after pumping our breath, eased it onto our shoulders. It didn't seem too bad. But we hadn't taken many steps before realizing we were carrying a *cross*, and a heavy one.

Too late! You're committed now! The Code boomed out. *Carry your cross, Sinners!* (Never mind that it was a *stolen* cross...)

Down the slope we plodded, toward the road that had to be crossed, waiting hidden for traffic to pass. We didn't want to be seen so close to the place we had "secured" our timber. Then we staggered across the road, and gained the overgrown wooded corridor on the other side that was our private avenue of escape.

By then, both of us were enduring difficulties. But would we embarrass each other and dishonor our gods by dropping the log? Certainly not – we might not be able to pick it up again! The shame would be unbearable. We silently repeated our mantra: *I won't be the one to drop it!* – and then, imposing further discipline, *Quiet that breathing, dog! You should be able to RUN with this!* It was about then that we noticed how sticky pines are, and how many branch stubs they have that were beginning to gouge into our shoulders. *PAIN!*

Passing by the Bailey property, we tried to run, but wavered and – may the gods forgive us! – *dropped the log.* We picked it up again hastily – maybe nothing had seen it fall...?

Sweating profusely, with insects starting to trail us and sticky resin beginning to glue our clothing to our bodies, we should have quit, but a deep need for punishment flogged us on.

Down the leafy tunnel that ran along the fence line we persisted. Through the fence, we could see the newly built Bailey house and its yard, but only someone standing in the yard close-by, looking our way, could see us. Unfortunately, that was exactly the case. The Bailey boy, nine or ten years old, saw us running with the log, and called out, "Whatcha doin?"

Oh, no – not him! He had a reputation as a plaguey nuisance, so we just grunted noncommittally, and moved away with all speed. He opened his mouth again, but by then we were out of range.

The tunnel ended after 100 yards at the gate to Kanes' field, and we stood the log on end, one balancing it while the other opened the gate. Both of us were pretty beat, but neither would admit it.

I said, "You want to rest awhile?"

"No," said Nick.

"Me, neither." (Liar, liar, pants on fire!) This meant, *This is as nothing to me.* This little bit of psychology was to make the other person wonder, *What kind of iron is HE made of?*

So we shouldered our cross again, weaving a bit, and were off. Our route followed the fence line through the most secluded part of the pasture, half grown-up in red cedars. We felt like Indians, furtively sneaking off with goods purloined from another tribe. *Watch out! Careful! Don't go that way!* The fantasizing renewed our strength and resolve.

The shadows were getting longer. So much the better, for going unseen! After a short way, the field ended in a fence under huge walnut trees. We dropped the log over the fence, climbed over ourselves, and retrieved the disgusting article again. In a moment of weakness, I almost chucked it wildly into the nearby ravine.

Now we were travelling through a valley of wild rose bushes on Grailville's property. *Rosa Multiflora* had almost taken over by the mid-sixties, and it was hard to pass. But we knew the route, and worked our way along the side, past the big beech, moving toward the "Robin Hood Oak," a stocky white oak, hoary with age and inviting to sit under. Lightning had knocked out its top years ago, but its girth of 26 feet made it a landmark, a member of the Sacred Groves. There, we turned right and crossed the low point of the wash without incident, both of us holding firm, too stupid to quit. It wasn't just a log – our honor was at stake!

The last fence abutting our property looked like the Promised Land! We were soaked with sweat, hungry, itching, badly bruised, and bitten by flies, but we arrived home triumphantly. The project was thriving.

We put the log in Grandpa's old toolshed, and Nick went inside. But I felt so inspired at our victory over the flesh that I hacked at it mercilessly with an axe before going in to dinner.

We left it there to season, but it didn't dry properly, and had so many checks that it wasn't usable. Maybe there was something about seasoning we didn't know... Two months later, it looked pitiful, with mold growing on it. And still no canoe!

That was the project's deathblow. Could it be the wages of sin? Or was it because we had dropped the log, betraying our Code?

Chapter XII.

Home on the Range

In the 1880s, when our house was built, door-trim was made better. It never fell off, and only creaked a little after many years of abuse. Using the doorframe for exercise was a habit of long standing with Nick, Gregory and me, and even Peter joined up, much later. The ledge at the top was only ¾" deep, and made chin-ups and leg-lifts tortuous, but all the better! No one complained – we just suffered in silence.

This particular morning, I had just eaten breakfast, and was hanging around the kitchen (literally), awaiting developments, or planning to cause them if none appeared. One exercise was swinging on the doorframe by my fingertips; another was jumping up and touching the nine-foot ceiling. The audience at the kitchen table was captive, able to witness (but hopefully not duplicate) any new records set. But what really mattered was to devote any spare moments to keeping in shape.

One of my objectives was to ferret out anyone who had lapsed from the "get tough, be tough, stay tough" religion, and I was beginning to have some trouble with Greg. He had arrived at that tricky age where he sometimes criticized my displays as immature, when he wasn't engaged in them himself.

Before breakfast, I had discovered that my fanatically grown patch of black raspberries was loaded with ripe fruit. They needed picking and freezing *now*, and we had to have black raspberry pie! I hoped to enlist help, to get the work done in a reasonable amount of time. Nick and Greg could be counted on, but Peter wouldn't do much, unless perpetually flogged.

Well, Mother would bake the pies, but wasn't going to make Peter work. (Maybe we'd worn her out on discipline by the time she came to him.) I had fumed and wrestled to make Peter help out so many times during my high school years—just to share equally in ordinary chores like cleaning out the garage, picking berries, mowing the lawn, scrubbing and waxing the kitchen floor, or cleaning the bathroom. But it was like trying to use a piece of cooked spaghetti as a threshing-stick, or molding water into a leverage tool. The Industrial Revolution proved it *could* be done, but it's too big a project to be practical at home, so I settled for revenge.

There was something about Peter that stimulated my imagination – the possibilities included whippings and fasting, or at least an upset stomach for undeserved, un-worked-for dinners and living provided. It was the reason I sometimes set him up for my own misdeeds. (You know how it is – technically, you know it's wrong, but in your heart, you also know he really deserves it. *Yes! Yes!* You exult to yourself as the switch goes up and down...)

But never mind, I told myself – *this time* he would do his part, or suffer the consequences!

I watched Nick eating breakfast. Good old Nick! – helpful and sturdy, even though he did seem almost middle-aged to me. Whenever I saw people going about their business quietly, just being good, I thought they needed stirring up, or at least poking a little. Why, they were almost *dead!*

But Nick was always there as a good companion, or ready to lend a helping hand, inside or out. He did what he was asked, without making a nuisance of himself, while I couldn't accept the commonplace, and made heavy work over small household tasks like the dishes. Or if I did agree to help, it was hard to pull me away from the task when it was time to quit: after doing the dishes, I would then proceed to clean the stove, the refrigerator, the floor, etc. Hard to start, hard to stop.

My attention was riveted by Peter at the table, idly adding spoonful after spoonful of sugar to his bowl of cereal, without stirring it up. Then he tasted it, and started to add more. I couldn't let that go. "Look at that! You always waste sugar! You're going to end up with a lot of extra sugar in the bottom of that bowl, if you don't stir it!"

Peter returned a weak, noncommittal smile, and continued what he was doing.

This drove me to action. "Mix it up, dummy! *You have to mix it up!*" I forcibly grabbed his hand. "Stir! Stir! Like this! Then you won't have to put so much in!"

But Peter didn't listen and wouldn't stir, and I almost smacked him on the back of the head. My mother said nothing... She was busy making some preparations for the next meal of the day. Part of my vehemence was to induce her intervention, but it didn't work.

Now my father entered the kitchen, looking disheveled and out-of-sorts, as usual before breakfast. *Food! Food! I want food!* His demeanor cried out.

Unfortunately, he arrived just as Peter had finished his cereal, and exploded when he saw the mound of sugar in the bottom of the bowl. (*Thank you, God!*) Generically addressing those present, my father spewed bitter accusations: "Look at that waste! I don't know why I bother to work... You stupid kids waste food. I might as well throw my money away!"

I tried to refocus attention on the offender by pointing out that the bowl belonged singly to Peter, but, for some reason, this didn't do the trick, nor did it assuage my father's temper. While my mother prepared his breakfast, he continued to expound on the various shortcomings of the household in general: his hammer was missing, and someone had ruined a paintbrush. (He had usually misplaced them himself, but always thought it was the kids. Sometimes it was true...) He still referred to us as "kids," even though all of us (except Peter) were in high school, and taller than our father.

Mother was still silent, not wishing to begin the day with futile wrangling.

Nicholas, meanwhile, had decamped, having nothing to contribute (by desire or nature) to the kitchen scene, and was now at the piano in the living room, doodling away at some assignment of Mother's. My ears were offended, and it didn't take me long to say so. "What a dumb exercise! Boring pieces like that would force a music-lover to quit!"

Mother had nothing to say, since she had assigned it, but I intended to put a flea in Nicky's ear privately. It might help him, especially if he planned a musical career.

My father was calming down. Sugar had entered the bloodstream, and would presently reach the brain. All would be well if he didn't see something in the paper to set him off again. But we were not so fortunate. He began to rustle his paper angrily, and started to animadvert through clenched teeth about "crooked GOPs," bankers, and Rockefeller, some of his favorite targets. After a minute or two, he wound down.

Enter my brother Gregory. By special arrangement, a famous sports commentator is here to tell the story.

"Hello, folks! This is Howard Martell, live with today's breakfast-cast! We're expecting a really good show today... and I see that Greg is already on the field, warming up. I've got to say, he sure looks hungry! Now he's moving toward the starting line, and I think he's getting ready to launch his breakfast – Yes! He's getting into the stove drawer, and making quite a din with those pots and pans, folks! I see that the dog Sam is playing goalie under the kitchen table. We know he's one of those calm players, but he's beginning to get nervous now that the star player is in position. Greg makes his choice, slams the cast-iron skillet on the stove, grabs the eggs and margarine, and starts breaking them into the skillet. Boy, those eggs are being fried at a furious rate!

"Everything's pretty quiet on the field – he has a clear shot. It won't be long now before those eggs are done, folks! Hey, they're ready! He grabs a plate in his left hand, a turner in his right! He's dividing them up! He chases them around the skillet with a turner! Uh-oh! One is escaping over the side of the skillet! He counters with his turner! He misses! He abandons the turner! The egg continues its slide down the stove-front, but he's close on it, trying to scoop it with his plate! He's almost got it! Now he's on his knees! He makes one – last – lunge – and scoops the egg onto the plate! He's got it, folks! Wow, what a play! But wait – there's too much momentum – he's STILL GOING, under the table, on all-fours! And the eggs are served up right under the goalie's nose! That dog is looking hard at the plate. Was there a foul? No – but I'll bet Sam's never seen service like that!

"You heard it here first, ladies and gentlemen! This is Howard Martell, signing off!"

At this finely tuned moment, Ruth Moore, a local schoolteacher and friend of Mother's, arrived to witness what appeared to be the last act of a three-ring circus: Greg on all fours proffering a plate of eggs to the dog.

Ruth remarked acerbically, "We wouldn't feed good food like that to our dogs at home, I can tell you!"

After Greg gobbled his breakfast, I asked all my brothers for help in picking the black raspberries, and everyone agreed (even Peter!) I knew he'd make a feint at it, if only to get some work-credit in a bankrupt bank (a veritable politician's move – he would think it wasn't whether you *worked* or not, but whether the right people [parents] *thought* you'd worked.)

Soon we were all in the berry patch, where a cool breeze played through the thin shade of locust trees. We all knew the rules of picking: begin at one end, and go through systematically to the other, making sure that every bush is picked clean before moving on. The berries were huge, and the bushes were loaded! We were picking as fast as we could with both hands, the buckets strapped to our belts. (Well... not Peter's. He couldn't bear the idea of doubling the work by using both hands.)

Silence prevailed for five minutes or so, except for my ongoing commentary on the berries. "Wow! Look at these berries!"

Every time I said it, Greg grew more annoyed, but I didn't notice. In my own private forge-ahead world, little attention was paid to other people's expressions.

Pretty soon, though, I saw Peter in the center of the patch, lazily picking a bush. "Hey, get back here, egghead!" I yelled.

This appellation was not a compliment to Peter's brainpower, but an expression reaching back to our cribs. Our oldest brother, Timmy, had derisively dubbed us all eggheads at some point, starting with Gregory, to make sure we knew our places. This brotherly endearment was usually accompanied by a dope slap and a sound like a spring unwinding, made by the perpetrator: "D-o-i-n-g-erl-erl-erl!"

My mother recently confided that, one day, Timmy had spied Peter, Nicky, and me walking out our lane, and been moved to say lugubriously, in a rare moment of brotherly affection, "There goes a head, an egg, and a pig." Mother didn't inquire further – she was a little surprised at this effusiveness.

In continuing to use the term *egghead*, we were just keeping the tradition alive, and, uh... "doing to others what had been done to us." Peter being the youngest, we felt that he represented the shallow end of the gene-pool, and had a lot to answer for. Years earlier, Greg and I had made a discovery: from aloft in a tree, we couldn't see Peter's body while looking straight down at him, but only a head with two feet sticking out.

"Wow! Look at the size of that head!" Greg had marveled, his voice tinged with awe and pride. For some reason (and to our delight), nature had authorized the growth of his head beyond that of his body. If that weren't enough, he had another peculiarity: his hair grew at an indecent rate, which, of course, only increased the head's apparent size.

With rare rapport, we proclaimed Peter "Head" on the spot.

Peter's head always figured in events. When he was five, he had crowned himself "King Peter" with a conical kitchen ricer, and it got stuck. My mother first tried putting butter on his head, to slip the ricer off, but every time she pulled, Peter was lifted off the ground.

My father was at work, so we called Uncle Lou, who lived next door at the time, and he brought his hacksaw. Being a barber, when he first saw Peter's predicament, he remarked regretfully that it was too bad he couldn't shave his head first – the crown would be easier to get off.

Peter saw the hacksaw coming, and started screaming in earnest. I think he was afraid they were going to try to save the ricer at his expense. He bolted, but the escaped monarch was brought to earth on the front porch, and forcibly (but painlessly) divested of his crown, after a nerve-wracking 20 minutes or so of screaming.

This sort of thing seemed only natural, for him. Another time, he got an aspirin bottle stuck on his finger (it wouldn't fit on his head), and we prevailed on Uncle Lou again...

* * *

Back in the berry patch, I shouted, "Hey, get back here, egghead! You don't start in the center of the patch! If we all wandered around like you, we'd miss half the berries. If you can't do something right, it's better not to do it at all!" Peter looked hopeful at this, and I instantly recognized my mistake. "Forget it! You're not going anywhere! Just do it RIGHT!"

Then I spotted several bushes Peter had picked before me. "Look at that! Do you call that picking? You idiot! You only picked them off the top! Just to show you how many berries you missed, I'm going to pick them again."

Five minutes later, I showed him the full bucket I had picked after him. He didn't seem impressed, and I considered making some tattoos on him where they wouldn't be seen. The three of us managed to herd him back to the berry-picking line. Five more minutes went by. I looked around, and he was gone!

"Where's Peter?" I asked Nick.

"He mumbled something about going to the bathroom."

I set my mental clock for two minutes, in expectation of his return. Normally, I would really have been enjoying myself by now in this natural heaven, but a sinner was jogging my aesthetic elbow continually, and I was getting irritated, just like the Lord.

"I'll be back," I told Gregory grimly. "I'm going weasel-hunting!" Greg only grinned.

Peter was nowhere in the vicinity of the bathroom. *Well, he's not in the house,* I thought, *so let's check around outside.* Not there, either, at least not in any of the obvious places. Then I heard strange noises coming from the basement, and crept down the outside steps. What did I see? A *weasel* with a contorted face, holding a contraband transistor radio near his ear. Worse yet, he was listening to WSAI, a local pop station!

I was too outraged to be ashamed of him. In our family, this was betrayal. You didn't smoke, drink, or swear. You ate only organic food (in theory, if not always in practice), and listened only to the finest classical music. (Well, my two sisters broke all of these rules, but they didn't count.)

I exploded at him. "I can't *believe* you are listening to that trash! You're not only a lousy worker, but you don't keep your word!"

Peter's vague, ingrown smile demurred, *Oh, but I didn't give my word, Your Honor...*

"Furthermore," I continued, ignoring that, "let me tell you, if you listen to music like that, you'll go straight to hell! It will corrupt the mind by tickling the ears, and then you'll be on the Devil's choice list. No one thinks the fires of hell are real, but we *all* die!"

Peter read my purpose, and fled upstairs, where he tried to hide behind Mother's skirts. I reported his crimes in detail, and appealed to her to enact the parental laws as old as time. Something had to be done.

But she made it clear that nothing was going to be done. *She* hadn't assigned the berry-picking. Deeply perturbed, I left, but gradually consoled myself with the cheering thought: *One serving of revenge coming up for the weasel!*

All this had taken only 15 minutes from my berry-picking, so I returned to the patch, and we picked 50 quarts of the finest black raspberries I've ever seen.

Now it was lunchtime, just the opportunity I needed. I offered to fix it (which was suspicious, in itself, since I didn't volunteer for domestic jobs). First I made several cans of tomato soup, then some chicken sandwiches, and liberally topped them both off with black pepper. Our Petrov was a finicky eater. Everyone else would eat the food, but Petrov would push his away, after a spoonful or two, whereupon I would eat his portion. It worked just as I planned. *But oh, what a paltry revenge, I thought. Not nearly good enough.*

When lunch was over, I generously made chocolate milkshakes, using extra chocolate, vanilla ice cream, and maraschino cherry juice. Finally, I blended a generous dose of "ExLax," and added it to the unregenerate varmint's drink.

After lunch, I froze all the black raspberries, saving out plenty for pies. Peter spent his afternoon in a small room that used to be the pantry in Grandmother's time, but now contained the necessary apparatus for his condition... a commode.

When I passed by the closed bathroom door, I whispered fiercely into the keyhole: *"Sinner!"*

Mother, sewing nearby on the dining-room table, looked up, slightly startled and puzzled by this epithet, since she knew I wasn't gratuitously mean. She said: "Aren't you being a bit hard on your brother?"

"Oh, no - not hard *enough!* But we're getting there!" I replied light-heartedly, leaving by the front door.

Chapter XIII.

The Sled Jump

A wet January snow had fallen in the hours before dawn. We were sitting around the breakfast table relaxing, basking in the wonderful Saturday feeling.

"Look how that snow clings to every twig and branch!" Greg marveled. "Those trees by the fence are nearly bent double, and the yard is *smooth*... It looks like no one's ever walked there before." Nick and I stood up, craning toward the window to see better.

"Let's get the sleds!" said Nick.

"Hey, why don't we open up the steep slope behind the barn!" I exclaimed. We'd never done that before.

Greg considered. "We'll have to clear a trail first. There are dead weeds on the slope, and willows at the bottom."

"And what about the creek?" Nick said. "We'll be moving so fast by that time that we'll go right into the water and the opposite bank." The creek was only two or three feet wide.

"Not if we build a ramp to take us across, and up the other side," I said eagerly.

"You're gonna spend your time working instead of sledding," Greg said.

"Not with three of us! It shouldn't take more than an hour."

"We'll give it a try. Let's get going!" Greg agreed.

"Boys, put away the food on the table first, and put your dishes in the sink." How did Mother think of these things?

"Okay," we muttered. Now was not the time for a sit-down strike.

We threw on our jackets and boots and trooped out the back door. Greg called, "Come on, Peter!"

"No, I'll be out later," Peter demurred.

Outside, every tree, bush, and dead weed was exquisitely gilt with snow, a fairyland. The small creek was a dark ribbon against white, dividing the house and yard from the barn area. At first, it seemed like a study in monochrome, but after a second look, you saw that the colors were there; they had merely been painted with a subtler brush. We noticed a tiny plant with red berries outlined in snow, its form delineated even more beautifully than in summer.

Greg said, "I'd like to paint that... it would make a nice watercolor."

"You'll have to use charcoal instead," I teased, treading on his turf. "There's no color."

He didn't notice I was kidding. "Shows what you know. It doesn't matter what medium you use – it's all to effect an illusion or revelation to the viewer."

Snow slid from a branch, hitting the ground soundlessly. Greg said, "The snow's like an acoustic blanket."

A sharp bark from Sam interrupted us. He was tied to his doghouse, and wanted loose! We hadn't noticed, but he'd been punctuating our thoughts and conversation with whining and impatient noises. We weren't used to his being tied, but, lately, he couldn't seem to stay home and be content with domestic life. And we didn't want the dogcatcher to get him on his periodical forays down Pfarr Lane. (Sam and other nearby dogs were addicted to a certain semiannual pilgrimage to Canterbury, or some such doggy sacred place, to see if they could generate more canines. It turns out they could.)

We trudged up the slope to the doghouse, and he greeted us exuberantly. Straining his chain, he snorted, smiled, curled his lip and whined with humble entreaty: "*Please untie me now! Hunh? I love you! (I'll have* to nip you if you don't hurry!) Mmm... That smells good – what did you eat for breakfast? OK, untie me _now_ (but don't touch my dish!) Then there was some nipping about the legs, to repay our having ignored him.

Unfortunately, as we tried to unhook him, one of us accidentally kicked the dog dish lying under the snow, and Sam lunged forward to protect his property, with a beastie explosion. "**R-r-r-rah**!" Then he stood foursquare over the dish, guarding with growl and snarl, daring us to touch it, so earnest that we fell down in the snow, laughing.

Sam enjoyed this game mightily. We often poked at the empty dish, or tried to snatch it when he wasn't looking, and occasionally he got so worked up that he broke the skin on our ankles. Usually, though, he knew just how much pressure to apply with those jaws.

He wasn't untied yet, but we needed a distraction to get his attention away from the dish. It came in the form of the neighbor's cat, which Nick spied a short distance away. (Sam thought that feline wore an "Open Season" sign.) It worked nicely, and Nick sneaked around his other side, quietly removing the communion tray.

Finally free, Sam came for us, forgetting the dish and cat, but remembering we'd mocked him, and proceeded to gnaw our ankles in retribution. We tried sweet-talking – "Sammy, Sammy, we didn't mean to do it." But you could almost hear him saying, like a judge, "You didn't mean _not_ to!"

We realized we were getting sidetracked, and went to get the tools.

"Where's Peter?" I asked, hauling the tool sled through the deep snow.

"He's still inside," Nick replied. "When I went in to use the bathroom, he told me he'd be out sometime later."

"Yeah, and we all know how much later _that_ will be," Gregory commented sourly.

"Peter heard the words 'clear' and 'dig' and felt faint," I quipped.

"We can arrange a special ride for him when he finally appears," Greg suggested gleefully.

"I like it!" I said. "'_He who does not work, shall not sled._' On the other hand, we can grant him _special_ sledding privileges. Yes, indeed, his lordship shall have a free ride on the backs of the Proletariat."

We arrived at the site with our arsenal of tools. At the swampy base of the hill, Greg and I began cutting willows and pulling their roots out of the semi-frozen ground. Nick grass-whipped a trail upslope through last year's dead weeds that still clung to a remnant of summer.

After half an hour, we were ready to build the ramp-bridge over the creek. We scavenged some wood in the barn, and constructed the ramp simply of 4-foot-long boards, secured by two wooden battens. Then, laying it in position, we staked it firmly so it couldn't move when the sled dashed across it.

The bridge didn't line up with the trail coming down the hill, so you had to steer hard-right to maneuver onto it. If you didn't quite make it, one runner would slip off, and you would flip over into the creek on your back. But it was the best place we had for the bridge, and it would be more interesting, anyway. Some unskilled incompetents were going into the drink today, but the Chosen would shoot straight across the ramp, go up a little rise on the other side, around the curving trail, and end up in our back yard.

The ramp was done, and after shoveling snow onto it, we were finally ready!

The hill wasn't long, but it was steep and fast, with rough ground at the bottom. You had to keep to the path – if you veered right or left, you might hit a willow stub that had escaped the axe, or a rock submerged in the snow.

One by one, at the crest of the hill, we hit the sled running, and flew down the slope, through the small trees, up over the bridge, and on to the high ground beyond. Sometimes hazards prevented you from reaching the back yard – you might slip, throwing down your sled, or something could get in the way – a dog or the neighbor kid.

The kid was Joey Monihan, four or five years old, whose predestined role was that of diddler. I guess he felt privileged to be around older boys, but for us it was more like a karate-chop at a critical juncture. When he saw one of us at the top of the hill running to make a slide, he would jump right out into the path of the oncoming sledder, and stand there, mesmerized, rubbing his cheeks with overwhelming excitement. As the sled approached, he had to choose which way to jump, but since he didn't have the brains God gave a fish, he crossed and recrossed the trail desperately, gibbering while the sled came ever closer – sounds like "*Unh, unh, unh, unh...*" We would yell: "*Joey! Joey!* Get out of the way! GET OUT OF THE WAY!" But his mind had vacated the universe, and he only grew more frenzied. Finally the sled would whiz by, somehow just missing him, but on one of Joey's bad days, the ill-fated lemming instinct would surface again.

Even when Joey wasn't in the picture, there were plenty of ways to mess up. You might trip over your shoelace or the dog, or someone might purposely distract you with a bit of song and dance at the wrong moment (or *right*, depending on your point of view).

Sam, who probably had better sense than any of us, learned to stay clear, and didn't often come to grief. When he did, he let you know exactly what he thought of the fun and games. Two or three years of guerrilla-training had given him remarkable savvy, and he wasn't often fooled about the culprit.

We sledded most of the day. Peter finally showed up in late morning (when all the work was done) and got his free ride. He was a wary sledder. As the youngest, he was torn between wanting to imitate us (in theory) and avoiding unnecessary risks. His habit was to lie low and quietly enjoy himself, since he knew the older ones would only crack down if he asserted his character. (We didn't really know if he had any.) But the role of the observer has its rewards – it may have forced Peter to do some thinking.

That morning, he didn't respond to any of our helpful suggestions about "doubling his fun" on the sledding field, but did cautiously agree to sit behind Greg, with arms clasped around his waist. It seemed safe enough, since both would pay if he pulled any tricks.

Greg headed straight for the ramp, even though he knew he couldn't build enough momentum to cross it with a passenger. He angled the sled perfectly on approach with some fine foot-steering, and came gently to a neat stop on the sloping ramp itself. He was on the uphill end, near the opposite bank, and Peter on the lower end, close to the water.

But after being hit by sleds all day, the ramp had become unstable, and began to tip sideways. Peter couldn't compensate for the sudden tilting, and fell on his side into the creek, while Greg, an "old master" with honed skills and confidence, avoided his fate by rolling over onto the high bank. Peter gave out a satisfactory shriek at the invasion of ice water, evoking a spontaneous cheer from the field of play. His overthrown lordship toddled back to the house much wet, and we went on playing, gladdened by the meting of justice.

By late afternoon, we were a little bored with the run. It needed more drama. Greg had retired from the lists for the day, so I proposed to Nick,

"What we need is a sled-jump right there, where the ground is steepest. That way, we could go flying through the air, and finish the course even faster than before."

"That's a good idea," Nick assented eagerly, "but I think we should wait till tomorrow... It's getting late."

We were tired and powerfully hungry, and cold was starting to nibble at our toes. Hanging up our sleds in the garage, we went in to supper.

Sunday intervened, and we had to wait till after Mass and breakfast. So it wasn't till around 11:00 that Nick and I began building the jump. The sledding trail had been packed yesterday and refrozen during the night, better than ever. I kept up a running stream of conversation while we were working, since I always had lots to say.

After several hours, the jump was done. Just as we finished up, Peter came out, curious. He smiled uncertainly at our engineering triumph, and shivered. "That doesn't look safe... I wouldn't–"

I didn't hear the rest of the sentence, since I was already running, sled in hand, to be the first off the jump. I was thinking, *Sailing through the air is going to be glorious!*

And it *was*. But when I came DOWN... *Smack!* I couldn't breathe! I couldn't even *talk!* But inside, I repeated my *mantra: Don't let anyone know, don't let them know!* Or all that work would be wasted!

Not if I could help it! With a prodigious effort, I wheezed, "Fine! It's fine!" and struggled to my feet.

From his vantage point on the hill, Nick couldn't see how pale I was, or hear my labored breathing. He had strong incentive to follow my lead, since he wanted to be an "old master," too, so he took his run, sailed through the air and came down. *Ka-wump!* went the sled. *Ooof!* went Nick.

"How was it?" I inquired innocently, though I knew very well.

But Nick rose nobly to the occasion, hesitating only a moment. "Fine!"

It was clear, right then, that Nick shared my plans for the whole neighborhood to go off that jump. There was also, from his point of view, the outside possibility that *I* was having fun, and *he* wasn't. Perhaps he had done something wrong the first time. He would have to try again. (Practice! Practice!)

So, for an hour or so, we stoically took turns going off the killer jump, pretending to enjoy ourselves while taking a bad beating. We paused at times to discuss the finer points of sled-jumping, and how much scope the jump had added to the whole venture. The point of this exercise was to put into practice our Indian Code, while trying to share the experience with as many as possible. There were several neighbor boys that we thought might benefit.

Peter was there again, sledding lackadaisically out of our way, and we halfheartedly urged him to try the jump. "Come on, Peter, it's fun! Don't hang-back... there's nothing to it! You'll come down as smooth as silk!"

Peter sort of allowed he might, but we knew he wouldn't... He hadn't even used the ramp over the creek by himself. After these attempts failed, I thought maybe a sermon was in order. "Take a good look at yourself! *Baby! Egghead!* You'll never get anywhere in life if you don't try things... You're pathetic! How are you going to grow up with any spine?"

Peter's reply to this homily was written on his face, which had adopted the shuttered look of the East. You couldn't really blame Peter for not being a good sport. He wasn't as strong as the rest of us, and had frequently met disaster through our encouragement.

Older brothers often make the youngest a scapegoat for all the things perpetrated on them by elders, schoolmates, parents, and others... things that made *them* feel helpless and angry. Although we believed in the Golden Rule, we felt family was the exception. Peter was ours! – handed over to us by God, through the family pecking-order, to fetch and carry, suffer for our misdeeds, and be the butt of jokes. We felt we should be able to control him completely, while molding his character for a higher destiny. In the meantime, he wasn't to move without our approval.

It turned out I couldn't get Gregory to try the sled jump, either. This was extremely annoying, since I was hoping to lure him in as I'd done in the past. He did come out behind the barn to look at it, but all he said was, "It looks like a *belly-smacker* to me. You'd be lucky to get your breath back, let alone stand up."

This boy was learning fast. But I smoothly replied, "We've used it over and over. It was fun! Of course, you have to practice a bit." This was a hook – the implication that his skills might be slipping.

"More fool you! I saw you a couple of times from the house, and you were moving awfully slow when you got up..."

"Well, that's true," said Brer Rabbit, suavely shifting gears. "But that was before I adjusted the jump for the right trajectory."

"It looks the same to me," Greg replied truculently.

"Well, you wouldn't notice the difference from here," I extemporized, "but only by the sled's path through the air, in relation to the ground. If the trajectory isn't parallel to the hill, or the sled fast enough, then you'll come down vertically on your stomach, but if it *is* parallel and the speed is right, your landing will be smooth, like skiing."

"Unh-HUNH," Gregory said slowly, the words full of skepticism. "Funny – I disremember you being that good in Science class…"

He was becoming a cynic, and I had to lead him away from wrong thinking. So I tried a different tack. "Look! I'll show you how smooth it is." (If all else fails, set a good example.)

But this didn't impress him, either. "Old master" was fast becoming "Ancient master." He just grinned when I belly-smacked the ground. This wasn't going anywhere, and I began to wonder whether he'd already tried the ramp, and was just enjoying my gyrations.

Oh, well, you couldn't win every trick… I would have to depend on neighbor kids and unexpected visitors who knew nothing of our wiles. We had many creative ploys and subterfuges on hand, depending on conditions and the personality of the intended victim.

One, Make polite, helpful suggestions to *try this* and *try that*. This works well with straightforward folk who simply want to have fun. They take your suggestions at face value (at least until afterwards).

Two, Be eager and enthusiastic – appeal to the player's sense of fun and adventure. This works well on optimistic types, because they're already more than halfway there. They only need a little push, and sometimes not even that. They may jump into the unknown under their own steam, before you get a chance to help them.

Three, One of the players may be a stubborn *macho* type. (He's the type who feels naturally insulted by your masterful presence, and can neither "sit nor stand" when it comes to listening to anything *you* might have to say.) So be tentative, and discourage him slightly. "You don't want to try that jump. It took Nick and me a while to get it." He'll almost certainly elbow you out of the way, especially if he's seen *you* do it.

Four, Demonstrate feats with practiced ease, and don't say *anything.* This is particularly effective on those who don't know you, and they'll automatically follow. If they ask, "Isn't that difficult?" you say, "Naw, nothing to it."

Five, Be bold. When anything daring is proposed, *you* be the first to do it. The odds are in your favor. Others, thinking to follow in your wake, will begin to have doubts that they can do as well, but social pressure will urge them to try. Consequently, they'll hang-back just a bit, spoil their aim, and mess up.

Six - The Inelegant Rule, Pursue the sledder that just shoved off. Tip his sled over (or push him off with your foot) when you catch him, then finish him off by rolling him in a snow bank and pelting him with snowballs. (Greg's style) This rule has been used by countless perpetrators and victims alike, perpetrators when they've had a dearth of victims that day, and victims of Numbers 1 through 5 who finally get the perpetrators in their sights.

I myself have undeservedly fallen victim to **Two**, **Three**, **Four**, and **Five**, above. You may think, from my succinct descriptions, that I invented them all, but I'm just a humble chronicler. (Though some would tell you snidely not to believe anything I say, unless you want to find yourself going off a ramp!)

Chapter XIV.
Modus Operandi

- *Don't play with fire – you'll die!* (True)

- *Don't use a knife like that – you'll cut yourself!* (Possibly, until you learn)

- *Don't run on the ice – you'll fall down and break something!* (Maybe)

- *Don't run on the playground – you'll fall down and hurt yourself!* (Thoreau knew that a man "...sits as many risks as he runs...")

- *Don't put so much food in your mouth – you'll choke!* (Almost never, if the food is good)

- *Don't swim alone – you'll drown!* (A pleasant thought to some, but not certain)

- *Hey, don't throw sticks like that – you'll put someone's eye out!* (A favorite, but unlikely)

- *Don't run when you're carrying a knife or scissors!* (Whyever not?)

* * *

In grade school, my viewpoint was admittedly subjective, but I felt that adults wanted to keep kids in straitjackets. I could tell, because they seemed driven to root childhood out of us. Armed with rules and cautions, they threw them at us like a knife-thrower tossing knives. The problem was, there were so *many* of them that they tended to obscure common sense and drew my attention away from serious things, like not playing with gasoline.

Whenever adults were around, they got tense just watching us do something perfectly ordinary, like running down steps. You'd think we were trying to destroy the world, as well as ourselves. Relations, teachers, neighbors and even strangers got into the act. It was a universal conspiracy!

Active kids would rather be dead than live the secondhand experience of failed lives – I mean, just *look* at the adults! They're *old!* Kids are positive that was a deliberate choice, and it's hard to forgive. But that's only the beginning. Look at what adults are interested in.

At gatherings of any kind, the mothers talk about family trivia – what the baby likes to eat, the time Johnny pulled Alice's hair, and how Bert kicked her last week when she tried to punish him.

Fathers aren't any better. They talk about their jobs – fascinating stuff, like how the third-shift production line at the ball-bearing plant broke down. This is discussed in excruciating detail, in monotone voices. It made our blood boil (and might have been the real cause of allergies!). But all we could do was rush out the door to get some fresh air.

From time to time we tried to resuscitate our parents by reminding them of certain rumored exploits when *they* were young. But the grownups only looked embarrassed (especially in company), didn't say much, and moved on, as though to disavow such putative history.

To fill all remaining time between rules and cautions (like mortar in a rock wall), there were "fuss and feathers" incidents. When I was eight, my mother left me at Gramma's one afternoon. Gramma invited me to sit down beside her on the couch, which was commonly adorned with pillows and a cat or two. With my neatly parted hair, freckles, and missing front tooth, she probably thought I was cute, and wanted to spend some time with me, not realizing that any indulgence comes with a price.

Well, I wanted the candy I spied on the coffee table, so I was agreeable to making a reasonable investment. But it wasn't ten seconds before she said testily, "Stop *fidgeting* – you're driving me crazy!"

Well! That was a little mystifying – I didn't think I'd been moving. But I was a tractable kid, so all I thought was, *O-kay...*

She handed me a piece of candy. (*Ah, yes! About time, too!*) Two seconds passed. Then she burst out, "Quit doing that to the pillows!"

Doing WHAT? I thought, as she peremptorily snatched the pillows away. *So you can't even squeeze pillows? Have it your way,* I sighed to myself. I always tried to see the positive, so I embarked on petting the cat, who was clearly begging for attention.

This evoked, "*Don't* pet the cat like that – she doesn't like it, and she'll leave!"

This was getting annoying, and I might add that the cat was perfectly happy until it caught the negative vibrations from its owner. The cozy visit with Gramma was fast becoming un-cozy, but I was prepared to endure a lot for the sake of candy.

So there I was, rolling the candy around on my tongue, when, out of the blue, she yelled, "Look out! Your feet are going to knock over the candy bowl! Keep them under the table!" Hunh? But my feet weren't anywhere near the bowl, at least not now... I didn't *think* I'd been swinging them.

After another minute, she exclaimed, "Would you *please* hold still and STOP SQUIRMING!" At this point, the brackets around Gramma's mouth were about as firm as they got. I still had some candy left, but she had finally reached her threshold.

"Oh, for heaven's sake! Go *outside* and play." She got up hastily, forcibly pressed another piece of candy into my hand, and propelled me to the door by my elbow, her head bobbing up and down with her shuffling walk.

Outside and free! But, *no* – Grandpa was lurking out there. (Probably he had been put out earlier.) Now it was his turn, and darned if he wasn't just as fractious! When I started to play with the old antique wagon with its iron wheels, he hovered nearby, and nervously warned, "Slow down, or you'll tip over and skin your knees!"

When this disaster failed to materialize, he yelled, "Watch out for that flower bed – you're going too fast!"

After I was done playing with the wagon, having demonstrated my obvious capability by ignoring all cautions, I wandered over to the apple tree and began to eat green apples. This got Grandpa going again. "Hey, those green apples will give you a stomach ache!"

Well, green apples never gave me a stomach ache, but I *was* starting to get a headache... Didn't they know that things were for use and enjoyment, and not to make you miserable? First I was nonplussed, and then I was annoyed. Hadn't I been on my best behavior with both of them? Even getting a skinned knee wasn't as bad as needing a shrink!

The real root of the problem in our family was that, as children, our imaginations fed on classic adventures – King Arthur, Robin Hood, Swiss Family Robinson, Treasure Island, and Huck Finn. As we grew older, "The Last of the Mohicans" and Altsheler's tales of Daniel Boone and Henry Ware assumed the guiding role.

To us, these were solid reality, much more so than what we saw at school and elsewhere. We patterned ourselves on them, and those books don't encourage social conformity, restraint and obedience. They aren't for stay-at-home, quiet types who probably won't break any rules, anyway, since they avoid the field of play (unless of course they are accidentally run over by the other type, while reading on the sidelines).

The safety-mongers might as well have saved their breath. My brothers and I didn't need all that. We would never do anything *really* dangerous.

* * *

Our back door banged behind me as I rushed outside and scanned the area restlessly. My prowling eye lit upon a beautifully smooth, grapefruit-sized rock at the base of the plum tree, and I held it, enjoying the feel in my hand. *How far can I throw it?* I wondered. I had been practicing the shot put all week at the high school... It was irresistible. With all my strength, I hurled it towards the patch of sky over the barn, 40 yards away, hoping it would clear the roof.

No sooner had I let-fly than I spotted Sam, running hard, 90 degrees to my right, chasing a rabbit along the boundary fence. "Yip! Yip! Yip!"

Could he possibly get there in time for the rock to hit him? I caught my breath sharply. *No way*, Common Sense replied, even though the rabbit path *was* going to intersect the rock's course behind the barn. It was just <u>too</u> far...

But I stood there, frozen. The rock moved upward in slow motion toward the barn roof. Sam kept running, getting closer to the barn.

The rock climbed faster.

Sam started to run faster.

Oh, man...!

The rock cleared the roof by a good six feet.

Sam disappeared behind the barn.

Nothing.

Then...

"YIPE!!!"

I'VE KILLED HIM! I anguished. How could I have been so *STUPID*, to throw that rock when I couldn't see where it would land?

But just as I started running, he came yipping out the other side of the barn, *still* chasing that rabbit! I broke out laughing from sheer relief.

Sam never did have any idea what hit him, and I never told him.

* * *

"FEET!" the upperclassman yelled, as I came down the hall. "Look who's coming!"

The cry was picked up and amplified by others, lounging at their lockers.

When I first went to high school, I was the smallest boy in my class, with very fair skin, huge moon-eyes and a baby-face. Unfortunately, I also had the largest feet in the school – size-12 boaters. (I quickly found it was a mistake to buy *white* ones.)

Although I was in excellent shape from my outdoor life, my appearance made me look like easy meat. When they passed me in the hall, I could just see the dogs thinking, *I know I can take dat cat, look how small it is...*

I soon realized that keeping everyone off my back was going to take some devious tap-dancing. My mind, like Brer Rabbit's, worked furiously, creating schemes to fool Brer Fox. ("Please, Brer Fox, whatever you do... *p-p-please* don't throw me into that briar patch!")

There was a boy named Joe Tracy, a pale-faced hood with black pointed shoes and his hair all ratted-up like Elvis's. It was one of his ambitions to get me to fight, and he would grab me by the collar and slam me up against the wall in the restroom, where he went to smoke and hobnob with his buddies. My mild suggestion that smoking was going to weaken him in any turn-up didn't curb his ardor. (They thought it would make them *real men*, even before nature had completed its work.)

Teachers interrupted this *tête-à-tête* several times, not to help *me*, but to catch the smokers. Of course, this only frustrated the aggressor, who had to wait till the next time the lone cat moved into his sights.

Fighting was a complex issue for me. My instinctive response was to lay Tracy out, but my Christian upbringing wouldn't let me. It also demanded that I try to instill some rudiments of morality into him, and eventually convert him to my faith.

So the next time Tracy cornered me, I threw him off balance by suggesting he might like to stand on my stomach.

"Hunh? What for?"

"Oh, I just want to find out if you're tough enough to hold up in a fracas with me."

"I can whip your butt any day, *Pfarr*," he bristled, shoving his face close to mine.

"Well, I don't know," I demurred, "but the gym's right outside. Let's go and find out – first you stand on my stomach, and then I'll stand on yours."

Standing on the softest part of my anatomy (and maybe accidentally jumping on it) didn't sound bad to him, so he agreed, cackling along with his pals.

Tracy's buddy said to him, aside, "What's a fracas, Boss?"

"Like an ignoramus," I answered coolly.

"You better shut up, Pfarr... You're digging your own grave!"

We went into the gym, where the usual group of boys was playing basketball, and others were just hanging around. Coach Mihalik was at his post, swat-paddle at the ready to make sure things didn't get out of hand. Swats were passed out generously (if not entirely justly) at lunchtime for various gym trespasses, the main one being hard shoes on the court. The coach thought that learning to take your swats was part of being a man.

Among the bystanders, I spotted Kevin Barry, an overweight boy I knew from grade school. This gave me an idea. I hailed him, and he came over, smiling good-naturedly.

"Whaddya know, Paul? How's the 'ole stomach?' " he added, with a twinkle. He knew my tricks of old, since we had traded stomach jumps several years before to solve a dispute.

"Kevin, I need your help. Would you show these boys how to stand on my stomach?"

"I don't need any help with *that!*" my adversary snapped.

"Well, maybe not," I said. "But –"

"Aw, let him, Boss," his henchmen said, guffawing when they realized how heavy my friend was.

"All right – go ahead," Tracy said uncertainly, trying to see some disadvantage, but not getting it.

"You ready?" Kevin asked genially.

"Yeah," I said, quickly laying myself out prone and hardening my stomach muscles. Kevin, who weighed at least twice what my unfriend did, stepped on me nonchalantly. I didn't even tremble, and the punks' support group began to make negative rumbling noises. One of them mumbled, "He'll never hold up under that pig!" Before getting off my stomach, Kevin took the time to tell that one to watch his mouth, unless he wanted a pig sitting on his face.

I was beginning to enjoy myself, and the enemy was looking pale and nervous.

It was Tracy's turn. He swore, but lay down with false bravado. "If that little runt can take it, so can I."

One of his cronies demurred, "I dunno... maybe you shouldn't have eaten lunch."

"Shut up, idiot!" Tracy fired back. I started to get on his stomach, but he said, "Not *you* – the big guy!"

"You don't have to do that," I said solicitously. "My stomach's been in training."

"Get the hell out of the way, Pfarr!"

Kevin said warmly, "Anything you say, *Boss.*" He winked at me, and stepped on Tracy's middle.

For about 2 seconds, all seemed well, but suddenly "Boss" let out a sound like, "A-a-a-arrrgh!" as his stomach collapsed and the air whooshed out of him. Kevin wasn't a mean fellow, and got off quickly, but when Tracy sat up, something besides air came out. Lunch.

Throughout the proceedings, I noticed Coach Mihalik observing us with a sly little smile on his face. He could hear us talking, but wasn't going to interfere, since we weren't breaking any rules he could see, but just engaging in a test of strength, wits, and creativity. I could see that, as a coach, he liked that (even though his hand itched to use the swat-paddle).

Tracy was embarrassed, but when he came back from the restroom, he reiterated, "It's not over, Pfarr. I'm *still* going to whip your ass!"

"Don't worry," I reassured him speciously. "We'll get to it, but I don't want either of us to be sorry. Why don't we do a few more things, since we're here?" (I was moving in for the kill. Punks didn't like to work out – too much sweating. They preferred making other people sweat.)

"I'm not going to do any more of your shit!" he snarled. Once uttered, his mistake was plain. It looked like he was afraid to tackle gym work.

"You can climb dem ropes, can't you, Boss?" one of his henchmen queried nervously.

"Sure I can, retard!" Tracy retorted.

This was going better than I expected.

There was a 25-foot climbing rope hanging from the gym ceiling. Tracy took the initiative and began to climb slowly, using his feet and hands. His cronies yelled encouragement. "Hey, we knew you could do it! Show 'em!"

When Tracy came back down, he dropped heavily to the floor, and almost lost his balance.

"Not bad," I said, stretching a point.

Then I skittered up and down in a flash, using no feet. Coach Mihalik nearly fell off his chair.

Tracy's cronies muttered, "Gawd!"

"Did I say you could speak, morons?" Tracy flashed.

I waded in disingenuously. "Just because I'm better at rope-climbing doesn't prove anything..."

Tracy only stared, his face stony.

"Let's run the other courses – first the pegboard, and then the chin-up bars," I said cheerfully. "After that, if you're still good-to-go, we'll finish up with the track. If you can keep up with me there, I'll know we're evenly matched."

"I told you to shut up!" Tracy bristled, but less viciously than before. He was trapped.

It was pathetic. He fell off the pegboard halfway up, and only made it through several chin-ups. The track was out of the question – he couldn't make it that far.

He almost said something to me as he left, but thought better of it.

Coach Mihalik came over. "Nice going, son. I saw what you did with that punk."

"Yeah – he was crazy to fight me, but I didn't think he was up to it."

"You want to try out for some of our teams?" he offered, with untypical generosity.

"Maybe... I'll think about it, Coach. Thanks."

There were no more problems with Tracy. When we passed in the hall, he stared straight ahead, as though he didn't see me. I'd seen that look before on our dog Sam's face when he had to pass a mean cat that meant business. He pretended not to see her, but avidly pursued the neighbors' cat instead, tromping it whenever he caught it out in the open.

I don't think I instilled any morality in Joe, but I did find out later that he was a lapsed Catholic, so my intended conversion effort would have had only a mediocre effect, anyway.

* * *

None of the five boys in our family were joiners. We didn't play sports in high school (except for track, that loner's paradise) – we were having too much fun at home. This frustrated the coaches no end, but they learned to give us our due. Back then, most kids involved in organized sports only trained during the season, but we kept in shape year-round, which gave us the edge.

Since the coaches couldn't have us on their teams, they reverted to using us as benchmarks in gym class, to measure their athletes. (Well – not

Peter, and Timmy was in the Air Force by then)

When I was a senior, walking past the gym one day, I happened to glance inside. A game of medicine ball was in session, though I couldn't tell that at the moment. What I saw was a tangled mound of boys, slowly inching across the floor mat. They were yelling and screaming, "Stop him! Stop him!"

Coach Mihalik shouted, "C'mon, you panty-waists! STOP him!" And then under his breath, "I don't *believe* this!"

The pile kept crawling, so the coach blew his whistle, motioning all the boys on the sideline to pile on. He was going to stop that renegade under the pile.

But the pile refused to recognize higher authority, and continued to move inexorably to the edge of the mat, in spite of the 20 boys piled on top. Reaching the goal, Nick wriggled out, triumphantly holding the ball. Coach just shook his head grimly. He wasn't happy when a nonconformist showed up the system.

I had a similar experience. The coaches had set up an obstacle course, involving parallel bars, tumbling mats, pegboards, climbing-ropes, jumps, and running-and-dodging. Standing around, ready to begin, I heard Mihalik saying to one of his football players, "I don't think you're in that good shape, Moss."

"Yeah, I am, Coach... I been working out for a couple of months!" the student protested.

"Unh-hunh... I bet you won't even beat Pfarr, standing over there."

"Sure, I will! He's not even on the team!"

"He'll still beat you by a mile!" Coach taunted.

"We'll see about that," Moss muttered sullenly.

"If he does, *you're mine* for the next six weeks," Coach promised.

That day, I set a school record for the obstacle course, and left Moss thinking about the Zen of keeping in shape.

But I knew that being in shape wouldn't solve all my problems. There were worse bullies out there than Tracy, so I devised heavyweight stratagems to hold in reserve for big game. Any formula for success required doing the unexpected, never backing down, and not showing fear.

I also had to be prepared for the occasional jerk who would just haul off and hit me in the middle. So I perfected putting on my "iron shirt" stomach instantaneously, and practiced pulling back a fraction, to minimize the impact. Then, instead of returning fire, I just looked them in the eye as if to say, "So?" Their imaginations would overheat, wondering what would happen if I *did* decide to reciprocate. It was pure profit for me - they left me alone, and I didn't violate my ethics.

Like the stomach trick with Tracy, sometimes I would offer the criminal a target, such as my neck to choke (if they hadn't already made a grab for it). That made them feel really funny and uncertain - *what was going on here?*

Once, in the Army, I was unexpectedly attacked by one of my co-workers, who didn't like the home truth I had just pressed on him. He tried to choke me, but I was sitting down at the time, and just tightened my neck muscles to resist, while calmly staring him in the eye. I knew he didn't have enough strength in his hands to accomplish what he intended, and, after a strained minute, he felt foolish and walked away.

But my favorite ploy was arm-wrestling. When bullies lost publicly to "baby-face," it never ended in a fight, because they were demoralized. If they couldn't beat me arm-wrestling, how could they expect to win in a fight? Not necessarily true, but I never told them that.

Jimmy Ackerman had shown me early on that it takes more than a strong arm to win at this sport. You have to understand the mechanics and psychology:

- Lock yourself into position as though you're rooted to the ground. (think *T'ai Chi*)

- Always pull the opponent's arm *toward* you, never sideways.

- Let him wear himself out - it's much easier to defend a fort than to take one.

- Never show any emotion.

- Prepare to be there all day.

It worked really well. At one point, the whole school caught the craze, and actually seemed to forget about settling disputes out back.

But there was a price to pay for my methods. None of those ploys would have succeeded if I hadn't been workout-mad. Still, I meant to be left alone, and was willing to pay the extortionate price of constant training. My mantra was, *Turn the other cheek, yes – but be strong – be prepared – and never be forced to fight.*

As high school progressed and I grew in inches and form, I had fewer difficulties. The gym-class grapevine spread our family's reputations. My most elaborate plan never had to be used, but I came close one January with Lenny Totterhouse. We were to run six miles up the railroad (after swimming the icy creek), then follow up with my usual workout of rope-climbing, pushups, sit-ups, and hanging by the neck until dead (okay – not *quite*). The fight would make a glorious end, if he made it through the hanging.

I don't think Lenny really believed in my course. He didn't have much imagination, and just thought I was going to get him away from school, then jump him. That suited him fine – he didn't have a nerve in his body. Besides, the rewards were so attractive – if he could claim he had whipped the weird Pfarr, his reputation would be made. He brought a crony along as witness – they always made that mistake.

They arrived at our house in an old car when a music lesson was in progress. The Johnsons were a black family Mother had known for years, and Connie Johnson's older brother Frank was waiting for her in his car, with the window open halfway, because it was a warm day for the time of year.

When Lenny got out of his car, the first thing he saw was the hangman's noose, dangling from my favorite workout tree.

"What's that for?" he said belligerently.

I answered, "It's a hangman's noose."

"I know that, *Pfarr!*"

"I practice on it... I figured we'd end our Strong Man course with hanging by the neck, to see who's the toughest. After we swim the creek, run six miles, and work out."

"Swim the creek! It's freezing! The ice just melted!"

"Well – if you can't take it –" I trailed off.

"I can take anything you can dish out, and still whip your butt," he said, thrusting his face in mine. (Real men always talk that way.)

"Yes, but I don't want it on my conscience if you have to face your

Maker today. Are you ready to walk through those pearly gates?"

A little unnerved, Lenny tried to bluster his way. "I just might send *you* there first!"

"I wouldn't mind," I said. "I've always wanted to go..."

This was confusing. Thinking wasn't his forte, and religion scared him.

"Don't worry," I told him kindly. "I'll hang myself first, at the end of our course. You can go after me."

He brightened. "Hell, let's see that course of yours."

So I took him out to Long Pond Cliff and showed him the first item, swimming the creek.

"Are you ready?" I asked.

"Let's just do it!" he yelled at me.

But I knelt down, folded my hands, and began to pray.

"What are you *doing?*"

"I just want to prepare," I answered innocently.

"Whaddya talking about?" he growled.

"Well, with the cold water and all, one of us might have a heart attack."

That tore it. Shaking his head like a dog, he said, "You know what? You're *crazy!* This is getting too spooky. I don't have to do any of this! Go swim, yourself! I'm going home! Come on, Russ!"

I took a step toward him, but he backed away.

"Get away from me! You're nuts!"

He and his buddy started running. They didn't even look back.

There wouldn't be any more trouble with that boy. The religious element had pushed him over the edge.

I strolled back to the house, hands in my pockets. Frank Johnson was lounging against his car, smoking. He gave me a crooked smile, and said, "Those boys come hurrin' back to their car, and tore out o' here like they see'd a ghost. I heard what you said to 'em right here 'bout hangin' and all. Man, you nuthin' but a jive turkey - you know dat!" And then he gave me high five. "Right on!"

Walking down the hall at school a few weeks later, I saw a new kid approaching with some of the riff-raff, and heard him say, "Look at that pansy! I can take *him*!"

But one of his newly acquired buddies was Lenny, and he said, "Forget it! Don't mess with Pfarr!"

"But I *know* I can do it," the newcomer gibbered.

"If he's asleep, *maybe*, but I'm telling you, leave him alone unless you want to find yourself in an ice-cold creek in January – he's *weird*. And he *prays*, too!"

I eventually met a really hardened criminal-to-be, Roger Fein, a 16-year-old boy from the city who had a bad reputation, having been known to use razor-knives on students. Ironically enough, we never tangled. He lived close-by, and I used to play pool with him at his house occasionally. While he was touchy, I think he knew I wasn't afraid of him. The path of his life didn't turn out well – he made the FBI's "Ten Most Wanted" list, and was finally gunned down by Federal Marshals at the age of 48.

* * *

I was one person at home and another when dealing with the world at large. School seemed bleach out my personality. I felt colorless in the classroom, a prisoner to someone's strange agenda, and couldn't understand their purposes. From the start, I could hardly learn there at all. Over time, I managed to get along, but never to feel comfortable.

But at home, I took control in the areas of *my* interests: gardening, woodlore, and botany. My preferred modes of travel were running, riding my bike at breakneck speed, and Olympic walking – anything, as long as it was flashy. (*Please, God – not the dull way <u>ordinary</u> people do things!*)

If you've ever watched Olympic walking, you know it seems very choppy and uncomfortable. The walker seems to have disjointed hips, and looks as though he were trying to rototill the ground with his legs. But appearing foolish to others didn't bother me, as long as I could leave them in the dust. They would never catch me to criticize. Besides, they were probably jealous of my speed – who wouldn't be?

Fences in my way were invitations to jump. Those too tall to jump were made for vaulting, and I sometimes carried a pole. Of course, I seldom *looked* beforehand – if Indians were on my trail, I couldn't afford it. Besides, real skill showed up when you were surprised, and performed well, anyway. It was a poor specimen who carefully figured and measured every move he made. In my book, he was dead long before the grave claimed him.

The Brothers Three (Greg, Nick and I) practiced pole-vaulting, broad-jumping, shooting a bow-and-arrow and shot-putting with rocks. We threw spears, climbed ropes, swung in trees, and used a real sling with egg-sized rocks, like David of old. Our vaulting poles sometimes doubled as quarterstaves, for Robin Hood encounters.

One particular fall day, when the air was crisp and clear and the leaves had turned in Schemel's Woods, Nick and I ran mile after mile, wild like deer. We jumped fences and logs, and navigated ravines. Over fields, through orchards and woodlots, our hearts raced to the chase. Were we the hunters or the quarry? Leaves whooshed out of our way, stirring and crackling, shoved wildly aside by our feet.

After a while, our clothing was torn and we had picked up various scratches. Blood was trickling from my knee, where a barbed-wire fence had caught my jeans, and Nicholas had a scraped elbow, but this encouragement only goaded us to surpass ourselves. At one point, we jumped a low fence and fell into a ravine, invisible until we landed. We rolled until we gained our feet, then clambered out the other side, covered with leaves and dirt. Up and running again!

When our nervous energy wore off, we gradually slowed to a walk, like horses cooling down. Our breathing subsided, and we finally dropped down to rest. Above, a rust-red beech shone like a torch against the deep blue sky, and we heard a bird rustling softly in a bush nearby. Nature had achieved its purpose – we were synchronized with its rhythms. All was one.

* * *

Grailville's head farmer, Prudence, was a strange character of Native American extraction who always had an eye to business first (and last). With her iron-grey hair and sour expression, she reminded us forcibly of the Corn Engrosser in Robin Hood, which nettled us to assume Robin's devil-may-care attitude. It piqued us further to find later that she had graduated from college *summa cum laude*. That wasn't the grade *we* assigned her.

At one of Grailville's celebratory events, with the community attending, Prudence happened to see Nick and me, and took the opportunity to spread a little cheer. "You're smashing our fences where you climb over them. They're getting lower and lower, and the cattle will get out!"

Little John and Robin were taken aback. This was an attack on our honor, woodsmanship and athletic prowess, _and_ contrary to unwritten rights-of-way existing from time immemorial.

"That can't be," I replied. "We don't climb 'em – we _jump_ 'em!"

Nick nodded firmly.

She crossly replied, "Now you know that's not true! Some of those fences are too tall to jump, and some are topped with barbed wire. I bet you've fallen on them, and made them worse!"

I contradicted her coolly: "Oh, we use poles to vault them, when they're too tall."

Game, set and match!

She didn't seem to be pacified, though, but retreated stiffly from the field of battle. She may have been nonplussed and speechless, or felt we weren't safe to be around. (Or maybe she was struggling against an atavistic Indian urge to scalp us.)

Nick and I shrugged our shoulders and proceeded to address more germane issues at the food table. While most saw this kind of occasion as a chance for social mingling, we were there for the food, and used everyone else's activities as a cover for how much we ate. Of course, we practiced some subtlety, circulating around the room and talking to various people we knew, between trips to the food table and intermissions outside, where speed of eating went unobserved.

Prudence was remarkably consistent. Every time she crossed our path, she behaved with the same obnoxious materialism. One sweltering summer day, Grailville called and asked for help with some farm work. Gregory, Nick and I always needed money, and thought it would be nice, clean work in the great outdoors. We didn't ask what the wage would be, trusting that people we knew would treat us fairly. So we went up to the main barn, and who was there to greet us but the Corn Engrosser, waiting with a hay wagon. Our first instinct was to return home – something had gone seriously wrong. But we knew Grailville needed the help, and decided to stick it out. After all, what could she do?

"You think you boys are up to bringing in the hay? I'll give you 50 cents an hour," she said sourly, as though she couldn't bear to talk about parting with money.

It was a disappointment – our uncles paid us as much as $2.00 an hour. But we didn't complain – it was an opportunity to demonstrate what good workers we were, for future job prospects.

Prudence went on to tell us that a nephew of hers, a beefy football player, had been helping her recently. Looking us over critically, her manner implied that she doubted we would do as well. Suddenly, she said gruffly, "Come on, boys – hurry up and get in the wagon! We haven't got all day!" (As though *we* had been delaying her!)

We rode to the field. The work didn't seem too bad for a while, and we worked like fiends, putting hay on the wagon as fast as we could. Even Prudence found nothing to criticize. The temperature was over 90°, and the bales weighed 150 lbs. After 4 hours, when the field was three-quarters done, we noticed that clouds were gathering. Prudence harassed us again to hurry, as though we weren't already breaking our necks!

Thunder and lightning were approaching, but we finished the field before it arrived, and barely got it all piled safely in the murderously hot barn. That was miserable work – our noses and eyes were itching and streaming from the hay in that high, closed space.

The day finally ended. They owed us six hours' wages each, which was $3.00 apiece. But when she paid us, there was only $2.25. Taken aback, we asked her why, and she said she wasn't paying for time we had spent riding in the wagon to and from the barn! We were speechless. The Corn Engrosser had struck again! The boys of Sherwood Forest were itching to return the favor, and certainly wouldn't be going out of their way to pull her out of a ditch again!

Some time later, Robin Hood and his merry men decided they needed a secret camp. Nicholas and I found the perfect place near Grailville's dump, off in a camouflaging thicket on the hillside. It seemed ideal for an underground house with sod roof. We would give it a stone floor, a fireplace or stove, and a small entry door concealed on the ravine side. We immediately marked out a 10' by 10' space with sticks, and came back later with shovels and mattocks. For several weeks, Nick and I dug like frenzied badgers, piling the excavated dirt around the walls. By then, it was a huge pit, and we were ready to build.

But the project began to pall, and, with fall coming, it slipped our minds. One day in early November, I came across the pit and was shocked at how exposed it seemed, now that the leaves had fallen. We'd never thought of that. And, boy, it sure was larger than I remembered, and held a foot of water!

It was then that I spotted Prudence plowing in the field below. Just as she drew opposite the pit, she glanced my way, did a double-take, and stopped the tractor dead. *Oh-oh... now the fat's in the fire!* I thought, and ducked down, scrambling away under the sumac on all-fours, in case she came closer to investigate. But I was delighted at the frozen, shocked look on her face, which did something to balance our past accounts!

> "Now the Corn Engrosser grew pale as white linen, and
> went his sorrowful way barefoot that day."

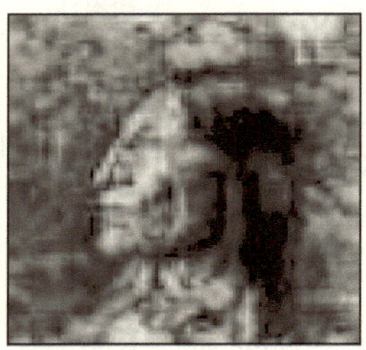

Chapter XV.

The Code

Nicholas, Gregory and I lived by a personal code, incorporating what the Church and our parents taught us with our own social disinclination and addictive devotion to woodlore and Indians.

This coalescence was woven seamlessly into our consciousness, and, if asked, we would have replied, "What code?" But it influenced our behavior constantly, especially in late high school, when we knew our entry into the outside world was imminent. The thing was, we liked our world just the way it was, and were determined to keep it safe and moral (if not exactly predictable).

How could we protect ourselves from a society that was godless, materialistic, and venal, and which certainly could not be trusted to preserve the Sacred Groves? But it was very *large*, and it was *everywhere*. The danger of becoming normal was insidious. Would religion alone be enough to defeat it? We doubted it – look at all the normal people, even in the Church!

We knew that Christianity was divinely noble in its aspirations, but sensed that, though Church teaching emphasized "not being of the world" and "dying to it," it was aimed more at preparing one for the *next* life than providing the nuts-and-bolts instruction manual we needed to make our way through *this* one, without joining up. By now, any hope of becoming child martyrs was gone, so we really needed that concrete guidance.

Our Code filled that need. It kept us case-hardened in the face of temptation, and helped us cope with a wide variety of problems. People who had contact with us fell into two camps: Some (the heathen and those of limited intelligence) thought we were impossible, eccentric, opinionated, and intolerant. The other faction considered us original, creative, and interesting – artistic precursors of the New Age ushered in by the '60s. (These were the enlightened, the intelligentsia, the benefactors of the race – and the Saved, of course.)

The Code was invoked as smoothly and quietly as an electric motor, and was adhered to without complaint. Sometimes it transformed personal adventures into uncomfortable struggles, and cut up our peace temporarily, but we never let Outsiders see that. After all, didn't our *official* religion hold, as a central tenet, that right-doing might cause you to suffer or even die, and that this was tragic, but irrelevant? The Code was similar, and when we came up with the grit necessary to follow its dictates, it increased our self-respect (like Klingons, of whom we knew nothing at the time).

**recept:** **The body is our temple, and nothing shall be allowed to defile it.**

**pplication:**

§   **Nothing but good organic food shall be eaten.**

We broke this one sometimes, to keep ourselves humble, but the principle was good. We longed for junk food like candy, potato chips and pop, but they were hard to come by, so we didn't feel that our principles were much compromised when we did get them. Some things would wash out – others wouldn't. Besides, sometimes the spirit was more important than the letter. (What decided? Some have cynically suggested it was the *food*.)

§   **No Smoking!**

Smoking was for people who were emotionally crippled and needed constant soothing, like a pacifier. The consequences of breaking this rule were really bad, since it set off a chain-reaction: Smoking ruined your health, and you wouldn't be able to run. If you couldn't run, the girls would catch you. That would be the end of the world, as you knew it.

§   **No Alcohol!**

Drinking caused the same problems as smoking, in addition to even nastier side effects, on yourself and others. The fact that we found alcohol distasteful in no way lessened our credit for avoiding it.

§ **No Coffee!**

Indians do not need stimulants! And coffee would stunt your growth! If that happened, the girls would definitely catch you, probably the runts - who else would want you? I know many of you will protest, "Aw, man, what's so bad about being caught by the girls?" If this is you, read no further - there's nothing here that can help you.

§ **No Getting Fat!**

Not even five pounds, you lazy sinner and son of a turtle!

§ **No TV!**

Indians do not need TV! It will pull you into the world of soap opera and beer drinking.

Precept: Walking can cure the body of many things.

Running WILL cure *everything* – body, mind and soul!

Application:

§ **Walk everywhere you go, or, preferably, RUN!**

This will keep people from talking to you - teachers, girls, and "your peers." (Despicable expression! Who were *our peers?*) If you're moving fast enough, all you'll hear in the school hallway is, "Hey, that boy is–!" It also keeps you in shape (Need I say more?) and makes ordinary tasks exciting. And if the Indians try a sneak attack, you'll be ready to run all the way to the Great Lakes and back! (Badly needed in *our* times!) If you must merely *walk*, save it for the Sacred Groves.

 **recept:** Indians never show surprise, emotion or

physical distress.

 **pplication:**

§   **Don't give in to the body, and never let your face betray you.**

This gives you the edge, and protects you from cheap shots. When engaging in any physical feat, watch your breathing! Don't pant or even breathe hard through your mouth. Suppress it, and sneak-breathe through your nose, whilst smiling and looking relaxed and cheerful. Your comrade will think that your physical condition is so far above him that he can't hope to equal it, except by prayer. Or he might possibly ask you for instruction (if you have the time for dilettantes). This psychological strategy generally worked quite well on the uninitiated. They were impressed, though I can't remember any of them ever taking instruction.

My brothers and I never let on to each other – just reciprocated in kind, silently. Our pride was at stake! I can tell you one thing, though: this produced a lot of frustrated, repressed sneaky-breathers!

Precept: **Be prepared at all times!**

Application:

§   **Walk silently in the woods.**

If you get a thorn in your foot, don't stop to pick it out. It's nothing.

§   **Expect a sneak-attack at any time.**

§   **Always be ready to run the gauntlet.**

§   **If someone ties you up, know how to get loose.**

Don't count the cost, and don't complain.

§   **Die before letting anyone beat you at "Indian Wrestling" or any other test of strength.**

**recept:**   **Don't join up!**

**pplication:**

§   **You must stand alone. If everyone's doing it, it's wrong!**

It *must* be, or the world wouldn't be in such a mess! Our path was the way of the stoic and mystic, independent and tough. This didn't mean we couldn't do *anything* others did – we were allowed to *eat*, for instance – but must never follow any social dicta.

§   **You don't *have* a "peer group."**

Never desire to belong, or seek the approval of those your age. Don't go to them for advice – this is worse than consulting adults! Be glad when they cast you out – you're really getting somewhere now! You are an example to others, though it may choke them.

§   **Don't be a "teenager!"**

(You'll notice I still handle that word carefully...) Teenagers were emotional, unstable, and unreliable. Who needed that? Worse yet, they went through puberty. *That* was a self-limiting state of mind we would never allow. (*If you don't open Pandora's Box, you won't have Pandora's problems!*)

§ **Never listen to anything but classical music, and be very selective even with it.**

Classical music is just very fine, beautiful music, with no agenda. You can listen to it without worrying about your safety. But popular music is a social tool, used to bond its members together emotionally. (Think about what the word "bond" really means!) And it all starts so innocently...

"Do you want to come over to my house and listen to some jazz?"

"No!" you firmly reply.

The Devil's advocate persists, "Hey, man, this is *cool* jazz, with a New-Age theme – it's what's *happening!*"

"Sorry – I can't do that. I play by the *Old Age* Rules–" (Think 18th century!) "– but I'm glad you told me what's coming into fashion... it will be easier to avoid."

You are being pleasantly invited to tread the primrose path, and if you divagate from *your path* only a trifle, you'll set your foot on that slippery slope where there is no holding your place. Little by little, you'll slide down it to the bottomless pit. It will seem harmless enough on the way down, but, one day, you will discover that your backbone is missing.

All the while, *they* will tell you everything is okay – I'm okay, you're okay, *everyone's* okay. But at the end, it will be "NO ONE'S OKAY!"

Precept: Never become an adult!

Application:

§ **They are pale shadows of what they once were – serious, dull and straitjacketed.**

You won't have any fun, and your life will get tangled past unraveling. Besides, just look at them! As Thoreau said, their hands have grown too coarse from ordinary living, and can no longer pick the finer fruits of life.

§ **Don't "share" projects you're planning with them.**

Even if they don't stop you, you'll lose your enthusiasm when you hear their take on it.

**recept:**   **Don't desire material things!**

pplication:

§   **You must have few wants. "A man is rich in proportion to the fewness of his wants." – Thoreau**

Indians need few material possessions! Once you get them, *they've* got *you!* It will require a job to keep you supplied, and then there's *maintenance.* So you'll have to buy a car to go to a job to service those possessions. Once on that job, sure enough! – Some girl with no judgment will see you. The dating cycle will begin, almost against your will (due to our flawed nature).

§   **You don't need a watch, either.**

I don't? **No.** It's only for running on someone else's schedule, like working in the factory. You must learn to tell time by the sun and the North Star! The Indians did.

§   **Never covet your neighbors' possessions.**

(Except food on your brother's or sister's plate.) Otherwise, it's gonna be *jail,* and maintenance on *stolen* goods. (Thieves don't often think of this, probably since they plan to steal again before maintenance problems occur.)

§ **You MAY have fishing and hunting gear, and camping equipment.**

These will enable you to better observe the Code, and keep safe.

§ **Never get a car!**

If you do, boys who never gave you the time of day before will now ask you to go places *neither* of you should go!

Nick and I met a man squirrel-hunting on Grailville's property, near the small footbridge that crossed Bear Creek on the way to the new church. After exchanging pleasantries, he expressed interest in what motivated us, as "teenagers."

"Don't you want wheels?" he asked. "Boy, when I was 16, I couldn't think of anything but wheels and a girl."

Oh, brother! We thought.

This gave us a rare opportunity to assume the pulpit and expound some very unusual ideals to this poor man, who thought he was in the woods that day to hunt and enjoy himself. Nicky and I talked in turns, each picking up where the other left off. It gave us quite an advantage – one could talk while the other reloaded.

We told him we had *no* interest in cars, and even less in girls, and that we preferred to walk, run, or bike to our destinations.

He was mystified. "What do you do with your time? I'd be bored sick!"

Nick and I looked at each other. This man really needed help!

So we treated him to a whole array of things he could do to avoid boredom and improve himself: studying woodlore, taking up gardening, making maple syrup, learning to paint, play the piano, or speak a foreign language, and more.

When we mentioned playing the piano, he said, "I thought that was only for *nancy-boys*."

We didn't know that term, but it made us uneasy, so we skipped right by it, and gave him a list of improving reading: Thoreau, Emerson, Christ, etc. We also recommended prayer, but only if he took Catholic instruction first. Otherwise, it was time wasted.

I don't recall his saying much to all this, and I wasn't into reading subtle expressions, especially when I was *telling* someone. We were a little disappointed that he didn't inquire further about the conversion option. Didn't some people *care* about their future well-being?

He wasn't a *bad* man – he just looked like a French goose that had been force-fed more than it could easily grind and swallow. It would take him a while to figure out just what he'd eaten.

§   **Don't get a driver's license!**

This sounds innocent enough, if you don't have a car, but it enables you to wreck someone else's car and encounter the same miseries and pitfalls detailed above. Then you'll have to get a job to pay for the destroyed or damaged car, in addition to the car you'll have to *buy* (almost certainly on credit) in order to get to work.

Even worse, you might be in jail, or the hospital, resulting from the accident. Recovering from your injuries may be easier than from a relationship with a nurse. She might take an unreasonable fancy to you (*unreasonable*, because you're such a poor risk for her future prosperity and happiness). If this happens, you could end up with a job, a wife, considerable debt, and possibly limited physical abilities to begin your new life, and all because you *had to have that driver's license.*

Precept: **Never talk to girls, or even notice them!**

Application:

The area where we needed the Code's help most of all was gender relations. We found the Church's approach remarkably androgynous, and, being young men with natural urges, we knew it wouldn't be a good idea to wander around aimlessly until some girl picked us up as strays.

So we looked to our Code to close that gap, and devised practical ways to counter the threat.

No dating! No dancing! No social graces! That was all girls were going to get from us. What girl would possibly want the tough, strongly opinionated, graceless and cold persons we presented?

We had a low opinion of girls. Any person (*thing*) that could be won over by candy, flowers, or jewelry was unworthy of our regard. TV had amply demonstrated their weaknesses, and our sisters seemed to confirm them. To associate with girls after you knew this meant only one thing: you were following your baser instincts, and would end up losing freedom and eternal life all in one throw, not to mention sinking lower than a worm.

After my eighth-grade summer, I knew there was no hair-trigger to the MSBCBBM phenomenon, but you still got a life-sentence if they caught you. (It was really more of a drawn-out death-sentence, like being nibbled to death by lemmings.)

Observing those who succumbed over time, we detected the following formula in action, and immediately codified it, for our deliverance:

This dread formula motivated us constantly to avoid even *looking* the wrong direction! It was just too dangerous. And by the time you learn how vicious the formula is, it's too late. The law mandates that you maintain that family, so you can't even afford the satisfaction of telling your boss what an unprincipled bigot he is, or where he can go (for starters). You lose your self-respect, eat too much, start drinking beer and compulsively watch TV in the evenings to escape.

If this downward cycle doesn't begin when you discover you can't reveal your boss's true quality, it will when you have to baby-sit the children you've acquired (almost overnight, it seems). Rationalization says clearly that you might as well be watching TV during this harrowing activity, to keep your sanity. The beer-drinking starts as soon as you learn how much crying the baby does, and how many times you have to change diapers. Beer deadens the senses, and helps you not to mind getting no sleep. Did I mention smoking, to calm lacerated nerves? Oh, well, you've got the idea. What can you do, besides growing fat and dull, and starting to feel that you're leading the life of a slug?

But you can look forward to this: later on, seeing the sorry picture you present, your kids will have the temerity to tell you you're not really alive, and won't listen to a thing you say!

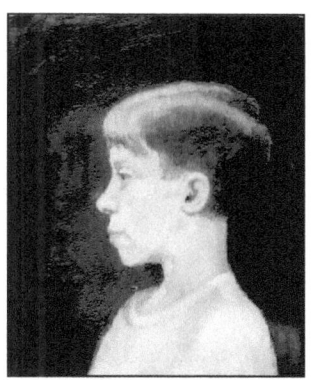

Chapter XVI.

Peter's Harvest

Peter was only three years behind me, but it always seemed more like six. He had the unforgivable quality of going his own way, instead of trying to imitate his older brothers. To me, "his way" was "no way," and I felt so self-righteous and saintly when I lectured him about the old saw, "A *coward dies a thousand deaths, and a brave man only one.*" But he appeared to have Attention Deficit Syndrome at such times, and it never changed him one whit.

The youngest in the family has a special karma. It is his lot to eat a large portion of humble pie, and be content to be left alone (which, of course, he is *not*). Peter was never allowed to forget his lowly place, at the feet of the Masters. Our attention was given to what he couldn't do, what he *wouldn't* do, and where he was supposed to be (but wasn't). We wanted to form his character properly, while there was still time.

I had a cute dog once, named Sassafras. When thrown outside for such doggie crimes as being a nuisance in the kitchen, generally doing everything wrong, and finally getting stepped on and yiping, she would proceed to kill ants with her paws on the front steps, one after the other. *Hail, Lord of the Ants!*

Peter's older brothers, too, were sometimes driven by unconscious forces. A six-year-old peers jealously into the playpen and sneers, "*Baby!* You stay in there until I *say* you can climb out!" (And that just might be *never!*) He longs to feel superior to *something*, since he's had to take a lot of interference from parents and older children. Perhaps he really sees a younger, more vulnerable, version of himself, and it frightens him.

I still wonder that all our well-intended criticism proved so ineffectual. (Though it's true I did leave home early and left off his training sooner than expected...) The inscrutability of the East, in some past existence, must have case-hardened his soul against our improvements. In spite of our easy talent for repression, we weren't able to prevent Peter from growing up, and he turned out surprisingly well, even without following much of our excellent advice and examples. (There *must* be another well!)

By the time I was in high school, Peter and I often did things together – berry-picking, riding our bikes, or fishing and camping. It vexed me that he was the better fisherman, but I was always keyed up (even when I thought I was almost asleep). I wanted the fish too badly, and they knew it, somehow, telegraphed through the pole and the line. I rarely caught anything, but Peter had cultivated the habit of doing nothing (that I could see), and seemed transparent to the fish, just part of the shrubbery.

Sometimes we would go rock-hunting up the O'Bannon, looking for fossils of prehistoric fish, shells, and trilobites. Occasionally we found large ones imbedded in huge limestone slabs, and would gaze longingly, wishing we could extract them whole from their rock prisons.

Early one fall, we decided to take a camping and fishing trip. There was an abandoned orchard that seemed perfect on Grailville's property, not far from where Nick and I had purloined the pine log. It was overgrown, but there was still enough grass under the trees for good bedding, *and* ripe fruit for the taking. We dreamed of apples roasted on sticks and cooked with the fish we were going to catch in Grailville's lake. I had actually caught a 3-½ pound bass there once, after a rain—it provided enough hope to keep me angling fruitlessly for years.

We planned to arrive at the lake after lunch, allowing plenty of time to catch and clean the fish, and set up camp. Not much gear would be needed – sleeping bags, a cast-iron skillet foraged from the stove drawer, and the indispensable Bowie knife. Then there was the fishing gear and Nick's old backpack, famed in song and story for its excruciating design, but which did, also, convey goods. We wouldn't need the old canvas tent, since the weather was still very warm and dry. This would be an opportunity to get closer to nature and the stars – though we did take some M-80s along to enliven any dull moments. We saw no inconsistency.

By the time lunch came around, our packing was done. I looked fondly at my Harrington & Richardson shotgun, but it wasn't hunting season yet, and it might seem a little insensitive to be holding it when asking permission to fish.

Our house was about half a mile from the lake. Taking a shortcut through the neighbors' property, we stopped at Grailville's communal bakery to see Elise, the manager. The policy of asking permission was new, and it irked us, since we had always run free in the close-knit neighborhood. But the big city was inching closer, and they wanted to know who was on their property. Our family was respected in the community, and Grailville never refused us, though the Corn Engrosser would have been highly tempted. She later got back at us – or so we imagined – by cutting down all the willows around the pond on some pseudo-logical premise. The pond became muddy, and most of the fish promptly died.

Carrying our fishing gear, we took the gravel road past the women's dormitory, the dairy barn, the pottery and silk-screening house, and the new barn, all of them white, with green roofs. On our left was a large sweep of field and sky, culminating in a hill surmounted by a large wooden cross. They called it Calvary, and it drew the eye for some distance. When I was very young, I thought it was the original Golgotha, and it made me pay serious attention in church. Christ had been crucified *right in our backyard!* I could never pass it without feeling sober. Even later, when I knew better, my reactions were fixed, and I was back in church momentarily, till the cross was out of sight.

We came to the lake at last, its edges still dotted with willow-shade, and excitedly started fishing, but the catch was poor that day, in the heat. We were hopeful, as always, but all sensible fish seemed to be on siesta, and we only caught a few scrawny minnows that didn't have enough wit to stay in their reedy beds, as their elders had told them. After a couple of hours, we threw in the towel. *Oh, well,* we thought, *the day's not over yet – on to camping! Apples can be pretty filling, can't they?*

The old orchard was only a short distance across the fields. We hadn't asked permission to camp, but didn't see how they could object, though it was comforting that our site was hidden from the casual eye.

Golden leaves lay on the ground beneath the trees, dotted with apples, and everything seemed idyllic, even the gentle hum of bees. Feeling serene, we began to set up camp, choosing the most comfortable spots for our sleeping bags, and I started to gather dead wood for a fire. Soon I had it built. It was... rather large. Oh, well, no matter! It would burn itself out. We began to roast apples on sticks. They were pretty good, but you can only eat so many on an empty stomach, and somehow it didn't satisfy the need for solid food.

It looked like it was going to be a lean night, but it turned out that Peter had stowed away ham sandwiches and potato chips, hidden in his gear. My first impulse was to administer a dope-slap, and lecture him for his non-adherence to principle, but, for once, salivary secretions managed to halt hasty speech.

Peter didn't notice the ripple of annoyance crossing my face – none of us were in the habit of being "sensitive" to each other. We *were the way we were,* and people just had to adapt. Anyone who didn't like it could take his medicine straight up. (A satisfying approach, when you're in the driver's seat) We thought it was all normal, for a large family – though we did know *some* families who would actually ask one another how they were feeling, or if they had slept well. They might even ask if something were too heavy for their sister to lift, and always said, "Please," "Thank you," and "You're welcome!" Like Tom Sawyer, we felt suffocated, just watching them – they *couldn't* be for real...

To soothe any qualms of conscience, I pointed out to Peter that the sandwiches were more entertainment than food, while the apples, being organic, were healthier and would carry more nutrition.

As we finished our meal, it was getting dark. Not talking much, we sat around the campfire for a while, trying to fill up on apples, and finally decided to turn in – staying up would only give us more time to think about unsatisfied appetites. So we got in our sleeping bags, expecting to repose gently in the sweet arms of nature.

Just as I started to drop off, I heard a high-pitched hum. When I raised my head to listen, it quit, so I closed my eyes.

After several minutes, it began again. The sound reminded me of something... but what was it?

When it started for the third time, I had an idea. I turned on my flashlight and carefully inspected the ground.

Nothing!

Then something made me pull back the sleeping bag gently, and I finally knew what the sound was.

BEES!!

Yellow-jackets had built nests in the ground under the bag. With a yelp, I got my bag and myself out of there! Peter made a similar discovery, and effected his own escape. Fortunately, the bees weren't quite so active at night, and we avoided being drilled, but this kind of activity doesn't exactly sing a lullaby to an agitated psyche. We moved our bags to an apparently un-buzzy place.

So far, so good. We settled down again.

In five minutes, I started to hear rustling noises in the bushes. I sat up. "Did you hear that, Peter?"

"Yeah, I think it's an animal."

"Shine the light!"

Nothing to be seen.

O-kay. Back to bed.

Immediately, we discovered that numerous ticks were in our bags and on us. After removing them from the world, we tried again, and achieved a half-sleep for a few minutes.

Then I heard Peter cry out, "Something walked over my bag!"

Well, that got *him* up. Just before that, I'd been hearing more noises. In the bushes. Again. It sounded like a small army of little animals.

So we shone the light. Again.

Nothing to be seen.

By now, we were getting a little peeved. We had moved beyond the "reverence-for-the-little-animals" stage.

I said, "I know, let's clear the place with the M-80s. That'll scare off everything, and then we can get some REST!"

We threw several into the dark. It jarred us to hear just how *loud* they were, at that time of night. Just over the hill were the Rogans' residence and another small house belonging to Grailville. It didn't occur to us that M-80s might attract their attention. We didn't think about the campfire being a giveaway, either.

One of the M-80s started a small grass fire, just to keep our interest keen. We didn't know that could happen! But it was quickly stomped out.

Then we made a thorough investigation of the area with our light.

No animals anywhere.

"Well, I think that's done it," I said, with satisfaction. "That'll clear the little varmints out!"

We went to bed again, this time with the smell of black powder in our nostrils, but determined to try one... more... time. My imagination, however, started to work overtime. *What*, I thought, *if one of those little animals is a skunk, and it gets on my bag and sprays me right in the face?*

That tore it for *my* sleep. But then... it was so quiet, all of a sudden... I began to think that maybe this *was* going to work, after all. I started to doze, for one whole minute.

Then... *something walked over my bag!*

And the bushes literally boiled with the noise of small animals –

—and the bees got excited all over again –

– and the ticks riposted vigorously, moving in the reserves!

Peter and I jumped up, harassed and whining, and proceeded to break camp. We hadn't realized that the four-footed mammals liked apples as much as two-footed ones! While we'd been anticipating camping and fruit, so had the animals and insects. The yellow-jackets wanted the rotten apples, while the ticks wanted the blood of whatever showed up to eat them. Everyone was waiting for night to fall.

After divesting ourselves of the remaining ticks, we packed our gear quickly, and headed home, taking the long way, by the railroad. Trudging down the tracks, we were starting to feel a little pulled. It was around midnight, and we had that funny feeling that comes when you've had a long day, and stayed up too late. We also discovered that chiggers, too, had lived in the orchard, and a lot of scratching commenced between us.

But it *was* a warm summer night, soft and quiet. No humans or cars were about, and the world was still and peaceful. The insects' singing was subdued, a flat, horizontal sound on the air. Peter and I were subdued, too.

The trip was uneventful, except that it seemed to take a lot longer than normal. We crossed the creek in the usual spot at Theodore's Pond, and went up the cliff path and over the field to home.

All the lights were out. No one was up. We entered the house through the back-porch door to the kitchen, and made straight for the refrigerator. We were starving! We ate everything we could forage, topping it all with "Chill Whip" that Mother had made, as though our camping *débacle* had been intuitively foreseen.

And no sooner did we sit down to eat at the table than Mother herself showed up. She had a knack for this, when anything unusual occurred in the house. She always said it was because she heard us, but I never believed that.

"What are you boys doing back? I thought you were camping out?"

"We came back," I said unnecessarily.

"Animals," Peter said, chewing his sandwich.

She didn't ask any more questions. She never did — I think that's how she survived.

All she said was: "Put the dishes in the sink when you're done, and the mayonnaise in the refrigerator. And turn the light out, when you go to bed."

"OK," I said.

Peter wasn't going to put away anything... That wasn't his style, but he wouldn't say so.

We finished eating, and started to sink into unconsciousness.

"Let's go to bed," I said, scratching.

"Okay."

"You know... camping isn't so bad if you can come home to "Chill Whip."

"Yeah," he said. "Night..."

* * *

Another time, we coincidentally became partners-in-crime. It was a dreary school morning in late February when Peter and I simultaneously fell ill with stomach ache and headache, possibly induced by yesterday's school or unfinished homework.

Our illnesses always revealed themselves before we got up, or at least before the bus came. I always thought this showed good judgment and consideration, since it would be awkward and inconvenient for everyone if you went to school, got sick, then had to come home in a taxi. Taxis were expensive, so I figured we saved Dad a lot of money. In fact, I can't recall a single time any of us was so thoughtless.

As usual on sick days, Peter and I spent a quiet morning. First we slept in, then got up and ate some breakfast, being careful to eat only half as much as usual. To underline our poor condition, we shuffled around in our bathrobes, trying to look subdued and meek. (We didn't actually *limp* – that would have been too much.)

By afternoon, we were almost completely cured. (This was reasonable for a stomach-ache and headache, we thought.) By 2:30, we would start getting very active, and Mother would caution, "Aren't you overdoing it, boys?"

Either we would ignore this, or say, "No, we're fine now." It was true. We felt amazingly good when we knew that school was out. There was a lightening of the air. (Though I remember one time that I stayed home from school with plans, and actually did get sick later. Now, *that* was disgusting. What a waste of a day! Worst of all, since I was *already* supposed to be sick, no one was very sympathetic!)

It helped that Mother wasn't a rigid believer in kids spending every possible day in school, though it did bother her a little that she had to write "stomach ache" on notes so often, since she was a good cook. I remember her saying laughingly that she was embarrassed to give that excuse to Mr. Guest *again*. "What must he think of my cooking?"

She wasn't fooled any more than she wanted to be by our temporary illnesses. She figured there must be some reason we didn't want to go to school, if we weren't really sick... either it wasn't a good school, or there were bullies, or we just needed a mental break. This was pretty tolerant of her, since, when she was a girl, she liked school and was a good student. (When she confessed this, it took us a long while to comprehend, and even longer to forgive.)

On this particular day, she phoned her mother to relate events and chat. Well, Gramma must have heard us talking in the background, because we heard her say sharply, "What are the boys home for?"

"Oh, nothing much – they've got headaches and stomach aches," Mother replied.

"Again?" Gramma said. "Are you sure you're feeding them right? What did they have for dinner last night?"

Mother's boat was filling up fast, and she hurriedly started to bail: "Oh, I fixed *Moussaka*, milk, bread..."

"What's Moussaka?" Gramma asked testily. She was of English extraction, and her cooking was hearty, traditional English fare: roast beef, potatoes, gravy, peas, etc. She never quite got used to her daughter's excursions into foreign cuisine, and resented them. What was good enough for her should be good enough for Mother.

"Oh, it comes from the Balkans. It has eggplant, bread-crumbs, hamburger, Parmesan cheese, and tomato juice." Here she started a long explanation of how to prepare it, but Gramma cut her off at the pass.

"Humph! No wonder they're sick, eating that foreign food. Sounds too rich for kids." Foreigners didn't have a lick of sense, so you couldn't trust their food, either.

Hearing the part about our sensitive stomachs, we had to smother our laughter in pillows on the couch. Our stomachs were like cast iron.

But it was rather pleasant to hear our mother being criticized. Gramma was always pleased to add more of her daughter's shortcomings to her list: Mother didn't dress her kids properly when they went out to play, or it was too cold for them to be out – didn't she know that? Or how to discipline them properly when they did something? (Why else why would her daughter tell her about it? Just more evidence that – as she had always suspected – Mother wasn't up to *her* level of competency and wisdom, when it came to raising kids.) Then, too, there was always the underlying theme that she "shouldn't have married *him*, in the first place." *He* was a Catholic, and Mother had converted – reprehensible, to Methodist thinking.

So, although Gramma couldn't put her finger on it, these conversational exchanges with her daughter made her feel better. She subtly inferred from them that her daughter still needed advice, just as she always had, and probably always would.

From Mother's point of view, she was merely chronicling events, not requesting advice, but no subject seemed safe from Gramma's commentary and exclamations of "Oh, for heaven's sake!" The phone was hung up at last, without acrimonious words but often a wry twist of the mouth, as though Mother had tasted a lemon.

We would have loved it if schools had been declared unhealthy or unsafe, like so many today. It was a wonderful day for us when the school furnace failed during below-zero weather. Perhaps the schools *were* unhealthy, and we were just environmentally sensitive, ahead of our time. Not only did we not feel well *at* school, but even thinking about it at home could bring on weakness at the knees (and certainly in the brain). Maybe asbestos was affecting us, or lead in the drinking water – I don't know. But we knew when we'd been shot out of the sky, and school did it every time.

This afternoon, Peter and I were going to be home alone. That didn't happen too often, and it would provide fertile soil for creativity, since we wouldn't have to play any role. We could relax and focus.

After lunch, Peter was lying in his bunk bed upstairs, desultorily drawing mustaches on various personages in magazines. ("National Geographic" was a favorite.) It didn't bother anybody in the family much, but was mostly for the edification of the music students and their parents, who casually perused the magazines while waiting for a lesson to start or finish. It gave them the opportunity for revelations: "*I didn't know Indira Gandhi looked like that in a mustache!*" I always thought this was pretty poor sport, appropriate to the marginally sane, but it wasn't my lookout.

I started my own amusement in the kitchen, throwing wadded-up paper balls into the kitchen wastebasket, with the ample supply of unwanted materials from school. Peter immediately forsook his drawing, and joined me in a duel. I lost, because I got too intense and spoiled my aim. It rankled to be beaten by the youngest, but it was a baby game, anyway, and I wasn't surprised an idiot won it. Who cared? *He probably cheated,* I thought, though I couldn't figure out how.

After these intellectual pursuits, it was about 2:00. We were tired of diddling, and a little bored. But our energy was picking up fast – school was defeated by now!

At this point, we noticed our dog, Sam, peacefully sleeping by the kitchen door, and instantly felt obliged make his life more interesting. We began by thumping his tummy and speaking to him in growl-speech. This elicited only meager response, in the form of soft "orumphs" and "groomps," punctuated by the silent lifting of the lip to show teeth, which plainly said: "Buzz off!"

Peter and I looked at each other, miffed. We couldn't have an unresponsive dog — we just *had* to liven him up. Then we remembered a story our parents told about Uncle Tony - in the time of the Great Depression, he had mail-ordered a disguise kit, and dressed up as a bum. Then he came to their back door, asking for a meal. His parents never recognized him.

What effect might this have on Sam? We decided to try dressing up, one at a time, and coming to the door as strangers. Peter quietly left the house first, after borrowing clothes from the hall closet. He used the old garage as his dressing room, and I removed myself to the back porch to observe the fun.

After a decent interval, the "stranger at the door" announced himself by thumping the brass knocker. This in itself was suspicious, since the knocker wasn't used much, but Sam was cool. He opened one eye and stirred a little, but didn't get up, as though to say, "I can accept that."

Now, Sam was a congenial, low-key hound dog, though he had plenty of courage when cornered. I once saw him whip five dogs in our front yard, two of them larger than he was. They were just passing through, and jumped him for no apparent reason. I couldn't believe his reaction - during most of the fight, he kept making 180-degree turns in midair to cover both directions.

But he was always very sensible. By the time he was six, he was on to almost everything we did. We had used every means we could invent to keep him at his most sentient and stirred up, and he had become such a good actor that you never quite knew whether he was fooled by our antics or faking. That was what goaded us to keep devising ever-more-ingenious games.

Peter knocked heavily, three times, like the sound of doom on that old door. Then he opened the door slowly, a little at a time, and poked his head through. That head was framed by a large, flowered straw hat, with ties under the chin. He presented an outlandish picture, in a dress that was too large and dragged the floor, and my mother's winter coat, open at the front, with an umbrella held cane-like in his right hand. In a high, falsetto voice, he sang out, "*How do de do?*"

Sam quickly changed his mind... *something was* WRONG. That was just *too* peculiar – it *had* to be a real, live monster! He began growling, deep in his throat, with his hackles up.

The stranger was now completely inside, and beginning to shuffle and tap its way across the hardwood floor in high-heeled shoes. That did it! Sam jumped up with his hair bristling, but held his position.

The thing kept advancing slowly. Sam started barking furiously, warning it not to come any closer. *"Alarm! Fire! It's the devil herself!"*

But it wouldn't stop! – It just kept coming, clicking and making strange sucking-noises. Sam tried to retreat, but he was cornered, so he ran under the table and then to the back door – but it was closed! With all his talents, he couldn't open it. *"Help!"*

No good – he was going to have to fight. He turned fierce. *"One more step, and I'm going to have to bite you real bad!"* his stance shouted.

We were delighted – we couldn't have asked for a better reaction! Peter started to laugh so hard that he fell over on the floor, clutching his stomach. Sam discovered his mistake, and started gnawing on Peter's ankles and growling in chagrin. Then I broke out laughing, too, whereupon he meted out the punishment equally.

We tried to soothe him with sweet-talk: "Sammy! Sammy! We were only playing... It was just a joke!" But he meant to make us pay, and nipped hard enough to hurt. *"How dare you tease a mature, dignified dog who was just minding his own business?"*

After Sam calmed down, I thought I would try *my* luck at the "odd-stranger" role. It was too good to use only once. So I gathered my chosen wardrobe, and sneaked down the outside cellar-way, through the unlighted basement to the cellar stairs. There, I put on my costume, and climbed the stairs slowly, dragging my feet in a sinister fashion, and pausing to sniff vigorously every so often. At the top of the stairs, I rattled the doorknob, then slowly pushed it open a few inches, since it was held by a chain. I growled a few half-words through the crack, producing wonderfully alarming reactions on the other side. Sam threw his body hard against the door, snarling ferociously. We vowed *never* to forget this, and added it to our repertoire, for the next slow day.

Before my mother came home around 4:00 and started fixing supper, we had carefully gotten rid of the evidence. She asked us what we'd been doing, and we made the classic reply, "Nothing..."

Sam gave a loud snort in the corner, which said emphatically, "*Liar!*" and put his head back down on his paws.

Chapter XVII.

Making Maple Syrup

The maple trees in the yard were leaking sap. After a cold night in late January, the wind had died and the sun was shining. By 10:00, the thermometer had reached 35° and was still rising. On the ground, the snow of a week ago had finally released its grip, and dry patches showed last year's leaves shining coppery. Tree branches were warm and still. I looked up at the pinkish trunk of the huge maple in the back yard, and saw sap running from a broken branch. *Why not make maple syrup?!* No one was around to nay-say, and my plans went forward.

Inside, I checked Collier's Encyclopaedia for anything on the subject. There wasn't much, but it did say you needed warm days and cold nights. The season lasted roughly from January 29th to April 17th, depending on your locale. You had to drill a hole in the tree no deeper than the sap layer— ½ to ¾ inches deep. When the sap started flowing, you'd know it was right. After collecting that sap in a bucket every day, you could boil it down to make the syrup. It took 35 gallons of sap to produce *one* of maple syrup.

I made my announcement to the family. This was never very productive, but it was my style, and I earnestly believed in sharing my ideas. My news release created diverse effects among the brethren.

Dad hadn't had breakfast yet, so he stated unequivocally that it couldn't be done, at least by us. Apparently we not only lacked the right knowledge and equipment, but there was also a vague inference that we didn't have the brains. This was a little puzzling, since the basic idea is to put sap in a pot, and boil it until syrup is produced. (Oh, I forgot – you do have to stir it, at times.)

However, being an optimist, I took this to mean, "Go forth, favored son. You're resourceful – you'll find a way to do what needs to be done!"

Mother was at her post, doing the household chores, and forbore to counter this dictum. Peter wasn't allowed to say anything (but was permitted to watch the show). I could see Nick was interested, so we exchanged a "*We'll talk later*" look. Gregory was interested, too, but knew better than to contradict Dad while he was feeding.

This was my project, so I expected to do a lot of the work, though I knew I could count on Nick from start to finish, or whenever I most needed help. Greg was dependable, too, provided he agreed to it in the first place, but he was a junior in high school, and busy with track, art projects, and brooding. (A requirement for budding artists) Peter... well, one didn't include him in practical matters, unless to go fishing, or maybe to eat a pancake with maple syrup on it. Though even that was not certain, due to inefficiencies – wasted pancake, wasted syrup, inordinate time to eat, etc.

Right after breakfast, Nick and I went next-door to parley with Old Man Monihan about the black cast-iron kettle in his barn. When we asked him, he said, "That thar kettle was used to render lard in m'pappy's tahm!" Then he added, "Sure, y'all kin use it if yer kin git it out o' th' barn!" He smiled, peering over his gold-framed spectacles, showing teeth stained yellow from long tobacco-chewing.

After we left him, grateful for the use of the kettle, Nick mused, "I wonder what he was smiling about."

"He was probably looking forward to seeing us handle that kettle. It must weigh a ton," I said.

So, after lunch, we went to retrieve that witches' cauldron. It held 35 gallons and weighed around 150 pounds. The weight was nothing to us, but it was awkward. The cast-iron bail kept unhooking itself – that is, when it wasn't trying to pinch your hand, or anything else that got in the way. We wrestled and slid our trophy home, getting nipped and bruised in the process, but with no real difficulty except at the boundary fence, which sustained some damage before letting us by.

Now we had our kettle. But what were we going to do for wood? We knew it would take a lot. There were plenty of dead elm trees around, so we logically decided to cut elm. When every decision pointed to more hard work, we felt better and better. We were **men!**

At first we planned to fell the trees with axes, but if you've ever tried to cut dead elm with an axe, you know where this is going. Our first candidate stood near some big catalpas on the edge of our property, and after we spent a couple of hours gnawing through its 2-foot trunk, we learned that *axes* are for <u>green</u> wood. *Saws* are what you use to cut dead wood.

Once we had made this discovery, the devil pointed out a saw we could use: a six-foot, two-man saw that had belonged to Grandpa Pfarr. In its day, it had undoubtedly cut many cords, but now it hung in our garage, looking over 100 years old, handles needing repair and teeth dull and ground-down. But we didn't know about that until after a little experience, which sounded like this: "*Swish-swish, Swish-swish, Swish-swish, Swish-swish, Swish-swish, Swish-swish, Swish-swish,*" for thousands and thousands of strokes, until there was nothing else left in the world. With each stroke, tons of sweat rolled off us, but only a trickle of sawdust came out.

It took half an hour to saw through a 12-inch log. *Ok, that's fine,* we thought. *We're building the biggest muscles in the County.* The saw's only reply was, "*Swish-swish, Swish-swish, Swish-swish.*"

After a while, we were so hypnotized by its sound and rhythm that we almost *couldn't* quit. Neither of us would even think of stopping until a log section was sawed through, however agonizing – that would indicate you were out of shape. But when suppertime came, it was quitting-time, mid-stroke or no. You *couldn't* fly in the face of parental authority.

After two weeks of nonstop sawing in all our free time, we finally had a pile of wood, which we wheelbarrowed to our chosen pyre-site in the backyard. Even we realized we couldn't go on this way. I told Nick, "There's GOT to be a way to sharpen this saw!" But our work mentor, the Evil One, told us, "You'll lose time... *just keep sawing!*"

Still, we visited the saw-sharpeners in town, but no one seemed to know how to deal with a two-man saw any more. They looked at us as though we had committed a crime against modernity, not in wanting our saw sharpened, but in actually using a *handsaw* to cut wood. This forced me to point out to one of them that if you avoided work, you would end up with a big potbelly. He didn't take this advice in good part, probably because his own middle was beginning to swell considerably.

Well, Old Scratch won that day, so it was back to the salt mines. By good fortune, we stumbled across a Swedish bow-saw in the garage, and purchased a new blade, or we might *still* be in that clearing, sawing away.

The next torture was splitting trunk-sections into firewood. You see, God did not intend elm to be split. This was one of the woodworking commandments passed down to Moses on the mount (but evidently not to *us*). God-fearing early pioneers knew about it – that's why they used it for wagon-tongues, because it wouldn't break, no matter how many times it was twisted under load. Despite this fact, we chewed our way through logs, using a sledgehammer and wedges. It was so bad that one wedge had to be *burnt* out of the log in which it had lodged itself. (My dad was gaining points.)

Getting enough wood was only part of the project. We needed containers for gathering sap, a brace-and-bit to drill holes in the trees, and short lengths of pipe to channel sap into the buckets. Our evil genius showed us copper pipe that was perfect for the job, but it turned out not to be such a good idea – toward the end of the season, I noticed green slime growing thickly on them, but didn't know what it was – something called *verdigris*. (Later, I knew. Nothing seemed to come off in the sap, though.) None of these things daunted us, and we continued with *esprit*, but the burnt offerings Nick and I made that season probably helped alleviate significant karmic debt.

I persuaded Loveland Bakery to give me six 5-gallon tins that had contained lard and flour. They weren't nearly enough, so I ransacked every pot and pan of size I could get from the house. Another day, I drilled all the holes and drove in the copper pipes.

Next, we had to build a primitive crane, so we could suspend the kettle and lift it off the fire when necessary. We used two vertical 6" locust posts with natural Y-crotches at the top, then cut a locust pole (notched in the center for the bail) to span those crotches, and hold the kettle. When the fire got too hot at the wrong time, we would lift the pole to take the kettle off the fire, and set it on the ground to cool.

It wasn't till one Saturday in February that we were ready to start boiling sap, and the buckets were overflowing. Collecting them eagerly, we filled the kettle to the brim and started the fire. Annoyingly, the flames didn't know they were supposed to stay *under* the kettle. It was windy, and the fire alternately tried to singe and choke us whenever we got near the pot to stir.

Coughing and with streaming eyes, we kept circling it, trying to escape the small purgatory we'd created. (What iron stuff were our early forefathers made of? Perhaps our father's pessimistic *credo* was worth a second look...)

As the fire raged on, I noticed that the locust posts supporting the kettle were beginning to ignite. We doused them with water, but the main problem remained: What were we going to do? _The_ _blasted_ _flames_ _would_ _not_ _stay_ _under_ _the_ _blasted_ _kettle,_ _and_ _the_ _blasted_ _sap_ _wouldn't_ _boil!_

At such a time, it's probably the better part of valor to stand back, reevaluate, and proceed later with fresh ideas. Nicky and I weren't old enough to know that, so we stood fast and added *more* wood, grimly thinking, *Whatever it takes!*

Now it was no longer a blaze, but a veritable inferno, and a highly mobile one. But never mind – we were young, and could really run and dodge. So we ran faster and faster around the fire, with the flames and smoke licking close behind. At one point, Sam came out to keep us company, but took one look at the blaze, turned tail and slunk back to the house.

Uncle Marshall, stopping by to see his sister Catherine, inquired, "What are the boys doing in the yard?"

"Oh, they're making maple syrup," Mother said.

"That'll be something to see," he commented ironically. "They look like Indians on the warpath. Look how black their faces are!"

Despite detractors, the sap began to boil mightily. Now it was just a matter of time before we would have our first taste of maple syrup. By the end of the day, we did get that sap boiled down. But we had burned most of our two-week wood supply in one afternoon! If there had been any observers that evening, they would have seen two boys with blackened faces, burnt fingers, and the whites of their eyes showing in the dusk, standing around the kettle, remarking on its contents in the bottom.

"It smells a little burnt, don't it?" one boy said wearily.

"Naw, not much. I think it's just maple flavor," said the other.

Then we used a wooden spoon to sample some, after blowing on it.

"It looks gritty, too. Where did all that come from?" I wondered.

"From the wood ashes in the fire, maybe," replied Nick.

"How come there's only a quart of this stuff left?" I said.

"I dunno – maybe the dog ate it."

"Oh, sure... What would try to steal something this hot?" (except Lincoln's fabled opponent) "Besides, it says in the book that 35 gallons of sap should make a gallon of syrup," I complained. "Where did the other three quarts go?"

"They evaporated, maybe?"

"No, the *water* evaporated, <u>not</u> the sugar syrup... *where is it?*

"Pixies?"

"You've been reading those English fairy tales again... Tell me, how many pixies have *you* seen? No, never mind – I don't want to know."

"Well, *some* people have seen–" Nick started.

"Well, *other* people have seen enough to void all the laws of the universe!" I snapped. Nicholas didn't take any offense – he never did.

The day had been trying, but underneath we were content. Hadn't we triumphed over Mother Nature for the moment, wresting our first quart of (gritty) maple syrup from the elements? What if we *had* invented a new grade of syrup, called "Grade D?" So what if we were a bit toasted around the edges, and smelled like fresh smoked meat? It was nothing compared to the trials the Indians and the saints had endured.

But one thing was certain: neither of us was looking forward to another day's syrup-making. We had to solve some practical problems first, or maple season would be over. Not only the wood-supply problem, but the sludge... Oh, well. Tomorrow would be different.

Tomorrow was Sunday, and it dawned fair and clear. After church and breakfast, I went outside to consider the syrup operation. Twenty feet away, by the creek, was a pile of concrete rubble. I had tossed it there last summer, after demolishing a concrete slab, the remains of my grandparents' chicken coop. We could use that rubble to build a kiln around the kettle, to make the burning more efficient!

I started stacking it immediately, and Nick soon joined in. By dinnertime, we had the kiln completely built, surrounding the kettle closely on all sides except the front, where we left a large gap for loading big chunks of wood.

It went really well. Once the kiln was hot, anything would burn, even wood that had been lying in the creek. It also solved the wind problem, and the flames no longer scorched the posts or us. The rest of the season took no more wood than we had burned our first day!

From here on, all the boys (except Peter) took their turns at kettle-watching. Even my father became a convert. It was his slow season and he didn't have much work, so he would fire the kiln in the morning, and then stir and watch the batch all day when we were at school. For once, I was prudent, and didn't confront him about his change of heart.

We learned to improve the grade of the syrup by straining the sap through cheesecloth, and covering the kettle with a large, round aluminum cover we found in the dump, along with a wooden cane, for stirring. We did have to go back to sawing, but didn't mind this time, since we knew our wood was going to stretch a long way.

In all, we made 14 quarts. It was very good, but dark and still not clear, though we had solved the grit problem. By accident, I found the way to clarify it one day a couple of months later, when I happened to be in the cellar on an errand. Glancing up at the syrup we had put away in quarts on the shelf, I saw the late afternoon sun shining through jars of clear syrup! All the minute debris had settled to the bottom, and all I had to do was decant it.

Some critics said the resulting syrup was still only "Grade C," but after Uncle Marshall gave me a taste of his "Grade A," I definitely preferred our open-air, smoke-flavored product. You only needed two tablespoons on pancakes to completely satisfy the maple-craving, and it also took much less in baking.

Attempting to recycle our mistakes, we proffered the nutritious sludge to Sam. (Dogs eat grit all the time, right?) He sniffed it cautiously, took a lick, curled his lip slightly, and walked away, apologetically wagging his tail.

Chapter XVIII.

The Bacon Chicken

Getting the blue-and-white car had changed Steve's behavior, just as our Code predicted. Without letting anyone know he was coming, our cousin and his friends, Dutch and Red, rattled up our driveway in the '57 Ford one chilly August day. About to finish four-year sentences at Chaminade High Penitentiary, they decided to have one last fling before the year commenced. Of course, we were always ready to go camping, though having Steve's friends there made it a company occasion, without the old camaraderie. Sam knew his duty when strangers appeared, though, and barked at them helpfully.

Red was shorter than Dutch, with orange hair and freckles, and a mania for playing tricks. His restless ways got to me a little... maybe he was encroaching on *my* territory (but in a crude and vulgar way, of course - he had no subtlety at all). I strongly suspected him of having relatives among the rooster clan - he did a lot of mindless scratching and fussing in the dirt when otherwise unoccupied, though I never saw him eat any bugs.

Dutch was conservative, for a teenager - more an observer and chronicler of events than a rabble-rouser. That was Red's job. With black hair and glasses, he looked like a staid, engineering type, and had learned the amazing knack of not saying everything he thought or felt. We instinctively took this as a challenge, and by working at it, did manage to elicit a few startled expressions.

He wore a sweatshirt with the original motto, "You can't beat the Dutch!" I wasn't *inclined* to beat the Dutch - just the *Irish*, in the form of a red-haired kid.

Steve always exuded natural charm, and went on to become a salesman after college. I later heard rumors that he could charm people's money away from them (even fiscal conservatives!), and they'd thank him for the honor! It wasn't words and logic that performed that deed, but innate talent.

His sunny personality made him a popular guy at school, and since he was also a top student and a joiner, he became Valedictorian the following spring. We figured he was probably learning to dance, too. The Code told us.

Of course, we were his opposites. While the Church, Thoreau, and Nature guided us, we also had an excellent role model in our Uncle Marshall. Working as a rural postal carrier all his life, he was a Renaissance man by modern standards – healthy and strong, a knowledgeable organic gardener, Civil War scholar, and admirer of Lincoln and the Concord Transcendentalists. A great Democrat in the best Kennedy tradition, his generosity and intellectual ability were hard to match. Though he belonged to no organized religion, he was always helping people and animals, and tried to live the stricture, "Judge not." He never married – what could marriage have added?

When Steve's party headed out toward the creek, it was late afternoon. We weren't ready yet, so, after gathering our gear, we joined them about dusk. They had made their camp, but its location surprised us a little – near a small stone enclosure that looked like a pigpen. We had built it years ago, and called it a fort, a relic of our cowboy-and-Indian fights. The site was about 12' above the creek bed, but back from it, behind a barbed-wire fence. And their campfire was on the *other* side of the fence. To tend the fire or get water, they had to climb over the fence every time! Greg and I exchanged looks. *Greenhorns!*

Not wanting to intrude, we made our own camp a little distance away, in the bottom behind Theodore's Pond. Last winter we'd built a lean-to there with logs, brush, and bark, and slept out as a survival experiment. Despite our fire, it was chill, and after restive sleep, we awoke to wet snow, but feeling triumphant.

After taking care of our camp, we strolled over to Steve's, and, on approach, heard him saying cheerfully to his friends, "Wait till you get a load of these guys – country briars all the way! I tease 'em about being hicks, but they're OK – pretty colorful, and over-serious, but full of woods lore. Don't let their peculiar notions rattle you!"

We considerately coughed to signal our arrival. They were sitting around smoking, and beginning to enjoy themselves. Remembering previous years' treats, Sam was single-mindedly searching their gear, especially Steve's. He was excited – his body language exulted, *Wow! Three smokers – a bonanza, for sure!* Steve hastily cautioned his comrades, "Watch that damn dog! He'll sniff out any cigarettes that aren't in a lockbox, and eat 'em!"

Dutch and Red stared blankly, not comprehending. Maybe they were thinking, *What's a cigarette or two between dogs?* (I mean, *friends*) In any case, they apparently ignored the warning.

Next morning, we learned that Sam had made a successful raid, leaving the camp in a shambles. Steve was laughing, "You should have seen the looks on Dutch and Red's faces when they woke up this morning, and saw your dog standing over their gear, munching cigarettes! He'd already eaten three packs by the look of it... I never saw Dutch move so quick, to save his smokes! Sam had at least four dangling out of his mouth, and was swallowing fast. Red cussed at him, but all Sam did was give him a look that said 'Find your own – I'm not done eating breakfast yet!'"

We couldn't believe it! Lightning had actually struck twice, and Sam was doing the Lord's work again! Funny thing, though – he never showed any ill effects from it, like humans. (The cigarettes, I mean – not the Lord's work.)

After things decelerated, they started telling us about strange noises in the night, and how the fire they built in the stone firepit kept mysteriously exploding.

"Who built the firepit?" I asked.

"Red did," said Steve.

We could see this one coming. "Unh-HUNH! Where'd you get the stones?" Greg's eyes gleamed.

"In the creek, of course!" Red answered impudently.

"I *know* that, but were they underwater?"

"Some of them..." A weasel-like smile lurked at the corners of Red's mouth.

Apparently he'd wanted to liven things up. Besides, his science teacher had *told* the class not to do this on any account, since it might kill you.

We began to understand why they had tar-and-feathering before there was recourse to litigation. Dutch vented his emotions by singing an impromptu ditty: ♫ "*Oh, how I'd like to blister his hide...*"♫ Then he stopped. "We should handcuff him by the fire for the rest of the day!"

Next it transpired that the veteran campers from Dayton had forgotten to provide breakfast.

Red told us cheekily, "*You* know these parts – go out and kill a chicken, and get us some bacon!"

Momentarily dumbfounded, Greg and I tried to figure out which part to attack first. But Steve just snorted with exasperation, and dope-slapped Red. "For crying out loud, didn't you learn *anything* in school? Bacon comes from *pigs*, not *chickens!* PIGS!"

"I knew that," said Red.

"*Sure* you did!" Dutch kicked the ground contemptuously.

Steve was embarrassed – he was hoping the old "city-slicker" image would die of malnutrition, and this moron had given it a megavitamin shot. After some silent grinning on our part, I volunteered to provide real bacon from lawful sources. "I can get some eggs, too, from our refrigerator, if you want..."

"I didn't know you had refrigerators in these parts," Steve teased.

"I wouldn't harp on that, if you want the food –"

The red-haired kid had been silent for a while, struggling hard to get his foot out of his mouth, where he had earlier injected it with some force. He finally managed it with a "Pop!" and was back in top form: "I'll go with you to get the eggs! I'll race you!" he added.

Wryly, Dutch quipped, "It should have taken you a week to recover from that one!"

"Come on, then – let's race! Hey, wait! Where are you going?"

Sure enough, the rooster was headed the wrong way, down the creek bed. "This way's quicker!" he said.

"No, it's not – come back!" I knew this small end of the woods, even at night, and raced off the shorter way, not bothering to see what he did.

The other three stared after Red. "What's that idiot up to *now?*" Dutch demanded. "He'll be eating *crow* for breakfast!"

"Only if he knows which animal it comes from..." Greg muttered.

Instead of the regular path, I took the mountain-goat way, up a dry wash, in case Red was faster than he looked. After scrabbling to the top, I tore straight through the small wood, and never caught sight of a red weasel anywhere on the way, either direction.

But when I got back with the food, there was the menace, lounging by the fire, and I realized it was all a fake-out – he wasn't going to risk losing face again.

We sat around the fire, cooking and eating breakfast, surrounded by an aroma of bacon and eggs frying and a haze of wood smoke. Surprisingly, Red managed to eat his full share of the food. The idyllic scene was interrupted occasionally by exploding rocks. *"Bang!"* After sparks, stones, and ashes flew everywhere, eating resumed – *if* no glob of ashes had landed in the middle of your plate, and *if* the plate itself weren't blown away, and *if* no one was killed outright! I personally elected to sit behind someone with red hair.

After breakfast, all of us were still alive, so Greg and I casually demonstrated the power and range of our homemade slings, which could throw egg-size rocks a quarter-mile with tremendous force. When one hit a far-off tree, you could hear a reverberating ***KNOCK!*** cutting the air like a shot, louder than the crack of a bat at a ball game.

Red was in love! In a dazed voice, he begged to borrow the sling.

Dutch groaned, "Heaven help us!"

Steve winked at Greg and me – he'd already tried this fickle weapon in the past. We really knew better than to let that *git* use it, but couldn't resist the thought of the sling's boomerang-effect on the unwary. So we finally agreed, but not before spying out our foxhole in the stone fort. Greg smiled, and I crossed my fingers, hoping for divine retribution on the annoying mosquito.

Red fumbled awkwardly, putting a stone into the leather pouch. While he was occupied, Greg and I signaled Dutch and Steve to take cover in the fort, and we started inching that way ourselves.

He finally figured it out, and wound up with terrific force. Dutch yelled, *"Incoming!"* and all of us dove into the fort.

Red let fly!

"*WHOOSH!*" The stone viciously ricocheted from tree to tree. Red held his head in the air-raid position, doing a little dance out of sheer terror, and the rock somehow missed him on its many rebounds. The scene ended with a strangled cry, and we poked our heads above the fort walls, to see the leather sling-cords neatly wrapped around Red's neck. YES! *Thank you, God!*

But he was recovering much too fast again, like Toad after his motorcar accident. "Wowee! What a trip! I guess it takes a little practice, though."

"Just a little!" Dutch replied acerbically. "Now just pass that sling over here, nice and easy..."

"Yeah – get that thing away from him at all costs!" Steve agreed.

Now the group began to re-savor the drama. "You should have seen the dumb look on your face when you were dancing around, trying to avoid the stone and holding your head! I wish I had Dad's movie camera!" Steve grinned.

Red wasn't celebrating that. "Yeah? Let's see how *you* do, Steve! C'mon – I dare you!"

"Oh, no!" Steve shouted. "I was initiated a couple of years ago by these guys! Wait till I tell *Cindy*..."

"You're not going to tell her anything!" Red flared.

"Oh, I think I might, if you don't mind your manners," Steve taunted.

"Then I'll tell your father what you did that night with his car!" Red retaliated.

"You promised you wouldn't!"

"My, oh, my – skeletons in the closet! And the Class President, too!" Dutch marveled.

Conversation lulled. The silver fog that had moved in during the night was dissipating, and the sun started to burn through. We radiated wood smoke, and were all tired and comfortably full from breakfast. It was time to go.

Dutch wondered aloud, "Red hasn't said anything for five minutes..."

"I think the *bacon chicken's* asleep," said Steve.

"God, I hope so!"

Chapter XIX.

The Sound of Music

My mother, the piano teacher! What a wealth of opportunity this provided for my brothers and me, though only Nick ever made any *musical* use of it.

Before she met and married my father, Mother had studied to become a concert pianist, and, although she didn't pursue that career, she always kept proficient. The sound of classical piano music was a running thread down the years of my growing up, and many nights were serenaded by Chopin, Bach, Mozart, and Liszt. Since we never had much money, she gave piano lessons for many years, to pass on her skills and bolster the budget.

Like dogs, my brothers and I felt rather territorial about the continuing incursion of *foreigners*. Not only did they distract our mother's attention from wonderful *us*, but they also seemed a rather hapless lot, submitting themselves to instruction, and endlessly plunking and annoying us. Despite our own pronounced distaste for the humbling learning experience, we felt infinitely superior, and viewed the students as our natural prey.

The lessons were held at the old Steinway in our living room. With my mother and the students tethered to the piano, we had the advantage of the high ground, like snipers, able to hear everything that went on without the encumbrance or potential embarrassment of being present. While enjoying the benefits of anonymity, we could make a disembodied jibe or unidentifiable noise, rattling the student thoroughly. The stairway was excellent for this, adjacent to the piano area, but walled away from view.

In addition, students and sometimes parents had occasion to witness the playing out of high domestic drama, though Mother couldn't quite understand *why* that had to happen during the precious half-hour. Events peaked during the lesson of a student named Mindy Biddle, when we were in high school. A well-behaved, mousy girl of 13 or so, she struck us as a little slow, but I now suspect she was just ordinary. I considered anyone "slow" who was less than flamboyant. We also felt that someone who could take music lessons for years without audible gain must be somewhat lacking. Poor girl, I learned later that it was her mother who *really* wanted the lessons.

Anyway, there Mindy sat, innocently doodling away at some corny John Thompson selection (and not that well, by the sound of it). Teacher and student had no warning of approaching turmoil, except for distant rumblings emanating from the kitchen. Probably they were concentrating, and had tuned us out like the buzzing of flies until the battle broke right over their heads.

As a junior in high school, I was obsessed with keeping in shape, running three, six, or occasionally twelve miles in a day and supplementing that with exercises – 100 pushups and 200 sit-ups, as well as chopping wood, pole-vaulting, modest weight-lifting and climbing ropes.

My brother Gregory grew tired of all this Roman devotion. Perhaps I had inadvertently awakened some confused spiritual instinct, so he decided to become jury, judge, and, if possible, hangman, to counter my excesses. (I really disliked this judgmental quality in him.)

My rope was suspended from a large maple tree in the front yard, coincidentally handy to the view of parents waiting in their cars. In addition to climbing, I practiced hanging by the neck to strengthen it, which I thought might be useful someday. (The phrase "born to be hanged" comes to mind.) Besides, I rather liked the potential shock-effect on watchers, though I was chagrined at how placidly some viewed the spectacle.

On this particular day, when I went to the rope, I found it lying on the ground in a heap. Could it have come loose? No! It had been *cut! Deliberately!* GREG!

This demanded blood-price! I steamed towards the house. On my way, I met Nick, who confirmed my suspicions. He didn't know why Greg had done it, but *I* knew. It was *sheer wickedness*, and called for instant revenge. This was war!

My mind leapt to the vulnerability of Greg's paintings. Maybe it would be justice to retaliate in kind, striking-down what was precious to *him*. Then I admitted regretfully, *I can get another rope, but he couldn't replace the paintings...* I knew that much, from being around artists. No, I would bring Greg *personally* to book in a way that would also impress Mother, who I felt did not always perceive rights and wrongs accurately in settling disputes.

Coming through the back door, I yelled dramatically, "Where is he? Where's Greg! Are you afraid to show yourself?"

Apparently he wasn't. Relaxed and shirtless, he lounged at the kitchen table, eating a peach with a satisfied grin on his face.

"Is something wrong?" he asked evilly.

"You had no right to cut my rope down! What did you do it for?"

"I got tired of watching you do exercises all day long! It's time someone put a stop to it."

"Well, *I'm* tired of you spending all your time on those paintings... maybe I'll just get rid of them!" The threat didn't hurt anything.

It did nothing to calm the tension, either. "That's not the same at all!" He boiled back.

"Yeah? *Sure* it is! And I think I'll do it, too," I said, coolly fanning the flames. "Let me see... which one shall I start with? The one of the cornfield in fall is nice..."

Now Greg wasn't just angry – he was *incendiary*, but I went on. "And I'm going to put my rope back right now!"

"And I'll cut it down again, as many times as it takes!"

Now *I* was mad! I grabbed the butcher knife from the kitchen drawer, and flourished it dramatically, making a mock lunge at him. Incredibly, Greg fled the kitchen, and his unplanned escape route took him right through the living room, where Mindy's music lesson was still plodding along resolutely. He headed for the front door, with me chasing hard after him, yelling original threats like, "I'll get you! You won't get away!"

Butcher knife in hand, I arrived in the living room just as he escaped to the front porch, but I didn't follow. I had made my point. Besides, I hadn't expected him to run in the first place, so I was well satisfied.

Mindy, the recipient of this unsought drama, who had no brothers or sisters at home to entertain her, sat there silent and pale, her eyes huge and mouth open. My mother, concerned, but demonstrating phlegm in the best English tradition, said sternly, "**Boys!** *BOYS!*" We had her attention at last.

But the play was not over. There was a going to be a last act. Greg opened the storm door a crack, and taunted: "You need a *knife* to deal with me! You don't dare put it down!"

Of course I instantly tossed it on the couch (Mindy shuddered), and replied, "See? No knife!" showing my empty hands. "Come back, if you're not *scared*."

He came with alacrity, and we started fighting like two wolves, right there, between the phone stand and the front door. My mother was trying to get between us, like a boxing referee, and not succeeding. After landing several hits, and sustaining a few, I knocked Greg down. He recovered and bolted out the front door, shouting over his shoulder, "I'm going to get in shape, and whip your ass!" He never used language like that. None of us did.

Well, Mindy's music lesson had almost reached its unnatural end. My mother and I were catching our breath when a rock shattered the upper part of the storm door, showering glass everywhere and hitting Mother in the back. Greg's parting shot – it was the last I saw of him that day. He was heading out to the railroad track to start his conditioning program. (Mother saw him later, though, and vigorously expressed her opinion of the rock-throwing.)

After a week of working out, Gregory apparently decided there were things more important than fighting, and possibly realized that I might hang myself, in time, if he gave me enough rope. He went back to devoting his time to artwork. It was a good choice – he is now a professional artist.

I never told Greg that I would never have used that knife, but only wanted to get Mother's attention and make a strong statement, so he would take me seriously. I guess it worked. He hasn't cut any more of my ropes. As to those early paintings I thought of destroying, like so many other artists, he did it for me.

* * *

Mother's piano lessons continued even after we were grown, always in the background like the score of a movie. One afternoon, after I had moved away but was visiting again at home, another music lesson was in progress. Shirley Schuler was a nice lady who had taken up the piano late in life, and probably made a welcome change for the teacher from all the children-under-duress who comprised her usual clientele.

That day, I needed to borrow Mother's car keys to go on an errand. So I entered the room unobtrusively, and waited for an appropriate pause to interrupt: "Do you know where the keys to the car are?"

"They're in my purse," she replied offhandedly, quickly looking back to the sheet on the piano.

So I started to rummage energetically through the purse on the coffee table. There was a lot in there, and it didn't look that familiar. Why was my mother keeping pictures of other people's kids in her purse? Why didn't she tell anyone she was taking medication? I would have to ask her about that.

When I couldn't immediately find the keys, I called on my German ancestry for a more systematic approach, and started to remove things one by one, arranging them on the coffee table so there would be no mistake. Student and teacher paid no attention.

By the time I had pulled out more than half the contents, I began to feel a little uneasy. The room had fallen silent. Everyone was looking at me.

"What?" I said. Shirley and my mother stared, bemused, at the objects I had spread out, but I had finally found the car keys, and held them up. "You know, these keys are strange! Did you change your ignition?"

Shirley was looking at me with a startled, intent look on her face, her eyes open *very* wide. She must have been thinking, *Either he is the most nonchalant pirate that I've ever encountered, or the greatest innocent!*

All at once, my mistake overtook me: This was *Shirley's* purse! Utterly chagrined, I tried to apologize, but my ready tongue was paralyzed.

Despite a slightly stunned expression, Shirley moved brightly into the rift, beckoning generously. "That's all right! Help yourself! Help yourself!"

* * *

A mountain lion was loose in our area. For years its loud, breathy screams had punctuated the night, sounding eerily down the O'Bannon valley. *WHOW! WHOW!* It didn't worry us – anything that shy couldn't be much of a nuisance.

However, there were other creatures in our community who also liked to scream, but for entertainment, and in broad daylight. They were lions of a two-footed pride, not at all shy, and some of them were *definitely* a nuisance.

At our old house, every Saturday afternoon in the '50s, local singers would come to perform music around the piano – usually opera, Gershwin, or Rodgers & Hammerstein. They enjoyed the large, acoustic living room with its tall ceiling and fireplace, but, more importantly, my mother was an accompanist *par excellence*, someone who not only possessed remarkable sight-reading skills, but could stay with the singers when they messed up.

The group consisted of Kenny Taylor, Jack Crest, Nick Barone, Leo Bennett, Mildred Archer, and Leon Jones. At least four of them showed up, most weeks. I was only eight or nine years old, but would listen to them for a while, until I got restless and went outside.

Leon Jones was the organizer, inviting former voice students and people he knew from the city. He also sang, but his bass voice lacked the spark and clarity of tone possessed by most of the others. Kenny Taylor had a powerful tenor voice in the *bel canto* style, reminiscent of Nicolai Gedda.

Jack Crest was a tall man, very dapper and neat in the style of Clark Gable. His was a clear, lyric bass, with a forward placement that held his pitches true and not muddy. I can still hear him singing the "Song of the Volga Boatmen" in Russian. Magnificent!

Leo Bennett, a very strong black man, had a penetrating natural baritone with a tenor coloring. If you wanted a classic folk singer to perform "John Henry," he was the one. He shoveled coal in a foundry.

Mildred Archer was a decent lyric soprano with a wide range and a lot of natural talent.

Nick Barone worked at the fireworks company, and was a less-frequent visitor. He had a pleasant baritone, but disliked the restraints classical music required, and was a little bitter about *those hoity-toity classical-music people who thought they were so superior.* Musicals suited him better.

Around the time I was born, Leon Jones, having studied voice, decided he was going to become our town's *konzertmeister* and voice teacher. Unfortunately, he was an advocate of the "fish method," which required the vocalist to thrust his lips forward and hold them open (fishlike) for the duration of the song. All pronunciation was forced through that ridged opening. (A few of his students, who couldn't hack the regimen, had to be treated for seizures of the lips.) Leon always said it improved the tone throughout the vocal registers. I won't give a professional opinion on that, since everyone's vocal apparatus is different (Who cares, anyway?), but I can tell you it was fascinating to watch. It so riveted my attention that I didn't become aware of the words until somewhere near the end. Kenny, Nick Barone, and Leo Bennett inexplicably declined to follow the method.

Leon was the classic jolly, rotund man of short stature. When he talked to you, his head bobbed up and down slightly in hopeful agreement, and he smiled with eyes twinkling. His jokes were rather ponderous, but people didn't mind because he was so friendly, and he could have played Santa Claus anywhere in the land, without suit or beard.

An ambitious dilettante, he had more *chutzpah* than sense or musical accomplishment. To fulfill his chosen role, he directed various local choirs, put on performances of the "Messiah," and even managed to organize and conduct operas at his place, Briarknoll. I'm forced to admit that some of his performances were bearable, but as time slipped by, he grew more foolhardy. The decent group that practiced at our house in the '50s, anchoring Leon in sensibility, gradually dispersed: Kenny started giving his own lessons and attending college in the evenings, Mildred got married, and the rest pursued their own activities.

But Leon didn't want for new material. He went out into the streets and got it, welcoming all and sundry (especially *sundry*). He would take people who could hardly carry a tune, subject them to *kamikaze* training, tell them they were as good as the singers at the Met (sometimes true), and then shove them out on stage to sing arias like *"Che Gelida Manina."*

Most of his audiences didn't mind, since they had no interest in that kind of music, but just viewed it as a sort of gong show, and thought later, "So that's opera, huh?"

The few genuine opera-lovers sat biting their tongues and nails, or pulling their hair to soften the impact, though not many had the *sangfroid* to tell this nice man exactly what horror he had perpetrated. Even if someone had, he wouldn't have believed it. My mother was Leon's friend, and not critical in spite of her highbrow training, but even she was forced to smile behind her hand at some of his antics.

Still, he did build up the confidence of a lot of people who couldn't really sing, giving them a new sense of identity, and providing amusement for Lovelanders, who wondered just what he was going to do next. One of his students, Emily Barton, even made it to college to study music. At sixteen, she was a wisp of a girl with stringy blonde hair and a pleasant voice. But several years of conservatory training achieved her amazing transformation to a commonplace, full-blown, very loud soprano. Sensitive listeners found themselves instinctively backing away when she sang. I think the regimen of vocal weight-lifting and forgetting to keep the iron clamps on vibrato was responsible, or maybe it was really the fish thing that got her.

When conducting his group, Leon held forth in an avuncular way, his demeanor suggesting that he shared a secret joke with the choir. Baton in hand, and smiling good-naturedly over his reading glasses, he instructed them pleasantly, making simple puns like "Don't say 'Shirley' when singing '*Surely* he hath born our grief and carried our sorrows.' No matter how execrably his group performed, he not only wouldn't quit, but also encouraged them outrageously with sayings like, "Loveland is the musical tail that wags the dog in Cincinnati."

I always thought they were more like the fleas that tormented the outraged dog. In today's world, those in musical high places would fantasize about sending Ninjas to get him, if they could only figure out how to use grant money for the hit.

One day, when Nick and I were taking a walk in Schemel's Woods, we heard a high wailing that ululated wildly. Electrified, we stopped dead.

"Could that be the mountain lion?" Nick said.

"Too high, I think... It must be around a high C!"

"Yeah," Nick agreed, "but that's not a *musical* sound!"

"That's for sure! I guess it *could* be the lion..."

"Maybe they make other noises besides 'Whow!' " Nick hazarded.

"I don't know," I answered, "but I'd say that sound rates somewhere between a chainsaw murder and an outraged space creature!"

Whatever it was, it didn't come again. We finished our walk and turned toward home.

That evening at dinner Nick and I told them about it. When I imitated the sound, I noticed that Mother wore an odd expression on her face, and started to laugh. She had just come from attending Leon Jones's production of "La Traviata" at Briarknoll, not much more than a mile from where we were walking.

"It was the funniest thing I have *ever* seen. I can't describe it! That murderous sound you heard was the tenor hitting his high C. It nearly flattened the audience! Some of the kids held their hands over their ears, and it was all I could do not to embarrass Leon by doing the same! At one point, the dying heroine cast herself too vigorously onto the couch where she was supposed to expire, and a huge cloud of dust rose up to choke everyone. It was more like vaudeville than opera! A lot of people were guffawing, but those who knew Leon were trying not to... And Leon *actually* had the nerve to invite a music critic from the 'Cincinnati Enquirer!' I was sitting right next to her, and her face was painful to see during the performance. Ruth Moore was sitting with me, and when she went back to use the portable toilets, she saw the critic laughing and crying uncontrollably, beating her chest and gasping, 'Oh, my God! Oh, my God!'"

It was discovered afterwards that the soprano had shattered some of the windows in Leon's house, and, after the tenor's special aria and high note, Leon's goats refused to give milk for a week. They did a lot of bleating, though, and some musically inclined neighbors said it sounded like the opening lines of "La Traviata," but I never believed that.

Sunday morning we looked eagerly for the musical review in the "Enquirer." The critic, who might understandably have employed Lizzie Borden's axe, decided for mysterious reasons to be merciful. This was impressive, when you consider that she was hoodwinked into coming by Leon's genial written invitation and buildup, and then subjected to the ordeal. Maybe she just didn't want her colleagues to know she'd been made a fool. Whatever her motive, she chose her words carefully, saying "The word 'farce' doesn't quite reach into the musical dimension where this director took his group." She added that it was a most unusual experience, and really rather mediaeval.

* * *

My senior year was problematical. Just making it through high school seemed doubtful – I felt I had no stamina left. And why should I, anyway? With the Vietnam War in full swing, I might still be drafted if I didn't go on to college. *More school?* I missed a lot of time that year, and was ready to quit, but my World Government teacher, Nancy Neumann, hunted me down and strongly urged me to stay. She told me I was smarter than most of the students there, and could easily make up the missed work. This was news! No one had ever said anything like that to me, so I followed her advice, and events justified her prediction.

On the other hand, I also had to find a career. That wasn't going to be easy, unconventional as I was – I didn't really seem to fit anywhere. My favored activities and talents did not seem likely to pay me – athletics was lucrative only if I were spotted by a scout and joined some team. But I wasn't a joiner, and besides, I wasn't *that* good at anything except pole-vaulting. Running wild in the woods as a profession wouldn't work out, not in this century. I was good at gardening, but it wouldn't make a living, and farming (agri-business) was anathema. I despised all forms of commercialism – this meant no factories, no advertising, no business, and, *Dear God!* – no sales! I was much too sensitive for law enforcement or fire protection.

So what was left? Being a game warden or forester appealed at first, until I realized it was just another kind of policeman. Law and medicine required too much schooling, even if I could have accepted them in my mind. There was the monastery, but the Church was changing, and they didn't seem too interested in me.

It came into my head that it was time to make *my own* music, and I unearthed two options. Both were suitably difficult and painful, and I thought they might reasonably kill me in the space of a few years (if the War didn't get me first). Possibly I felt a karmic need to atone for my sins, and so proposed to ensure lifelong penance.

Plan One – Become a **ballet dancer.** (God knows why, since I had no training – maybe that's why I was attracted to it.)

or...

Plan Two – Become an **opera singer.** This may have had something to do with my early exposure. Could I sing? I had sung in the Schola several years ago. Maybe I could now, if I tried.

I immediately trumpeted these deathwishes to my family, but they were too inured to my sudden manias to give it any mind-room. But when Kenny Taylor showed up in late spring, offering to give me free voice lessons, it seemed providential. That cinched it – *no tights for me!* I still wonder how he knew I could sing, when *I* wasn't sure. Maybe he was just following in the Leon Jones tradition, but mostly, I think he wanted to give something back to my mother for all the free piano accompaniment down the years.

At first, Kenny encouraged me toward church music, but I rapidly realized there was no living in it. Opera, on the other hand, was exciting, and paid well if you could make it to the top. And it did seem to dovetail with my personality – not that I was a showoff or anything...

After a month or so, Kenny thought I had potential. He called my voice *tenore robusto*, and suggested I try for a scholarship at the new college of music in Cincinnati the following spring. From then on, I began studying piano with my mother, and at Kenny's instigation also took up the guitar to accompany myself. Since the only time I had previously spent on piano lessons had been to tease and criticize the music students, I was ill prepared for my career of choice.

But this never stopped Do-it-the-wrong-way Pfarr! I knew I could make up any amount of lost ground by brute force and ferocious persistence. No vocalise or piano exercise was too dull or exacting for my diligence. The inmates of our house must have been almost crazy, enduring discordant strumming, brazen howling, and excruciatingly hammered piano exercises. *Gone* was my old life, like smoke on the wind – this was the *new* Toad, with no regrets to cloud his horizon!

My uncle Marshall abetted by taking me to guitar lessons every Thursday in Norwood. One winter morning, he came to pick me up while Mother was giving a music lesson. It was snowing outside, and he was patiently waiting at the curb in his green Rambler. Getting my equipment and leaving naturally required interrupting the music lesson. I rushed in, threw on my coat and hat from the hall closet, grabbed my guitar and music stand, and ran for the door.

Music stands are tricky. Unless folded and clamped with a steel band, they like to surprise people by springing open suddenly, and possibly poking someone's eye, spearing sheet music, or maybe oversetting another stand nearby. Even when apparently stable, they can fall over mysteriously, or trip other musicians trying to get past. Many a petty injury can be traced to them, including bruised knuckles and pinched fingers, usually from trying to muzzle them in disgust.

That day, I was out of time, and my stand wasn't closed. Trying to get the guitar and open stand through both doors at once caused quite a clattering and banging, but at least I could see that my coming had given my uncle hope for a timely departure. I escaped the doors, using great agility, only to find myself skating across the snowy porch on one foot, the other leg extended wildly in the air to keep my balance. At the end of the porch, I sailed down the steps on my one leg. *Thump! Thump! Thump! Thump!* Still holding on to my stuff, I slid across the walk to the waiting car, doing a fast shuffle to stay upright. The car stopped me with a thud, and I got in nonchalantly after another struggle with the equipment. Uncle Marshall just hunched over the wheel, shaking his head. He didn't even laugh – maybe he didn't want to lend countenance to the forces of chaos.

* * *

In April of 1967, I actually won a full-tuition scholarship to the Cincinnati College-Conservatory of Music. I was as shocked as everyone else, but the professor who auditioned me happened to be an opera coach, and didn't want to let anyone get away who could scream like that.

Unfortunately, Leon Jones felt the same way. After this, his pursuit of me was hotter than ever, and, during the next year, I experienced some instant karma. Remember those music students I had stalked and tormented? Now *I* was being stalked by the affable Mr. Jones, with repeated invitations to participate in his productions. The problem was, I was so deadly serious about my new career intentions that I couldn't see his good qualities. The only thing I could think of was protecting my musical virtue from assault, so I declined, as quickly as savage civility would permit. It needed 24-hour vigilance to counteract his jovial menace – he would only hear "Yes" when you were saying "No!" You could see him thinking, "*You'll change your mind when you realize what a wonderful piece we're putting on,*" or, "*If you would just listen to us practice!*" I was hoping to God that no one in my conservatory had heard of him, or would know that I lived in the same town. It took me years to cool down and realize that he was really a decent man, just not someone I wanted to be guided by musically.

One day, late that summer, I was vocalizing in the barn, exiled from the living room by piano lessons. Nick later told me about a conversation between Mother and the student's parent, waiting outside in the car.

"*Madre de Diòs!*" The parent exclaimed, reverting to his native tongue in the grip of strong emotion. "What is that awful screaming?"

"Oh, that's Paul vocalizing in the barn," Mother answered him matter-of-factly.

"That barn way over there? I can barely see it," he said incredulously.

"Well... he *has* a big voice..."

The man asked suspiciously, "Is he the same boy that was hanging himself by the neck in that tree over there, last year?"

"I don't know about that," Mother replied truthfully, "but he did have a rope there."

"Sounds like someone's hanging him now," the parent said, with apparent satisfaction.

"I doubt if a person could make that much noise with a noose tightened around his neck," Mother rejoined, laughing at last.

"I wouldn't bet on it!" The parent stated emphatically. "That one's got talent!"

* * *

I feel compelled to say something about the professions that so attract artistic types. Since most of us fail (in the end) in the worldly sense, perhaps it is time for a little honesty. These vocations are really *spiritual* quests, not *material* ones. If only we had recognized that, early on, we could have quixotically embraced the trials, poverty, and disillusionment, instead of being continually surprised and discomfited. So I've developed some formulas for *real success* in achieving worldly failure, and have listed them in order of their lethal potency.

1. *Ballet Dancer*

These artists are 110% guaranteed to receive only pains for their labor. First of all, you have to have a compliant personality (not to mention a pliant body), starting so young that you're not sure of your name, the members of your family, or your gender. Even at that age, you will probably work hard to avoid the lessons your parents have sacrificed to give you. But if you persist (or are *made* to), one day you may say, "This isn't so bad! Maybe I'll become a dancer." Your teacher will only shrug in a bored way. She's helped destroy many young students' lives by encouraging this line of work. She will say, "One more is sad, but *c'est la vie.*"

After many years of toil and suffering, you and your teacher may begin to have hope, but more likely, you will hear the bad news: "You are too slow!" "You are too big and dance like ze elephant!" Or, "You lack a certain *je ne sais quoi!*" (And then there are the *injuries.*) Even if you get through the passage of fire, your troubles are only beginning. *Where will you get a job?*

Suppose you do manage to break through and have a stage career for a few years. Then, how do I say, "You are too *old.*" (*Already?*) Of course, there is always "the teaching," which can be done for many years... your final revenge, to prevent as many students as possible from escaping back into the outside world of opportunity. I mean... just look at your teacher's scrawny, emaciated body, which bears its own testament for all who have eyes to see... *Ça suffit!* (Enough, already!)

2. *Poet*

This vocation runs neck-and-neck with ballet dancer, giving you at least a 100% chance at failure. (More, if you're very original) And there are many perks: You can live as you like, starve in unfettered bliss, dressing as you please, and best of all, run yourself to perdition following your own schedule. A college education doesn't really help you here, since no one will be able to grasp what your poetry is about, anyway. Holding a university chair may help to entomb you. Mostly that is for those who realize they will never be Poet Laureate, and bitterly decide that no one else is going to be, either. So they put on erudite airs, as guardians of the portal, while being cynical and snide, joy-killers whom nothing pleases.

To succeed at poetry, you must be romantically inclined. So, if being completely misunderstood, outcast, and impecunious is your *forte*, go for it!

3. *Opera Singer*

Careful! Chances of worldly success are increasing slowly, but not significantly. Don't panic – they're only up to 20%. There are some perks, though. Demented behavior is excused if you make it big. It will be written off to artistic inflammation of the ego, and if they ever want to hear you sing again, they will do your bidding. Opera may not always be that nice to listen to, but remember, as the *perpetrator*, you get to do the screaming at everybody on stage, even the audience. If you shout "You SOB!" in Italian at the conductor during a performance, who will know? (Not at La Scala, obviously – use another language there.)

4. *Artist*

Not 100% guaranteed to fail, but about the same as Opera Singer. Still, that 15%-20% chance of success can be scotched easily, especially if you have original ideas, don't teach at a university, etc. Also, be sure to shut yourself away during your productive years, before you get rich or famous. That way, no one will be able to buy your work until after you're *dead*.

5. _Writer_

You may write and write and write. And you may be a _good_ writer with something to say, but sometimes all you hear from the publisher is "Not interested." So you say to yourself, _They probably didn't read it._ (True)

So you think, _If I talk to them on the phone, I may get some one-on-one interaction._ If you can get past the recording that says, "Not interested. Not interested. Not interested," and somehow get a live person, it's probably only the copy boy/girl, who says, "I've only been here a week," in a pathetic nasal voice.

You say, "I need to speak to someone important, like the editor."

She hesitates, and says, "Oh, all right, he won't know _I_ transferred you. After all–" an afterthought "–I may be speaking to another Hemingway," she giggles.

When you get the editor, and explain that you just sent a book last week, he says, "Oh, that was probably part of Batch 1,264 that I gave to Maria. Let me connect you."

"No, wait!" you gasp. Too late. _Buzz! Buzz!_

"Maria here. What can I do for you, dear?"

"Listen, this is Mr. Blank. I'm a writer, and I sent you a manuscript recently..."

"Oh, one of those," she says disparagingly, through her nose.

"Yes, I fear so," you reply.

"Let me see, I think it's in batch 1,265."

"The other man said 1,264...."

"Oh, _he_ doesn't know! He's only the editor. _We_ do the work."

"What's the 1,265 stand for?" you ask, beginning to feel overwhelmed.

"That's how many we're assigned this month to take home and read at night."

"How can you possibly do justice to all of those, on top of your day job?" you ask.

"Oh, I have a system. First, I separate all the irregulars, like the ones that have the wrong kind of paper clips, or have sections separated with three asterisks (my boss detests those), or are tied with pink ribbons. You know, anything that doesn't appeal, or conform to the rules sheet..." You can just see her wrinkling her nose.

"Well, no," you answer, "but I'm beginning to..." Then you ask, "What do you do with that first cull, cherish them?"

"Oh, you're funny! They go into the trash, of course, unless an SASE was sent – sometimes we pitch them anyway if the return envelope was the wrong size."

"Don't you even send a rejection letter with the returns?"

"Oh, sure, I've got a pile of them made by the copy girl," she says, tinkling at your naiveté. "But that only gets rid of a couple of hundred or so," she volunteers.

"And the other 1,065?" you ask reluctantly (but driven).

"I reduce them again by sending back every other one. You see, there are so many irregularities: the wrong format for the query letter, or maybe they sent the whole manuscript."

"That doesn't sound fair to the authors," you protest. You're really thinking, *It's outrageous!*

"Well, we have to run a business, you know."

"I thought I knew that, but...." You try again. "That leaves 532½. Then what?"

"I divide that batch up into Monday, Tuesday, Wednesday, Thursday, and Friday. Monday is a bad day – I'm still fagged from the weekend, so I throw that batch out, or send it back, depending on the details... We're not heartless, you know. Then I actually do scan Tuesday's, Wednesday's and Thursday's, but Friday goes into the trash out of hand. After all, I need a social life. That cuts it down to a little over 300, sweetie. Still too many to read, but I try my best."

"I can't believe this!" you say. "Does your editor know?"

"Oh, heavens, no! If he asks me, I say sweetly, 'Ask me no questions, and I'll tell you no lies.' That satisfies him. He doesn't have time for my problems."

Then she adds speculatively, "Look, why don't you get an agent? I have this brother-in-law..."

Now it's your turn to cut *her* off. "Not on your life!" You slam the phone down.

* * * (*Rejection!*)

A university would seem a good environment for writing, but administration has its own idea of proper form and procedure, and what you should do with your time. That time is filled with seminars, and you are constantly threatened with "publish or perish." (They will let you know what they want you to write to complement their agenda.) It's like Clint Eastwood putting a gun to a violinist's head, and saying, "More expression!"

Then there's teaching your students how to get by your assignments without really thinking. But if you're the hard-as-nails type and can't be penetrated at all, you *may* succeed. Just take a tip: If you have any creativity left, make sure everyone knows about it, so they can stop you. If you keep it secret until your work reaches the market as a *fait accompli,* there's a real danger of success.

* * *

There are other professions not listed that will also guarantee hardship (I mean, *success*). I've only listed the ones that are near and dear to my heart, or at least experience.

As a general rule-of-thumb for artistic types, if you're mad about a certain thing and willing to sell everything to obtain your "pearl of great price," you've probably sealed your fate already. On the other hand, if some occupation or idea (such as yet another fast-food joint) irritates you, or is even against your principles, there's probably money in it.

For those of non-artistic temperaments, you have your own formula for success, and part of it is steering clear of people like me. If this is <u>you</u>, *perdoneme.* Don't let me confuse you further. (I know – I should have been hooked off the stage a while back...)

Chapter XX.

The Smiter is Smitten

Leaves rustled softly overhead, and the sand squished under Dennis's feet. The dark was warm and friendly as he sneaked through the wooded bottom behind Theodore's Pond, on a mission. The older Pfarr boys were camped on the small beach at the edge of the woods, and he meant to steal their supply of pop. Conveniently nearby, he and Peter Pfarr had their own camp on top of Long Pond Cliff.

As he moved forward, he noticed that someone had cut paths, giving him an easy approach to the target. Dennis giggled. This was perfect! Even the nettles were mown-down. He drew close to the enemy's site, and started to crawl the last 25 feet on hands and knees, ignoring the sand trickling into his shoes.

Now he was right behind their tent, shivering with suppressed excitement. He decided to calm himself by resting a minute and listening in on their conversation. It wasn't every day he got to hear what older boys talked about by themselves.

At the moment, Paul was pacing restlessly. "You know, I *was* going to have us camp at our usual place on the cliff, but those two cretins, Peter and Dennis Hutzel, got there first!"

Dennis almost choked.

Johnny replied, "That's okay. I don't mind camping by the water."

"Yeah, I know, but it just doesn't seem right... We ought to teach them a lesson."

"Did you hear that fish jump over there?" Greg pointed to the south end of the pond. "It must have been a foot long!"

"Yeah, look at those ripples coming to the shore... Had to be a big one," Johnny said.

Everyone scrambled for rods and reels.

Dennis lost interest. He never could hold still for long – besides, he wanted that pop! He looked around while they settled down to angle, but the only bottles he saw were empty, lying on the beach. *Rats! Foiled!* The pigs had drunk it all!

Unfortunately, at that puissant moment, a mosquito bit him on the ear, and he instinctively slapped it. That tipped him slightly off-balance, and a stick snapped under his knee. He held his breath for a moment, hoping no one would notice.

* * *

"Sshh! Did you hear that noise?" Johnny whispered.

"Sure did!" Greg answered, in a low voice.

"What noise?" I asked. I could distinguish birdcalls a quarter-mile away, but often missed the obvious.

"Over there by the tent," Johnny said.

"It sounded like a foot snapping a twig," said Greg.

"I don't care," Johnny said. "I just want to hold still for a while after eating... Throw a rock in there, and see what it is."

No one objected to this practical suggestion, so I tossed a small rock into the weeds. Immediately, a kid's voice squeaked, "Don't! Stop! It's me, Dennis."

He stood up quickly, then spun on his heel and raced away, apparently deciding to avoid embarrassment and count coup by escaping. From the commotion he was making, it was clear he'd missed the trail, but apparently not the nettles that grew off it. His location was telegraphed to us in the dark by small yelps whenever he jarred against an unseen rock, tree, or nettle patch, very like my dog Sassafras, who yiped as she coursed the woods when barbed wire, bees, or a snake surprised her.

"After him!" I exploded.

We all jumped for it. I was first out the gate, since my grudge over the campsite was still simmering. Dennis had a headstart, but the chase turned out to be short — I caught him in 50 paces, just before he reached the cliff trail.

When I collared him, he went dejectedly limp, his body language signaling that it was all over - no pop, no escape, and nabbed, to boot! But Dennis (being Dennis) recovered in two seconds flat. "Wait, let go! I've lost my shoe! I have to find it or my mom'll kill me!" His parents were terrors, and very strict. If he didn't find that shoe, it would probably be bread and water for days. He bent over and started scratching his legs madly. "Creepers! My legs itch like fire!"

"Wait! Don't scratch 'em! Nettles make nasty water bubbles! Wait five minutes, and the itching and burning will quit."

"I can't - I'll go crazy!" Dennis writhed.

"I know, but it's the best you're gonna do..."

Gregory and Johnny joined us, and we spent 10 minutes looking for that shoe, alongside the hobbling Dennis. But it was just too dark. Dennis said he was going to come back later with his father's flashlight, which he had at his camp, and we dispersed.

* * *

Earlier that day, we had been mowing the lawn, but after lunch it reached 90° in the shade. Greg and I draped ourselves lethargically over the back steps, trying to get interested in something. The heat weighed us down like a damp, warm blanket, addling our brains. The locusts had geared up. Their hypnotic, sustained accompaniment sounded like Philip Glass, but without the benefit of harmony — one big wall of sound that played tricks on the ear.

"We could go swimming," Greg proffered dispiritedly.

"Sounds like a cool idea," I answered. But neither of us moved.

We were still sogging when the phone rang, and Mother came to the door. "It's Johnny Pfarr. He wants to talk to you."

Greg went inside, and came back after a moment. "He wants to come over and go camping tonight!"

Johnny was our cousin, who lived across town. He was Greg's age, but shorter. That didn't bother him – he had an easygoing disposition, like his father, Uncle John. "That's great! We can go swimming and cool down before we set up camp!"

We revived miraculously. Mosquitoes made the Eddie Bauer tent a necessity, and we fought our way to the back of the garage to snake it out. Fishing gear and other requisites were gathered, including my specially ordered 14" swashbuckling cutlass (complete with knuckle guard). My excuse was that it served as a machete, and did a surprisingly good job of cutting brush. But really, it was a totem... *He who carry this knife get heap big respect and glory.* It *was* glorious, a pirate sword worthy of the Spanish Main!

Our usual camping place wasn't far, so we weren't very careful about packing. It was easier just to pick up all the gear we could carry, and make another trip if we couldn't manage it on the first.

Now we were ready for Johnny.

He rolled up our drive in his Rambler half an hour later, got out with his sleepy smile, and asked, "What have you guys been up to?"

Sam ambled over, sniffed him desultorily, and after approving the DNA, moved in for petting.

We gave the stock reply, "Oh, nothing much – mowing the lawn, taking walks, fishing and swimming."

He pointed at the sword and the Bowie knife slung on our belts, and laughed. "What are those pig-stickers for? Is that a cutlass? Expecting trouble with the savages tonight?"

We merely smiled knowingly, and shrugged. Johnny would have had one strapped to *his* belt in a second, if he had the chance. Greg wordlessly handed him the Buck knife, which he accepted without demur. The knives made us feel that we *were* the law on our home turf - somehow older, wiser, taller, and dangerous to invaders.

Shooing Sam away from the food for the second time, we set off together. Johnny's gear wasn't much different from ours, except for the soda pop and potato chips he'd brought. Our involuntary Ramadan of fasting from junk food (due to meager funds) was going to be over.

The usual campsite lay directly across the field, near Long Pond Cliff, but Dennis Hutzel and Peter were already in residence. Greg and I were annoyed, but, constrained by Johnny's presence, forbore to brangle or administer a dope slap. Chewing silently on the slight, Greg and I looked at each other meaningfully. Petrov was a marked man. Punishment would somehow find him, in the natural course of events.

So we moved on to our other campsite, taking the cliff path down to the creek. Every year we cut steps into the blue clay of this steep and sometimes slippery path. At the bottom, we crossed a small gully on a log, and followed the sandy trail through the small woods to Theodore's Pond.

Theodore's was a good place to swim, camp or fish. Well... honestly, we had *fun* fishing there, but never caught a lot. The pond lay at a bend in the creek, and every year, high water deposited fresh sand, renewing its beach. In spring, just after the ice on the creek had broken up, strings of groundnuts could be seen hanging from banks. Those edible tubers had sometimes kept the Indians from starving, and we sampled them ourselves once. They were better than daylily roots, but couldn't compare with mashed potatoes.

Theodore's Beach was backed by a narrow band of trees and a field that was part of Grailville's bottomland. This lower field ran up the creek for a quarter-mile, bounded on one side by a low, wooded hill, and along the water by an ancient, dry-laid stone retaining-wall. In many places, tree roots had taken possession of the wall, gripping it as though for support. But the wall was laid so cunningly that it seemed to have been there for all time, and always held a fascination for me. If it had been built to protect the field from flooding, it never accomplished that in my time, since the field flooded almost every year. Of course, it might have been effective 200 years ago, when the water table was held in check by heavily forested land.

In the early seventies, after I had left home, the creek washed out a large section of the lower field. On one of his walks, Peter saw the tops of stone walls there, laid in regular patterns. Other primitive sites of Indian worship had been found in Clermont County, along creeks and rivers. But the Corn Engrosser, instead of investigating or calling in any experts, quickly plowed over it for the summer's crop. Still, the discovery of the buried walls excited conjecture – perhaps Indians, rather than settlers, had also built the creek retaining-wall.

* * *

We began to make camp on the beach, starting with the tent. Though it was made for two men, we had once managed to sleep four boys in it crosswise, when the weather was cold. It had its own peculiar smell – woodsy and pungent, probably from a combination of preservative and damp canvas.

Then we all went swimming, and Peter and Dennis came down and joined us. In late afternoon, interesting shadows began to fall across the pond. Theodore's wasn't large (only six feet deep, at most) and would have warmed up quickly in the hot sun if it hadn't been blessed with cold springs.

After swimming for an hour, we decided to see if we could catch any fish for our supper. *No.* They were probably sitting under a ledge somewhere, sulking about the dog days of summer (and fasting).

So we built the campfire. I don't know exactly why, but our fires always turned into bonfires. This one started out small, too, in keeping with the Indian motif, but everyone gathered dead wood so joyfully that it soon became a monster.

We all knew that you were supposed to wait till the fire died down before trying to cook, but we were HUNGRY! That was okay – we had plenty of experience with bonfires, and with only a modicum of hustle, were able to produce and happily devour a meal of burnt hot dogs, potato chips, baked beans and pop. The freedom to make these decisions was one of the attractions – if an adult had been there, we would have had to wait on the fire, lay out a tablecloth, wash our hands and *maybe* even say prayers!

Our campsite felt remote because of the terrain, but we weren't really far from home. Only a cliff, a patch of woods, and a field lay between us, which was handy if you forgot the skillet, or needed Miracle Whip for your hot dogs. Someone could run and get it, without much compromise to ethics. (After all, the primary guilt for purchasing such items lay with our parents. Our part was to eat, and hide the evidence.)

Dusk imperceptibly settled. There was a faint glow in the sky, and the bullfrogs started to grate, hailing their nocturnal day. Time for dessert!

We cut some green willow sticks, and began to roast marshmallows. Now, we all knew how to produce a light-brown marshmallow, but that took too long, so we just flamed them charcoal-black and popped them in our mouths as quickly as possible. You could accelerate the process if you held the marshmallow lightly in your teeth, and hyperventilated it cool. (If you were a fuddy-duddy, and roasted yours properly, the other guy would be 15 marshmallows ahead of you.)

Then we sat around the fire and talked about the stars, UFO's, and plans for college. Years before, we would have talked about ghosts, but they hadn't been seriously on our minds (or chasing us) since Jimmy left town.

Extraterrestrials had never bothered us, either, but that was different. Scientific odds were in favor of intelligent life in the universe, and it *could* be part of our future. Wouldn't it be a kicker if we had to live out our days not under Communism, but under the foot of an alien regime from otherwhere? We didn't dwell on it, but saw the inherent irony. Still, our interest had more to do with the excitement of new frontiers and adventures in science than fear of enslavement.

Johnny asked Greg what he was going to do, now that he was out of school. Gregory had thought about going to the Art Academy in Cincinnati, but wanted to stay out of school a year. Johnny was planning to attend Xavier University in the fall. He asked if I had any plans yet, but I didn't, other than being a senior next year.

"You better plan ahead for college," Johnny warned.

I couldn't see it. In my family, we had the mindset that there was no money for college, and it didn't occur to us (or *me*, at least) to work our way. But I was full of energy, and felt immortal. There was endless time.

While Greg and Johnny were still talking, I seized a firebrand by its unburnt end and began waving it in the air. Greg and Johnny must have felt an atavistic response, because they quickly grabbed their own brands, to engage in fiery swordplay. Johnny and I clashed at the waterside, sparks flying everywhere in the night like fireworks. What a show!

We backed off, then engaged again, but this time a coal hit Johnny's arm and he hurried to cool it in the water while Greg and I took a turn. As hot debris flew from the brands, it made fiery trails before hissing out in the water like spent comets. Circling each other like ancient Celtic warriors, the combatants were invisible but for the dark-red light reflecting from their faces. Only the glowing ends of the sticks shone, brightly circumscribing light-circles in the dark at each thrust and parry.

When the best brands had all been used, we tired of the sport and reconnoitered.

Johnny said, "Boy, I'd sure like some ice cream about now. Why don't we go to town and get some?"

There was no opposition to that.

"We wouldn't all have to go," Greg said. "I could be back in about 20 minutes, if I hurried."

"I wouldn't mind the walk," Johnny said.

"OK. Let's put out the fire." Throwing the burning brands high in the air made fiery trails, as they spun end-over-end before landing in the black water with a splash and a hiss.

The railroad was our back way to town. (It's always handy not to have to go past the parents' front door.) It was usually against our ethics to mix the venal and commercial experiences of town with camping, but we *wanted* that ice cream. Besides, L & J's store was just at the near edge of town, close to the tracks, and the whole way there was country. The darkness added allure – soft, green and soothing.

We had to cross a railroad bridge with no side rails and gaps between the ties. (Of course, we *could* have used the road-bridge that stood 75 feet away, but not one of us considered it. Miss traversing the railroad bridge in the dark?!)

Inside the store, fluorescent lights glared harshly. Hasty consensus approved butter-pecan ice cream, RC Cola, Canada Dry grapefruit pop (my favorite) and Hershey bars for entertainment on the return journey.

Walking back, we listened to the night sounds, ate chocolate and drank pop, as the ice cream grew soft in its double freezer bag. Back in camp, we were still able to slice it into three portions, and pass it around. The dripping carton was Sam's.

After that, we were all holding ourselves rather carefully, milling around the remains of the campfire, and not saying much. We were too full to go to bed, and, anyway, the evening couldn't be over *yet*. But group digestion had ascendancy for the moment, and the only sound was an occasional soft groan.

I recovered my power of speech first, and suggested, "Let's go for a walk!"

In my family, this was always a powerful suggestion. It would get them going even when ill, and could cure any problem, spiritual or physical... (I did find that it was no substitute for Saturday Confession, though, no matter how much one rationalized on the walk.)

Everyone assented. It might not cure our stomachs, but it would be another adventure to add to this night, and also staved off the boredom of going to bed.

We started off up the creek bed, before crossing at the usual place, near the Indian stone. Then Greg pointed back to the woods behind our camp, and asked, "What is that light moving over there?"

"I bet it's Dennis, looking for his lost shoe... He said he'd come back with his dad's flashlight, remember?"

"Hey, Dennis, watch out for big mosquitoes!" Johnny yelled into the woods. "I saw one as big as a dragonfly earlier!"

"And look out for nettles!" I added.

"Ha! *Very* funny, you guys!" Dennis's high voice floated to us over the riffles. "Be careful to check your beds for critters, when you turn in!"

"What!" "Did you hear that!" We all replied spontaneously to this implied threat.

"He's just out of diapers, and has no respect for his elders! Maybe we need to put him back in his playpen," Johnny suggested, in a carrying voice.

"Sounds good to me. Shall we baptize him in St. Theodore's Pond?" I queried.

"You better not!" Dennis yelled back. "I'll tell Mom!"

"Let him be for now. We want to go on our walk," Greg said.

But it sure was an entertaining notion, having a late-night religious service and "lessonin'," all rolled into one.

We scrambled up the embankment, and started walking the tracks at a subdued pace, a little uncomfortable, but, like Sam, determined to have a good time. The only sound was the crunch of cinders under our feet.

Johnny broke the silence. "Do you think they'll dare do anything to our beds while we're gone?"

"Naw... Dennis knows we'll come after him, if he does," Greg replied, grinning.

We savored the imagery of a born-again Dennis that this conjured up, and speculated about whether Peter should be included in the rebirth.

Johnny volunteered ingenuously that he'd been doing a lot of running in the spring, and thought he was in pretty good shape.

This was a call to arms! We quickened our pace at the mere mention.

Looking him over with the fanatical eyes of a high priest, I doubted he was especially fit, but forbore comment. We would soon know.

"Greg and I are in pretty good shape, too," I countered.

The walking was growing rather strained, but it was Johnny who threw down the gauntlet. "Let's run! It's only a mile from here to Pickleville."

The test of faith had come. Now all of us would be measured by a Spartan god who required sacrifice and pain. Our stomachs were no better, but the evening's adventure had shifted from a pleasant walk to heartless competition. There was suspicion of immorality amongst the congregation: someone was probably *out of shape!* (And it better be Johnny!)

Sinner! Greg and I gloated to ourselves. *Soon, soon, we will know <u>who</u> it is! He will be flushed out, and the quicker, the better!"* I had at least part of that right...

Stomach pain began almost immediately, but no one complained as we ran heavily along. We had been training ourselves for such impromptu Indian events for years, and it was understood that physical strains and irritations were *not* valid excuses to shirk any test. If a person were really in condition, it wouldn't matter one bit. We knew that Indians were surprised while eating, and had to run for it, sometimes for days!

So there we were, running in the dark over the railroad cinders, none of us *thinking* any more than Sam, trotting alongside. However, the body has its own ways of expressing postprandial misery, which we were about to experience.

At the ¾-mile mark, I realized I would have to make my move or lose this race to the lowly gut. *But how <u>can</u> I?* I groaned inwardly. *My stomach is killing me!*

"Sinner!" roared my spirit guide. "You <u>will</u> overcome! You <u>have</u> to! If you don't, all those hours of devotion were wasted! Shame on you! <u>Move!</u>"

With that inner voice to spur me, I began to pull away from the group. *Agony!* But I heard Greg hard on my heels, lashed by the same whip, emitting his own sounds of distress.

As we ran, ground fog began moving in from the creek. Johnny was falling behind, hardly visible and calling for us to wait. He was more of a social animal than either of us, and definitely not into pain. I could hear him groaning and gasping for breath.

"Wait up! Slow down! Come on, guys! Wait for me!" he entreated.

But the cruel god had taken full possession of the Brothers Heathenov, and Johnny's cries came only faintly to our ears.

At last, I saw the finish posts looming ahead, and with one final spurt of energy, I reached them first, 15 feet ahead of Greg. My emotions surged – *You are saved! Thank God, the sinner wasn't you!*

Now that "who was who" and "what was what" were established, it was time to be magnanimous to the fallen. As we stood around, breathing very hard, with our hands resting on our knees, I said: "Well, both of you probably could have beaten me, another time. I guess I just got lucky. Sometimes, even if you've trained better, you have a bad day. Or maybe it's because you had a cold more recently than I did."

"Yeah," Johnny croaked.

"I know what you mean," Greg said huskily.

We were feeling pretty companionable, like becoming friends after you fight with someone. The journey back was uneventful, except for natural interruptions when we dropped out one at a time to visit the bushes. Each reappeared much relieved, no one explaining what version of bodily revenge he had endured.

We arrived back at camp around 11:00, hot, pale, and a little tired.

I said, "Hey, let's go swimming again!"

"Can't – we've eaten too much," said Johnny. "We'll get cramps."

Greg replied seriously, "I don't think it will matter, after that physicking... We're pretty cleaned out."

"Don't! I don't even want to think about it!"

We stripped down to our swimshorts and slipped into the water, too tired for much exertion.

A gibbous moon was rising over in the east, casting tree shadows and lighting the pond with silvered nets. The katydids were still at it, filling the night. After half an hour, we felt relaxed enough to go to bed, and tried to get some sleep.

Our tent was pitched on sand, which conformed to our bodies nicely at first, but grew increasingly hard like rock, so we didn't sleep very well. All of us woke around 3:00 AM (regulated by how many hours of discomfort a body can endure). We got up, and stood around the remains of the fire, wondering how to fill the hours till dawn. Then yesterday's theme rose in my mind, like bad cream.

"You know..." I proffered slowly, "Peter and Dennis are probably sleeping soundly about now, like little rabbits."

It was satisfying to see how my offhand observation kindled an answering gleam in my compatriots' eyes.

"Let's go!" Johnny cried. "We'll give 'em a surprise!"

"We've got some M-80s!" Greg contributed gleefully. It seemed I wasn't going to be alone at Confession, come Saturday.

We ran through the woods silently, like avenging Indians, and flowed up the cliff path like weasels. *Gone* were our petty ailments.

The three marauders stealthily approached the rival campers, who *were* sound asleep, as the seer had predicted. We were delighted, but hastily conferred in whispers – what should we do? We mustn't spoil the moment and accidentally deny ourselves a dramatic awakening...

"Throw an M-80," Greg said. "That'll wake 'em up."

I lit one, and threw it. **KABOOM!** Do you know how loud an M-80 sounds at 3:00 in the morning, in a quiet woods? Even the insects quit chirruping for a full two minutes.

But nobody even *stirred!* We looked at each other, incensed. Peter wasn't going to get off *that* lightly. Besides, *no one* had the right to sleep that well. (except maybe God) Now it was imperative to get their attention in some remarkable way.

Dennis and Peter had put their sleeping bags partly under the old lean-to, with their heads in the open.

"Well," I said, "we could light a small fire at the back of the lean-to, well away from them. That would get them up in a hurry."

"Yeah, but it would take too much time, and wouldn't burn very fast," Johnny demurred.

My guardian-demon whispered helpfully in my ear, *"There's some gasoline in the red can in the garage..."* As soon as I shared that idea with the others, I had second thoughts. But I wasn't going to play second fiddle in any unfolding drama.

For some reason, this idea transformed Johnny. At the mere suggestion, this genial, low-key person became someone else, with a wild light in his eyes and devilish laughter bursting forth. *He* had been the one to refuse the bait earlier, when I proposed punitive action upon our camping brethren. But, of course, that was after supper, and far removed from the primal energy of 3:00 AM. The new Johnny gave us a glimpse of what might lie under smooth waters.

At the garage, he grabbed the gas, still laughing in a smothered way. My parents' bedroom was close by. We streamed back across the field to the campsite, where the sleepers were still dead out. Perfect!

Johnny eagerly poured what he thought was a small amount of gas at the back of the lean-to, and struck a match. The fire took hold of the structure with a loud WHOOSH! And Peter jackknifed from prone to standing in one second. We were shocked. With all our athletics, we had never managed that kind of levitation. Then Johnny started screaming, "My leg! My leg!" In his haste, he had sloshed some gasoline on his legs. (Oh, well, to make an omelet, you have to break leggs...)

The fire was crackling wildly in its zeal for oxygen. We had no idea it would burn like that! But Dennis *kept on sleeping*, and the fire was getting closer! We were dumbstruck. How could anyone sleep through *that?* Peter tried to wake Dennis by shaking him. That failing, he grabbed hold of the sleeping bag and dragged Dennis, bag and all, away from the fire.

Dennis finally woke up, rubbed his eyes and said, "What's going on?" and then, "Where's my shoe?"

"Down in the bottom, where you lost it, remember?" I said.

"No, the *other* one," he insisted, worried.

"I saw you put it under the lean-to when we went to bed," Peter said, trying not to laugh.

"Oh, God, it's burnt up! Mom's going to kill me!" he lamented, for the second time that night. "Now it won't even help if I find the other one! And Dad's going to kill me, too. I lost the spring from his flashlight, looking for the first shoe."

But the fire was shooting flames 25 feet into the air, singeing green leaves and scorching branches. Victims and perpetrators alike stood amazed at its fierce energy. Shoeless, taking care not to step on any stray embers, Dennis watched with as much interest as any. He held no grudge – he would have done the same to us.

We watched until it burnt itself out, never once thinking that the woods might have caught fire or someone been injured. Then we looked up, surprised to see light coming in the east. The night was over.

Our nerves felt strangely pulled as we moved slowly across the field, not saying much. The camping gear could be retrieved later. Johnny's legs were bald, and all of us were smudged with soot and reeked of smoke. We quietly put the gas can in the garage. It was early yet, and my parents still slept peacefully in their beds.

We were starving, and headed for the kitchen. But my mother was already standing by the kitchen stove, getting breakfast.

"Heavens! What happened?" she said. "You're all covered with soot! And look at Johnny's legs! They're all red!"

"Yeah, he got too close to the fire when he did his Boy Scout Indian dance," Greg said wickedly.

Mother, who was often psychic, said, "I don't know why, but I kept dreaming of fire. It seemed so real, I thought I could smell smoke when I woke up at 3:00 AM."

Back in the corner, Johnny was grinning. I glanced at Mother. Her back was toward me. I put my finger to my lips and shook my head, mouthing *No.*

"You probably smelled our campfire," I temporized quickly. "That carries a long way, sometimes."

"I guess so... but what is that other smell? Gasoline?"

We had maneuvered pretty well till now, but I started to feel a little nervous, and decided to sacrifice Peter.

"That's probably because Peter and Dennis don't know how to start a fire without gas." (Peter was laughing up his sleeve.) "They probably spilled it on their shoes or something." (Whew! I barely squeaked out of that one.) Mercifully, she never did press us very hard. She had too much work to do. Or possibly she felt it was better not to know too much.

After breakfast, things slowed down a lot. We were tired. The day seemed bleached out, not like a *real* day. But before we could hit the sack, we had to bring our things back from camp. If we waited, local hoods like Lonnie Disco might steal them.

It was around 8:30 when we got back with the stuff. Johnny loaded his car and got ready to leave.

"It was fun, guys. Maybe we can do this again, sometime."

"What are you going to do today?" Greg asked.

"Same as you, I expect – go home and sleep."

"Yeah, right."

It wasn't going to be much of a day, but we didn't care – just show us the beds. We hoped Mother didn't have chores in mind, just now.

When Dennis returned home early that morning, his parents had no inkling what a night he'd had. We never did find out how he explained the loss of his shoes, or the wobbly makeshift spring in his dad's flashlight that didn't work like the old one. But he couldn't have ratted on us – we would have heard about it, and his parents would have grounded him for life. I guessed Dennis would rather face fire than his parents. (I knew a little bit about his mother, and couldn't argue with that.)

The next time I saw him, though, I noticed he hadn't followed my advice. There were oozing, watery bubbles all over his legs from the nettles.

Chapter XXI.

Home for Christmas

Christmas was a big deal at our house, on both the religious and secular sides. Every year, four Sundays before the Day, we got out the flat wooden cross my father had made, its arms all of equal length with tall nail points straight up at the ends. Then we cut evergreen boughs, binding them in a circle large enough to cover the nails, and adorned it with pinecones, tied on with black thread. Finally, we wrapped it with purple ribbon, and carefully set the wreath over the flat cross on the sideboard in our dining room. Four tall candles were stuck onto the nails, three purple and one pink, rising out of the greenery, and in the center was the tall walnut statue of Mary that my father had carved. It was an Advent wreath, and each candle represented a thousand years of waiting for the birth of Christ. The pink one was lit on Christmas.

The Old Church pushed penance during Advent, to purify its congregation for THE EVENT. As kids, we felt the burden keenly – those 4,000 years of waiting and yearning, represented by the candles, were always before our eyes. What a clever way the Church had found to make even the children participate, long before Santa! I remember waiting for next week's candle to be lit, and it really did seem like a thousand years, even though our distress came mainly from longing for our presents, and wanting to sink our teeth into the holiday goodies.

My mother started baking special Christmas treats several weeks in advance – date nut bars, Christmas Stollen, brownies with black walnuts, iced gingerbread boys, and many others. Even earlier than that, she started to make the *un*-special ones: an evil cookie called *pfeffernüssen*, or peppernuts, that could break your teeth, and then the everlasting fruitcake.

It took a well-stocked store to get all the ingredients for fruitcake, and hard labor to produce it. Now and again, we would stop by the kitchen and watch Mother at her Herculean labors – endless chopping of ingredients, then dumping and mixing them in a huge, bottomless bowl. My mother was a strong woman, but this recipe needed all her strength.

The ritual went on all day, and even throughout the month, since, once baked and cooled, the cake had to be wrapped in cheesecloth, and *brandy* applied regularly. We were horrified. Here she was, making this object technically called "cake," which was barely edible with milk, even fresh out of the oven. (Where do you suppose the saying "He's a fruitcake" came from?)

But NEXT, we had to watch it gradually recede entirely from the world of food, getting blacker and nastier each week as she poured the brandy over it. Finally, once it was completely disgusting even to starving wolves, they had the gall to serve it on Christmas, as a special treat. I remember feeling, *Why now? Why me?*

If it wasn't edible fresh, what would make anyone think the ruined version would be good after a wonderful Christmas dinner? But my conscience always pricked me – it *ought* to be good, since my mother had worked so hard. So I poked desultorily at the vile object with my fork, trying to get up steam to ingest it. My mother would offer helpfully, "Do you want some milk with that?" But I didn't want to spoil good milk.

I now think there may have been more going on than met the eye. Maybe fruitcake was really a seasonal social weapon to send the message to people you didn't like: "*Never darken our doorstep again!*" Or perhaps it expressed the social standing of the recipient in the eyes of the giver. Either way, a lot of people were sending that message, since everyone always seemed to have a generous supply of ammunition on hand. Why else would someone give my mother a fruitcake, when they knew she made the best (worst) darn fruitcake in the county? Got to be a message there somewhere...

Probably my dad was the only one who really liked it. He said it was an acquired taste, like wine and Limburger cheese. I vowed privately never to age with the cheese, and it must have worked, since those dubious tastes have yet to overtake me.

I have to confess that I would eventually be brought low enough to eat some of the fruitcake by the end of the holiday season, when the supply of wonderful baked goods ran out and I was growing thin from the travails of winter. I remember feeling a little sorry for myself.

Oh, well, in late winter (and beyond), when the starvation period was in full swing, there would always be *pfeffernüssen*. They were eternal – even mice wouldn't risk their teeth on them, and they lasted until the end of April. Occasionally, in early summer, while mowing the yard, we would come across one in the grass that someone had deep-sixed in December – still sound, but without its powdered sugar. This long-lived food was remarkable, when you consider that there were seven hungry bears in our house. Maybe the "rock cookies" were a ploy on my mother's part to guarantee having something around to serve company and dunk in her coffee. (And that's what she had – *something*.)

I thought about getting a petty revenge on the fruitcake and rock cookies by not mentioning them at all, but realized that they were as much a part of the season's penance as the other requirements of our religion.

* * *

Getting the Christmas tree was an event. As soon as Thanksgiving was over, my brothers and I began looking out for that special tree on our walks. When we were younger, our father would sometimes go with us to get it, especially if work was slow for him that season. In our locale, red cedar grew in modest abundance around the countryside. This humble relative of fancier conifers was looked-down-on by some, but it grew wild, and was free, though prickly to handle. Birds loved to nest in it at night, and when cut, it sported red-purple wood inside. The *smell* was <u>heavenly</u>!

On our own, we made an expedition out of it, especially if it happened to be snowing or sleeting, and sometimes passed up trees close to home – the Tree was not to be cheaply come by! Suffering *must* occur if we wanted to keep covenant with the Code and other gods we served. When we returned from the sacred mountain with this seasonal relic, we were supposed to have strained every faculty to the limit: spiritual, mental, and physical.

To think I was critical of the Germans with their worshipful, "O Tannenbaum!" I instinctively felt that it was too much, a kind of heathen hymn for a pagan object, howled by burly, bearded baritones after a huge dinner, but perhaps now I ought to make some meager apology for hypocrisy: maybe it was a recessive gene (I almost said, *recumbent*) left over from our own German ancestry that claimed us against our wills during the Yuletide season.

One of the requirements our tree must meet, besides having elegant conformation, was that it be the tallest and largest our living room could possibly accommodate. It always perplexed us that, once inside the house, a three-foot tree stood six feet – a six-foot tree towered nine – and so on. Every year Mother would exclaim, "Isn't that tree too large?!" But this was uniformly ignored, and evoked no reply except possibly a groan or stony, incredulous stare.

Over the years, the family dynamic changed as the older ones grew away. By December of '64, at the new place, Timmy was in the Air Force and Gregory almost out of high school, his mind on the future. Nick and I had just finished the first semesters of our freshman and junior years, and knew *we* were now the Elect to make the journey.

One morning we realized that the 25th was only a few days away – we needed that tree *now!* When it started snowing around 10:00 in the morning, it was clearly the blessing of heaven. We quickly dressed for the weather, and gathered matches and survival-rations to sustain us on the long trek into the wilds of southern Ohio.

Sam was rousted from under the kitchen table, balking and splaying his legs at the back door when he saw the wind and snow. Mrs. Claws, the outside cat, naturally took advantage, causing Sam a very nervous moment as she dashed through his legs to attain the Nirvana inside. We finally managed to shove him out, at which point he gave in and accepted his fate, since we were out there with him.

I told Nicholas, "He thought we were just going to put *him* out in the snow, without taking a walk."

"Yeah, looks like it," Nick laughed, thumping Sam on the back. "Is it too c-c-cold for you, S-S-Sammy?" he teased, in a commiserating-shivering way.

Sam, finely attuned to self-advantage, commenced to shake and chatter his teeth, making little whining sounds.

I joined in. "Are you fr...fr...freezing *R-R-REAL* bad?"

This excess of sympathy caused Sam to fall down and convulse, forgetting that it was colder lying in the snow. He was a consummate actor, and really enjoyed these games – *cold, mistreated, pathetic, wretched Sammy...* But you could see his tail wagging a little during his afflictions.

We went out to the old garage and picked up a dull axe. When Sam saw this article of the religion, he knew we were going for a walk, so he dropped the act and ran around in circles, barking. *"Come on! Let's go! Hooray!"*

We set out eastward towards the Grailville Oratory, across the rutted field that someone had plowed but not disked. After crossing the much-beleaguered cow fence bounding Grandpa's old property, we cut around the hill behind the chapel and headed up the little rose-choked valley that shortly passed under the road to Pickleville. Emerging on the other side, we were almost within sight of the college's milk barn and other buildings, but partly screened by willow trees and a drop in the land. Like Thoreau, we didn't care to be seen, so, under cover of the snow, we continued up the shallow wash, skirting the "Hill of Calvary" on our left, with its large wooden cross.

Walking was becoming difficult, with the snow six inches deep now and treacherous. We were wearing those shiny black boots that buckled up, good for rain and slush, but not much on traction. Wind-thrown sleet stung our faces, and our feet began to slip constantly. Every now and then one of us fell down in the wet snow, but we knew each other – neither would dream of turning back. Besides, we were beginning to enjoy ourselves acutely.

Halfway across the field, we got wet to the knee accidentally stepping into some troughs disguised by soft ice. That was how we discovered the downside to our galoshes: what's waterproof on the outside is a leak-proof container on the inside when gallons of water pour in. But never mind – this complication only cheered us. Things were getting better and better! True, we had to grit our teeth and reach deep inside to mine the "raw-bits" nourishment from this chastisement, but we understood way before its time the phrase, "No pain, no gain!"

Supporting each other in turn by the elbow, we drained our boots. (No sense in volunteering to sit down in wet snow... you get plenty of punishment without pushing it.) Funny, though, how it could freeze the hands and feet so quickly. To warm them, we began to run toward a line of old sassafras trees that marked a fence in the distance, and arrived there somewhat warmer, feeling that we were giving Trouble a hard time.

The snow was thinner there, blown away by the wind, and we paused to catch our breath and greet our old tree-friends. These sassafrasses were ancient, and the finest specimens I have ever seen, the most remarkable over two feet through, its stylized branches reaching more than 60 feet into the air. By intuitive ring-counting, we figured it to be around 100 years old. Its five brethren were almost as large, and all in their prime.

Once, when I was visiting the Mound Builders at Fort Ancient, someone pointed out a "large" sassafras tree to me, but it was only 12 inches through and 25 feet tall. The first time we encountered the Grailville trees, we didn't even recognize them – their bark was so deeply furrowed and blackened at the bottom. But after close inspection of the branching habit, the lobed leaves, the pinkish bark, and the taste of a twig, we knew its identity beyond doubt. The blackening was caused by the questionable farming practice of fence-line burning to control growth.

My brothers and I always had a reverence for specimens like this, and felt some anxiety about their fate – would some farmhand in the future even *know* what rare trees he was cutting down without a thought? The Corn Engrosser wouldn't.

Nick reminded me to move on. "We'd better go get our tree."

There was only one problem. Our hands and feet were starting to freeze in earnest, and it would be shameful to fall victim to lowly frostbite. The storm had renewed its vigor, pelting us harder than ever, and when we spied a small wash on our right, we decided to shelter there.

The same creek we had left earlier now wove its way through a lightly wooded bottom toward Route 48. We crossed it, choosing a tussocky place by an Osage orange tree to build a fire, and managed to get it started with our Indian skills, using shredded cedar bark and twigs from the lee side of the tree. The natural oil in red cedar keeps its wood dry and ready to burn. But it was still hard to light a match with numb hands in that wind and wet, so we had to remove a section of bark from a dead elm nearby to shield the flames from the wind.

We proceeded to heat- and smoke-dry everything that was wet, and brought out our sandwiches. Then I spied some peppernuts in Nicholas's bag, and demanded, "How did *those* get in there!"

At that point, Sam burst into our camp, smoothly switching from *wabbit*-hunting to begging. Continuing to chew, Nick finally answered, "I put 'em in there." (He always could eat anything, and fast, too.) "You want one?"

I didn't, but had an experiment in mind, so I said, "OK." He tossed me one, which I deftly caught and later sneaked into the fire, to see if it could withstand that – would it burn, or just sit there impervious till it crumbled like a bone in the stove? The latter proved to be true.

We sat by the fire for an hour on more foraged elm bark, feeling we had mastered the elements and ruminating about that terrible Christmas long ago at Valley Forge. We could identify with the plight of Washington's soldiers.

Eventually we were ready to leave, and putting out the fire with snow, resumed our quest with two more fields yet to cross. Like doctors making their rounds, we checked up on a massive black cherry tree before arriving at the final fence, near a large stand of red cedars. Climbing over, we found an opening in the green mass, and stepped inside a world that was still, with no driving wind, and snow that only swirled in gently over the cedar tops. Occasionally a bush would shed its mounded snow with a swish and a plop, so we took care not to brush them. Birds rustled at our passing, making small twitting sounds as they discreetly flew and crept about. Further on, we disturbed a flock of Juncos who flitted in front of us, displaying their white tail feathers. It was peaceful and much warmer here, out of the wind. It took about ten minutes to locate and fell the Chosen Tree with our axe, purple chips scattered everywhere and the scent of cedar all-pervasive. About nine feet tall from base to tip, the tree would barely squeeze into our living room by the grand piano. Perfect!

Wet, tired, scratched, hungry *again*, and smoked thoroughly, like codfish destined for immortality, we took turns dragging the tree home over the winter fields, hooking the axe-as-handle around a sturdy branch near the bottom. Was this better than buying a tree at the local store, or *what?* We felt a sense of relief – the required year's-end rituals had been performed; the new year's sun would rise again, granting us indulgences till next year.

* * *

Our first house, in pseudo-saltbox style, had a large living room with hardwood floors and a fireplace at one end, framed by bookcases and a window-seat. Its tallest wall was around 17 feet high, and the opposite wall

10 feet, with redwood beams running across the air-space overhead and into the high plastered wall. In the middle of the room, a medieval wrought-iron light fixture sat on one of the beams. We always tried to get a tree that tall.

Conventional decorations were not for us. We wanted the tree to be unique, and reveal Nature in all its glory. Things collected in the wild were made into adornments, though we also had electric lights and some ornaments. There was a magical angel that crowned the tree. When I was eight, I thought it was the most beautiful thing I had ever seen.

My brothers and I gathered milkweed, acorns, pinecones, bittersweet, sycamore balls, and blue vineberries on our regular long walks. The blue vineberries and the bittersweet found their places entwined around the front door wreath.

The milkweed silk was white fluff, and floated easily on the air when the pods burst in late fall. If you waited too long, most of the silk was gone, taken by the wind to distribute its seeds. When blown gently onto the tree after all the rest of the decorating was done, it gave an effect like angel hair or snow, and formed spun pools of light, nestled around the Christmas tree bulbs.

The pods that housed the silk were like little boats with pointed prows at each end, rough grey on the outside and light gold within. Sometimes we bound five or six together, then gilded them with glue and glitter. *Voila!* One gold or silver sparkling star for our tree. Pinecones we hung plain, or painted the tips – white to mimic snow, or red. We might also sprinkle glued cones or sycamore balls with glitter to make them dazzle.

We usually trimmed the tree on Christmas Eve day. It was a noisy affair, with everyone keyed up and all trying to decorate at once. (Except Timmy – and, of course, Peter) But Bea, Greg, Angela, and I would each be pushing to do it *our* way, and Nicky would be quietly helping anyone who had conscripted his services for the moment. Bea would demand, "Give me that ornament ... *I* want to hang it!" Angela would be throwing icicles on the tree any-old-how, while I pulled them off again, complaining, "That's a mess! We'll have to hang it straight, or it will look as bad as the Hills' tree!" Angela would be petulant at my criticism, and Timmy, moved to rare speech by the sight, might add his two-cents: "Maw's decorating... look out!" Then Angela would yell and stamp her foot. "Mama, make him shuddup!"

Nicky and Greg would be trying to find the best place for our milkweed star, while Bea yelled, "Get Peter, he's going to pull the tree over!" All this against a constant background theme of clattering pots and Christmas music coming from the kitchen, underscoring the din.

Finally, the tree would be done. We would struggle to put the angel on top, using a stepladder and pruning shears, and one of us would plug in the lights. Presto – pure magic radiating from the tree! We would all pile on the mangy couch by the upright piano to admire it, looking forward to midnight Mass, each wondering, *"What will I be getting?"* and *"Will we be allowed to open our presents early, after midnight Mass, or will we have to wait till morning?"*

That was Christmas at the old house.

* * *

In 1962, Greg, Nicholas, Peter, and I received our first ice skates for Christmas. Our parents couldn't normally afford such costly presents, not to mention the scarcity of ice on the creek anytime in December – we usually had to wait for the 10th of January, or thereabouts. But, that year, we had skates *and* ice by the 25th. Our mother must have been psychic when she purchased the skates back in November.

We could hardly wait till breakfast was over to try those beauties out, and eagerly rushed down to Martins' Pond, even though we had to shovel a snow path all the way around the pond first. Nick, Gregory and I (but not Peter) worked like fiends for an hour to get it done. None of us had ever skated, but that was insignificant – once we strapped the skates on, we would just *know*.

Well... it didn't turn out *quite* that way. The truth was, we spent most of the day just trying to stand up – skating wasn't even an issue. Being reduced to a two-year-old state again is humbling, especially for self-styled "old masters." But we were determined – it **had** to be today!

We stopped only for Christmas dinner around 2:00, and were back by 4:00 for more punishment. Our reputations were at stake – we had to be able to say we had learned to skate in one day. It would give us the edge in any conversation where the subject of skating surfaced.

By dark, Greg, Nick and I could stand up and move around a little without clinging to each other. (We wouldn't have done that, anyway – that was for *girls*. We preferred the splendid isolation of crashing into each other, the ice, or the creek bank.) We also exercised the novelty option of hurling ourselves up to six feet, a desperate act of skating, before wiping out, usually face-down.

Our meager progress was paid for by a certain portion of our anatomy. We could hardly walk home, but had achieved our goal, and were already planning future exploits on the ice. Visiting our relatives that season, we had to endure snide remarks from Uncle Pete, like "How's your skating coming? Don't wear out the seat of your pants, heh, heh, heh..." He wasn't the only one not-so-secretly pleased by those fringe benefits, figuring they were long overdue.

Then there was Peter. He managed to get his skates on that day, but I think he spent most of his time avoiding us, and studiously not trying *anything* we did. Somehow, somewhere, he did to learn to skate, probably alone, when he could catch his breath and collect his thoughts, away from our censorious eyes.

By the end of January we could skate comfortably, and were jumping logs and playing ice hockey with Billy Martin, using a tin can and sticks. We yelled and chased each other up and down the pond until the sun sank low behind the trees, turning the sky, riffles, and ice orange in its passing. The farther sky showed a pale turquoise that complemented the orange and promised another frigid, sunny day tomorrow. When it was too dark to see, we trudged home up the lane, skates tied together and draped over our shoulders, bouncing gently. We didn't talk – our raging energies were stilled, and frustrations forgotten. It was time for supper, maybe some TV, and then bed.

Every year from then on, those skates enlivened our winters. In 1967, I was home at Christmas break from my first semester of college. The shock of being flushed out of my natural habitat was still with me, and I hadn't done well scholastically. Now, however, I was HOME, and felt the need to re-center myself, so the wilds would take me back. Reading Howard Pyle's Robin Hood again seemed a solid starting-point. (We knew about affirmation even back then.)

Next, I went on an Indian raid. Peter slyly informed me that, while I was in college and Gregory in Korea, the Bigwood kids had built a sort of pigpen-camp in Long Pond Bottom, littering it widely with garbage. As soon as the creek flooded in the spring, it would all end up in the river – nails, glass, and cans.

Peter was really probing to see whether my old character had eroded from college living. *It hadn't.* Here was a way to channel some Robin Hood energy to a purpose! I launched into a diatribe against the Bigwoods and all other barbarians – ruining the aesthetics of the place, *and* infringing on our territory! The blot had to be expunged. We laid our plans.

After Mass on the Sunday before Christmas, Peter, Nick, and I were to be seen wildly flowing across the field with streaming torches, on our mission. When we arrived at the camp, the offenders weren't there (probably attending a later Mass). That was fine – this was an ecological raid, not a battle. We thoroughly cleansed the sacred ground, taking away in bags what wouldn't burn.

The raid did much to restore my equilibrium, and I felt at home again in my coverts. But the vacation days melted away, and soon I must face my chosen major of punishment again. Before then, though, our brother-in-law Chris Hammond came to visit, and we all went skating. What happened is introduced here by my alter ego, Robin Hood.

§ **Wherein** Now perchance the reader thinketh to himself that the
pride goeth author appeareth in too rosy a light, always stealing the
before a fall advantage, playing tricks, and getting off without a
drubbing. But <u>not so</u>, as this story showeth.

It was as bitter a day in winter as Maytime is sweet and fair. Not only was it cold, but the wind blew wildly, kicking up the snow, and swirling it in our faces. Greg was home briefly on leave from the Army, soon to return to Korea, and all of us were together for the nonce. We were determined to have fun in spite of the weather – only the weak and timid would let *that* keep them housebound.

I always tried to skate confidently and nonchalantly where no one else dared, thereby inducing others to follow in my skate-steps. This meant getting awfully close to thin ice and rocks showing through, and I had to play constant footsie with open holes that hadn't properly frozen, near moving water. It was remarkable how many times I *didn't* come to grief, but the one after me did. It makes sense, though, since the chances are the ice will hold *once*, but that risky passage certifies a trap for the next skater. If you made it look easy enough, the person following might unthinkingly relax, and wipe out. You could also engage in conversation at a critical moment: "Did you see those Juncos flitting around over there?" or "Maybe it's going to snow again..."

The only difficulty with my style was that Greg had perversely adopted the same one, and it caused tension between us. Being a year and a half younger, I was supposed to take a back seat to *his worship*, but the back seat gaveth *me* a rash! However, meekly pretending to accept the place appointed by fate could be useful. If it helped you accomplish your nefarious goal, there was no shame attached.

One of the stratagems to get the jump on Greg was to get my skates on *fast*. That way, I could control the game by always being one step ahead, and he <u>had</u> to follow, else it would say plainly: **"Thou fearest!"** Strangely, he took the smug view that if *I* could do it, *he* certainly could.

When I succeeded in tripping up *his eminence*, I wasn't allowed to laugh, cough, or express anything of my inner feelings. (Was he using Timmy as a role model?) Gregory was very observant on these occasions. He would eye me narrowly, acting for all the world as though he *knew* the secret smile in my heart, and was going to sock me. **(Lest the reader lay down these pages in disgust, I must aver that I am completely penitent of those past actions, and have turned me over a new leaf.)**

At Kane's Pond that day, we were all hurriedly putting on our skates, and nearly freezing our fingers. As usual, I rushed to be first out.

Chris didn't hurry forward, but sat back to watch the entertainment. He was a new member of our family, and got much amusement from going with us on our jaunts or just watching us at work. Our harum-scarum approach kept him astonished, off-balance, and frequently in stitches. He was always saying things like, "Man, I can't believe he did that!" We just thought, *What a wonderful new canvas for us to paint on!* St. Ælfreda had delivered into our hands someone with a fresh perspective who could witness our exploits and reflect our glory back to us. We thought him an estimable companion (and intelligent, since he found us enjoyable).

We were certainly colorful and opinionated – art, music, religion, temperament, nature-worship, and organic gardening all struggled together in a uniquely provincial yet *avant-garde* way. I can only suppose Chris's own family did not amuse him nearly as much (but then, it never does).

Peter was looking around carefully for a *safe* place to skate. **(But methinks nowhere was safe from us.)**

Nicky had the look on his face that said, **Sithee, I'll bide myself here a bit, and see how things fall out between Greg and Paul.** *Will they be antagonists or friends for the day?* Then he would slip into his position accordingly, choosing one or the other to follow, or sometimes both, if that weren't too tricky. It would do no good to get in the way when either of us was on a tear. Nick wasn't looking for competition, but joined in with *joie de vivre*, and was such a good sport that he almost never came to grief.

I got my skates on first, so I shot off, straight for the shallows. Greg called after me, "Watch out for that place near the riffles! Looks really thin!"

"Naw, it's all right. Come on!" I shouted, gliding in ever-widening circles toward the lower end of the pond.

But why was no one following? Not Greg. Not Peter, of course. But not even Nick? Chris was gaping and grinning, "Man, oh, man! He's going down, for sure!"

This sounded sweetly in my ears, much better than I had hoped – a *really* attentive audience. Greg wasn't even smiling. But I congratulated myself. Hadn't I always gotten away with this sort of thing? Wasn't I as light as thistledown, and the envy of slow, ordinary folk? (Wasn't I the Toad, the incomparable Toad?)

I skimmed even closer to the shoals, deciding to give the onlookers a real show. But the ice suddenly began to quiver in a sickening way, like a mere skin over the water. My stomach went all hollow and queer with presentiment. But with weasel cunning, I thought, *Coast out quietly and softly as a mouse! ... NO! Belay that order! Lie down and spread yourself out as far as possible!* This was a technique I had seen much touted in books on ice safety, so I floated down gently to the ice. *I made it!* Stretched out prone, I began to inch cautiously towards the creek bank, and felt a surge of triumph.

Then the whole ice-section slowly subsided, shattering into fragments. From a great distance, I heard a shriek that sounded more like a mad hyena than human, and fairly exploded out of that pond, heedless of abrasions and bruises, coming closer to levitation than ever before or since.

Apparently the ice had been only a quarter-inch thick. In disgust, I realized that if I had just stayed upright, only my legs would have suffered.

On the creek bank, the clamor was uproarious. Chris was rolling on the bank, alternately slapping his knees and grabbing his stomach, overcome. He gasped: "You better run for it, Paul, or you'll freeze to death!"

Greg chimed in, eyes gleaming. "You'd better take the high field home!" Then he started singing, " ♫ Oh, ye'll take the high road and I'll take the low road... ♫"

"Yeah, he's already found the low road, in the pond..." Chris sputtered. "But if he goes that way, we'll find him later, freeze-dried!"

Running *was* a tempting solution, and it would keep me warm. But I didn't want to let go of the day's entertainment before it started! Greg had matches, so a fire was kindled with some difficulty, despite the wind. Then I had to take off every piece of clothing, wring it out, prop it on sticks in front of the fire, and proceed to cook myself dry with the clothes. But my Indian soul rejoiced in this severe ritual. I thought grimly, *Was I driven out, like "normal" folk? No! Did I lose control of my agenda? Again, no!* I gloated over the thought that most would have gone home. (Toad was obviously making a day of it.)

It took me a long hour of thorough smoking and basting to get everything sort-of dry. My shoes were a little burnt, from being too close to the fire, and my clothes had some pinholes in them from sparks. During the process, I had to endure repeated jibes, like, "It's not too late to start running for home..." or, "I'll have to remember that trick of spreading out, when the ice starts to break..."

Ha-Ha! Very funny, I thought. **But one must always be sporting when the joke is on oneself... Still, methinks 'twould ha' been funnier if they had fallen in!**

After skating ourselves silly, we all went home by that "high road." It was at least zero, with the wind still lashing, and the 20-minute walk felt endless. But finally we all trooped into the warm kitchen, our eyes darting about for FOOD!

There was a scented lavender envelope waiting for me on the table, from... Molly Doherty! Curious — we had met again unexpectedly at college, talked, and taken some walks, but a perfumed envelope? I pocketed it surreptitiously, hoping for anonymity. No use letting anyone get the wrong idea. But Chris saw me and smirked. Now it was unlikely that anyone would fail to grasp the implications, even the dog, who probably knew the sender's blood type.

We all sat down at the table - a pathetic hint to the cook of the house that we were famished. As though on cue, Mother came in briskly, saying, "Supper won't be for another hour," and then added, "Does anyone want some fruitcake?"

Was this fair, taking advantage of our debilitation? She knew how to move tenth-rate food. On the other hand, maybe those secret messages were at work again...

She cut the slices at the counter, passing them on small plates to each of us in turn. Nick, of course, had quietly served himself earlier, upon arriving home, so he was almost through with his before the rest of us had finished considering her question. I was cornered, and certainly didn't want to risk my health by waiting an hour till dinner, so I sighed and gave in.

Oh, well, I thought to myself, *my Gramma always did say that everyone had to eat his peck of dirt!*

THE END

Wild for an opera career, Paul Pfarr won a voice scholarship at 18 to the Cincinnati College-Conservatory of Music. He was caught there by his wife Justice (Molly!) (still in captivity), caught by the Army during the Vietnam War (paroled), and caught by the back-to-the-land movement in the 1970s (exorcised).

With Justice, he wrote <u>Build Your Own Log Cabin</u>, Winchester Press, 1978. Suspect has two computer-related degrees, and is webmaster of **http://www.choosing-natural-health.com**. But writing, especially humor, seems necessary to keep him away from the cliff. Paul is still not a joiner, but no longer hangs himself by the neck (even by request).